Anyone But Him

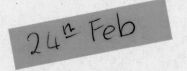

24ᵗʰ Feb

Also by Ronali Collings

All the Single Ladies

Anyone But Him

Ronali Collings

embla books

First published in Great Britain in 2025 by

embla books

Bonnier Books UK Limited
HYLO, 5th Floor, 103-105 Bunhill Row, London, EC1Y 8LZ

Owned by Bonnier Books
Sveavägen 56, Stockholm, Sweden

A CIP catalogue record for this book is available from the British Library.

ISBN: 9781471417887

This book is typeset using Atomik ePublisher.

Printed and bound in Great Britain by Clays Ltd, Elcograf S.p.A.

Embla Books is an imprint of Bonnier Books UK.
www.bonnierbooks.co.uk

To Malcolm
My best friend, my love, always

Prologue

April 2013

Ingrid took a deep breath and imagined she was lying on a lounger in the south of France, the sun kissing her skin . . . or taking a breezy stroll by the Thames with a cup of coffee in her hand . . . or luxuriating in a bath full of lavender-scented bubbles. Although who was she kidding? She'd give the right arm that was currently holding her decidedly heavy and grumpy baby for just *five minutes* alone on the toilet.

How could she have been so naive as to believe those soft-focus nappy ads selling a glamorous, spotlessly clean life as a new parent? Even her own sister hadn't prepared her for the 1 a.m. carrot vomit down her back. Nor did anyone mention the exploding poos, covering Lily from neck to toe, that only occurred when out and about with three wet wipes left in the packet and no change of clothes. Added to that, she was trying to hold down a full-time job and was now hosting her entire family for Sunday lunch.

She looked out of the kitchen window and snarled at the cherry blossom tree in the garden, heavy with perky, pale-pink petals, tempting her with its promise of spring and sunshine, as if she'd have a chance to enjoy any of it. And what was that smell? Surely Lily's nappy couldn't need changing already? Oh God, it was her. Showers these days

1

were hurried affairs with Lily strapped into the car seat with a few toys at the bathroom door, and they often ended with Ingrid hopping out of the shower stall, still partially soaped up and having to placate her impatient daughter.

Was motherhood supposed to be this hard? Was she really this crap at it? Why could she never get to work without some kind of puréed food on her shirt? Why were the toilet stalls at work the only place where she could be alone? Why was she always running from one place to the next with an overarching sense of guilt and failure?

And why couldn't *she* be the one going on a two-week holiday to California? Frankly anywhere would do as long as she could sleep.

'Let me help with that,' said her sister, Audrey, nudging her out of the way with her hip and grabbing a plate out of Ingrid's hand.

Ingrid snatched the plate back. However rubbish she felt, there wasn't a chance in hell that she'd admit to her annoyingly capable sister she couldn't handle all of this on her own.

'No, I can manage.'

Audrey held out her arms. 'At least give me the baby.'

Lily took one look at Audrey and buried her face in Ingrid's shoulder, small hands gripping tighter. Audrey didn't exactly exude warmth.

'She's a bit grizzly today,' Ingrid said, grimacing in apology and moving Lily further away from her sister.

Audrey touched Ingrid's arm for a moment as though poised to say something more, but thought better of it as their mother's voice took up all the space in the room.

'So, Matthew, tell me where you're off to this time? You're so intrepid. Always doing new things.'

A plate slipped through Ingrid's fingers and clattered into the sink.

'It's fine!' she said, with everyone's eyes suddenly on her.

If the tables had been turned and Ingrid were the one who

was about to go on a trip with her mates while she had a six-month-old baby at home, she was positive that her mother would not be using the word 'intrepid'. Ingrid swallowed the bubble of resentment that rose like acid in her mouth. There was nothing to be gained by saying anything. It never made any difference, and all she wanted right now was peace.

'We're going to Coachella in the desert,' said Matt, looking very pleased with himself before spooning another dollop of her chocolate mousse into his mouth.

Ingrid stared at her husband. There were times like this when she wondered what she'd ever seen in him. So he was good looking, but that only took you so far in a relationship. She wasn't even sure she liked him much these days, partly because he seemed to think that looking after their baby was her responsibility alone.

'The desert sounds so challenging,' said Mum, leaning towards him. Ugh, was she fluttering her eyelashes at him?

Ingrid stole a glance at Audrey whose eyes had rolled so far back in her head that she thought her sister might fall over.

'There isn't much challenging about going to a music festival, Ammi,' Audrey muttered.

'It's important we follow our passions, isn't it?' said Matt, like an earnest guidance counsellor.

Ingrid stared up at the ceiling, wishing she had time to even figure out what her passions were. In between work, taking care of Lily and being the one sibling who was always at Mum's beck and call, she had no time to think, let alone sit online for hours to nab tickets to a music festival on another continent.

'And while you're following your passions, Ingrid's left here holding the baby and trying to work at the same time.'

Ingrid bit her lip, her eyes darting between her sister and husband. She didn't need Audrey charging in with her good intentions.

'Ingrid's fine with it, aren't you, darling? She loves her job,' said Matt, rising to come and put an arm around her – a gesture that felt claustrophobic rather than comforting.

She nodded. Even though at thirty-four, she didn't quite qualify as a geriatric mother, she felt like one, because this motherhood lark was so exhausting that even thinking of a response to this question was too much trouble.

'Maybe Grace will be there,' said Mum, lifting her coffee cup to her lips for a sip.

Audrey and Ingrid exchanged an amused glance.

Their sister Grace was a violinist in a New York-based orchestra, the geography being the only part of her career choice that their mother had felt was worth boasting about to her friends. The fallout from Grace's failure to conform in the way Audrey and Ingrid had, with their solid careers as doctor and accountant respectively, had been one of the main drivers of her escape to the Big Apple.

Lily nuzzled Ingrid's neck, burrowing down for a nap. Ingrid loved cuddles with her daughter, but she also wished she could put her down. She might be a baby, but Lily knew when her mother was absent during the working week and only wanted to be in her arms if she were at home. Most of Ingrid's nights were spent in the rocking chair in Lily's bedroom, holding her, so most of her mornings were a blur of bleary eyes and the new major food group in her life: caffeine. The baristas at Starbucks were usually ready with her triple-shot espressos in the morning, no longer alarmed by Ingrid's slightly manic eyes.

The weekends should've been easier but were somehow worse, as Matt seemed to think that, just because Ingrid was at home, it was fine to spend hours on end at the gym. Goodness knows what he did there because he still looked tall and stringy with nary a flexed bicep in sight. And she was sure that these family lunches were Mum's way of testing her, lounging about like some Roman emperor while Ingrid fetched her things in between dashing back to the kitchen to check on the food.

If she'd accepted Audrey's offer of help earlier for instance, Mum would have started on at her about how she was a failure because she couldn't look after one child. How she'd had to trudge seven miles every day with all three of them on her back, fetching water from the well, when really they'd been brought up in Rayners Lane with the Piccadilly Line running along the back of their tiny garden and a bus stop right outside their front door.

'And shouldn't *you* have a job?' Audrey asked Matt, standing well within his personal space, challenge in her eyes.

'You know I gave up my job to look after Lily while Ingrid went for partnership.'

Audrey glanced at Ingrid, who busied herself with looking at Lily. As her canny sister no doubt suspected, she hadn't wanted to go for partnership yet. It was a tough process and not too many women made it, particularly if they'd just had a child. But Matt had insisted that they put their house on the market and look for somewhere bigger on one of the premier roads in Pinner – framing the months that followed as him altruistically giving up work to care for Lily, allowing Ingrid the opportunity to work for their future. In reality, he had failed to get another contract as a software engineer, but still wanted a big house to show off.

Things hadn't quite worked out as expected, with Ingrid rushing home to pick Lily up from the nursery that Matt had enrolled her in, while he was doing goodness knows what. She was simply too busy and too tired to question it. And if she did, there would be an inevitable argument, with no resolution to the situation. Audrey probably thought that Ingrid was a doormat, but she had enough on her plate. It took all her effort to simply get going every day.

Surprisingly, Audrey took her cue from Ingrid and swallowed whatever acerbic comment she'd been about to make. 'So you did.'

'We'll be fine, won't we, Lilypad?' Ingrid said, kissing her daughter's head softly as Lily edged closer to sleep.

At that moment Ingrid's phone rang, startling them all.

'Oh goodness, child. Is that work?' said her mother, frowning.

'It's fine, Ammi,' said Matt. 'She needs to work. I understand completely.'

Someone had to pay for all his holidays.

'You're so supportive,' said Mum.

'Matt, why don't you take the baby so that Ingrid can take her call?' said Audrey.

Matt waved her off. 'Oh, Ingrid's a dab hand at taking conference calls with Lily in tow.'

Audrey stared at him, momentarily incredulous. Ingrid gripped her sister's arm, restraining her.

She was fine. Not everyone could be like Audrey and Nathan, sharing the parenting as equally as possible. And perhaps some couples needed a little distance for their relationship to last. She could handle this.

'Hey, Will, give me a sec to get somewhere quieter,' she said as she passed the packed rucksack in the hallway. Two weeks was a long time to be away. But who was she to complain? There were so many women out there doing this all alone.

She was fine.

Absolutely fine.

1

The Wife

June 2024

Ingrid stared at her open wardrobe, her brain buffering. Something had gone wrong. Where was the blouse that went with the peacock-blue pencil skirt? She felt tears begin to prick her eyes.

One of the unexpected upsides of Matt's year-long sabbatical pursuing his 'passions' was the development of Ingrid's foolproof, time-saving morning routine. Wake at 5.30 a.m., work out for an hour, breakfast, check emails, shower, wake Lily, and finally get dressed.

But it was Ingrid's wardrobe that was the cherry on her somewhat obsessive cake. Long gone were the mornings spent dithering over what to wear, hunting around under the bed for matching shoes, and detangling necklaces from the jumble inside her drawer. Her wardrobe was now a thing of Marie Kondo beauty, with colour-coded sections and Polaroids of outfits pasted inside the cupboard doors. Fourteen of them to be precise, rotated over a two-week cycle. Along with accessories that were neatly lined up on shelves and in a jewellery box with separate compartments for each piece. It gave her so much joy that sometimes she'd sacrifice precious seconds just staring at it in front of the open doors, running her hands along the soft fabrics.

This morning, she riffled through her blouses, time slipping away. Past the one with ruffles, the one with carefully placed breast pockets, the tasteful floral one, the peplum. Where was the plain silk shell that went with her Thursday skirt? She mustn't cry, partly because it was only a top, and partly because she didn't have enough time to redo her makeup. Her routine didn't allow for contingencies, but perhaps with Grace in the house these days, this was a big mistake. Despite having completely different taste in clothing to Ingrid, some habits died hard and Grace had a habit of borrowing random items, completely messing up Ingrid's system.

If Thursday's top was missing, perhaps this was a sign that the rest of the day was going to be a complete disaster. After all, Matt was returning today, and instead of being desperate to see him after a year apart, her reaction was distinctly indifferent, which didn't bode well for their reunion.

'Mum!' Lily shouted as she raced past the open bedroom door.

Lily was the polar opposite to Ingrid, preferring the adrenaline rush of leaving everything until the last minute, shooting Ingrid's cortisol levels through the roof.

Lily raced from room to room, most likely in search of the PE kit that Ingrid had suggested packing last night. They both had to be in the car in twenty minutes if Ingrid had any hope of dropping off Lily and getting to the station car park before the only spaces left were the ones at the very end where a minor flood of unseasonal but entirely British summer rainwater meant that she'd need waders to be able to exit the car.

She let out a loud groan of frustration, relinquishing her quest for the Thursday blouse, and picked the one for next Tuesday, which would do, although wearing the wrong blouse at the wrong time would irritate her all day like an itch that couldn't be scratched.

'Mum!' Lily shouted. 'I can't find my white T-shirt.'

Grace had done a whites wash two days ago, so Lily's T-shirt would probably be found in the utility room. Ingrid shimmied into her skirt, pulled the wrong blouse over her head, tucking it into the waistband, picked up her handbag and shoes, and stomped downstairs, huffing loudly.

'Get your stuff ready, please, Lils. We need to leave on time today,' she called behind her.

'But, Mum . . .'

'No buts, just get *your* butt down here.'

She skidded into the utility room, her eyes searching the airer for the PE top.

Which was now pink. And hanging up with her newly pink silk shell top, Grace's now-pink knickers and the offending red sock.

'Grace!' she screamed.

She was going to murder her sister. How on earth could a forty-year-old woman still be so domestically useless? Grace had made being the baby of the family her profession, never growing up despite her age. It was no doubt why she was living with Ingrid at the age of forty, having been made redundant from the New York-based orchestra where she'd been playing the violin for the last ten years. The pandemic hadn't been kind to musicians like Grace, and of course, Ingrid sympathised, but sometimes that was hard when Grace lounged around Ingrid's house like a teenager, eating food that she didn't buy or replace, left her stuff all over the place while playing video games with Lily, and turned the laundry into bunting.

Grace appeared in the doorway, hair wild, sleep crust in the corners of her eyes, her body clearly trying to adjust to being awake and operational at 8 a.m.

'What? Is there a fire or something? Why on earth are you screaming at this time of the morning?' Grace followed Ingrid's gaze to the airer.

'Ah, that. I was going to tell you, but you were . . . it's not the end of the world, is it?'

'I was going to wear that *very expensive* silk top today, and Lily needs that T-shirt for games. Didn't you check the washing machine before putting the whites on?'

'I did, but you know sometimes socks appear from nowhere. Like there's this black hole in the machine that gives as well as receives. Anyway, look, my knickers are the greatest casualties. You've got loads of clothes up there. This top looks great with that skirt.'

'But this is a *Tuesday* blouse,' Ingrid muttered.

'Oh right, the Polaroids,' said Grace with a smile. 'Why are you wound so tight anyway?' She screwed up her face into a frown and then as realisation dawned, slapped her forehead with her palm. 'Oh shit, it's today, isn't it? Don't worry, Sis, it'll be fine.'

Her sister had a rosy, balcony-seat view of her marriage, where everything looked perfect and a little out of focus. It was naive to think that things would go back to normal, whatever that had been. A year away was a big statement. And she hadn't heard from him once. Not even a crummy postcard, no card on Lily's birthday. It was as if he'd fallen off the face of the earth. The biggest surprise was finding she was just fine with that.

She'd been antsy from the moment Matt had finally called last week to announce his imminent return. He'd been so over the top that she was surprised he hadn't issued a press release in the local paper. What would it be like to have him back in what was now *her* space? She wasn't sure she even wanted it anymore. But she couldn't tell anyone that. Not even Grace or Audrey. Grace was a hopeless romantic, who despite being an adult, continued to fall hook, line and sinker for the Disney romance fallacy. And Audrey's years-long hatred of Matt meant that she'd have Ingrid packed and out of the house before she could finish her sentence.

Grace clutched Ingrid by the shoulders and looked her straight in the eye. 'Lils can borrow one of my white T-shirts. And don't worry about tonight. You look incredible and he'll be desperate for you.'

Ingrid rolled her eyes. 'Just get the T-shirt, would you?'

Grace raced up the stairs, passing Lily and ruffling her hair on the way.

'Is that my T-shirt?' asked Lily as she peered into the utility room. 'I couldn't find the other one. Oh my days, why is it pink?'

'Aunty Grace did the laundry. But you see? This is exactly why we have a spare top. On the bright side, at least it looks quite nice in pink.'

'Do you think the same about your top?' Lily shrewdly observed.

They both looked at the ruined silk shell. 'Good point. Anyway, Aunty Grace is going to give you one of her T-shirts.'

Lily was horrified. 'But Aunty Grace's shirts are . . .'

Ingrid held up a hand at her daughter. 'I know, but you'll have to make do today. I'll take the heat from any teachers who have a problem with it.'

Grace wasn't the type to conform to age clichés when it came to fashion and continued to favour tight cropped tops, preferably with graphics or slogans, so finding a plain one could take a while. And Ingrid didn't have a moment to spare.

Ingrid sighed and accepted her fate of the worst parking space. She had to admit that having the tornado that was Grace in the house, while periodically annoying, had helped immeasurably. Aunty Grace was always available to play Mario Kart or Minecraft, to bake cookies – leaving an almighty mess for Ingrid to clean up – and to do a whole host of fun things that Ingrid simply didn't have time for with her increasingly demanding job. And for all of that, she *should* forgive her sister for her shocking laundry skills and basic student mentality.

'Is Dad really coming home today?'

Ingrid stroked her daughter's silky long dark brown hair. 'Yep.'

'I don't want to see him.'

Ingrid chewed her lip. As much as she disapproved of Matt's failure as a father, she was determined not to allow this to affect any possible opportunities for him to reconcile with Lily.

'But he's been away for a year, darling. He'll want to see you.'

'He didn't even remember my birthday, or that I was going to secondary school.' Lily hugged her tightly.

Ingrid hugged her back. 'How about we give him a chance?'

'Alicia thinks that you're going to get a divorce. She said that her mum said that no one stays away for as long as Dad has and wants to be a family again.'

Thank you so much, Alicia. She hadn't wanted Lily to think like this, even though this was exactly what Ingrid herself had thought on many nights when she'd stared at the ceiling rose in her bedroom. But divorce was failure and surely this was why she'd spent all their years together swallowing her complaints, putting her needs last, keeping calm and carrying on? Had that all been for nothing?

'Of course not,' Ingrid said, feigning a confidence she didn't feel.

'I wouldn't mind, you know. If you got divorced. It's not like things would be that different.'

Ingrid wasn't so sure of that. Her daughter's bravado often hid her vulnerability. Was there a child unaffected by their parents' divorce? She doubted it.

'Try not to worry about it, okay?'

Which was more than could be said for Ingrid. Damn Alicia's mum.

2

The Partnership Myth

God was definitely having a laugh with her because her annual farce of a partner assessment meeting had been scheduled for the same day that her errant husband was due to return. Like a repeat of a tired old sitcom with stale jokes, every year the powers-that-be allocated her a lower than average profit share while ignoring the significant revenues Ingrid brought in on her clients. Once again, she'd be found wanting in comparison to her peers. But for the life of her, Ingrid couldn't figure out when they did any actual work because most of them spent infinite amounts of time in pointless three-hour meetings to discuss why they had pointless three-hour meetings, and the rest of the time filling up on Pret subscription coffees with younger members of staff.

And this year would be exactly the same. That insufferable cuckoo, Tim Woodstock, would get more cash again after adding his name to every single one of her projects, while doing absolutely no work on them. And it was her fault really because she didn't have the time to complain about this in between getting her work done, winning new clients, going to parents' evenings and generally running around between work and home as she juggled all her responsibilities.

She tried to keep her soul-deep loathing for the smug,

public-school bastard, with his 'ya's and that bloody signet ring as though he had a coat of arms displayed in his house or something, in check. She hated the clip of his heels across the lobby, that smug arsehole grin of his, not to mention his nineties Hugh Grant floppy hair.

Partnership had turned out to be a complete misnomer, as Ingrid found that the more work she won, the more she had to look over her shoulder for the inevitable stab in the back by the Tims of her world, partners looking to increase their share of the pie while starving her. And yes, she knew that alliances were key, but when the hell was she supposed to make them while constantly firefighting her life? She sighed.

'You okay?' asked Kerry, her personal assistant. Should she mention the perm Kerry had got over the weekend? Ingrid guessed not, as Kerry had accessorised it with a scarf that covered a large proportion of her head.

'Yep. Matt's due back today.'

'And you have that meeting about your performance, right? Crap day. Sorry. Let me get you a coffee.' Even Kerry knew how this was likely to go.

'Thanks, but the last thing I need is a shot of caffeine right now.' She'd already had three espressos and her hands were definitely shaking.

'Grace called and said she's taking Lily to Puttshack at Westfield after school, and then to the movies and dinner with Audrey and Nathan.'

Ingrid was never sure whether she should be grateful for or wary of her sister's close relationship with her PA. In many ways, it was a godsend, but she was sure that Grace's inability to apply a filter to her mouth meant that Kerry knew far too much about their family.

'And your sister Audrey called too. She tried you on your mobile but it kept going straight to voicemail.'

Ingrid checked her phone. The do-not-disturb was still on and when she disabled it, there were twenty-five messages, ranging from her sisters wishing her luck for tonight, to the dreaded parents' WhatsApp group asking about the geography field trip next week, to Matt confirming the time tonight, to senior partner Chris telling her that the meeting had been moved up to 10 a.m.

'Shit, shit, shit. Didn't anyone tell you that the meeting time had been changed?' she asked Kerry who looked nonplussed.

'No, what? Wait.' She checked her emails. 'Oh my God, I'm so sorry, Ingrid. I got an email in the last ten minutes. Quick.' Kerry took Ingrid's bag from her left hand, pressed her leather folio into her right, dusted some fluff from Ingrid's skirt and steered her in the direction of the conference room. 'Good luck, boss.'

As Ingrid shot into the room in the least flustered entrance she could manage, Chris stood from his place at the conference table, clearly pleased that she looked so discombobulated by the time change. Then the bastard actually checked his watch pointedly before indicating that she should sit on the chair opposite him. She slid onto the seat, careful to smooth her skirt down to cover her knees, and suddenly grateful to Grace for tie-dyeing her Thursday V-necked blouse and forcing her into the Tuesday high-necked one.

Chris was one of those dinosaurs of the accountancy world for whom sexual harassment claims were just women being oversensitive. She'd been in many a meeting with him where he'd stared at her boobs or 'accidentally' brushed his hand against her thigh. He'd been in the running for the Chairman of the Board role, but once he'd disclosed the fifteen personal relationships he'd had with staff, his dreams of accountancy domination ended abruptly. Now he ran her part of the business with Not-Nice Tim as his golden boy.

'I'm sorry I'm a little late. I just got the message about the change of time,' she said.

Chris settled into his chair and steepled his fingers. 'So, you've done well this year in terms of fees and feedback from your staff and other partners. But you know that we can't reward our partners based on this alone. We have to assess you across many criteria and I'm sorry to say that, once again, you're falling short.'

Ingrid uncrossed and recrossed her legs. If she were Audrey, she would be telling him that there would be no firm at all if people like her didn't go out there and win work that brought in actual fees. But then she'd probably have no job. She took a sip of water.

'There's still some work to do on diversity and inclusion.'

Ingrid snorted the water up her nose. Had he noticed that she was brown and female? Clearly they preferred someone who jumped through their meaningless 'tick box' hoops but achieved no real change, while Ingrid actually tried to help every member of her staff progress while embracing their differences. Which was all in the upward feedback. But of course, no one read that unless it was negative.

'And you're not very collegiate. Tim has had an awful lot to say about how protective you are of your clients.'

Funny, because he had no problem claiming that all her hard-won work was his.

'And he's not the only one.'

Who else had been saying this? Why was this all so difficult? She didn't have time to make friends and form alliances at work. But the joke was on her because, when it came to the nebulous justification of partner share, this counted more than bringing in the money. Something that Not-Nice Tim clearly understood with all his lunches at his private club.

By now she was fuming, but she had to keep her mouth shut.

'Here's the number.' He slid a piece of paper in front of her.

She peered at the rating. Three. Distinctly average. And the money. Less than last year, despite inflation. But she'd learned a long time ago that it was never a good move to complain outright, as it would only count against her in the future. Anyway, it was way more than she'd ever dreamed of earning while sharing a tiny box room with Grace in Rayners Lane.

'Thank you,' she said, standing. She'd perfected this nonchalant exit over the past few years. It was best to get out as soon as possible. 'Have a good day, Chris.' She delivered the usual fake smile.

When were things going to get easier? Certainly not this evening, that was for sure.

3

The Return of the Husband

Ingrid was momentarily speechless as she stared at Matt on the other side of the front door. Before he'd left, Matt had taken on that shabby, can't-be-bothered dad look of band T-shirt – to show that he used to have a much more interesting life at some point – along with shapeless, dirty jeans. His work outfits had been only marginally better, with a selection of checked button-down shirts, well-worn corduroy and sturdy, rubber-soled shoes.

This Matt looked like he was trying out his best David Gandy impression. His once thick, curly hair was styled into a faded back and sides with a hint of his natural curls on top. He wore a crisp white shirt – unbuttoned to contrast with the golden tan on his chest and neck, his sleeves rolled up to reveal a selection of leather and stone bracelets, tight faded jeans and light grey suede desert boots. The pièce de résistance was an artfully wound long, woven scarf draped down the length of his torso.

He moved forward and kissed her on the cheek. He'd overdone it on the aftershave though – one inhale of it made her sneeze.

'Ingrid. Good to see you,' he said, his tone unexpectedly formal. Had she just forgotten what he was like because this wasn't the same man who'd left a year ago?

She peered behind him. 'No luggage?'

'I'm staying with a friend.' The look in his eyes made her wonder if the friend was a woman. Did she care?

He stalked past her, heading straight for the kitchen where she'd left an open bottle of wine on the table with two glasses and a small charcuterie platter she'd bought from M&S on the way home but hadn't bothered to remove from its plastic container.

Matt looked at the platter, a wry smile on his lips, taking the glass she offered him.

'You look different.'

He smiled, clearly pleased with himself. 'You like it?'

'It's good.' He was so smug, she kicked herself for saying anything at all.

'Thanks.'

She waited, but there was no reciprocal compliment – something about Matt that hadn't changed. He had always been so much more preoccupied with himself, but its absence still stung. Logically, Ingrid knew she was in good shape for her age, with all the morning workouts, but maybe this part of her life was over and she should consign herself to the middle-aged-woman waste heap of invisibility and asexuality.

'Look, Ingrid, so much has changed.'

Here we go. She braced herself.

'We used to have something good, but somewhere between becoming parents, getting so busy, moving home and so on, we lost it all. And I needed to find out who I was without you.'

'And did you?'

Throughout the course of their marriage, he'd been away so much that it was a mystery to Ingrid as to why he didn't already know this.

'I wasn't happy before and being away helped me to realise what I want from my life. I found the real me . . . It turns out I like myself so much more when I feel free.'

She managed to suppress a hysterical snort. How on earth was he managing to say all this with a straight face?

His eyes fixed on a spot behind her, a little to the left of her head, and she recognised the signs of disengagement. Still, she had to ask the question that bubbled up within her.

'Did you find someone else too?'

He looked away, unable to meet her eyes. 'Not exactly. But I . . . I enjoyed sex with someone else. Well, other *people*.'

Ingrid took a deep breath. So while she'd been running around to keep still, he'd been shagging other people.

'But we were, *are* still married. Did those marriage vows mean nothing to you?'

'Of course they did, Ingrid, but we were on a break and I thought . . .'

'*You* were the one on the break, Matt, not me. You were always on breaks. And you never discussed any of it with me.'

'You were always so busy, you never had the time for me to *try* and explain. I mean, I've been away for a year, surely you had sex with someone else?'

She laughed. 'When exactly would I have done that, Matt, between looking after Lily and work? It's not like we haven't gone without sex for that long before.'

Matt looked at his feet. 'It had all become a bit stale for us, hadn't it? You have to admit that. Sleeping with other people made me realise how much I enjoy sex.'

Seriously?

He was the one who'd rebuffed every advance she'd made before he'd left, leaving her feeling foolish and unwanted as she took off the sexy silk underwear and put it carefully back in the drawer. Had he just not enjoyed it with *her*? Was it too much of a habit? Was she too old for him now? It wasn't as though it had all been fireworks for her either, but at least she'd been willing to try.

The tears that had begun to pool in her eyes dried up as her body heated, indignation boiling deep within her. Her usual tight control on her emotions battled the anger threatening to engulf her.

She wondered how much he'd 'enjoy' it if she pulled hard

on the ends of that stupid scarf around his neck. He was a selfish, immature, man-boy who had never taken her feelings into account and had put himself before everyone, even his daughter, without giving a thought to the destruction he left in his wake.

Ingrid usually left the emotional outbursts to the rest of her volatile family. But his nonchalance, arrogance even, had provoked her beyond belief.

'It's been such a liberating year. I've found new purpose.' As what? *A middle-aged gigolo?*

'Matt,' she said, desperate to stop whatever this display was. But he was on a roll.

'I think we should get a divorce.'

'What?' It was no surprise, but the word still landed heavily on her.

'A divorce. You know, a dissolution of marriage, a split of all the assets, custody and all that.'

'*Custody?* Of what?'

'Lily, of course.'

At the mention of custody, her mind was razor sharp, her anger so red hot that she was calm.

'You mean the daughter you abandoned without a word for an entire year, and didn't even wish happy birthday? Not to mention all your trips away over the years.'

He dusted an imaginary piece of lint from his sleeve. 'Now there's no need to get emotional.'

'What? How is pointing out a fact an emotional outburst?'

But she knew why he thought her simple statement of fact seemed emotional to him. Their marriage had been one decision of Matt's after another with no push back from Ingrid, even if she thought his plans were hare-brained and ill-conceived. She wasn't a doormat. She just wanted peace. And it was easier to go along with things and steer him gently back onto the sensible path without him ever realising her involvement.

'Are you upset?' he asked.

She didn't know how she managed not to scoff at him, but she was deeply grateful to her bodily instincts for holding it together and giving the appearance of calm. She stared at him.

'I'm sorry, Ingrid, I just assumed that after all this time, you'd probably moved on too.'

'Honestly, we both know that you moved on years ago. I don't care about the sex part, but you know that you've only shown a passing interest at best in our daughter. Why on earth do you want custody?'

'She's my daughter. And my time away has made me see that she needs more stability than you're able to give her with that job of yours.'

She looked at her wine glass, and before she knew it, she'd thrown the contents in his face, drenching him in a fairly average Cabernet Sauvignon.

'What the fuck?'

Ingrid bit her lip to hold back the laugh that threatened to break loose as wine droplets fell from the drooping strands of his hair.

'Have you completely lost your mind?'

'Is the wine not to your taste then?'

Matt stared at her in surprise for a moment, then grabbed some kitchen paper and began the futile job of trying to get red wine stains out of his suede boots. He looked up from under those long eyelashes that had once been so attractive to her.

'You've changed,' he said with something approaching appreciation in his eyes.

'It was about time, wasn't it?' she replied with clarity. Why had she put up with all his bullshit for so long?

'You know that we're over. We have been for a long time,' he continued.

Of course, she knew that. But knowledge was quite a different animal from acceptance.

'We got married so young,' he said, wiping a droplet of wine from his face.

She turned away to hide the laugh that erupted from her. They'd been thirty-two when they'd married, which wasn't old, but wasn't particularly young either. They had both established their careers and lives, but the ticking clock in her ovaries had made him the best prospect for a family at the time.

He dabbed ineffectually at his crime scene of a shirt. She didn't imagine that his year away had included a 'how to do laundry' segment.

'Maybe I should file for full custody of Lily,' he said, shooting her a dark look as he straightened up. 'You're clearly not mentally sound.'

Her anger was now white hot, threatening to destroy anything in its path. 'Are you insane?'

'You have to admit that with your job, it's pretty hard for you to be a mother. And now this.' He gestured to his clothes.

'I'm *always* a mother, Matt. I'm the one that does the laundry, buys and cooks the food, holds her when she cries, celebrates her triumphs, listens to all her troubles, helps with her schoolwork, reads to her, gets her hair cut, buys birthday and Christmas presents, takes her to the doctor – all while doing that job you resent so much. That job that bought you this house, fed you, clothed you, paid for your holidays every year. That job that just paid for you to *find yourself*. Of course you thought you were a great dad when you spared a little time for trips to the Natural History Museum where you could pontificate for hours. But cleaning up vomit at one in the morning, that was Ingrid's job. Yes, Ingrid, the one with the big fancy job that pays for everything. You've got an absolute cheek coming here after abandoning our daughter for a year and suggesting that there's a court that would actually give an irresponsible arsehole like you custody. And I'm mentally just fine, thank you very much. This is what you call a proportional response to my husband returning from the self-indulgent, mid-life crisis holiday *I* funded, and telling me he wants custody of *my* child.'

She took a deep breath. Where the hell had that come from? She hadn't said a word when he'd announced that he simply had to get away and explore his passions, which as far as she could see, comprised hours in the gym and collecting vinyl records, and certainly didn't require him to leave the country, not to mention his family, for a whole year. But when he had dared to mention custody, the valve within her that regulated what she said had clearly come loose.

He stared at her in shock and she allowed herself an internal smile.

'We'll see,' he said.

What was that tone? He had never spoken to her like that. Supercilious, even a little smug. All pretence at kindness had disappeared, the gloves were off now. She couldn't overplay her hand any more than she already had. She didn't even know what her hand was. She needed time to process.

'You should leave.'

'And I want half the house.'

He was literally *asking* her to strangle him with that stupid bloody scarf of his. She felt every iota of self-control struggle to break free within her.

'We'll see,' she said, carefully enunciating his earlier phrase so he could feel the full weight of its insolence. 'Now leave.'

He pushed back his wine-slicked hair and flashed a fake smile before stalking out of the house.

As soon as the front door closed, Ingrid reached for her phone with shaking fingers.

4

Code Red

Sitting alone in the encroaching dark at the kitchen table, Ingrid listened to the rhythmic drip of the kitchen tap. Since Matt had left she'd been rooted to her seat, unable to get up and switch on the lights, watching the colours of the wine stains on the floor and table changing from deep red to black.

Drip, drip, drip. All she heard was 'fix me, fix me, fix me'. There was always something to fix or arrange, her life one long 'to do' list. She'd always been the one carrying the burden of being a homeowner, from paying the mortgage to arranging the boiler service. And what on earth had it been for? She was living with her daughter and her sister in this money-pit of a house that *he'd* wanted. She was exhausted.

Even the knick-knacks and furniture were more a reflection of the interior designer's taste than either of theirs. When they'd first bought the house, Ingrid had excitedly browsed design websites, ordered fabric swatches and picked up paint samples. But Matt had laughed at her. What did an accountant know about interior design? They should leave it to the professionals. He'd reminded Ingrid that she was far too busy to think about colour schemes and themes, and that she should trust Honor's judgement and her sodding mood boards. *He* would take care of all the liaison with Honor so Ingrid didn't need to worry about a thing – not even the long honey-gold hair she'd found in her bed that was suspiciously similar to Honor's dye job. God, she'd been a fool.

And now Matt wanted half. Did that mean he wanted to sell it? She fully resented this implication because, although it hadn't been her choice to move there, it was her home and, more importantly, it was Lily's home. Did the bastard expect her to buy him out? Where on earth was *that* money coming from? She thought of her conversation with Chris earlier that day and put her head in her hands. She was like a broken dam, unable to stop the relentless tide of bad news that kept coming her way.

The front door opened and closed and she heard the familiar shuffle of her sisters as they made their way down the narrow hallway to the kitchen. She'd sent the Code Red as soon as Matt had left the house.

Ingrid was usually first responder to a Code Red. She wasn't accustomed to sending her own, the last one being when she'd gone into labour with Lily. But this evening had demanded it. Feelings were jostling and tumbling within her and thoughts were ricocheting around her head.

The kitchen was suddenly bathed in bright light and Ingrid squinted, covering her eyes with her palm.

'What happened?' asked Audrey with her usual lack of preamble, normally irritating, but this time very welcome.

'Where's Lily?' Ingrid asked, looking behind Grace.

'She's playing Wii Sports with Nathan,' said Audrey. 'Don't worry. She's fine. But what's going on here?'

'He wants a divorce,' said Ingrid before taking another gulp of wine.

'You didn't murder him and bury his body in the garden, did you?' asked Grace, pointing at the red stains on the table and floor.

'I thought about it, but no, that's wine. I threw a glass at him.'

'You what?' they both said, whirling around to face her. She shrugged.

'Grace, get another bottle and some glasses,' ordered Audrey.

'Always so bossy,' said Grace as she slouched off to do as she was told.

'And?' Audrey could never be accused of lacking self-awareness. She turned back to Ingrid. 'What happened?'

'He's had a makeover. He's all skinny jeans and unbuttoned shirts with a tan.'

Audrey grimaced. 'Sounds sleazy.'

Ingrid managed a laugh. Maybe his fashion had caught up with his personality.

'Talking of sleazy, he's spent the last year having mind-blowing sex with other women, not that this is something entirely new.' She took a long sip of the wine Grace had handed her in a new, full glass. It was much better than the one she'd thrown over her soon-to-be-ex husband . . . 'Apparently, he didn't know he could enjoy it so much.'

'So the bastard finally admitted it,' said Audrey, watching Ingrid carefully.

'You knew?'

Audrey shrugged. 'I suspected. Wasn't there something shady going on with that interior designer you hired?'

Ingrid rolled her eyes. So many missed conversations. 'You didn't say anything?'

'I thought you knew and were fine with it.'

'I did. I wasn't. Anyway, he finished it all off by announcing that he wanted a divorce.' Ingrid took another deep gulp of wine. 'And then he said he would file for custody of Lily.'

Audrey smacked the table hard, making both Ingrid and Grace jump. 'That cretin is nuts if he thinks any judge would give him custody. And anyway, Lily doesn't want to see him, does she? It's not like a judge would ignore that either.'

Ingrid had thought the same, but was relieved to have her opinions validated.

'But Matt loves you,' said Grace. 'He's probably going to change his mind pretty soon.'

Audrey and Ingrid gaped at her.

'What? I mean, it's Matt. We know him, don't we? It sounds like a midlife crisis. He'll change his mind.'

'Please tell me that you're joking and that you can't possibly be this naive,' said Audrey.

'It's not naivety. It just that the Matt we know wouldn't do something like this.'

'Did you hit your head, Grace? He is *exactly* the type of man to do this. He took off for a whole year of self-indulgence – all on Ingrid's tab, lest we forget – leaving Ingrid to bring up Lily, pay the bills, you name it. And it sounds like he's been having quite the time of it,' said Audrey.

Ingrid raised her glass to toast Audrey's common sense.

'Sounds like that wine bath was the very least he deserved. I mean, he actually said that he enjoys sex now that it's with other women?' Audrey asked, still a little incredulous.

Ingrid winced at hearing the words repeated back to her so baldly. But then this was what she relied on from Audrey. No bullshit, no sugar-coating. It was why she'd been an excellent doctor before she gave up work to be a full-time mother, able to emotionally distance herself from her patients.

'That was the gist of it,' said Ingrid, still smarting.

'Who says something like that when asking for a divorce? You know I've always thought he was a waste of space. Now I think he can be downgraded even further to total fucker.'

'Aude, he's our brother-in-law! You can't talk about him like that.'

Audrey turned in her seat to look at Grace. 'Pick a team, Gracie. There's no nuance here, or "listen to his side", or objectivity. He came in here, stomped all over our sister's heart, told her she was crap at sex—' Ingrid winced '—and that he wants to take their daughter away and get half of the house. How are you even wavering over this? And in case you still haven't a clue, let me give you a hint, you *always* pick the Perera side.'

'Okay, okay, keep your knickers on,' said Grace looking contrite, and Ingrid almost laughed as she remembered Grace's pale pink knickers hanging on the airer in the utility room. 'It's just that they've been together for so long and they were so perfect.'

'There's nothing perfect about a marriage where one person buggers off on a gap year without any proper explanation, not to mention all the sex with other people,' said Audrey.

'Hear, hear,' said Ingrid, raising her glass in another toast.

'Are you okay?' asked Grace. 'I mean, it kind of looks like you've had an out-of-body experience.'

Ingrid shook her head. She wasn't okay. How could she be?

'I think he'll see how hurt you are and he'll change his mind,' said Grace.

Ingrid barked out a laugh. 'I really don't want him to, Gracie.' She glanced at her sister, who had so many of their mother's facial features that it was almost unsettling to look at her . . . Oh God. Her mother. She snapped up straight in her seat.

'I have to tell Ammi and Thatha. They're going to lose it,' she said.

'Correction, Mum will lose it while Dad tries to calm her down,' said Grace.

'Listen, Gracie, Ammi and Thatha are going to have plenty to say about this. And you have to promise not to sit this one out. You *have* to back Ingrid,' said Audrey.

'I really resent that,' said Grace.

'Don't even pretend that you're not a coward when it comes to them. Your whole MO is to keep out of things just in case they start on you and you become collateral damage,' Audrey continued.

'You can't blame me. I'm like their favourite punch bag.'

'Then get a job,' said Audrey.

Ingrid waved her hand at her sisters. 'Excuse me? Code Red for *me*. Can we not get distracted here? What am I supposed to do now?'

Audrey took Ingrid's hand in both of hers. 'Can you get some time off work?'

Ingrid shrugged. She hadn't had a holiday for over a year, but she wasn't sure if taking a break would look like some sort of protest against the partner profit share that she'd been allocated this year. And what about Lily? And the dripping tap and the million other things on her 'to do' list? *She* wasn't the one who ran away from things.

'You should go away for a bit, Sis,' said Grace. 'Get your head together, pamper yourself and then you can think about what to do. Don't worry about Lily. Between Audrey and me, we can manage.'

'She's right.' Audrey pulled Ingrid's laptop to her and opened it. Miraculously, it had escaped her wine toss. 'Password?'

Ingrid leaned forward and typed it in. Audrey tapped the keyboard then turned the screen towards Ingrid.

'What about this place? It's in the Lake District. A spa retreat. I've been meaning to go myself.'

Ingrid peered at the screen. It was a bit difficult to see without her glasses, but she saw photos of white rooms accented with bright green foliage, massage tables, plush bedrooms and lush scenery.

'They have availability for a *New You* package next week. Sounds perfect. Go have a few massages, some good food, soak in a tub. And then you'll be ready to fight.'

'I don't know,' said Ingrid.

What on earth was she going to do on a spa retreat? She'd never been one of those women with the time or patience for a long string of regular beauty appointments, only having gel polish applied to her nails because she couldn't be bothered to take care of them herself. She was allergic to so many things that the facials would probably bring her out in dermatitis, and the last time she'd done any type of group exercise was about three years ago when she'd tried yoga and farted so loudly during a downward dog that she'd been too embarrassed to go back.

'You know I don't say this often, but I think Audrey's right. You need a change of scenery.'

Maybe a solo holiday *was* what she needed. Matt had had a whole year for goodness' sake. Couldn't she have a week? Ingrid pictured herself in a fluffy robe, sipping a cocktail, leafing through the glossy pages of a magazine and daydreaming as she was massaged into relaxation. She could eat gourmet nutritious meals that she hadn't had to cook herself, and laugh and bond with new friends on a leisurely forest walk. She didn't mind the idea of glowing with health when she had to face Matt again either.

Yes. She deserved it.

'Okay,' she said, 'I'll do it.'

Audrey tapped some more keys and then typed her credit card number in. 'Done. This is on me, Sis. And let me sort you out a lawyer. You know my friend Cheska, right? She's a shit-hot divorce lawyer who'll crush Matt and any delusions he has about custody.'

A lawyer. It was all too real.

Suddenly Ingrid felt very ready to escape for a while.

5

Retreat

On reflection, Ingrid was definitely an indoor person. There was far too much fresh air out here. She scratched the midge bites she'd sustained when she'd made the cardinal mistake of popping out onto the balcony of her tree house with her bottle of water on the first night to enjoy the view. And now, she was trudging her way up what felt like an almost vertical incline in trainers that certainly weren't up to the slippery, rocky path.

Not for the first time she resolved that this was the last time she would ever allow Audrey to book something for her. She was going to have a stern word with her when she got home. Or, better still, book her in for the same deal as her fiftieth birthday present. The *New You* package at The Tree House Resort had been a week of little to no relaxation. The fluffy robes, gourmet food and nice gentle massages on the website were nowhere in sight. Instead, the timetable she'd been handed as she'd checked into her tree house room had been as packed as her Outlook calendar at work. Sunrise power yoga, followed by a tiny breakfast, a personal training session, an even tinier lunch, a yomp up hills, a minuscule dinner à la eighties nouvelle cuisine, and an early bedtime that wasn't even relieved by the ability to chill out with a Netflix drama because the Wi-Fi was almost non-existent.

No wonder people lost weight in this place. They were practically starved to death and exercised into oblivion. Ingrid didn't even need to lose weight. But maybe this retreat *was* working, because the mental image of Matt standing in their kitchen dressed in that bloody scarf had receded in the face of hunger. Or maybe it was that the summer wind and rain in the Lake District had cleared away the fog of shock that had enveloped her since that day. Despite all the hurtful things he'd said, she'd known that this was coming. And now she just had to deal with it.

She watched the women ahead of her, prancing up the hill like a herd of mountain goats, all clad in waterproofs and walking boots and casting occasional glances at the idiot behind them in her 'comme ci, comme ça' sweatshirt, jeans and unsuitable footwear. They kept their distance, no doubt picking up on her foul mood and perhaps sensing that she had booked onto this retreat by mistake.

Would she at least be able to get a decent mobile phone signal out here? Then again, she didn't want to pull out her phone in front of everyone and advertise her blatant disregard for the 'digital detox' promoted by the retreat. She'd promised Lily she'd call every day, having no idea she'd be in the dark ages. And now she was desperate to speak to her. She'd decided not to tell Lily anything about the divorce until she was over the worst of her anger, although she worried that Matt would get there first. Audrey and Grace had promised to keep him away until she got back, but she needed to know if she should return home for any reason. Or maybe she was looking for an excuse to escape and get herself a nice juicy steak and a large glass of wine . . .

And when her emails had finally downloaded in the middle of the night, a request for advice for a client had come through, which she desperately needed to see to. This retreat had been a huge error. What had she been thinking? She had a life back home and she couldn't do a Matt and leave it all behind on a whim.

As she strategised on the best way to extricate herself from the group and sneak a quick phone call, she slipped and fell hard on her bum, her already damp clothes now covered in mud. Could this get much worse? She was a grown woman. Why was she persisting in doing something that made her this miserable? Because that's what she always did, wasn't it? She made do, told herself that this was life and she shouldn't complain, and suppressed every desire of her own while helping others to fulfil theirs. And where had it got her? Sitting in a puddle of mud, up a hill in the Lake District.

She pulled herself up, trying to clean her hands but succeeding in getting even more mud on her jeans, and looked around for the rest of the group. She was alone. Never mind that she had been actively trying to give them the slip, those hill-walking, map-reading, sensibly dressed bitches had left her in the middle of nowhere in the pouring rain. Ingrid took her phone out of her pocket. One bar of signal. She could work with that. Time to make some phone calls.

Two hours in steady rain showers and the flirty one bar of signal having deserted her almost immediately, Ingrid's phone battery had ten per cent left and she was soaked to the skin. She could have been back at The Tree House by now, and even if the next meal was an artfully presented crumb, at least she'd be dry. Instead, her hair was plastered to her head and her clothes were so sodden they were weighing her down. She should have rushed to Gaynor's in Ambleside to get suitable gear when she'd realised Audrey's mistake, but she'd been too busy silently raging about the whole thing to do anything practical about it.

Even though it was summer and the sun didn't set fully until after 9 p.m., the light was dim, the 6 p.m. sun hiding behind thick grey clouds. She was sure that she'd seen the Narnia-style signpost on the path ahead of her at least once before in the past hour, and the realisation that she was walking around in circles brought tears to her already wet cheeks. As she shuffled forward to try and interpret the sign into something that would get her safely down this wretched hill, she slipped again.

For a moment, Ingrid gave in to the despair as the reality of her situation sunk in. She was going to die of hypothermia in this place, her body preserved in mud. In summer. It was hours since she'd followed the other people on the hike without paying any attention at all to her surroundings, which all looked the same anyway. She'd been so busy simmering about the indignities of the retreat that she now had no clue how to get back to it. She put her head in her muddy hands, hoping that if she shielded her face from the driving rain, it might give her a little clarity of thought.

'Are you okay?' said a deep male voice next to her.

Ingrid was so startled that she jumped off the boulder she was perched on, yelped, and fell in the mud yet again. When she looked up to see who had spoken, she felt even more of a fool, if that was possible. Before her was a kind-looking young man dressed in sensible waterproofs and sturdy boots with one of those walking poles and a rucksack. What had she been expecting? The Yeti of the Lakes? She shivered, and wondered if it was from the cold or the thought of her own appearance. No one who saw her now would think that she was a hot-shot partner who managed teams of people and a multimillion-pound annual budget in one of the world's leading accountancy firms.

The man knelt next to her in the mud and pushed his hood off his head so that she could see his face. Well, sort of see his face. Everything was blurry in the rain.

'I'm going to take a wild guess here, but you must be from London with that get-up. You're not the only one tramping around the hills in unsuitable clothing,' he said with a wry smile. Unfortunately, Ingrid's sense of humour had gone on its own holiday as soon as she'd entered The Tree House.

'Yes, I'm from London. Somewhere I would much rather be right now, instead of here being mocked by you.'

'Alright then. I'll be off.'

He walked past her. Was he actually going to leave her here?

'Wait, wait.'

He turned. 'Yes?'

She sighed and tried to look as dignified as possible while soaked and covered in mud, which she knew was not very dignified at all. 'I have no idea where I am. I need help to get back to The Tree House Resort.'

'Ahh, you're one of those.'

'One of those what?'

'The detox and yoga brigade.'

She crossed her arms, vaguely offended, despite the circumstances. 'Do you know the way there or not?'

'I do.'

If she hadn't been so desperate to get somewhere warm and dry, she'd have stomped off in the opposite direction by now. This person was exasperating.

'Would you tell me?'

He stared at her for a moment as if evaluating the mud-person in front of him. 'I'll give you a lift there, but first we'll have to get back to my cottage so I can pick up my car.'

Cottage? Oh God, she was going to be chopped up and served to pigs or something. She looked down at herself. Was it worth the risk for some dry clothes and a place to sit down? Honestly, things couldn't get much worse.

'I'm not sure. What if you're an axe murderer?'

'One, why do people say that? Murdering someone with an axe sounds like an awful lot of trouble. And two, if I *were* an axe murderer, I'd probably have used the axe by now. You're safe with me, but . . .' He took his phone out of a zipped pocket on his jacket and handed it to her. 'Here, keep this if it makes you feel safer.'

A fat lot of use that would be with no signal around here. But she took it nonetheless. Despite their exchange, there was something in those deep brown eyes of his that told her that she could trust him.

'Okay. How far is it?'

'Just round the corner.'

Ingrid looked around. What corner? All she saw was miles of hills.

He walked a little ahead and turned back to check she was following. 'Are you coming?'

No matter how far it was, she had no choice. She moved forward, trying to step into his footprints, but her trainers didn't have as much grip as his walking boots and she slipped again. Except this time, one of her shoes made a bid for freedom down the hillside. She groaned as she landed in the mud once again.

The man turned around and approached the snivelling lump of mud that was Ingrid, as this time she gave in to self-pity. He stooped to her eye level as if she were a child.

'What happened?'

'My . . . my shoe,' she sobbed.

'Did you see where it went?'

She shook her head. Between the rain and the tears, she couldn't see much.

'I might have to carry you.' He transferred his rucksack from his back to his front and squatted down in front of her, indicating that she should hop onto his back like the five-year-old she'd become.

She shook her head. She could manage with one shoe, couldn't she? She wasn't sure she could handle the indignity of being carried by a total stranger. 'I'll be fine,' she said, standing and promptly slipping again as her socked foot skidded through the mud.

'Let me carry you.'

God, she was going to have to accept this piggyback. She looked at him, unconvinced that someone who looked so slight could carry a grown woman on his back.

He put his hand on her arm. 'Look, we're both soaking out here. Let me carry you. It isn't far.'

6

The Cottage

After twenty of the most mortifying minutes of her life, a white stone cottage with a thatched roof and a chimney finally came into view. Ingrid gripped the man's shoulders as his slow and deliberate tread carried her under a trellis archway and onto an uneven stone path. It seemed an unlikely place for a murder, but then horror movies would tell her otherwise. An innocent white cottage could be the perfect backdrop for an unexpected bloodbath. Desperation had dampened her usual instinct to weigh the pros and cons of all her decisions, leading her to take the kind of risk that was complete anathema to her as an accountant.

But there had once been a different, more carefree Ingrid, who'd existed before she was a teenager. A young girl who snuck out to the sweet shop around the corner when she'd been expressly told to stay at home, or who insisted that the school hadn't set any homework only to be discovered when Mum had marched into the office and demanded to know why they weren't teaching her properly. The Ingrid who'd existed before a crippling need to be valued and liked for the things that she did rather than the person she was had emerged. And in this moment of clinging to a complete stranger in the pouring rain, there was more exhilaration than fear, because there was a tinge of freedom in her potentially ill-advised decision to ask this man for help.

But really, was anyone this kind? He must be exhausted from carrying her all this way over uneven terrain in foul weather. He put her down just outside the cottage and opened the front door. Ingrid peered into a blinding sea of white from the floor, the ceiling, the walls, even the furniture. The clean-up from a murder would be a nightmare in a space like this. She stepped inside gingerly, not from fear of potential violence, but because she was coated in mud.

'Something wrong?' asked the man, removing his boots by the door.

'I don't want to get your house dirty.'

He laughed, a low, sonorous sound that helped to put her at ease. 'I don't think we can avoid that. Come in. The bathroom's that way.' He pointed down to the end of the white corridor. 'You can take a shower and I'll get some clothes for you to change into.'

The interior of the cottage was so relentlessly bright that Ingrid shut her eyes for a moment of respite.

'Um, here's your phone,' she said, removing it from where she'd stored it between her stomach and the waistband of her jeans.

He took it from her between his thumb and forefinger as though she'd handed him a rat, and she had no doubt that he would be disinfecting it as soon as she was in the bathroom.

'I'm Jacob, by the way.'

She took a proper look at him as he removed his waterproof jacket. He was young, perhaps late twenties or early thirties, with a lean, muscular physique, dark hair pushed back from his symmetrical face. He smiled at her, two dimples appearing in his cheeks, and her breath caught. Something that felt very much like attraction stirred within her for a moment before her common sense quickly quashed it.

'Ingrid.' She held out her hand to shake his but then hastily withdrew it. 'Sorry, I'm filthy.'

He grabbed her hand anyway and shook it, his skin surprisingly soft for a rugged outdoor type. 'So am I. Nice name, Ingrid. You can use the landline to call the resort if you want. Based on previous experience with this weather, the road up there will be flooded. But you should call and check.'

She couldn't remember the last time she'd used a landline, but she was immensely grateful for one now. She could at least confirm Jacob's story. She took the handset he offered and stared at the keypad helplessly. She had no idea what the phone number was. She extracted her phone from her pocket, but the black screen told her that it had either run out of battery, or drowned in the downpour. Now she wouldn't even be able to call Lily, because who remembered phone numbers these days?

'Let me plug this in and see if we can bring it back to life,' Jacob said, his hand covering hers as he took her phone from her. 'And here,' he said, unlocking his mobile phone and handing it to her. 'You can look up the number for the resort. The Wi-Fi still works even if the phone signal is patchy.'

She took his phone, careful not to touch his skin as she did so, and dialled the resort's number. 'Oh, hello, I'm Ingrid Perera. I'm a guest at your resort but I got lost during a hike. A . . .' She looked at Jacob who smiled. 'A friend says that they can drive me back but that it's likely the road is flooded. Could you confirm if that's the case?'

'Thank goodness, you're safe. We were about to send out a rescue team. I'm so sorry, madam, but as usual, excessive rain has caused a road closure. From experience, I'd say that it takes at least twelve hours for the ground water to recede. Do you have somewhere to stay?'

Ingrid wanted to cry, but had to hold it together. This holiday was an unmitigated disaster. Now she would have to ask a stranger who had already carried her to safety on his back to take her to a hotel somewhere that wasn't flooded, if they could even get there. And how the hell was she going to pay for it? Her cards were back at the hotel and her phone seemed to have drowned.

'Are you okay?' Jacob mouthed at her.

'They're asking if I have somewhere to stay. Can you take me to a hotel in town perhaps?'

'You can stay here.'

'I can't impose on you. You've been so kind already.'

'It's no trouble, honestly. I have a guest room and plenty of food. And no axes in the house,' he said, grinning.

So some people really were this kind.

'You're sure?'

Jacob nodded.

'Yes, I have somewhere to stay,' Ingrid said to the woman on the phone.

'Wonderful. We'll see you back here tomorrow.'

Ingrid hung up and faced Jacob. People were unlikely to help you out in London, preferring not to get involved with other people's business. She'd become an expert herself at the wilful blindness required to survive life in the capital.

'Thank you. I really appreciate all the help you've given me. And I'm sorry for being a bit of a cow out there.'

'I'm used to cows,' he said with a wink. 'Anyway, it's no problem. I wouldn't leave anyone out there in this.'

'And yet, you were walking away.' She kicked herself the moment it came out. How ungrateful could she be? The circumstances had stripped away her usual filter.

'Yeah, sorry about that. It's just that we get lots of tourists around here and there's always a few who set out on hikes without the right gear when the weather can change in a moment. Then other people have to risk *their* lives to save them when they get into trouble.'

Ingrid bit her lip. She hadn't known that the 'stroll' mentioned by the organisers of the *New You* package would turn into a full-blown hike – and yet everyone else had come prepared. She probably was one of those thoughtless people Jacob had just described. Even so, she was going to be having a word with the resort people.

'I'm sorry. You're right. I should've planned better.'

'I blame the hotel really. Anyway, why don't you go and clean up while I heat up some soup or something? That shouldn't interfere with whatever diet they've got you on in that place.'

Ingrid's stomach growled on cue. 'About that. Funny story. I didn't actually realise that I was signed up for the ascetic living package. My sister booked me onto this thinking it would be full of massages and gourmet food, not hikes and morsels. I've been starving for the past week.'

He laughed. Gosh, he was handsome. Deep brown eyes, black hair, a long nose with a slight bump in it, full pink lips. No, she shouldn't look at his lips. She was a bedraggled forty-five-year-old woman who was about to get divorced, and she shouldn't be noticing that *anyone* was good looking, let alone a man as young as this one. But then again, why shouldn't she? They were never likely to meet again, and perhaps a little light flirting with a beautiful man would be even more of a confidence boost than a luxury spa retreat.

'We can't have that. How about pasta?'

'Oh my God, yes. I've literally been dreaming about spaghetti and I don't even eat carbs.'

Another of those deep laughs resonated and Ingrid swore she could feel it in her body. 'Okay. But now you really must take a shower before your mud becomes a permanent feature on the stone floor.'

She managed a small, nervous laugh before inching her way down the corridor to the bathroom. Another temple of white that served as a frame for the picture window taking up a large part of one wall with breath-taking views of the lush green landscape, a Victorian-style bathtub with claw feet and shiny chrome taps just below it. The shower stall stood in the corner. And the floor . . . well, it was muddy now, but the tiles underneath were white too.

She removed her clothes and placed them in a small pile by the door then tried to work out what to do with the two different space-age knobs attached to the wall. Freezing cold water cascaded out of the shower head, and just as she hopped out of the shower stall to avoid it, the bathroom door opened. She turned her body to face the door, where Jacob stood, a neatly folded pile of clothing in one hand, his mouth open as he stared at Ingrid who was completely naked.

She could plunge herself back into the frozen water in a vain attempt to preserve her modesty. Or she could act like the mature person she was, the one who had checked in her dignity when she'd given birth, legs splayed wide, dilating vagina on full display to a roomful of medical professionals, and thank him for the clothes.

She opted for the latter, meeting his eyes as she did. As embarrassing as the situation was, she couldn't help the tiny satisfaction at the way he looked at her, cheeks pink. She'd been out of the dating game for so long that it was hard to tell, but she thought that there *might* be a spark of something more than just embarrassment there.

Jacob gulped. 'Sorry, so sorry, I should've knocked. I've been living alone for so long that I didn't even think . . .' he gabbled, placing the clothes on the floor and backing out of the room, but not taking his eyes off her.

For the first time in a while, Ingrid smiled to herself. Maybe she should embrace this opportunity that the universe had presented to her?

7

Carbs and Confidences

Ingrid emerged from the bathroom and entered the modern farmhouse kitchen with its deep butler sink and an assortment of copper pans hanging from a frame on the ceiling. One large pot bubbled, while a frying pan filled with fresh tomatoes sizzled next to it. Jacob was a tall man, so she felt like a child wearing adult clothes as sleeves and trouser legs bunched up at her wrists and ankles.

'Oh my God, the sweet smell of carbs!' Ingrid inhaled deeply, forgetting her determination to stay well away from that food group for the sake of her middle-aged waistline.

He laughed and handed her a grissini stick with another one of those smiles. 'Here, this should keep you going while I get dinner ready.'

Seriously, who had a box of grissini lying around their kitchen just in case bedraggled Londoners showed up? From Waitrose no less. Jacob clearly wasn't just the rugged mountain guide she'd thought he was.

'Oh, and here's your phone,' he said, pulling it out of his back pocket and handing it to her. It was warm in her hand. 'I charged it for a bit, and it works. Also there's a decent signal here if you want to make any calls. I'll be back in a tick. Just off to shower.' His hand momentarily pressed onto her arm.

'Do you need me to deliver your clothes too?' she asked with what she thought might pass for a flirty smile, but being so out of practice may have looked pained instead.

He turned, his eyes meeting hers. 'Hmm . . .' He pretended to consider the offer. 'Tempting, but I'll manage for the moment.'

She felt a blush starting at the base of her neck, and if she wasn't mistaken, the tips of his ears were tinged red.

He pointed to the bathroom. 'I should . . .'

She nodded and he padded off to clean up.

Ingrid wasted no time in looking for a good signal by the window and dialling Lily's number, thankful that she'd finally given in and bought her daughter the much longed-for smartphone.

'Mum! I miss you so much,' said Lily, the sound of her voice prompting a deep need to see her daughter and hold her in her arms.

'I miss you too, baby. What have you been doing today? How was school?'

'School was so-so. And I played Fortnite with Aunty Grace, but she's so bad, it's not that much fun.'

Ingrid chuckled. 'And you're fine otherwise?'

'Yeah. Dad came round.'

Ingrid froze.

'Mum?'

'Yes, darling.' She tried to keep her voice light and even. 'Are you okay?'

'I don't like it when he comes over.'

Ingrid had to agree with her daughter on this one, and if Matt insisted on his ludicrous custody battle, perhaps this was a good thing.

'I'll talk to him, alright?'

'When are you coming home?'

'Tomorrow.' She wasn't going to stay up here any longer than she had to. It turned out that she could run away, but she couldn't outrun her life.

'What time?'

'Not sure yet, but I'll text when I'm leaving.' She prayed that the road would be accessible in the morning.

'Mum, I've got to go, I've got another game starting in a minute.'

'Not too long on the computer, Lils . . .'

But she was gone.

Ingrid would not cry again. She had to be strong for both herself and her daughter. Her life with Matt had played across her mind for the past week, visions of them like a sepia-tinted movie that haunted her every moment. Their first meeting at a mutual friend's wedding, the way he looked in the morning with his hair a little dishevelled, bringing Lily home from the hospital, the three of them together at Disneyland Paris as an enchanted Lily gazed at the characters with eyes like saucers. But there were many more not-so-great times like when she'd be late on the rare occasion that he'd cooked dinner, or how he turned away from her in bed, his back an impenetrable wall, the way he'd leave to go to the gym and return hours later, the strange perfumes on his clothes, the sulks when she wasn't able to give him her full attention, the constant suitcases in the hallway as he prepared for yet another trip away.

And in truth, the last year without him had been much easier than she'd thought it might be. She, Lily and Grace had fallen into comfortable and happy routines, and she'd been less burdened by the need to walk on eggshells around Matt, pandering to his enormous ego to maintain the status quo.

Was there anything worth maintaining? It was time for some forward momentum in her life and she couldn't do that while hiding away in the Lake District.

She looked around the cottage. Cosy, well-equipped, but a little soulless. Not one photograph anywhere. Not even any artwork. It screamed rental.

'All good?' Jacob asked, entering the room as he towel-dried his hair. Her breath caught in her throat for a moment as she noted the shape of his body in his T-shirt and joggers, the strength in his corded arms, his lightly tanned skin with stray droplets of water. She wasn't used to seeing people like this up close in real life rather than on a screen or in a magazine.

'Um, er . . . yes. Actually, I just called home.' Should she mention that she had a daughter? No. There was no need. She would never see Jacob again.

'Is everything okay?'

She ran her fingers through her wet hair. 'Yep. I said I should be back tomorrow.'

'Cool. I've got an alert set for when the road opens, so I can take you back then. Hopefully it will be early in the morning if you're driving home.' He pointed to her wet hair. 'I have a hairdryer somewhere.'

She shook her head. 'No, it's fine.'

He approached her with his towel. 'At least let me help you dry it with this.'

He began to gently rub thick strands of her hair in the fluffy towel that was still a little damp from his own, his fingers occasionally brushing the back of her neck, sending shivers down Ingrid's spine.

'You're from London?'

She nodded, remembering his dim view of Londoners.

'The accent and lack of appropriate clothing were a dead giveaway, huh?'

His hands rested on her shoulders, his palms warm. She wanted to lean back into him. Would that be too much?

'Sort of. You just seem like someone who works in the City.'

'You mean rude and brash?'

His hands pressed down on her shoulders, kneading a little. 'Stressed and mistrustful.'

She couldn't disagree with that, and she was too distracted anyway. She wanted him to continue, to feel his hands on her and she swayed towards him as her stomach growled again. He swung her round to face him.

'How about I promise I won't start the murdering until after you've had something to eat?'

'Okay, so I'm hoping that if you were a real murderer, you wouldn't say something like that unless this cottage is actually made of gingerbread. Can I help?'

He walked to the kitchen, poured what seemed like half the bottle of red wine into a fishbowl-sized glass, and pressed it into her hand.

'Trying to get me drunk?' Ingrid asked before taking a long gulp.

He leaned towards her with a smile. 'And why would I do that?'

Oh God, she was an amateur at this flirting thing. 'Surely a drunk person would be easier to murder.'

He laughed, then looked her up and down. 'You're pretty small. I reckon I could manage the murdering without any form of incapacitation.'

Ingrid decided it was best to hide her embarrassment in the glass, bringing it to her lips for a sip while Jacob checked on the sauce. Had she accidentally stumbled on the perfect man? He was cooking from scratch when Ingrid would've fished an almost out-of-date bottle of pesto from the back of the cupboard. The pan bubbled with fresh tomatoes, garlic, capers and basil. She watched as he grated a large wedge of Parmesan into it.

'Can you grab a couple of bowls from that cupboard?' He indicated one next to his left leg.

She nodded and crouched beside him to extract two large pasta bowls, brushing against him as she stood when he made no attempt to get out of the way. She couldn't be sure, but it felt like he wanted to be near her as much as she was drawn to him. Was she imagining this? She felt a little breathless. Or maybe that was the effect of the wine that she'd just knocked back.

'What brings you up here?' he asked, spooning sauce over the pasta.

She could either talk about her troubles with this man or she could go along with whatever this energy was between them for just one night.

'I've been working pretty hard, so it's just a break.'

'And you said that your sister booked you on the health thing by accident?'

She smiled. 'Yeah, she'll think it's hilarious that I'm on the special diet version of a spa break.'

He handed her a bowl full of pasta. 'Especially when you're already in such good shape.'

From the way he avoided her eyes, they both knew that he was referring to seeing her naked. She couldn't remember the last time someone had looked at her like that. Matt had avoided and ignored her for so long that she'd convinced herself that she was no longer attractive to anyone, especially at her age. But Jacob had noticed, hadn't he?

He guided her to the oak kitchen table, a bowl in one hand and the other at the base of her spine and she tried not to react to the physical contact. They both sat. The rain continued to batter the windows as their forks clattered against the crockery, twirling long strands of spaghetti. Was she imagining this charged atmosphere between them?

As Ingrid registered the sweet taste of pasta and tomatoes, the whirl of thoughts in her head came to a brief standstill as she allowed the dopamine hit of comfort food to wash over her for the first time in years. She groaned with delight.

Jacob watched her. 'That good, huh?'

'I can't tell you the joy that this meal has just brought me.'

'I heard it.'

'God, that's so embarrassing.'

'No, I liked it.' He leaned forward. 'You should never be embarrassed about your pleasure, Ingrid. Even in the small things in life.'

She was suddenly very hot and wished that she could take off the sweatshirt she was wearing, but she had nothing on underneath it.

She nodded. 'Shouldn't I be telling you stuff like that? After all, I'm the one with the life experience.'

He smiled wryly. 'You're not much older than me, are you? But I'm sure you could teach me a thing or two.'

Ingrid nearly gasped but managed to control herself. Was this utterly gorgeous man who was possibly two decades younger than her really flirting with her? It seemed like it. Was he just buttering her up before the axes came out? God, she was no good at this. Flirtation wasn't something that she ever really did, because someone as rational and practical as her always thought through options before she said anything. Now, having leaned into this attraction, she couldn't handle it. She stuffed more pasta into her mouth, trying hard not to make any sounds as she did so, while Jacob smiled and looked down at his bowl. After a few minutes of slightly awkward eating, she managed to break the silence.

'How long have you lived here, Jacob?'

He looked up at her from under very long eyelashes and she instinctively blinked in response. 'Not too long. Actually, I'm originally from Kendal, but I'm visiting for a bit, seeing my mum. Considering my options.'

'You have some decisions to make?'

He put down his fork and leaned back in his chair. 'Yeah. I've been in Singapore for the past five years. And Mum wants me to stick around here for a bit. But she doesn't get that my job isn't one I can do in the Lakes.'

Ingrid nodded. She had been fulfilling her parents' hopes and dreams for as long as she could remember. 'I'm much older than you and even now my parents would have a fit if I left the country.' They still hadn't forgiven Grace for going to live in the US for so long, particularly because she'd decided to be a musician, a career that was too unstable and didn't carry enough professional kudos for her traditional Sri Lankan parents.

'Yeah, Mum wasn't too pleased when I left. But I wanted to get out of here, make money and all that.' He sighed.

'Actually, I've already accepted a job in New York and am due to start in December, but then . . . stuff happened, and I'm back here. I feel like I owe it to Mum to think about staying.'

'Isn't it *your* life?' The irony of Ingrid, who lived her life for every other person in it, saying these words to him wasn't lost on her.

'She has her reasons. Maybe it's time for me to grow up and stop being so selfish.' From the sound of it, he'd been thinking about this a lot.

Their eyes locked. There was sadness there. She wanted to ask why he'd come back to the UK at all, but she sensed that this wasn't something he would want to talk about with her. After all, who was she? A wretched vagabond he'd picked up on the side of a hill. She took a grateful sip of the red wine he'd topped up for them both, suddenly shocked that she'd already drunk so much.

They stared at each other again, and there was a zip of electricity between them.

She cleared her throat and looked out of the window, feeling a little bad about being so cagey when he'd been so forthcoming about his life, but she didn't want to break the spell. Something about being at this table with this lovely man, eating this divine food, was everything she needed right now.

'So how do you usually choose your victims? Are they all middle-aged saddos crying in the mud, or is it a little more sophisticated than that?'

He barked out a laugh. 'I try and mix it up a bit, but it's the middle-aged saddos I like best. I can fill them up on pasta and wine and the slaughtering is so much easier. No axes needed.'

They both laughed.

'Thank you for helping me, I'm not sure what I would've done if you hadn't come along. It's pelting down out there,' she said.

'It's turning out to be quite a pleasure, Ingrid. And yeah, it's unlikely that road will clear tonight.'

She avoided his gaze. Was his eye contact this intense with everyone? She cupped her wine glass as though it were a mug. 'So do you usually live alone?'

Why the hell had she just said that?

He nodded as his eyes flashed towards her ring finger. She'd taken off her rings as soon as Matt had asked for a divorce, but the telltale tan line remained.

'How about you? Do you live alone?'

She hadn't done this for a while, but she was pretty sure that you didn't flirt with someone by telling them about the daughter and sister you shared your house with.

'Yep.' The lie came out slightly strangled, and she looked away. But she could feel him smiling at her as he stood to take her empty bowl to the sink.

Ingrid jumped up to help him, unable to prevent her body from leaning towards his, as though yearning for contact. When his arm slid across her to reach a sponge, Ingrid inhaled his woody scent. A sudden panic gripped her as she knew instantly that she didn't have the guts to take this further right now. If there was a further . . . She had enjoyed the surprising sensation of what she thought was some serious flirting, but now was the time to step away. And there was always the chance that she had read things wrong. She *was* feeling slightly delirious . . .

Ingrid forced a yawn.

'Maybe you should get some sleep,' said Jacob on cue, looking down at her with those brown eyes.

Her eyes fixed on his lips. They looked soft. Would they feel soft?

'Yes, I should sleep,' she stammered.

'I'll show you to the spare room and if the road opens earlier than tomorrow morning, I can wake you up and take you back.'

He motioned to her to follow him to the spare bedroom,

which was, surprise, all white. 'I'll let you know about the road.' With one brief but loaded look, he left the room, closing the door behind him softly.

Ingrid sighed. It was probably only about 8 p.m. and far too early for bed, but the exhaustion of the day caught up with her and before she could fully finish her thought, she was asleep.

8

Departure

Ingrid was woken by the loud call of a bird outside her window. Weak early-morning light leaked into the room through the gap in the thin linen curtains at the leaded glass window. The constant rain from yesterday had stopped. Her head was heavy and foggy with excess sleep, having slept deeply and dreamlessly for the first time since Matt had come home. There was a moment of confusion as she tried to focus on the unfamiliar walls, the strange white dresser, the iron-framed bed. No, she wasn't in a white-walled cell in some strange sci-fi movie, but the cottage. With Jacob.

She ought to have been unsettled with a strange man sleeping somewhere nearby or at least as restless as she'd been in The Tree House Resort, where she'd found the extreme quiet and the pitch-black sky disconcerting. Perhaps it was all the fresh air from yesterday, the relentless rain, or the carbs. Or maybe something had snapped free as she'd made decisions that were completely out of character.

Her skin heated as she remembered her evening with Jacob. The way he'd looked at her. His hands on her shoulders. She smacked the side of her face. No more pathetic attempts at flirting today. She had things to do. A life to get on with.

She headed into the kitchen where she found Jacob already up, heating something on the stove.

'You're awake early,' he said, turning to smile at her.

So much for not flirting – she'd been in his presence all of a minute and already couldn't take her eyes off his mouth. She cleared her throat and ran her fingers through her hair, pushing it behind her ears, then crossed her arms and tucked her hands under her armpits, suddenly very aware that she was standing there in a sweatshirt that hit her mid thigh and his boxers. Jacob glanced at her legs then back to her face.

He was freshly showered, in another figure-hugging T-shirt. She tried to adopt her most professional facial expression, desperately hoping that the fact she was swooning at the sight of him wasn't written all over her face.

'So are you.'

'The road will be open at six, so you have about forty-five minutes to eat and get changed. Your clothes are clean and mostly dry. Hang on, let me grab them for you. Could you stir the pot?'

She nodded while he ducked the low beam that bisected the kitchen and the room behind it where she presumed the washing machine and dryer lived. Jacob had been preparing porridge oats on the stove. She picked up the wooden spoon and continued to stir the unappetising thick sludge.

He reappeared with a neatly folded pile of her clothes. Instead of being tactfully hidden between the sandwich of jeans and sweatshirt, her bra and pants lay proudly on top. Ingrid was instantly aware that he knew her bra size, and that she preferred Bridget Jones maxi briefs to the sexier bikini ones. She had to be thankful that they were both still white and not pink after Grace's laundry skills, or even the well-worn, slightly grey, most comfortable underwear she reached for when tired and upset. She grabbed the clothes from him, pulling them from his grasp as he grinned.

'What are you smiling at?' She couldn't resist asking him.

'I didn't picture you in such sensible underwear.'

'You pictured me in underwear?' Dear God, what was she doing this early in the morning?

It was his turn to blush. He rubbed the back of his head sheepishly.

They both laughed awkwardly, and Ingrid placed her clothes on the arm of the sofa before returning to her place by the stove. A moment later, Jacob joined her, reaching around her for the spoon, his body so close that she could smell faint traces of spearmint toothpaste on his breath, his fingers brushing hers. She looked up at him. He glanced at her for a moment, a strange current passing between them, before turning back to the porridge. Did he have no issue with their proximity? She was struggling to breathe normally . . . She felt the warmth of his body along her back as his other hand reached out to adjust the heat. If he carried on like this, she might pass out. Pushing on his arm lightly, she released herself from the enclosure.

'I should've asked if you like porridge.'

'Er, I do.'

'Any preference on what you'd like on it? I have honey, jam, some blueberries.' There should be a law against voices like his around women who hadn't had sex in two years. Every word was as sensual as a Nigella food commercial.

'Whatever you're having. I should change.'

'You're welcome to keep those clothes, you know. I did my best with yours, but they may still be a little damp.'

He was right about that. The jeans were still a little wet. And he probably didn't want the underwear back now that she'd worn it.

'At least let me pay you for them.'

'No need.'

She looked down. The telltale polo pony symbol on both items of clothing told her that they weren't cheap. 'Are you sure?'

'Absolutely.' He handed her a cup of coffee, the smell of the roasted beans immediately helping to disperse some of the fog in her head. 'You look like you need this.'

She cursed herself for not checking the mirror before she'd

wandered into this man's kitchen. She had no doubt that she looked as though she'd spent the night in a wind tunnel. Her hair was tangled and messy in the morning at the best of times, her skin tired. It was possible she even had a bit of drool on the corner of her mouth. Having not had to worry what she looked like in the morning for at least a year she was out of the habit. At least she wouldn't be seeing Jacob again.

'Thanks,' she said, sipping the delicious brew with gratitude. She felt less enthusiastic as he slapped porridge into two bowls and added a few blueberries with a drizzle of honey. She'd lied about liking it because he seemed to have gone to so much trouble to prepare it. She couldn't tell him now that even the sight of porridge made her queasy.

She closed her eyes as she stirred the sticky mixture, then gave up and sipped her coffee while watching Jacob polish off his food with gusto.

'You should've mentioned,' he said, nodding at her bowl.

'Excuse me?'

'That you don't like porridge.' He moved closer to her so he could look into her eyes. 'I wouldn't have been offended. I could've made you something else.'

'No, no, it's fine. I'm just still a bit full from all the food last night.'

He held her gaze again for a moment and another current of electricity zipped through her. She might never be seeing him again, but she wasn't going to forget this breakfast in a hurry.

He smiled. 'Okay. Do you want to get back now?'

'Will the road be open?'

He checked his watch. 'If we leave now, it should be open by the time we get there.'

Jacob's electric car was eerily quiet as she sat next to him in the passenger seat, too nervous to take in what she was sure was plush, green countryside as she looked out of the window. He calmly navigated the twists and turns, the passing points, the narrow lanes, with the distinctive Radio 4 beeps faint in the background.

The now familiar buildings of The Tree House Resort came into view and she guided him to park near her room, which was separate from the main hotel. As she got out of the car, she reached into her pocket for her key. Shit, where was the key? Probably somewhere in the mud on an unidentifiable hillside.

'Looking for this?' Jacob asked, getting out of his side with the key card held aloft. 'I found it in the pocket of your jeans before I tossed them in the wash.'

She could've hugged him for saving her a trudge down to the main building. 'I seem to spend all of my time thanking you.'

He stood very close to her as he handed her the key. 'It's been a pleasure meeting you, Ingrid.' He bowed slightly and smiled.

'And you, Jacob. I should go,' she said, pointing at the stairs behind her.

'Need a piggyback?' he asked, pointing at the wellies they'd found in the utility room. A couple of sizes too big, she was wearing a thick pair of Jacob's socks to keep them on.

'I'll manage, but you may need a chiropractor after yesterday.'

'I'll add it to your tab.'

He kissed her on the cheek, then stepped away as she touched her face in response. 'Bye, Ingrid. Safe journey.' He climbed back into his car, waved, then reversed before she could say anything else.

Her heart sank at the prospect of not seeing him again, and that feeling alone told her that it was probably for the best.

9

Trouble

Ingrid's mood had begun to dip after about two hours of driving, and plunged closer to despair as she pulled up in front of her house another three hours later. Her fantasies of lying in bed with a newspaper and a cup of strong Colombian roasted coffee dissipated like wispy clouds as she saw two familiar cars parked on her driveway.

Her parents' metallic blue Honda Jazz jostled for space with Audrey and Nathan's obnoxiously large Range Rover. She knew that they would have called her instantly if anything had happened to Lily, so it was clear that something else was afoot. Drama was on the other side of her front door and for a moment she wondered if she should make a run for it and check herself into the nearest Premier Inn.

The door flew open before she was even able to insert her key into the lock and both Audrey and Nathan barrelled out of the house and propelled her backwards. Nathan grabbed her bag and Audrey gripped both of her arms. Dread crept through her bones and she saw Grace's face peering out from a gap in the blinds at the window.

'Mum,' said Ingrid. She didn't have the energy to glare at Audrey.

Nathan shifted from one foot to the other in the background.

'Er,' said Audrey, glancing at Nathan and letting go of Ingrid's arms.

'It's sort of my fault,' said Nathan.

'*You* blabbed?'

Audrey and Nathan exchanged one of those wordless married couple looks.

'So, er, I had a gap between shifts and helped your mum with her Costco shop yesterday, and she was asking about you and why you'd gone away,' Nathan began.

'Partly because *I* refused to give her any information,' said Audrey, tossing her long black hair over her shoulder.

'And then she . . .' said Nathan.

'She basically played him. You know how sneaky Ammi is. She told him that she knew you were getting a divorce and when Nathan told her that he was really sad for you, she exploded because she obviously did not get that information from Nangi or me.' Audrey smacked her husband on the arm, partly in admonition and partly to emphasise to Ingrid that she didn't condone this breaking of the sister code, which she obviously thought extended to Nathan.

'I'm so sorry,' said Nathan, clearly a little distraught at having broken the confidence to the worst possible person. Mum needed to be handled carefully and now she was probably on the other side of the front door like Cerberus, salivating and steaming about another one of her daughters who had failed to live up to her totally unrealistic expectations.

Ingrid couldn't help feeling a little sorry for Nathan, whom she had always liked. There weren't many people who could live with someone like Audrey. Often blunt to the point of rudeness, single-minded and bossy, her headstrong sister made lesser men run in the opposite direction. But Nathan was mature and kind, with an easy confidence, always encouraging Audrey to be her most authentic self. And when that meant that she gave up being a doctor, he was one hundred per cent behind her. It helped that he was almost ten years older than her and already a consultant, so money wasn't an issue. Their parents had almost lost their minds when Audrey quit, but it was Nathan who'd carefully steered them through it, who'd stood by Audrey's right to make her own decisions. Nathan's only failing was that he was so straightforward that, time and again, he failed to spot the traps Mum craftily laid to extract information about their lives.

Ingrid had always been a little bit envious of her sister's relationship. Nathan stood by his wife and celebrated who she was without trying to change her, whereas Matt was only interested in the version of Ingrid that suited him and his life goals.

'It's fine, Nathan. She had to find out some time. How bad is it?' asked Ingrid.

'It's bad,' he said, lowering his head so that she couldn't look him in the eye.

Audrey toed the ground with her Gucci trainers. The Premier Inn was becoming more attractive by the second.

'Spill,' said Ingrid to her sister.

'So, Nathan told Mum, who then called Matt and told him to come round here to explain it all to her. And when he arrived, Lily overheard, so she knows and she's locked herself in her room and won't come out until you come home.'

'*Matt*? What the . . . ? I mean, *what, why?* Who the hell does he think he is?'

Was she living in one of those K-dramas her mother loved to watch? She couldn't quite process this bizarre chain of events. Matt was here? Lily knew? Oh God, this was a lesson to her to never go away on her own again. She turned around and faced the road. Perhaps she could grab Lily and they could *both* head to the Premier Inn . . .

Audrey put her hand on Ingrid's shoulder and turned her around. 'Matt's in there talking to Lily now and I heard something about your job and coming second.'

'Oh sweet Jesus. This is *your* fault, you know,' said Ingrid, jabbing her index finger at her sister. 'You're the one who told me to go to that spa, which, by the way, was one of those weight loss ones that feed you a grape and make you hike up hills. With *no Wi-Fi*. And look what bloody happened!'

She'd known that she'd have to face the music at some point, but she'd been expecting a single, rather than the whole goddamn album at once. Like one of Lily's first-person shooter games, she'd just have to deal with each threat as it came at her. She squared her shoulders and made her way towards the front door.

'What are you wearing?' Audrey's eyes were slanted as she scanned Ingrid from head to toe, turning her slightly to get a better look.

Ingrid had been so keen to get on the road that she'd forgotten to change out of Jacob's clothes. 'Long story. Priorities, Akki.'

Audrey peered at her, suspicion growing. 'Okay, but at some point you'd better explain why you're wearing men's clothes.'

Ingrid rolled her eyes, hopefully distracting her sister from the automatic blush that rose to her cheeks as she remembered her strange night in the cottage.

'Look, in time I'll probably forgive you for making me enter an episode of *Dallas* in there, but you two can make up for blabbing by backing me up.'

'Absolutely,' said Nathan. 'Never really liked the bloke in the first place.'

'Seriously?' Ingrid asked. Whenever the brothers-in-law met amid a series of hugs and back slaps, she'd assumed that they'd liked each other. She looked at Audrey for confirmation.

'I never hid what I thought of the smarmy git in the first place. You should've guessed that Nate would feel the same as me.'

And yet, if Ingrid had ever implied that Audrey and Nathan had the same views, her sister would have given her a lecture about how married couples were capable of independent thought and Ingrid shouldn't be so Victorian.

As they entered the hallway, five foot three of righteous indignation rushed towards her second daughter.

Florence Perera was a force of nature, always battle-ready with a full face of makeup, blow-dried hair only slightly short of being a helmet, coordinated outfits complete with jacket and matching handbag, and a string of large round pearls around her neck. Today Mum was in full Iron Lady mode in a signature Thatcher blue suit complete with brooch.

Thatha stood behind her, hands splayed in silent apology. He rarely had to say anything as Mum managed to use up all the oxygen around them both. Dad was the complete opposite. A quiet and considered man, he was the perfect local accountant in his polyester-blend trousers, brown shoes and short-sleeved shirts, his greying hair slicked back with his beloved Brylcreem. She knew that if she hugged him, she'd get a whiff of his Old Spice aftershave. But there was no chance of that right now because Mum was on the warpath.

'You have some explaining to do, putha,' Mum shouted as she came forward to whack Ingrid with her handbag. What on earth did the woman put in there? She'd have a bruise the next day. None of them had escaped the plastic-soled slipper, but this was an upgrade in weaponry.

Grace, who was at the top of the stairs, smiled weakly at Ingrid and then noticed her men's clothing, a puzzled look crossing her face.

Audrey grabbed Florence by the shoulders and steered her away from Ingrid. 'Let's go this way, Ammi. You're not the priority here.'

Ingrid knew that she'd left her backbone for dealing head-on with her mother somewhere in the nineties and that she shouldn't hide behind her big sister, but she couldn't handle all that drama right now. She rushed past her mother and up the stairs, her only care for her daughter.

Lily opened her door as soon as Ingrid approached.

'Baby,' said Ingrid, pulling her daughter into her arms. 'I'm sorry you had to hear all that from everyone else and not me.' She rubbed Lily's back. 'Dad talked to you?' No doubt Matt had taken the opportunity to moot the possibility of Lily living with him.

Lily nodded. 'He said that you were getting a divorce because you didn't love each other anymore but you both love me.'

Ingrid sighed. At least he'd been sensible enough to tell her that. Ingrid wasn't sure if the change in her daughter over the past year, becoming more guarded and taking solace in her computer games, was due to Matt's disappearance. Had she thought her father didn't love her enough?

Ingrid knew that *she* hadn't loved Matt for some time. Had she ever? She'd been going through the motions of what she'd thought a long-term relationship should look like.

'And he said he wanted me to live with him because I must be fed up with you at work all the time. But I'm not! Mum, please, please, don't make me. I want to stay with you and Aunty Grace.'

Ingrid hugged her tight, burning with fury at Matt, who subsequently burst into the room as though her thoughts had summoned him.

Honestly, Nathan was a big bloke, couldn't he have blocked him for a few minutes?

'You see, this is exactly why I want custody. You're always off somewhere and leaving our daughter alone,' he shouted, a little winded from having run up the stairs.

Lily's arms tightened around Ingrid.

'Matt, now is not the time for this.'

'And what are you wearing?'

Why was everyone so obsessed with her clothes? Okay, Jacob's clothes . . . Her only thought had been to get back to Lily. She'd had no way of knowing that *he'd* be there when she returned, dripping poison. She didn't have time for this.

Audrey was next to charge into the room, followed by Nathan.

'Why are you in my house?' Matt shouted at them both.

'Mate, the last I heard, it was my sister paying the mortgage on this house.'

'Audrey,' said Ingrid, shaking her head and pointing at Lily.

'Why don't we go downstairs?' asked Nathan.

'I see *you* haven't changed. Still a supercilious arsehole,' spat Matt.

Ingrid stared in shock. She really had been oblivious. So focused on her job, on motherhood, on keeping the peace between her siblings and her parents, that she hadn't seen the animosity between Nathan and Matt. Lily buried her face in Ingrid's shoulder.

'Matt! You're upsetting Lily. And please don't come here and be rude to my sister and Nathan. *You're* the one who disappeared for an entire year. We should talk, but not now and not here, and preferably with a lawyer involved.'

Nathan pulled on Matt's arm, urging him to leave and he slapped it away, squaring up for a confrontation.

'Dad,' said Lily, turning to look at him with tears in her eyes.

Ingrid breathed out with relief when Matt stepped back. He wasn't so changed that his daughter's pleas no longer affected him.

'It's alright, Lils. I'll go.' He jabbed a finger at Ingrid. 'You'll be hearing from me.'

Matt shouldered past Nathan on his way out before thundering down the stairs and slamming the front door behind him.

'Lily, I'm so sorry. Everyone's a little upset at the moment, but I promise you it'll all work out. We both love you so much,' said Ingrid.

Lily didn't look too convinced, and who could blame her? Their family had turned into a soap opera and Ingrid hadn't been given the script in advance so she had no idea how it would all end.

'Ingrid!' Ammi screeched from the foot of the stairs.

Cue the next scene.

10

Wrath of the Disappointed Mother

For a moment, Ingrid considered taking Lily back downstairs with her to deal with Mum, relying on her mother's boundless love for her granddaughter to dull the intensity of the rage that was coming her way. But using one's child as a human shield from a rampaging matriarch really wasn't the mature path to take.

'I think it's best you stay up here for this portion of the programme,' said Ingrid.

'Lilypad, do you want to play Mario Kart with me?' asked Grace, putting her arm around Lily's shoulder.

'I recommend headphones,' Ingrid advised Grace.

'Let me get down there and try to calm her down first,' said Audrey, rushing back downstairs before Ingrid could stop her. Grace and Ingrid exchanged a panicked look. Audrey had never placated their mother in her life. She was like paraffin on a fire. Ingrid had to move fast.

'Nathan, please, please try and head your wife off at the pass,' Ingrid implored. He looked doubtful, knowing better than anyone that Audrey was cut from the same cloth as their mother. There was no stopping her when she was in full flight.

'I'll do my best,' he said as he slouched out of the room.

'Love you, baby,' said Ingrid to her daughter as she bent to kiss her on the cheek. 'I missed you.'

'Mum? Why are you wearing those clothes?'

'Good question,' said Grace.

Ingrid scowled. If she kept brushing it off, they'd be even more suspicious. 'I fell in the mud on a hike yesterday and someone helped me out and gave me a change of clothes. I should've changed, but I wanted to get back to you as soon as possible.'

Lily seemed satisfied with the explanation, which was essentially the truth with a few details omitted, and began to set up the game. But Grace wasn't so easy to fool. Her expression clearly conveyed that she would be revisiting the topic, and Ingrid shouldn't feel like she'd escaped the sisterly inquisition.

As Ingrid made it to the top of the stairs, it became apparent that Nathan had not been able to mediate.

'You're always so rude and disrespectful to me, Audrey. You know, every day I go to church and ask God why he gave me such a headstrong girl for a daughter.'

Ingrid winced as Audrey rolled her eyes at being called a 'girl' at almost fifty, knowing that Ammi had definitely seen it and it would do nothing to mollify her.

'Ammi, you know, this is not about you. Ingrid is going through some huge stuff with Matt right now. Her main priority is making sure that Lily is okay, and you shouldn't be piling on the Catholic guilt.'

'What do you mean, Catholic guilt? Are you not also a Catholic? Oh dear Lord, how have my children turned out like this?'

'No, I'm no longer a Catholic and gosh, Mum, we're all middle-aged now. Is there really no end to your perpetual disappointment in our life choices?'

This wasn't going well. Ingrid had to stop it now or her mother's wrath would reach thermo-nuclear levels by the time it was levelled at her. She caught Nathan's eye. He merely shrugged.

'Akki, leave it, please. Ammi, I know this was all a surprise, but honestly, it was for me too.'

'A surprise? Not according to your *husband*. And you know, your father and I have thought that man was a saint for some time.'

'Don't drag me into this,' shouted her father from the living room.

'A saint? I'll tell you what kind of saint he is,' began Audrey.

Ingrid shook her head at her sister, trying to shut her down. Being the eldest, Audrey often charged in to defend her sister out of habit, but it never helped and always riled up their mother even further. A quick glance at Mum told Ingrid that she'd dismissed the notion that Matt wasn't a saint instantly.

Mum had never been objective about Matt. At first, that had been a blessing. He'd charmed her with his knowledge of Sri Lanka, with his wit and intelligence, his good looks, and the fact that he wanted to marry her on-the-shelf thirty-two-year-old daughter. Ingrid had initially enjoyed the fact that not only was she the least troublesome daughter, but Ammi preferred Matt to Nathan. And she'd soon come to understand that the reason why Mum favoured Matt was because Nathan would always defend and protect Audrey no matter what decision she made. Mum couldn't penetrate their family unit at all. Even their three children were impervious to Mum's digs about their life choices.

'I knew that this job would be the end of your marriage. No man likes being emasculated like that,' said Mum, pointing a manicured finger at Ingrid.

Audrey stared at Ingrid, willing her to retaliate, but she knew that it was better to let Mum get it all out. Once she'd burned herself out, Thatha could escort her out of the house and into her car. These were just words and Ingrid would listen.

'You are always away. That poor child needs a mother.'

Ingrid flashed a look at Audrey who almost had steam coming out of her ears. Nathan moved forward to hug her from behind.

Clearly Matt had got to Ammi before Ingrid had been able to tell her anything. And everything he'd told her probably chimed with what she thought anyway. On the one hand, she'd wanted her daughter to be a partner at a large accountancy firm, earning a six-figure salary, and on the other, she wanted her to be a good little wife who didn't make her husband feel bad about her success, not to mention a stay-at-home mother.

'She has a mother, Ammi. I'm there for all the important stuff and for all the mundane stuff, like washing her clothes, taking her to the doctor, helping with her homework. Yes, sometimes I have to work overtime, but that's always at home. And sometimes there are business trips, but I keep them to a minimum and as short as possible,' said Ingrid in the voice she used for particularly difficult clients: slow, steady and calm.

'Matthew said that it was all the time.'

'Matt is wrong. And how would he know? He hasn't even been here for the past year.'

'But you must have done something to make him want a divorce?'

'Maybe I have? I don't know. He's been away for so long and all I've done is try to hang on.' Her tone remained low and her mother visibly deflated. 'Did he tell you that he wants full custody of Lily? And half the house?'

Thankfully, her tactic of shocking her mother worked. She was speechless. Matt had obviously been selective in what he'd told her. What he'd never understood was that, underneath all that disappointment, Mum would walk over red-hot coals in defence of her girls. She would criticise them until the cows came home, but she was the *only* person who was allowed to do so. It was the privilege of being the one who'd birthed them.

'Here, Florrie, that's enough now,' said Thatha, emerging from the living room now that the initial cannons had been fired and the dust had settled. He put his hand on her arm, which she shrugged off with a huff. 'Putha, you need a good lawyer.'

'Don't worry about that, Thatha, I've got that covered,' said Audrey.

'If he gets custody of Lily, does that mean that we won't be able to see her?' asked Mum.

'He won't get custody, Ammi,' said Ingrid.

'Is there no way you can patch things up with him?' Mum asked. 'I can't have a divorced daughter. What on earth will everyone say? And you won't be able to receive communion anymore either.'

Of course, Mum's priorities didn't include Ingrid's happiness.

Nowadays, Ingrid only made guest appearances at church due to her pitiful need for her mother's begrudging approval. It wasn't as though she really believed or anything, although she had been known to say a quick Hail Mary before a pitch, and even a rosary that time that Lily broke her arm. But her Catholic indoctrination ran deep enough that she felt the sting of not being able to receive communion as usual.

Ingrid found herself wondering if it was almost worth trying to patch things up with Matt. But at that moment she put her hand in her pocket and looked down at the soft grey sweatpants, remembered Jacob's smile, his kindness, his soft kiss to her cheek, the way he looked into her eyes, the spark of attraction between them. Amazingly, to him she wasn't the washed-up old has-been that Matt had made her see herself as. She didn't have to settle for a man who clearly didn't want her. She'd thrived on her own for long enough.

She sighed. 'No, Ammi. He's made it clear that it's all over for him. Look, I appreciate your concern today, but I've had a really long drive, I'm tired and hungry, and I need to rest and be with my daughter. Can we talk about this some other time?' *Hopefully never*. 'You should get home before the traffic picks up.' Honestly, what kind of traffic could there be between Pinner and Rayners Lane, a journey of five minutes at the most?

'Okay, putha. We'll leave you,' said Thatha, picking up on her cue and steering her spluttering mum towards the front door.

'We'll go too,' said Audrey, giving Ingrid a terse hug as she left.

As the door closed mercifully behind them, Ingrid went into the kitchen, made herself a much-needed cup of coffee and sat at the table. Her family was pretty dramatic at the best of times, but she was never usually at the centre of it, and she didn't like the criticism and disapproval that came with being in the eye of the storm.

And yet, her life hadn't ended. She'd spent so long trying not to upset anyone, but it had made no difference. Life had a way of happening without being able to control it. She'd given Matt her life for the past fifteen years and he'd thrown it back at her.

And now she was angry. At him. At herself.

Suddenly, Ingrid didn't want to sit quietly and continue to take whatever was handed to her. How would it feel to be like everyone else in her family and express how she felt? How would it feel to actually do something just for herself?

She didn't know yet. But she had to find out.

11

Sibling Solidarity

The next day, Ingrid flopped onto one of Audrey's plush new sofas, wishing that she could sink even further into the soft cushions and possibly disappear entirely so that she didn't have to deal with her life. Unfortunately, a day spent hanging out with Lily and picking up laundry, tidying the kitchen cupboards and cleaning the mould off the silicone sealant around the shower had done nothing to keep her brain from replaying yesterday's scene. And now that she was in Audrey's house with both her sisters watching her closely, she didn't want to talk about it.

'Nice sofa, Akki. Where did you say you got it from?' Ingrid asked Audrey in a hopeless attempt to divert her single-minded sister. Six months ago, when Audrey completely renovated her house as soon as the last of her three children left for university, she might have been successful. A tiny question like this could have brought her at least a twenty-minute reprieve while her sister banged on about how the scuffs in the skirting boards, dents in the walls, ink on the carpets and chips in the wood from years of footballs, tennis racquets, toy cars, frisbees and so on had all been replaced with glossy paint, Osborne & Little wallpaper and cream carpets. There were no husband-stealing interior designers called Honor for Audrey, who sourced every carefully placed vase and ornament, every tile, every light fixture herself, complete with an Excel spreadsheet and a project plan.

'You know where it's from,' said Audrey, shoving Ingrid's feet off the sofa to create space for her to sit.

Grace sat on the floor next to the coffee table in front of them both. 'How are you feeling about yesterday? I didn't want to ask in front of Lily.'

Ingrid sighed. These two were like bloodhounds sometimes, but it all came from a good place. 'And there's no need to ask now because she's upstairs and just an earbud away from hearing you.'

'Look, yesterday was an unmitigated shit show, which is, frankly, par for the course in our family, and there's no way you escaped from it unscathed. We're worried about you,' said Audrey.

Ingrid pulled herself upright to sit cross-legged, chastened by the genuine concern in her sisters' voices. 'Look, it was awful. My life is a disaster. End of story.'

Audrey and Grace exchanged a glance that told Ingrid they'd hatched some plan of contrition beforehand.

'I'm sorry I let everyone in,' said Grace, looking at her intertwined fingers in her lap.

'Honestly, you couldn't have stopped either of them,' said Audrey.

'I think she's including you too,' said Ingrid.

'*I* was there to help you out. No offence, Grace, but you're no good with Mum.'

'No offence taken,' said Grace, looking very offended.

'You're no better, you know. You just wind her up even more,' said Ingrid. It had been Thatha who had handled their mother in the end.

'That's a fat lot of gratitude from you. You know Nate was so upset when he realised that he'd set her off. He insisted I go round there with him to try and stop her.'

She felt really bad now. Nathan was literally one of the nicest people she knew. 'I do really appreciate it. I'm sorry, Akki. And please tell Nathan that I don't blame him at all.'

'Yeah, you know how sneaky she is,' said Grace. 'So, how are you?'

'Angry.'

'Really?' Audrey asked, incredulous.

'You?' asked Grace, wearing almost the same expression as Audrey.

'What? I get angry.'

'Hmm, but we never see it,' said Audrey. 'And frankly, I'm relieved. Does this mean that you might finally have developed a backbone?' If Audrey had a brand, it would be bluntness. Ingrid would be in a near constant state of umbrage if she took offence at every one of her sister's blunt opinions.

'Maybe?' Except she'd never really seen it like that. It took plenty of courage to keep her family together, to keep the peace. It was an active choice, and she'd needed all her strength over the past year as she managed both her career, her child, and her adult sister living with her. Partnership at a large accountancy firm wasn't for the faint-hearted. So she chose not to fight certain battles. It wasn't that she wasn't capable of fighting if she wanted to.

'I just think that perhaps my approach hasn't worked. Don't they say that doing the same thing over and over again and expecting a different outcome is the definition of insanity? I can't keep going through the same patterns and expect things to change. And I'm furious at Matt for involving Lily without talking it through with me first.'

'What about the other women?' Audrey asked, taking a sip of her white wine. It was always white these days as she wanted to preserve her cream palace.

Rationally, Ingrid knew that she was an attractive woman, but when her husband showed no sexual interest in her at all for at least a year before he left, and then was quick to shag anything that moved while he was away, she couldn't help the self-pity that appeared in moments like this.

'Am I really so disgusting?' asked Ingrid, the question bubbling up from deep within her. She must have looked as if she were about to cry because Audrey scooted closer to her and put an arm around her.

'Oh, Sis, no. You're gorgeous, beautiful. That bastard has made you feel like this and you can't let him win. He's the inadequate one, not you. The prick . . . You should be angrier that you haven't spent the last year shagging too.'

An image of Jacob flashed into her head: the look on his face as he'd walked in on her in the bathroom. In response, combined with her sister's words, the narrative about her that Matt had spent years constructing, that she was old and unattractive, receded into the background. He had made her feel that no one would ever want her, but now she was starting to wonder if perhaps that wasn't true.

'I still can't believe that he's being like this,' said Grace. 'He was so in love with you. How could he have changed so much?'

Audrey leaned over and smacked Grace's arm. 'Seriously? Is it any wonder that you're forty and still single? If you're in love with someone, you have the courtesy to tell them when you're unhappy, give them a chance to change or work things out. You don't bugger off for an entire year leaving the person you're supposed to be in love with to manage everything on their own.'

'But, he can't have changed that much, can he?' Grace persisted.

Ingrid couldn't listen to this anymore. She'd indulged Grace with every whim, supported every madcap decision she'd made in her life, held her as she cried at yet another failed relationship, and she needed her sister to do the same for her.

'Look, Grace, you haven't even been in the same country as Matt for most of the time he's been my husband. All you've ever seen is the man who comes along to family events and charms the pants off all the old people. It's not who he is all the time.'

'But you fell in love with him.'

'People change.'

But had he? If she were honest with herself, she had never been head-over-heels with Matt. Red flags had popped up all over the place while they'd dated. He always chose where and when they'd go on holiday, which movie they'd see, which restaurant they'd eat at because Ingrid's suggestions were laughable, apparently. And Ingrid told herself that she didn't care enough about any of these things, so she didn't kick up a fuss about a visit to a mosquito-infested island where she'd spend the whole time covered in calamine lotion and dosed on antihistamines; or she'd try not to nod off in a long Scorcese movie; or tell him that she disliked the cream and butter in French cuisine. By the time they'd been together for a couple of years, she was thirty-two and one of the only people in her friend group who'd remained unmarried, her biological clock ticking like an unexploded bomb. So, she'd ignored all the warning signs and married him. The best thing to come out of it had been Lily. She'd go through it all again to make sure that her daughter existed.

As time had gone on, Ingrid began to forget about her own preferences. And then, as he became more and more dissatisfied with the life he'd chosen for them, it had been easier not to rile him. She'd walked on eggshells every day to save his fragile ego. He was the one who'd pushed her towards partnership. He'd wanted a bigger house in a better area and his job as a software engineer wasn't going to finance it, so he'd pushed her, while simultaneously piling on the guilt about her absences. And she went along with it all, even though every departure for an overseas trip broke her heart as she hugged Lily goodbye. She loathed all those business dinners that he insisted on calling 'jollies' where she felt obliged to wait until the end to ensure her clients' happiness, endured leering comments and glances, or worse, assertions that her position was merely the result of affirmative action in the workplace and nothing to do with her competence. All to fund the lifestyle he had wanted.

'I was only talking about how it's hard for me to believe how much he has changed. Not that I don't believe that he's done all these things. The way he was yesterday . . .' Grace shook her head as she recalled the scene. 'That wasn't the person I've known. It's hard to process how he could go from loving Ingrid so much to being the way he was yesterday. Of course I'm on Ingrid's side. And you're right, I have no place giving you romantic advice. And thank you for not mentioning Luca.'

Audrey and Ingrid exchanged a glance. Luca had been the married concerts manager for the orchestra Grace had played with in New York, with whom she'd had an affair for two years before his wife found out and kicked him out. Grace had thought it would be the next phase in their relationship because he was the usual cliché of a cheating husband who'd convinced her that he and his wife were going through the motions but no longer wanted each other. His lies were exposed when he'd dumped Grace and begged his wife for forgiveness, moving back into their apartment a week before lockdown.

Grace had been devastated and all alone in her tiny fifth-floor walk-up in Brooklyn while her sisters attempted to console her via countless video calls. Of course, Audrey's comfort was laced with a healthy side of realism – like a salad of bitter, spiky leaves without a dressing. Ingrid had watched Grace's face crumple as Audrey reminded her that embarking on a relationship with a married man was destined for disaster and that she'd never wanted her sister to be 'that kind of woman'. Ingrid had taken the non-hectoring approach and tried to ease her lonely sister's broken heart, calling her every day, helping her through her feelings of abandonment mixed with the abject fear of someone living in a city so ravaged by a deadly pandemic. Audrey hadn't been a help with this aspect either, her medical training meaning that she presented information so clinically that Grace looked even more terrified at the end of each call than she had when it started.

'Mum was true to form yesterday, wasn't she?' said Audrey. 'And that bastard loved it. He was dripping poison into her ear, trying to get her on side. From the way she was raging at you, I thought he'd succeeded.'

'Mum might scream and shout, but oddly, it comes from a place of love,' said Ingrid.

'Sure it does,' said Audrey and Grace together, with the same scepticism.

They all laughed.

'At least she picked the right side,' said Audrey, pointedly.

'So, what are you going to do about the custody and the house?' Grace asked.

'I'm just telling myself there's no way in hell that any court would give him custody of Lily. And I'd rather not uproot her by selling the house, but if it's easier to do that then I will.'

'I spoke to Cheska and she said she'd be happy to make sure he gets as little as possible as well as crush his fantasies of getting any custody,' said Audrey.

Ingrid couldn't continue to wallow in self-pity. She wasn't a helpless person, despite appearances. All she'd ever wanted was a little parental approval, some praise and a quiet life, but had any of those things been worth all this? It certainly didn't feel like it. She would have to adapt and progress. She sat up, tightened her ponytail and straightened out her crumpled T-shirt.

'I'm ready for it,' she said with emphasis. And as weary as she felt, if this became about Lily's happiness rather than her own, she could endure anything that Matt threw at her.

'But can we also talk about those clothes you were wearing yesterday?' Audrey asked with a sly grin.

'Those bloody clothes. Why is everyone so curious?' Ingrid said.

'Because they were men's clothes and you looked a bit dishevelled . . . Is there anything you need to tell us about the Lake District?' asked Grace, grinning.

Why was she blushing? Nothing had happened. 'I already told you. I got separated from my group on a hike. I still haven't forgiven you for booking me onto the wrong break, Audrey, by the way. And it was raining, I fell in the mud, lost my way and had no mobile phone signal. Some very kind local found me and took me in. I borrowed his clothes.'

'His Ralph Lauren clothes,' said Audrey.

'How is that relevant?'

'Sounds like he has money,' Audrey continued.

'Again? Relevance? Look, he was just a kind person and that was the end of it.'

'Hmm,' said Grace observing her carefully. 'And what did this kind person look like?'

Ingrid picked at some lint on her top, her eyes down. 'Old and unattractive.'

'Right,' said Grace who was clearly assuming the opposite, but keeping her mouth shut in front of Audrey.

'Honestly, guys, there's no story here,' Ingrid proclaimed, without looking either of them in the eye.

'Okay, so what are you going to do about this mess in your life?' Audrey asked.

Ingrid topped up her glass.

12

Plans

Cheska handed back Ingrid's passport and utility bill along with a client engagement letter and scrolled through something on her iPad while Ingrid took another sip of her now lukewarm coffee. The glass-walled offices of Wardman, Hoddle & Dempsey with ergonomic furniture and state-of-the-art technology must cost an absolute fortune to maintain, every penny of which would be reflected in Cheska's fees. The hourly rate was much lower than Ingrid's own, but where accountants billed on value, lawyers billed for every letter, every photocopy, every moment one of their brain cells were occupied with your case, and it would inevitably bankrupt her. Although that might do her a favour because there'd be less for Matt to take.

She'd spent the last hour listening to Cheska outline the process for division of assets and how she didn't have to worry about Matt getting custody, and her head was spinning. It was as though she'd boarded a runaway train when Matt had announced that he was divorcing her and she had no way to apply the brakes or collect herself. But Cheska's plain, straightforward advice with no sugar-coating or false hope was strangely comforting. Like listening to her sister who never withheld her opinions and always delivered them with the sensitivity of a sledgehammer. It was what Ingrid needed right now. A dose of harsh reality to give her the strength to fight.

It was time to stop this cycle of appeasement.

Her phone vibrated with a message, and because Cheska seemed occupied with reading something on her iPad, Ingrid snuck a look at her phone.

> Hey, long time no hear. Can you give me a call when you get this? Big opportunity for you. Will

Will had been a senior manager on all of Ingrid's major clients before he'd left to join a hedge fund's finance department. She'd trained him from graduate level until he'd left and they'd developed a close working relationship, which had often infuriated Matt, especially when Will had called with client issues at the weekend or when they were on holiday.

She needed all her energy to fight in this divorce and she wasn't sure that she had the bandwidth to do more at work. There was no point in doing anything if every distribution ended up with her being edged out of the way by Not-Nice Tim Woodstock. But then, perhaps the reason this kept happening was because she allowed it. As she watched Cheska, so self-assured in this cathedral of glass and chrome, her calm sense of authority, Ingrid was positive that her sister's best friend wouldn't allow *anyone* to get the better of her in the workplace. Or out of it.

Ingrid stared at Will's text. Was she a masochist? For so many years, she was the one who had researched, who'd stayed up night after night putting the proposal together, who'd given the pitch, won the client, project managed the work, maintained the relationship, ensured exceptional service and collected the money. And even though she'd been the team player they wanted by never complaining when others took credit for her work, it had done nothing to increase her profit share. As one of the few women of colour in her position, she'd been setting an appalling example by never standing up for herself. She needed to change things. Her gaze rested on the word 'opportunity'.

'Right, that's all done,' said Cheska, slapping the conference table with her hands and sitting back in her seat as though she'd taken off her professionalism like a coat. 'Fancy a quick drink? You look like you need one.'

'Actually, I need to get back to work, but how about another time?'

'Sure. I know all of this is a bit bewildering, but don't worry, Ingrid, I'll make sure you get what you deserve.'

'Thanks, Cheska. I really appreciate you taking on my case.'

'I'm sure you know that if Audrey asks you to do something, you don't say no,' said Cheska, smiling. She ran her hands through her sharply cut blonde bob and took off her cat-eye glasses, laying them on the table. She rubbed her eyes. 'It's pretty handy that Matt took off like that, you know, it will act in your favour with visitation rights. But let's not get ahead of ourselves. I'll set up something with his lawyers and see what their opening salvo is. We can determine where we go from there. But don't worry about custody because that will be a slam dunk for you. Will you be alright being in the same room as him?'

Ingrid nodded. The thought of his smug face irritated her beyond belief, but she could put her professional, responsible face on to get through all this. He wouldn't intimidate her anymore with underhand tactics.

'Thanks, Cheska, that sounds good. Let's speak soon.'

Ingrid stood on the Strand, facing the law courts, trying to dodge the tourists that descended on London in July, as she dialled Will's number.

'Hey, stranger,' said Will, his voice light and cheery. She pictured his face as he spoke, thin and long with overgrown dark brown hair, his profile sharpened by his angular nose, and never without a smile, even at his most stressed.

'Will, so lovely to hear from you. How's it going over on the dark side?'

He laughed. 'Pretty good, you know. Although I still don't get to see my wife most nights.'

'Can't imagine Cathy's happy about that.'

'Not really, but it's paying the mortgage so . . . How about you? Any sign of Matt?'

'He got back a couple of weeks ago. And he wants a divorce.'

A bus roared past Ingrid as she stood at the kerb, so she wasn't sure if she'd missed Will's comment or if there really was silence from the other end of the phone.

'Will?'

'I'm so sorry, Ingrid.'

'You're not really,' said Ingrid, smiling. Matt had accused Will of having an affair with Ingrid during one drunken Christmas party, sending the office rumour mill into overdrive. Since then, the usually sunny Will hadn't been able to hide his dislike on the few occasions that they'd met.

'No, you're right. Can't say I am. Are *you* alright?'

Will didn't do pity and she didn't need it. She wasn't a helpless puppy abandoned by the side of the road. She was a partner in a big four global accountancy firm with a home and a car she'd paid for herself while bringing up her daughter.

'I'm good.'

She pictured him nodding and smiling encouragingly on the other end of the phone.

'Okay then. Blue Mark's work is going out to tender and I wanted to give you a heads-up.'

'Miss working with me?'

'Of course. But also, I don't want that arsehole Woodstock coming in here and giving our firm a bad name.'

'*Our* firm? You can take the man out of the firm . . . But seriously, thank you for the heads-up. When can we expect it?'

'Next week. And I've stressed how important *our* working

relationship is, so they'd better not put that man anywhere near this.'

'You're the best, Will. Thank you.'

'But, Ingrid, you have to promise me something.'

'What?'

'That you won't let anyone else take the credit for this. I want you on this job because you're the best. Please don't sit back and let them take advantage of you anymore.'

Ingrid winced. All she'd really been doing was trying to survive the long hours of being a partner and a mother. Added to that, she hadn't wanted to be labelled 'difficult' or 'pushy' or any of the number of labels a woman like her could fall prey to. But a fat lot of good that had done her as she took home the same amount each year, while the salaries around her increased exponentially thanks to all the income she brought in.

'I'm sorry. I've overstepped. I shouldn't have said that.'

'Listen, Will, you've earned the right to be straight with me. After all, you were the only person who cared enough to tell me that I had the hem of my skirt stuck in my knickers before that training presentation.' Will laughed. 'Funnily enough, I've recently come to a similar conclusion,' Ingrid continued.

'Really? I almost wish I could be there to witness an Ingrid Perera smackdown.'

'When have you ever seen one of those?'

'Oh, I've seen the way you dealt with those clients and their happy hands. I know you can put the Woodstocks in their place. You just haven't wanted to. Or maybe it was not having the time.'

At least one person had seen the real her.

The sights and sounds of the Strand buzzing around her were all too familiar, but the woman who stood looking at the wrought iron gates of the law courts felt different. Was this divorce setting her free in more ways than one?

'In all the years we worked together,' Will continued, 'you

never took any shit from me. It was always a mystery why you didn't stick up for yourself with the partners.'

'You were right about the time factor, Will. You know that Lily is the most important part of my life.'

'But being a mum never stopped you from being great at your job. I'm glad you're finally seeing your worth.'

'Thanks, Will. I really appreciate both the heads-up and the pep talk.'

'Anytime.'

As Ingrid hung up, she couldn't help but grin. She liked the idea of an Ingrid Perera smackdown. What would that look like in the office? Or even with Matt? It wasn't the moment itself that worried her, it was the fallout. Her job was an endless consideration of consequences and risks, but perhaps she'd been overcautious. There were some risks in life that were worth taking.

She remembered her chat with Chris as she'd been undervalued once again, then Matt's face as he told her that she was crap in bed. Anger flickered within her, stronger and more righteous than the resentment that had been in her heart for so many years. She embraced it. It would fuel her.

Ingrid turned towards St Paul's Cathedral, its famous dome glistening in the sunshine, and strode towards her future.

13

Rivalry

A week later, Ingrid tapped her fountain pen against the lined pad of paper in front of her. She'd spent the last half an hour of the meeting scribbling key words down in a vain attempt to push down the rage simmering within her.

Chris continued his spiel, everyone in the room focused on him. But not once did he even glance at Ingrid, his eyes continually resting on the pinstriped smugness of Tim who literally sat at Chris's right hand.

'Blue Mark LLC is one of the most dynamic hedge funds in the financial services arena and it's essential that we, as one of the largest global accountancy firms, win that proposal. Now, I've listed Tim's recent wins at length and . . .'

She should've expected this, but now it was crystal clear that Chris was going to completely ignore Will's request to have her on the client. She had to act now or regret it forever.

'Excuse me,' Ingrid said, laying her pen down on top of the pad and raising her hand with an exaggerated wave in case Chris felt inclined to ignore her as was often the case in these meetings.

'Ingrid, I'm just in the middle of this. Can we save the questions until the end?' said Chris, turning away to continue his speech.

'No, we can't, actually. Before you go on, I'd like to clarify a few things with Tim.'

'It's not the right time,' replied Chris, throwing her an annoyed stare that told her she wasn't supposed to behave like this.

'It really *is* the right time,' said Ingrid, standing and fixing her gaze on Tim who looked at her with a mildly amused expression.

'It's alright, Chris. Let her ask,' said Tim, smiling widely, clearly unthreatened.

It was at times like these that Ingrid was incredibly thankful that she was a Perera. She couldn't have survived their home in Rayners Lane without always being prepared for battle, either with Mum or Audrey, and it was time to bring that fighting spirit into her workplace. She was no longer going to let these men wilfully ignore her.

'Tim, would you remind us of Barton Finance's dealbreaker in their RFP? And also, what quantifiable contribution you made to the subsequent pitch. I think it's highly relevant to this RFP.'

'Ingrid, there's no need for this now,' said Chris.

'Actually, I'm very interested to hear what it is,' said Trent, a partner who had recently transferred to London from New York. Ingrid had met him when she'd been in the New York office preparing for the Barton Finance pitch and they'd hit it off immediately. He was equally baffled by budget Hugh Grant's rise through the ranks on nothing more than his charm and bloody signet ring.

Chris looked at Trent and nodded while Ingrid bit her lip. Of course he would sanction it now that a bloke had stated the same thing. 'Fine. Tim, please elaborate.'

'This is completely irrelevant,' said Tim, brushing an imaginary piece of lint off his pinstripe tailored trouser leg.

'Just answer the question so we can get on with this,' said Chris impatiently.

Tim squirmed, unused to being chastened by Chris. 'Um . . .

I was doing the networking and we all know that's what wins the work, don't we?' He looked around the room at the other partners, some of whom began to look very uncomfortable.

'So you can't answer the question?' Ingrid asked.

Tim looked away.

'Alright, how about this one? What about the pitch for Wharton & Sons? What KPIs were agreed?'

Tim shifted in his seat and shot her an irritated look. 'All of that was standard and there was nothing further to discuss.'

Chris rolled his eyes, probably annoyed that Tim hadn't remembered that the proposed KPIs were initially ridiculous before Ingrid spent hours renegotiating with the client. He must have been hoping Tim would take the credit for it.

'You know, I win so much work these days that it's hard to distinguish,' Tim continued.

Ingrid stood a little straighter, pressing the advantage that she felt in the air.

'For clarity, Tim's "networking" was on the golf course with a university friend who was completely unconnected with the client. He can't remember the KPIs for Whartons because he was never involved, and the Barton dealbreaker was that they wanted me as engagement partner because I'd worked with the COO for years when she was at another client. And the reason I mention all of this is because I know that Will Sturgess, who is the CFO from Blue Mark, specifically wants *me* and not Tim on this proposal. In fact, he went so far as to say that if Tim were on it, we wouldn't win the work.'

Wow, that was a massive risk. She almost held her breath in anticipation, but she was finally staking her claim and it felt good to hear her voice reverberating loud and strong in her head for once.

'Right,' said Chris, looking down at his papers. Ingrid knew that none of this was news to him, but he had banked on her not saying anything. If she hadn't brought it up in front of everyone right now, she'd have no chance of staking her claim. She was relying on Chris's hatred of looking foolish in public.

She looked around the room. Usually, it resembled what she'd imagined Thatcher's cabinet meetings were like: a bunch of nodding sycophants too worried about preserving their positions to state their opinions in front of their overbearing leader. But clearly Ingrid had had her head in the sand for the last few years because from what she saw it obviously wasn't just her and Trent who loathed Tim.

Chris stared at Tim for a moment, but it soon became clear that he'd decided to abandon his soldier on the battlefield. 'Right, well, Ingrid, it does appear that you're the most qualified here to lead the Blue Mark proposal.'

'But . . .' sputtered Tim who'd clearly thought that he had this locked down before he entered the room.

'Everyone else in agreement?' Chris asked, not even bothering to look up from his papers.

She allowed herself a moment of triumph as the majority of partners instantly agreed.

'That's settled. Ingrid, you're in charge. But because this is such a key potential client, I've brought in a consultant to help with the proposal.'

'What's their expertise?' Ingrid asked, resuming her seat, and now a little annoyed that Chris thought they needed outside help on this one, but then perhaps that was because he'd been planning on giving this to Tim who would have needed the help.

'He's an investment banker who's been setting up similar funds to Blue Mark's. A bit of a hotshot in the industry and we were lucky that he was looking for a little consultancy work as a stopgap.'

'If you think it will help,' said Ingrid, feeling that she needed to give a little after pushing Chris into a corner. She just prayed that it wasn't Tim 2.0 – another entitled arsehole who would take credit for her work.

Chris leaned forward and pressed a button on the satellite intercom in front of him. 'Would you send him in please?'

Ingrid heard the door behind her open and steady footsteps

on the felt floor tiles of the conference room. She felt a gust of cool air on the back of her legs as the consultant passed behind her and headed towards Chris. She looked up and saw the back of his head, his broad back straining against the material of his beautifully tailored suit jacket. Even from this angle he looked strangely familiar, but she couldn't quite place him.

'Everyone, this is Jacob Ellis,' said Chris, as Jacob Ellis turned to face them. 'And Jacob, this is . . .'

'Ingrid,' said Jacob with a wide smile.

14

Reunion

There was no amount of melanin to disguise the deep blush that rose to Ingrid's cheeks as Jacob turned around. It felt as though her entire body had burst into flames at the sight of the man who had seen her at her most vulnerable, covered in mud and crying, not to mention naked, a couple of weeks ago. It was deeply uncomfortable to encounter him in the space where she was supposed to be competent and professional, especially following her rare showdown.

Fighting a sudden urge in her body to sprint from the room, Ingrid forced herself to look up at him. Jacob's smile was almost intimate, and as if she was back in his kitchen again she found herself looking at that mouth . . . Oh God. As her blush continued to rise, she felt certain that every person in the room now assumed she'd had sex with him. Her skin burned even hotter at the thought, remembering how she'd imagined it herself when she'd been in his cottage.

Forcing herself back to the room, Ingrid swallowed and rearranged her face to its gamest expression. Then she stood to come forward and shake his hand, which she managed with some modicum of elegance and poise. His hand was warm, his handshake firm.

'You know each other?' Chris asked, looking between them.

'We met recently,' said Jacob with a glint in his eye and a smile flirting at the corner of his lips.

'It was a conference, wasn't it?' said Ingrid, her smile firm.

'Was it?' said Jacob, tilting his head, still smiling.

'You remember,' she willed him, gripping his fingers tighter, 'the one in New York.'

'I thought it was that retreat, but then you were wearing . . .'

If she were white, she'd be crimson by now. The look on his face told her that he was definitely remembering her hopping out of the shower naked. He was determined to torture her. She resisted the urge to stab him with her expensive fountain pen. 'You must be thinking of someone else.'

Was it possible to imbue a stare with everything that had preceded their reunion? Ingrid certainly tried and almost gasped in gratitude as Jacob read her expression and seemed to get the message.

'You're right. It was that asset management conference in November.'

Chris watched them with interest. 'It's great that you two already know each other, you can get straight into working on this pitch. Jacob here has been working in this field in the Far East.'

'Singapore, right?' said Ingrid, before she could check herself.

He looked her in the eye as he smiled again, this time reading the room. 'Right.'

'I think we can wrap things up here. Tim, can we talk in my office please? Ingrid, let's regroup by the end of the week to discuss a plan of attack. Jacob, we're a bit limited on space at the moment, so maybe you could camp out in Ingrid's office for the time being and when an office becomes free, we'll move you in there,' said Chris.

Oh dear God, this man she'd thought she'd never have to see again was going to be sitting in the same small office as her. And she knew how RFPs went. There were long hours, late nights and close proximity. She'd spent a whole evening blatantly flirting with him, safe in the knowledge that she would never see him again, and now here he was.

'That's no problem,' said Jacob as Chris clapped him on the shoulder.

'Good. Put something in the diary, Ingrid.'

'Sure,' she replied.

Tim passed by her on his way out, his expression murderous. She just caught him hissing under his breath, 'You'll regret this.'

In all honesty, she was afraid that she might regret it. This was exactly why she had done nothing about Tim and his ilk in the past. She had enough drama in her personal life at the moment to be dealing with threats at work. But then she'd been made a partner for a reason. She'd gone through a rigorous selection process, and she deserved her position. She had to own it. She couldn't let some supercilious little cuckoo and his protective 'uncle' take the credit for all her achievements. This wasn't a collective society where her work was for the greater good. This was business. And it was time that she stood up for herself.

'Just stating facts, Tim.'

He took a step towards her and she squared up to him.

'Chris is calling you,' she said. 'Run along, won't you, Tim?'

Tim glared at her, glanced at the two men, then clicked his heels and stalked out of the room while Trent laughed, Ingrid grimaced and Jacob looked puzzled.

'I'm Trent Daniels. I work with Ingrid,' he said, extending his hand to Jacob who shook it firmly.

'Nice to meet you. Jacob Ellis.' He looked at Ingrid. 'That seemed a little serious.'

She tucked her hair behind her ears and smoothed her skirt down. 'Long story.' She was still a little giddy from her uncharacteristic victory.

Jacob nodded.

'I'll leave you two to talk. But, wow, Ingrid. That was awesome! I'm so glad that someone finally stood up to that ass,' said Trent.

'Thank you for supporting me.' So many people, including her, were often too worried about their own positions to put themselves on the line for someone else.

'Anytime.' Trent nodded at her, gave Jacob a long look of appraisal, then a wave before leaving the conference room.

They were alone, but Ingrid was aware of the stares of many of the women in the open-plan office through the glass wall of the conference room. Jacob was a very attractive, unknown male, and like any shiny sandwich or coffee place that popped up around the office, the appeal of something new was undeniable. They'd be queuing up around the block for one of those smiles.

'So . . .' said Ingrid, aware that she'd be first in the queue.

'I didn't expect to see *you* here,' said Jacob with a smile. She had to stop looking at his mouth. It had been the same a few weeks ago, her eyes were continually drawn to those full soft lips.

She cleared her throat. 'Ditto.' She glanced through the glass wall. Sure enough, several pairs of curious eyes were on them.

'So, tell me more about that conference where we met,' he said, perching on the edge of the table and crossing his legs at the ankle. 'Because I need to make sure I sign up for that one again. Especially that bit where I brought you some clean clothes.'

He flashed her a heart-stopping smile.

'You'd be surprised at how good people are at lip-reading in this office,' said Ingrid, glancing at the glass and trying to ignore her heartbeat as it thundered in her chest.

Jacob turned so that his face couldn't be seen from outside the room. 'Understood. How have you been, Ingrid?'

'Busy, as you can see.'

He took a step back, his index finger resting on his chin, considering her. 'You know, when we met, I had no idea what you might do for a job, but seeing you here in your element, it makes perfect sense.'

She wasn't quite sure how to take that. She was an accountant.

'Are you saying I'm boring?'

He laughed. 'Not at all! Quite the opposite. I just meant that we're both in the same industry. And this outfit . . .' he looked her up and down '. . . is a big improvement on the other one.'

'Ah, yes, I do love to make a good first impression on my colleagues, you know.'

'I'd say mission accomplished,' he said with a wink and a laugh. 'Anyway, it's really good to see you again.'

She looked at him, his expression now so sincere and warm.

'It's really good to see you too.' It was *too* good. She'd just fought hard for this project, but how the hell was she going to get any work done with this god of a man in her office? She felt herself overheating again.

She was going to have to give herself a major talking-to. Jacob wouldn't be interested in her beyond their mild flirtation in the cottage. That had just been a forced proximity thing. She'd read enough Regency romances to know that. He'd been kind and that was it. For all she knew, his suggestive comments were just millennial banter. Her attraction to him was *her* problem, and now was the time to tamp it all down and be professional.

'And I'm looking forward to working with you,' he said.

'I'll show you to our office, and then how about we have a chat about how to proceed over lunch?' Ingrid asked as she gathered the rest of her things from the table. He had an unnerving way of holding her gaze, just like that evening in the cottage. She couldn't look away.

After what seemed like minutes, but was probably only a couple of seconds, she blinked, breaking eye contact. She could do this. She was a forty-five-year-old woman and she would share an office with this man, have meals and work with him without dissolving into a lustful mess. She could absolutely be professional and calm in his presence.

Ingrid was in big trouble. She knew it from the moment the waiter placed them at a corner table where they sat at right angles, knees occasionally brushing against each other in the limited space. She knew it when Jacob leaned forward so that she could repeat her sentence into his ear over the din of the busy restaurant. She knew it as his eyes tracked her hands past her neck as she secured her hair into a ponytail.

Discussions about financial products and fund assets did nothing to dampen her attraction to this man. If anything, it was fun to discover they talked the same work language. She had known Jacob was smart, but now she got to see his brain in action. Goddamn, it was sexy. Even though he'd been trying to help his Golden Boy, she had to admit that Chris had made a good call – with his insights and market knowledge, Jacob would be a great collaborator for this project. If it wasn't for whatever it was that caused her heart to race at a million miles around him. Whether she trained her focus on his eyes or his mouth, it was getting hard to concentrate on what he was saying.

She had to get a grip. Not only did they have to work together, chasing a very lucrative contract, but she was about to go through a messy divorce . . . as she was still currently *married*. She had briefly forgotten that over the cauliflower bang bang. And she had no idea how old Jacob was, but he was definitely too young for her.

Anyway, he was probably like this with everyone – watching them closely, not moving away when accidentally touching. Some people were just like that, weren't they? She was letting his style of interacting with people go to her head and scramble all the neurons that were waking up after over a decade of being dormant.

'So, did you scold your sister for booking you on that retreat?' Jacob asked, looking into his coffee cup as he stirred the thick black liquid with a tiny spoon.

'Yeah. I'll get my revenge and book her a hike up Kilimanjaro for her next birthday. Although, knowing Audrey, she'll train for it and make it up there in record time.'

'So you're all overachievers in your family,' Jacob put both elbows on the table and leaned forward, with another smile that threatened to send Ingrid off to the doctor for an ECG.

'Hmm, not exactly. I'm a bit of a failure at the moment because I'm getting divorced.'

What was that in his expression before he corrected it? She pinched herself to snap out of this level of over-analysis she was slipping into. It wouldn't lead anywhere safe.

'Hardly makes you a failure, but I'm sorry, that's rough. And now you have this proposal on top of all that.'

Ingrid waved her hand dismissively. 'I'm used to juggling it. My husband . . . almost ex-husband, has been gone for a year already. Things haven't been good between us for a long time, so it's just the legal stuff to sort out now.'

'He moved out a year ago?'

'Kind of. He actually went off on a trip to "find himself". He's been doing that for years, this was just the longest one. And he found several other people at the same time.'

'Wow! Do people really do that kind of stuff?'

'Apparently.'

'And you're fine with it?'

She shrugged. 'I had no choice. I made do.'

'And you have kids?'

'One, a daughter. She's eleven, so it's tricky.'

He raised his eyebrows for a moment, no doubt recalling her previous lie in the cottage when she'd told him she lived alone. Then he smiled. 'I don't really know you, Ingrid, but I suspect that you're amazing.'

She shook her head. 'Not at all. I just got on with things, you know. One foot in front of the other every day.'

'I think you're selling yourself short. I mean, look at your job. Not everyone can hold down a big four partnership, let alone be as good at it as you are. And then you're looking after your daughter all by yourself, going through a divorce, and you still look like you've got it all together. I think I'm right.'

Ingrid didn't know where to look. No one had ever said anything like this to her before. Her family assumed that she was perfectly fine while they erupted all over the place. No one had ever thought to tell her that she was doing a good job. After all that confrontation in the conference room today, she was afraid that she would sob if she met Jacob's eyes, but she couldn't dismiss his words by looking around the room. In the end, she settled for staring at her hands in her lap, her left one lighter without the weight of her rings.

'I wasn't doing a good job when you met me, if you remember. Pretty useless, in fact.'

He ducked his head to meet her eyes. 'You looked okay to me. Just like you weren't expecting to go on any hikes.'

He held her gaze for a beat, and she was now in serious trouble. What would those lips feel like on . . . Thankfully her thought process was broken when he picked up his glass.

She sat on her hands to prevent herself from doing anything embarrassing like trying to hug him. 'What about you? Have you decided to stay?'

'Not yet. I'm still due to start the new job in the US in December.'

She nodded, her head bobbing up and down as she took it in. He was leaving the country soon. Acting on her feelings would be an absolutely terrible idea. Wouldn't it? Maybe her libido had gone mad because of her long sexual drought . . . as though the dial was broken or something and she was either completely uninterested or in full heat.

'How weird is it that we met again like this? My sister, Grace, would say that it was fate.' Now she really sounded like a teenager. He was probably expecting her to whip out their astrological charts or some crystals. She smiled to herself, wishing she had one or both. In her experience, that sort of thing made people like Jacob run a mile.

He smiled and leaned towards her. 'It seems like the only logical explanation.'

'Hmm, I'm not sure that the concept of fate is actually logical,' she said, backtracking.

'Maybe not, but it's a handy explanation. Or we're living out the plot of an old movie and you're really a princess who took a day off in the Lakes.'

Ingrid smiled. She'd watched *Roman Holiday* with her mother countless times.

'I'm surprised a baby like you knows that movie reference. Are you physically able to watch films in black and white?'

'I've seen a few with my grandma,' he said with a wink.

Ingrid laughed.

'Wait,' said Jacob, holding up an index finger. 'Ingrid, Audrey and Grace? Did your mum like old movies?'

Ingrid groaned. 'Yeah, Mum is crazy about all those old movies. She used to watch them with *my* grandma in Sri Lanka when she was a child. We're her film stars, apparently.'

A shadow crossed his face as she spoke about her sisters, but he covered it with another smile.

'That's pretty cool. They're all great names.'

So much for keeping this professional. After Jacob had rescued her on that godforsaken hill there was a strange level of intimacy between them that she couldn't seem to shake.

'Don't worry, no one will ever know about how we met,' he said before taking a sip of his bitter-looking coffee.

What had happened to her poker face? She wasn't usually this expressive. How was he able to read her so well?

'I appreciate that. It's not easy being a woman in business, and I can't have people knowing about my personal life.'

'I assume they don't know about the divorce.'

'Only Kerry, my PA knows. And Trent. He's a good egg.'

'You're close?' Jacob asked. Was he being careful not to look her in the eyes? His usual eye contact was so frequent and intense.

'Let's just say that our interests are aligned. He supports me, I support him. Everyone thinks that partnership means that we all work in each other's interests, but really, the knives are out all the time. I'm glad he came over from the US because I was all alone before that.'

'So is that what the atmosphere was when I arrived?'

'Just office politics. Not at all relevant to your job here.' They still had the same easy rapport as in the cottage, but whereas before she was openly flirting with him, now she needed to keep a professional distance and stop this attraction from turning into feelings, which would be much more difficult to stem. She managed a tight, uneasy smile, then checked her watch, barely registering the time on the tiny face without her glasses on. 'Speaking of which. Shall we get the bill? We should get started with a plan of action.'

Jacob smiled knowingly, possibly reading her mind again, placed his hands on the table and looked at her silently. A long, slow stare directly into her eyes that made her feel as though he could see right through her. There was something about the length of it that felt intimate, and she flushed with embarrassment. As Ingrid looked away, she saw him nod. Had he been about to say something?

Ingrid flagged someone down to get the bill.

Shit. She was in so much trouble.

15

Sunday

Ingrid reached a little further, sweating in the July heat, her fingers brushing the worn suede on Lily's trainers under the bed. Knowing her luck lately, she'd probably become wedged under there with the dust and random multicoloured Lego pieces for company. The same tableau played out every time that they had to leave for Sunday mass due to Lily's reluctance to sit on a hard, wooden pew for an hour and a half when she'd rather be gaming.

'Lils, how many times do I have to tell you to put these in the cupboard by the front door?' Ingrid said, puffing some hair off her face and redistributing some of the under-bed dust up her nose.

'Sorry, Mum. I forgot.'

'This is the first time we've gone to mass in weeks and Aachi's going to kill me if we're late.'

'Tell her it's my fault.'

'For Aachi, your fault is actually *my* fault, you know this.'

'Mum, why do we have to go to church, but Aunty Grace doesn't?'

Lily could win awards in procrastination. This was a question that was often thrown out to delay proceedings. Ingrid had fallen for it in the past.

'Got it!' Ingrid pulled the trainer out in triumph and then

stood to dust herself off. There was no time to change so this mess would have to do.

'Mum? Aunty Grace?'

'You'll have to ask her that one,' said Ingrid, wishing that she hadn't started this little somewhat sporadic ritual with her parents. She didn't feel like going to church. Or more accurately, she didn't want to listen to any more of her mother's opinions after she'd successfully managed to avoid her since the scene at her house four weeks earlier. Mum had called her and threatened to come and stay for a week if she didn't bring Lily to mass, so she'd given in.

A part of her liked the ritual of the service, the hymns, the streaks of multicoloured light as sun shone through the stained-glass windows. There was some peace to be found in the calm tranquillity of an empty church, traces of incense and melting wax in the air.

Church attendance had always been compulsory in their family. The concept of the Sunday morning lie-in a complete anathema to the Pereras, who pulled their children out of their sleep, made them scrub their faces and dress in their best clothes, and dragged them to mass early enough for them all to sit in the same pew.

'Is it because she doesn't believe in God?'

This child was persistent. Though, she couldn't blame her; she was as reluctant to go as her daughter. 'If you know this, why are you asking me?'

'Do *you* believe in God?'

Ingrid resisted rolling her eyes, which would segue into another opportunity for procrastination as Lily tried her hand at an existentialist conversation at the ripe old age of eleven and three-quarters. 'We don't have time for a conversation on faith and the universe right now, Lily. We have to get to church before Aachi spontaneously combusts. And chances are that I'll be the one who has to clean up if that happens. Come on, shoo!'

Ingrid waved her daughter down the stairs.

'But Mum, *please* can I stay with Aunty Grace,' said Lily, spotting Grace at the bottom of the stairs, bacon sandwich in one hand and a large cup of tea in the other, newspaper tucked under one armpit.

'Lilypad, be a good girl and go with Mum,' said Grace, knowing all too well that she would also be blamed for Lily's absence.

Lily shoved her foot into a dusty trainer and scowled at her mother.

'Baby, I'm sorry, but you have to go. We all had to when we were your age and it wasn't so bad.'

'Speak for yourself,' said Grace, before munching her sandwich.

Ingrid shot her a glare. 'Not helping, Sis.'

'Sing lots of hymns for me,' said Grace as brightly as was possible through her mouthful of food.

Ingrid slipped into her loafers, checked her hair in the mirror for stray whorls of dust and turned to her sister. 'And remember not to let in people who shouldn't be let in.'

'Do you mean Dad?' Lily asked.

'Of course not, darling,' Ingrid lied.

Lily rolled her eyes. 'I'm not a child, Mum. I know you mean Dad.'

'Well, I have news for you, Lily darling, you *are* a child. And I didn't mean Dad.' She absolutely did, but she couldn't let Lily know that. It wasn't that she wanted to deny him access to his child, she just wanted it to be controlled and planned, not spontaneous and filled with poison about her. 'Let's go.'

Although most people these days turned up to church in the most casual of casual clothing, Florence Perera took the idea of wearing her Sunday best literally. Every week she wore a different suit, her wardrobe an array of age-appropriate colours. This week, it was a lavender trouser suit, a cream camisole, oversized pearls around her neck with matching earrings (she was possibly taking this Maggie Thatcher thing a bit too far), and white kitten heels. Ingrid was sure that she would have accessorised with white gloves and a hat if even she hadn't thought that they were a little too much. In stark contrast, Thatha seemed to own at least five of the same maroon shirt with a small gold button at the neck. This was paired with his poly-blend grey trousers and sturdy black Hush Puppies. Without a doubt, there'd been the usual argument about his refusal to wear a jacket and tie, one which escalated in winter when he insisted on wearing his comfy parka instead of a smart wool coat.

Ammi insisted on attending the 9 a.m. mass at Pinner parish church because it was a children's mass. Yet another reason why Ingrid dragged her daughter along. And even though Lily complained about attending, each week she'd squeal with delight when she spotted some of the friends with whom she'd studied for her First Holy Communion and then ditch Ingrid to go and sit with them. Ingrid could have done with the cover this week, because she was sure that her mother would use Lily's absence to lecture her.

'Nice of you to finally show up. And you're late,' Ammi hissed as Ingrid slid into the space next to her.

'It hasn't started yet,' said Ingrid, looking around.

'It's about to.'

Ingrid looked at her watch. It was 8.58 and these things never started exactly on time anyway. Mum was setting the tone for the rest of their interaction today. Whatever Ingrid did, it would be wrong.

'Hello, putha,' said Thatha with a kind smile as he looked over Florence's head at his daughter. 'Are you okay?'

'I'm getting there,' said Ingrid, while Florence huffed next to her.

'Jerry, I told you to stay out of it,' said Mum, shoving the parish newsletter into his hands. 'Here, read this and be quiet.'

Ingrid shot her father a sympathetic glance over Mum's

head. After almost fifty-five years of marriage, he knew when it was best to retreat when it came to his wife and her moods.

'You know you won't be able to come here anymore if you go through with it?' Mum said, pinching Ingrid's knee as if she were still ten years old and fidgeting on the seat instead of paying attention to the mass.

There were definitely perks to divorce then. She could be spared what she knew would be a repeated scolding about how she'd let her life get out of control and made all the wrong decisions just like her sisters.

'That's not a reason to stay with a man who doesn't want me anymore.'

'Divorce is a sin.'

Ingrid nodded. Mum had a knack of starting something at the worst times. A bell sounded from somewhere behind the altar and the entire congregation stood to welcome the priest. The organist gamely began to play the accompaniment to Hymn 118 in the hymnal and the makeshift choir, complete with screechy soprano and out-of-tune tenor, began to sing. The sudden cacophony and the general reverence for the mass that was about to begin would have stopped most people, but Florence Perera was the kind of opportunist who used the noise as cover to continue her lecture.

'And what about your daughter? Have you thought about her? She needs a father. Not to mention all the gossip. This won't look good for you at work either. You can't let people know that you can't hold onto a husband. They'll think you're incapable at everything else too. I won't be able to hold my head up in the parish hall,' she whispered loudly enough for the people directly in front and behind them to hear.

Ingrid considered her options. If she began to sing a hymn, Mum could literally explode in front of everyone. If she said anything in response, even if it were to ask her to keep it down, it would have the same effect as someone telling her to calm down in the middle of an argument. The third and best option was to bite her lip and nod as though her mother had made some valid points and maybe she'd settle down for the rest of the mass and concentrate on praying for less disappointing children.

Ammi glared at her before they all settled into the familiar rhythms of the mass.

Ingrid usually made a dash for it after communion on the pretext that she had to get some things from Marks & Spencer across the road, and she wanted to avoid the rush as the rest of the congregation had the same idea. But Lily was nowhere to be seen and Ingrid found herself hustled into the parish hall for coffee with her parents and their friends.

This was the part of the Sunday ritual that her mother lived for, which was somewhat hypocritical of her, but Ingrid wasn't going to be the person to pull her up on it. Florence maintained a firm grip on Ingrid's wrist as she herded her through the room, greeting parishioners as if she were the Queen at a garden party.

'Ingrid! We haven't seen you here for a while,' said Ethel, one of the elderly ladies who volunteered their time to clean the church, make flower arrangements and organise the refreshments every Sunday.

Ingrid opened her mouth to respond, but unsurprisingly, Florence headed her off at the pass.

'Oh you know, she's been terribly busy at work. She's got such a high-powered job and there've been a few business trips, otherwise she would be here. You know what a good girl she is.'

What did this moniker even mean? That she was the one who conceded to her mother's opinions on where her life should go? That she was the one who stayed at home and took care of everything while her husband went away to find himself? That she was the one who took whatever was dished out at her at work without fighting back?

Ingrid accepted the stark, cold truth of all these things. And she didn't want it anymore. She'd had a taste of the exhilaration of standing up for herself in the conference room, but shedding the persona she adopted around her parents wasn't as simple a process as presenting irrefutable facts. Emotions made things much more complex, which was exactly why she'd avoided it all so far. She hadn't wanted to hurt or disappoint anyone, and it was only now she realised that in doing so, she was the one hurt and disappointed.

'Actually, I'm getting divorced,' said Ingrid.

Mum gripped Ingrid's wrist so tightly that she was sure she'd be sporting a bruise in the next day or so, and Thatha choked on his sip of coffee and began coughing. Ethel was the only one with a vaguely normal reaction. She reached out to Ingrid and stroked her arm.

'I'm so sorry, my love. That must be very difficult for you and the little one.' Ethel turned to Ammi and Thatha. 'I know we're all supposed to think that divorce is a terrible thing, but I think it's a lot better than two unhappy people wasting their lives together.'

Mum clearly didn't agree because she glared at Dad who had recovered from his coughing fit and was nodding sagely at Ethel.

Ethel patted Ingrid on the arm again. 'I'll be praying for you, my love. May you find some peace and happiness.'

Ingrid almost grabbed Ethel to give her a hug and kiss in gratitude, but she restrained herself. 'Thank you, Ethel. You're so kind.'

As Ethel shuffled off on her rounds, Ammi hissed at Ingrid. 'What on earth were you thinking, revealing your private business to everyone?'

'Ammi, enough people heard you in the church at the beginning of mass,' said Ingrid, aware that she was entering unexplored territory with her mother by pointing out the obvious in defence of herself.

'Of course they didn't. You're the one spreading it around

and it isn't even certain you'll be getting a divorce. Matthew will change his mind, I'm sure.'

'Ammi, even if he changed his mind, do you think it would be right for me to accept it? He left for an entire year, during which he slept with other women, and you think it's acceptable for me to just go with it?'

Her mother stared at her.

'He did what?' said Thatha.

'These things happen with some men. You have to let them come back to you,' said Ammi.

Wasn't that what Ingrid had been doing? And he still hadn't wanted her. At some point, surely her mother should expect Ingrid's self-respect to kick in.

'No, no, Florrie,' said Thatha, placing his hand on Mum's arm. 'Ingrid stared at her father, a little shocked by his unexpected intervention. 'Our daughter is a jewel and he hasn't appreciated her. Whatever you say, I won't let him come back. Putha, you go ahead with the divorce, I'll be there to support you. Your mother's in shock and isn't saying the right things. Don't worry, it will be fine.'

Lily tugged Ingrid's sleeve.

'Mum, can we go now? I've got lots of homework.' Regardless of how accurate this was, Ingrid was grateful to her daughter for the handy excuse. If there was one thing that South-Asian parents could support, it was study.

'Yes, putha, you go,' said Thatha.

'But I haven't finished,' said Ammi.

'Let's stop now. It's time to support her. She didn't do any of this, it was all that man.' As she looked at her father's expression, she wondered if he'd ever liked her husband. 'Now let's go and get another cup, eh?' said Thatha as he steered Florence away from Ingrid and Lily.

What was this new feeling? Independence?

She liked it.

16

Dangerous Territory

Sadly, independence came with a hefty price tag. Ingrid surveyed the jagged peaks of the London skyline from her seat on the roof terrace where she'd taken her phone call with Cheska. Divorce was expensive. Her life would change irrevocably as she would have to sell the house, maybe even move Lily out of school if she couldn't find anywhere to live within the catchment area of her current one. And the thought that she would have to give Matt a proportion of her hard-earned money rankled. But according to Cheska, that was the easiest way to settle it. Ingrid wasn't sure if she could be bothered with the hard way, instead wanting to sever ties as cleanly and quickly as possible.

Her phone buzzed in her hand. Matt. It was like he had a sixth sense that she'd been talking about him.

'I want to see Lily.'

So this was how it was going to be.

'Okay. When?'

'I have time on Wednesday evening.'

'Lily has chess club that day.' If he'd been around, he'd have known that. 'But she's free on Thursday. Let me check with her first though.'

'Why do you need to check with her? She's my daughter. I should be able to see her whenever I want.'

'If she wants to. Her feelings are all I care about, Matt.'

'You're just trying to poison her against me.'

'I really don't want to do that. After all these years, do you still not know me?' He'd been so wrapped up in himself, it was unlikely.

He huffed. 'Alright, check with her and text me. I'll pick her up at six.'

He hung up. She sighed. Were all divorces like this?

Ingrid trudged back downstairs to her office, her eyes struggling to adjust to the artificial light. Jacob's desk was neat and tidy with no extraneous papers lying around, just a laptop, screen, keyboard, a leather-bound notebook, an expensive-looking ballpoint pen and a book on commodities that lay open. She wondered where he was.

She crossed the room to look out of the window. If she angled herself correctly, on a clear day like this, she could see a bit of Tower Bridge. An office with a view surely meant she'd made it, like that iconic scene in *Working Girl* where Melanie Griffith finally got the job she wanted with a view of Manhattan. Had she made it?

'Everything alright?' asked Jacob, behind her.

She whirled around to see him with a coffee in each hand and a paper Pret bag dangling from one of his pinky fingers.

Ingrid waved her phone at Jacob. 'Just spoke to my lawyer. And then my ex.'

'Rough?'

She shrugged and came to sit at her desk, facing him. 'Could be better.'

Jacob placed one coffee cup on her desk and the other on his, then extracted a Pret salad from the bag with cutlery. He brought it over, placing it on the desk in front of her. She caught herself staring at his forearms as he removed the plastic cover on the salad box, and he was close enough that she could smell his cologne – woody and sensual – and the faint scent of coconut from his shampoo. He tipped the salad dressing over the leaves and brought his index finger to his lips to lick off the excess while Ingrid's eyes followed.

Ingrid took a deep breath to calm her racing heart. If she'd had a medical during the two weeks that she'd shared this office with him, she would surely be on blood pressure medication by now. Her resting heart rate was up so much she'd had to disable the alarm on her smartwatch.

'I thought you might miss out on dinner, so I picked up the Pret salad you like.' He smiled.

This was who he was: kind and considerate. Ingrid was sure she'd seen him pick up food for Kerry before as she'd swooned gratefully when accepting it. He was just a nice guy and Ingrid had to stop reading more into these gestures.

Jacob nodded towards the coffee. 'Looks like you need that too.'

'Thanks, Jacob. The next one's on me.' Should she tell him she was having dinner with her sisters when he'd been so kind?

He nodded and sat in his chair, swivelling it around to face her. 'Divorce is hard.'

'God, yes. Even though I've known my marriage was over for a long time, there's no escaping that feeling of being a failure. And the whole process doesn't exactly help you to come to some sort of peace with it all.'

'I guess it's never going to be easy because you can't separate it from your emotions. You loved this person and created a life with them. It can't be a clinical process.'

'But we could make it easier. I really don't understand Matt. He's the one who wanted the divorce and yet he's being so aggressive about it.'

'It might feel like a failure for him too. Perhaps it's harder for him to go through the reality of it than he thought.'

She still didn't know Jacob's age, but to her eyes, he seemed wiser than however many years old he was.

'Maybe. I just wish he'd think of Lily.'

'Your daughter?'

She nodded and watched again for his reaction. He didn't seem in the slightest bit fazed by talk of her child, which was further evidence in her 'he doesn't fancy you' column because, of course, men of his age would be running a mile from a relationship with a woman with a child.

'I wish he could be civil about it for her sake.'

'She's eleven, right?' Jacob asked.

Ingrid nodded.

'I was about the same age as Lily when my parents split. I guess I kind of knew what was happening but I didn't have the emotional maturity to deal with it. And even though they told my brother and me that they loved us, we still felt abandoned. To be honest, to an extent we were. I haven't seen my dad for years.'

Ingrid sat and faced him. 'I'm so sorry, Jacob. It must have been traumatic for you. Your mum must have done a great job to fill the gap because you seem really well adjusted to me.'

Jacob smiled. 'Yeah, Mum's great. But this . . .' he said, pointing to himself, 'is the product of a lot of therapy as an adult.'

'Do you think I should look at getting Lily a therapist now? I think she already felt abandoned when Matt left on his gap year. She used to be so much more sociable, but now she's in her room all the time on that bloody computer.'

Jacob leaned forward and rested his elbows on his knees. 'I'm not trying to minimise the impact of having a parent disappear like that, but it could be a combination of a lot of other things too. She must have started secondary school and I'm pretty sure that kids tend to change then. And then there's puberty, which is a whole other thing. Perhaps a therapist would help. I can do some research for you if you like?'

'Thank you, but no, it's fine. I'd need to talk to Matt first. And then there's my family . . .' Mainly Ammi and Thatha. They were of the generation where mental health struggles were a sign of weakness and any sort of therapy was the source of familial stigma, much like divorce.

'Even if you don't go through some sort of therapy, as long as she has a loving family around her, she'll get through it if you keep talking and making her feel loved. My parents detested each other by the end and it definitely filtered through to my brother and me.'

She sat back in her chair with a sigh. 'I can only control *my* behaviour. And Matt can't seem to do that. Doesn't he realise how much it hurts Lily? Then there's my mum who's so upset about it all, and she's about as controllable as Japanese knotweed.'

Jacob laughed.

'Hey, you may laugh, but that woman is no joke,' said Ingrid, smiling.

'Noted.'

Ingrid pulled her silk scrunchy off her head, allowing her hair to cascade around her shoulders. When she looked back at Jacob, he was watching her, his eyes a little unfocused. Was that because of her? He was probably thinking of something, or someone, else.

She massaged her temples to try to stave off the tension headache she could feel building. 'And Matt's trying to file for full custody, because apparently my job is too demanding for me to be a mother. It's completely ridiculous, but it's one more thing to deal with and he's not making it easy for me to keep my temper.'

Jacob stood and came to perch on the edge of her desk. 'I'm sure that your lawyer has told you this, but judges do tend to give custody to mothers, even when the father hasn't been away for a whole year.'

She knew that, rationally, but until the papers were stamped there was a part of her that wouldn't rest.

'She's the one good thing that's come out of all this,' she said, hearing her voice choke on the words as tears appeared in her eyes.

Jacob took her hand in both of his and the skin-to-skin contact caused both of them to look into each other's eyes.

'That's the healthiest way to look at it.'

His thumb brushed the top of her hand, soothing her, and as she looked at his face she couldn't shake the feeling that they'd crossed an invisible line. Could it be that her feelings were getting harder to deny so she was imagining things, or was there something here? She watched his chest heave as he took a deep breath. She must have raked up bad memories for him.

'I should go,' she said, pulling her hand free and wiping away the tears. 'It's really kind of you to get me something to eat, but would you mind if I save it for lunch tomorrow? Lily's at a sleepover, so I'm meeting my sisters for a drink.'

Jacob looked at his watch. Whatever had been written all over his face a moment before was gone now. 'No problem. Give me a minute to shut down my computer and I'll walk out with you.'

'No, that's okay. You take your time.'

'I need to go now anyway. Wait for me?'

'Hot date?' *What?* She heard herself asking the question before her brain had caught up with her mouth. Was this her subconscious sabotaging whatever might be between them before it even happened?

To her relief, Jacob just smiled and shook his head. 'Boxing.' He retrieved a small sports bag from underneath his desk. 'Ready?' She nodded.

Ingrid tried not to think about how nice, how natural it felt, as they headed to the lifts together. Six o'clock was clearly the most popular time for leaving the office because they had to wait until at least three lifts stopped at their floor before they could get into one. As more people boarded, Ingrid was pushed further inside and she wobbled on the heels she'd forgotten to change out of before leaving in a hurry. Jacob moved behind her, his hands resting lightly on her hips to steady her as she swayed, protecting her from the crush of people around her. He leaned down to whisper in her ear and she shivered at his breath.

'I've got you.'

17

Truth and Tequila

'Here, have a shot!' said Grace as soon as Ingrid took a seat at their table in a restaurant next to her office in London Bridge.

'I can't drink that stuff.' Ingrid grimaced, pushing away Grace's hand.

'It's not the usual rancid tequila that'll lay you out cold and give you a banging twenty-four-hour headache, Sis. This is the good Mexican stuff,' said Grace, now holding the shot glass under Ingrid's nose.

Audrey held her glass aloft, ready to knock hers back as soon as the signal was given.

An unwelcome image of Matt popped into her head and Ingrid decided that Grace was right about the need for a straight shot of alcohol to her bloodstream. She took the glass and held it up to meet Audrey's and Grace's.

'To getting rid of the trash,' said Audrey with a wink at Ingrid. *Just how many of those had she had?*

'To getting rid of the trash,' Grace and Ingrid repeated and downed the alcohol.

Ingrid winced as the strong liquor wound its way down her oesophagus and burned into her stomach. She needed to eat something if this was the way the evening was going to go. And fast – as she caught Grace motioning to the waiter for another round.

Audrey's phone rang from its spot on the table, a photo of her youngest, Harry, popping up on the screen. As with most teens, he didn't like having his photo taken by his mum so his expression was sulky.

'Yes, darling?' said Audrey.

Grace and Ingrid picked up the menus to order some stomach-lining food.

'Separate the whites from everything else. Then wash at forty degrees. And you'll probably have to tumble-dry it as you have nowhere to hang your clothes, right?'

'You should give him some pointers,' said Ingrid to Grace, who smacked her arm playfully.

'You do like to hold a grudge, don't you, Sis?'

'Alright, bring it home at the weekend and I'll do it for you. Okay, bye,' said Audrey.

'Medical school going well for Harry then?' Ingrid asked.

'Who knows? He only calls when he doesn't know how to do something. Last week he called to ask for a soup recipe for some girl he likes.'

'You miss him?' Grace asked.

'I don't miss the piles of dirty crockery in his room, or the empty cartons of milk in the fridge, but yes, I never thought I'd miss the relentless thud of drum and bass in the house.'

Audrey dropped her phone into her bag. 'So . . .' she continued, leaning forward into Ingrid's space. 'Who was that delicious man who came out of your office with you?'

Both of her sisters stared at her as she took a moment to answer. Audrey was like a bloodhound, sniffing out untold truths with ruthless efficiency. And Grace had the ability to read Ingrid's usually inscrutable expressions with pinpoint accuracy.

She kept her tone as bland as possible. 'That's Jacob. He's working with us on this pitch.'

'Shame he's a bit young for you,' said Audrey, picking up the wine list and holding it at arm's length, having forgotten to bring her glasses with her.

Ingrid bristled. Was he too young for her? Probably. But hearing Audrey dismiss the possibility with such certainty rankled.

'Why? Nobody bats an eyelid when the woman is much younger. I mean, look at Leonardo DiCaprio. He's definitely breaking that French rule of half your age plus seven,' said Grace.

Ingrid took a moment to examine her elated reaction to Grace's comment.

'I'm positive that he gets a fair amount of flak for it,' said Audrey, her eyes raking the menu as another round of shots was delivered.

'To new beginnings,' said Grace, as they raised the tiny glasses. The three women clinked once again and drank the surprisingly smooth tequila.

'And what about all those other Hollywood actors whose love interest is usually about thirty years younger than them? No one says anything about that,' said Ingrid, leaning into Grace's argument.

Both of her sisters turned to look at her and she mentally kicked herself.

'Interesting. So you're not ruling out the possibility of having hot sex with a younger man?' said Audrey.

'And judging by the way that your eyes refuse to look at us, I think she might have even thought about hot sex with *this* particular man,' said Grace with a mischievous grin.

'Don't be ridiculous. We work together, that's all. I was just backing up your point,' said Ingrid, feeling rumbled by her overly perceptive sisters. Of course she'd thought about what sex would be like with Jacob, in the shower she found it difficult to think of anything else, but there was absolutely no way she would ever admit that to these two.

'If you ask me, hot sex with that divine man is exactly what she needs,' said Grace.

Audrey rolled her eyes as if Grace were a silly child,

completely missing the flush that was overtaking Ingrid's face and shoulders.

'What?' Grace asked, shrugging her shoulders. 'She doesn't have to be a nun, you know. And hasn't Matt been doing exactly that?'

'But she doesn't have to sink to his level.'

Ingrid placed her cold glass of water against her neck, leaving her sisters to argue about her non-existent sex life.

'Doesn't he want a divorce? Surely that means that Ingrid is a free agent. Having sex with someone else isn't sinking to any level,' said Grace.

'Fine, fine, let's order something to eat and stop talking about this, shall we? I can't even remember what sex is like so this is all a moot point,' said Ingrid.

'A year is a long time,' said Audrey. 'I'm not sure how I'd cope without the usual three times a week.'

Ingrid stared at her sister. Was that normal? The last time Ingrid had sex with Matt was two years ago and even before that, they'd have been lucky to manage once every two months, not to mention it was always the same routine that left her unsatisfied while he went to the bathroom to wash all traces of her off him.

'Why are you staring at me with that fish face?' Audrey asked.

Ingrid closed her mouth immediately. She typically didn't engage in any talk about sex with her sisters because what did you say when you didn't have any?

Audrey put down her menu and leaned closer. 'What's up, Nangi? You can trust us.'

The tequila had clearly gone to her head because she heard herself saying words she had never planned to speak out loud. 'We hadn't slept together for a year before he left, and hardly before that.'

Audrey and Grace stared at each other in shock for a moment before scooting their chairs around as best they could to put an arm each around her.

Ingrid shrugged them off. 'See, this is why I never said anything before. I don't need your pity. I'm fine.'

They looked at her, both wearing expressions that seemed to say, *really?*

'Honestly. It happened pretty gradually. And I was sort of okay with it. I can't say I felt like having sex with him anyway.'

'Two years with *no sex*,' said Grace, incredulous.

'So basically, you're saying that no one has seen you naked for the last two years except perhaps for a doctor?' Audrey asked.

Jacob's heated gaze as he'd looked at her naked body in the bathroom popped into her head. She realised he'd made her feel beautiful in that moment.

'Ingrid?' Audrey said. 'Where did you go just then?'

'Huh?' Ingrid pulled herself out of her thoughts and fixed her gaze on her sister.

'I'm sorry,' said Audrey in a rare apology for her. 'I shouldn't push you.'

'I told you. I'm fine,' said Ingrid, taking a large gulp of wine from the glass that had appeared next to her plate while she'd been daydreaming. She was beginning to feel light-headed.

'She needs to date someone,' said Grace. 'I'll sign you up to one of the apps I use.'

'And that's been so successful for you,' said Audrey, sitting back in her seat and crossing her arms.

'Well, I haven't had a sexual drought, so I would call that a success. I'm getting what I want.'

'Show off,' said Ingrid, smiling now. 'But no thanks. I don't want to sign up for anything.'

'And she shouldn't give Matt any ammunition in her divorce,' said Audrey.

And yet, it was alright for him to sleep with countless women and it would have no bearing on his ability to be a parent. Audrey would be horrified to hear how much she sounded like their mother.

'It's not like she's going to post about her shags on Instagram, Sis. You need to chill,' said Grace.

Audrey patted Grace's head. 'You do know that you're forty and are most definitely not down with the kids?'

'Oh, shush! I'm young enough to talk like that, thank you very much.'

'No apps!' Ingrid said, pointing at Grace who grabbed her finger and pushed her hand away.

'Alright, I get it. No apps. Just sex with the gorgeous man in your office.'

'Not a good idea,' said Audrey sternly.

Ingrid touched her ear, recalling Jacob's breath as he'd whispered to her earlier. She knew that her sister was right. And that she always did the right thing.

But was it time she did something wrong?

She needed to calm down. That voice in her head was not helping. Ingrid stood up, feeling the effects of the tequila as she swayed a little on her heels. She pictured the trendy, and crucially comfortable trainers she'd left under the desk in her hurry to exit the office and scowled. 'Just going to the loo.'

She managed to pick her way through the tables to the dark corridor that led to the toilets at the back of the restaurant. As she turned to walk down it, one of her stiletto heels hit the shiny floor tiles at the wrong angle and she felt herself pitch sideways. There was little she could do except anticipate the fall, but a hand gripped her waist and she was suddenly flush against a wall of warm muscle and a very familiar scent.

'It seems to be my life's mission to save you from ankle injuries caused by unsuitable shoes,' said Jacob's voice.

She looked up at him, momentarily confused but also very happy to see him. 'I thought you had boxing?'

Jacob smiled down at her. 'My friend's having some issues with his girlfriend, so he wanted to talk.'

'Ah,' said Ingrid, extricating herself from his embrace to regain her equilibrium. She really should have had some bread. 'Well, thanks for the assist.'

'Don't you normally wear trainers?' he asked, looking at her feet, or was that her legs? She couldn't tell in this dim light.

'Forgot.'

He nodded. 'Right. Anyway, I wanted to see if you were okay.'

'Why?'

Jacob looked a little sheepish. 'Well, we're only a couple of tables away from you, and your sisters are pretty loud.'

Was there a black hole at the end of this corridor? No, even that wouldn't have been enough to swallow the gargantuan level of embarrassment she was experiencing right now.

'What did you hear?' This was still salvageable if he hadn't heard much. She hid her face in her hands and wracked her brain to try and remember what had been said and when.

He waited patiently until she looked up at him, his expression kind, but there was a tinge of something else.

'For the record, your ex-husband is an idiot.' He stepped closer and she instinctively stepped back and hit the wall behind her.

'Well, I know *that*,' said Ingrid, trying to smile and dampen whatever this atmosphere between them was. But Jacob's expression remained intense. Perhaps it was the darkness of the corridor, or possibly the alcohol running through her, but she could have sworn that his eyes were boring into her.

'You're a beautiful woman, Ingrid.'

Now she didn't know where to look. Compliments like this were not an everyday occurrence for her. She settled on standing up straight and trying to muster her scattered dignity. 'That's very kind of you.' Oh God, she sounded like she'd just met him at a garden party or something. He must think she was bonkers. Or hopefully, just drunk.

Jacob pushed his hair back, taking a deep breath. She peered at his face in the half light, unable to read this situation. This was why she usually didn't do shots.

'Anyway, I hope you're alright.'

'Hmm,' she said, nodding her head.

'You know, if you need to relieve some stress . . .' Her heartbeat kicked up a notch. 'You should try boxing at my gym.'

What? This conversation had segued into unexpected territory.

'Seriously?'

He smiled. 'It's a great workout, but especially good for stress relief. And you have a lot going on right now. It might help. Hey, we can get a photo of your ex and stick it on the pads.'

She laughed, glad to feel on firmer ground with this kind of conversation with Jacob. 'That would be priceless.'

'How about tomorrow?'

'Wait, you're serious.'

'Of course.'

'But I don't know anything about it.'

'I'll teach you. You look fit so it shouldn't be too hard for you.' His eyes raked her body before they held her gaze again.

'Okay.' She was sure that she might burst into flames at any moment, the copious amounts of tequila in her system adding to the conflagration. Maybe Grace was right and she did need to have sex with someone else. At least it would stop her from throwing herself at this man.

'Great. And I'll take you out to dinner afterwards.' He put his hand on her arm. 'Enjoy the rest of your evening, Ingrid. And remember to send me a photo of your ex so I can stick it to the pads and the punch bag.'

She watched him walk back to his table.

What had just happened?

18

In the Ring

Ingrid inched her way out of the changing rooms, staying close to the wall like a bad spy. Music played in the background, but the gym's main soundtrack was the steady thwack of leather gloves on leather pads. What on earth had she agreed to? This place was utterly intimidating, filled with City workers and their controlled aggression. She'd thought that after reaching her mid-forties, little could throw her off balance, but clearly this giant step outside her carefully drawn comfort zone was her nemesis.

She leaned against the wall and took a swig of water from her bottle. An arm brushed against hers.

'Not thinking of backing out, are you? Not when I've gone to all this trouble,' said Jacob, who had come to stand next to her, with boxing gloves tucked under an armpit and pads in his hands.

Ingrid looked at the pads and burst out laughing.

'We agreed that I'd do this and then you reneged and didn't give me a photo so I had to get creative.'

'Where did you get that?' Ingrid pointed at an image of Matt that looked fairly recent.

'I asked Kerry his name and she pointed me to his Instagram account. As with most people his age, he hasn't kept it private.'

Matt had an Instagram account? Also, she'd be having a word with Kerry. 'Are you calling me old too?'

'I wouldn't dare.' He gave her a shove with his shoulder. 'Come on then, Ms Perera, let's get a move on before the osteoporosis kicks in, shall we?'

'Listen, don't blame me if I accidentally punch you in the face.'

'I look forward to it,' said Jacob with a wide grin. 'Here, let me put these on for you.'

He set the pads on the floor and helped her with the gloves, checking her face for her expression as he did so.

'There's no need to be nervous, Ingrid. No one here is looking. They're all in their own zones. You just need to focus on you, the pads . . . and my voice.'

Did he know he sounded like that? She was breathless before they'd even started. And, Lord help her, did he look good in his gym shorts and muscle T-shirt. Jacob's eyes meanwhile were on the gloves, checking that they fitted properly.

She cleared her throat as he looked up at her and smiled. 'They feel good?'

She nodded.

'I assume you haven't done anything like this before then?'

She forced a laugh to hide the attraction that was pounding in her veins. 'Only in my imagination.'

'Well, let's turn that into a reality then. Let me show you a jab cross first and we can work on that before we move onto the rest. The thing with boxing is to keep moving. You're left-handed, aren't you? So, right foot forward, left behind and shift lightly back and forth between the two.'

She tried to remember if she knew whether he was left- or right-handed but she couldn't. Had he been watching her more closely than she thought? Or was he usually this perceptive?

He demonstrated the technique and Ingrid tried to follow

him, but he shook his head and came to stand behind her. He lifted her arms so that her hands blocked her face, and tapped her right thigh.

'Right foot planted.'

Then his hand was on her left hip, pushing it forward.

'Most people think that boxing is all in the arms, but it has to come through the hip, the shoulder and the arm to land a good punch. Like this.'

He repeated the action several times, their bodies pressed close, and Ingrid began to feel overheated, unsure if it was the physical exertion or the proximity to Jacob. Did he need to demonstrate with his hands on her body quite this much? She couldn't help noticing that when he stepped away and slipped on the pads, his face was as flushed as hers felt.

'Right then, I'll hold the pads up and I'll call out some instructions like, three jab, or four cross, or one-two, which means jab, cross, then I'll tell you to duck, but you need to keep moving. Think you can handle that?'

'It sounds a bit confusing, to be honest.'

'You'll get the hang of it. Just remember to listen and to let go a bit. Look at this face.' He held up a pad with Matt on it. 'And feel free to hit the pad as hard as you can.'

'What if I hurt you?'

'You won't.'

'I might,' she said, looking at Matt's smug Instagram profile shot.

He smiled. 'Okay, two jab . . .' he began.

After a few false starts and a clobbering from one of the pads as she failed to duck when instructed, Ingrid began to get the hang of things. Once she let go of her worries of being watched and laughed at by the other gym-goers, she tuned out of the fact that it was Jacob holding the pads and focused on Matt's annoying, tanned, gap-year face, and punched it with all her strength. Power surged through her limbs, along with the euphoria of venting frustration that had bottled up within her with nowhere to go. With every satisfying thwack of leather on leather, it felt like she was taking back control of her life. This time, she wouldn't acquiesce to keep the peace, she would take what was hers, what she'd earned. *She* would be the main character in her story, no longer an extra. Her heart pounded, her limbs ached, her spirit soared, and it was glorious.

Ingrid took a huge bite out of the burger, a mixture of mayonnaise and ketchup escaping from the bun and beginning a slow drip down her arm. But she didn't care. She was ravenous after that workout and on such a high that she would never again question why anyone would want to go and hit something for an hour.

Jacob grinned at her from across the table.

'What?' Ingrid said before taking another bite.

Jacob shook his head. 'I love the way you love food.'

For a moment she considered how inelegant she must look, stuffing her face with sauce dripping down her arm, but then decided that she wasn't going to care about things like that anymore.

'I can't remember the last time I enjoyed a burger this much, you know? Like I've really earned it. I might have to have one every time we come here.'

Jacob leaned forward. 'So we're going to do this again?'

'It must have been pretty boring for you, right? You didn't even get a workout in.'

'Not at all. One, I have to brace my abs every time you punch the pads.'

No, no, thought Ingrid. She must not think about his abs.

'And by the way, by the end it was pretty bloody hard,' he continued. 'And two, I loved seeing you let loose like that. Your face was full of determination and power and it was honestly so . . .' He stopped himself from saying something. 'Er, inspiring.'

His ears were tinged slightly red.

She wiped her hands on a napkin and then touched his arm lightly.

'Thank you, Jacob. Really. I can't tell you how much I loved that. I feel so much more in control of my life. Does that sound stupid?'

He put his hand on top of hers. 'Not at all. It's why I took you there in the first place. You needed to let off some steam.'

She extracted her hand quickly and picked up her burger again. 'I have to ask. Just how much did you hear of our conversation last night?' She took a large bite.

'Just the bit about no sex for two years.'

Ingrid nearly choked, but managed to turn it into a brief coughing fit. As she wiped her mouth with her paper napkin, she considered that, while mortifying, this was still better than him hearing her sisters' banter about sex with him.

'Do women usually talk about sex when they get together? You know, like in that show with those old ladies?'

'Do you mean *The Golden Girls*?'

'No, that wasn't it.' He thought for a moment. 'Wait, no, I mean *Sex and the City*.'

She smacked his arm. Dear God, he was a zygote. 'They're not old!'

'I'm just teasing,' he said with a grin, wiping off the grease she'd just deposited on his arm with a napkin.

'I suppose for you, anyone over the age of forty is old.'

He leaned towards her, moving to pick up the napkin he'd dropped on the floor and brushing her bare thigh on the way.

'I happen to find age a very attractive quality. And confidence,' he said as he straightened. 'Like you right now, all energised and powerful. Honestly, there's nothing sexier.' Jacob bit his lip as the word that she was sure he'd swallowed earlier escaped his lips.

Ingrid slurped a large sip of cola. What did she do now?

Humour, yes, that was the safest way to deal with this situation.

'Listen, you can't go around saying stuff like that to us old ladies. We might get a bit overexcited and keel over.' To be fair, she was only half joking. Both his words and the endorphins had made her feel so good about herself she was giddy. In a way she hadn't been for a long time.

He reached for his smoothie. 'I reckon you can handle it.'

Quick, change the subject! her brain screamed.

'So when did you start boxing?' she asked.

He smiled, and fortunately went along with her diversion tactic. 'When I was about fifteen. I had a lot of unresolved anger to vent. Mum marched me to the local gym and asked them to teach me. I haven't looked back since.'

'Is that why you suggested it to me?'

'Has it worked?'

'Definitely. I had no idea how good it would feel. But you must actually spar with people, right?'

'It's a mixture. Mostly it's the bag or pads and sometimes it's in the ring with someone else. I can't say I enjoy hitting other people though.'

She nodded. He didn't seem the type to get into fights.

'So is your anger resolved now?'

'It was, but lately, I've needed this a little more. A bit of physical exhaustion to stop all the thinking, you know?'

She didn't know what he was referring to. Apart from a few clouded looks when they'd been alone together in the cottage, Jacob seemed like the poster-boy for positivity. She couldn't imagine what it was that preoccupied his thoughts enough for him to take out his frustrations in the boxing ring.

'Is it the decision you have to make? About staying or going?'

'It's related. But we're here for you today.' He leaned his elbows on the table. 'What are you doing this weekend?' he asked.

It was his turn to change the subject but she resolved not to mention it.

Ingrid groaned. 'Working. I've been neglecting all my other work while prepping for this proposal and it's piled up. I have to sign off on some fund reporting that has to go out next week and it's a nightmare. So bloody complex.'

He shrugged. 'Funds are my specialty. Let me help you.'

'Oh no, I can't encroach on your time like that. It's way beyond the scope of your contract with us.'

'It's no bother. It saves me spending more time in that nondescript flat all weekend. Let me help.'

With her workload, Ingrid was no stranger to working at the weekend, usually in her pyjamas with her laptop on the kitchen table, a nice big cup of coffee, and a fleece blanket over her knees. But after the conversation with her sisters and this nebulous conversation now, she couldn't invite Jacob to work in her home. If he were to help her, she'd have to go into the office.

She wondered if she could put off the work, but the deadline was immutable. Even though the Enron debacle had happened over twenty years ago, the echoes still reverberated through all the work that they undertook. There were no short cuts, and big mistakes would be the end of her career at best, the end of the global firm at worst. As a partner, she had to ensure that everything was by the book so as not to expose the firm to any risk.

In truth, she was worried about spending more time alone with him after today. Her attraction increased with every moment they were together, and he had given her enough signals now for her to suspect that it might be reciprocated. But Audrey's voice boomed in her head, reminding her of her divorce, of Matt. And Ingrid could never make a decision like this without considering Lily.

Then again, it would be great to have his help and the work would take half the time. She might even get the chance to spend some quality time with Lily, having promised to learn how to play Mario Kart with her. She looked at his face as he waited for her response and told herself that it would all be strictly business.

'In that case, thanks, Jacob. That would be great.'

Ingrid ran home from Pinner station, still high on her boxing-induced endorphins, her head full of Jacob, when she slammed into an almost purple-faced Matt at the end of her driveway.

'Where the hell were you?' he shouted, drops of saliva landing on her face because he was so close.

'Matt! What are you doing here?'

'The school called me after the dress rehearsal because Lily was the only one who wasn't picked up this evening.'

'What? Grace was fetching her.'

'Don't you check your messages?'

She stared at him. Why did today have to be the *one* day that her phone had run out of battery and she had neither a phone charger nor a battery pack to save her? She held up the black screen for him to see.

'Don't tell me you're so irresponsible that you didn't even charge your phone in case your child might need you?'

The bastard was enjoying this. Ingrid bit her lip to stop herself from launching into a lecture about responsibility. But she also couldn't deny that, somehow, she'd dropped the ball. Was there a message from Grace about a change of plan? She probably should have checked her phone before she went to the gym. Had she been so caught up in her attraction to Jacob that she had neglected her maternal duties?

'As I'm sure the school told you, this has never happened before. Look, I'm sorry, Matt. Where's Lily? Is she alright?'

'Oh, *now* you think of our daughter. I mean look at what you're wearing. It's obvious that you put yourself first and our daughter's welfare second. Or maybe even third or fourth. You're a terrible mother, Ingrid.'

There was no doubt that Ingrid had made a mistake here,

but she wasn't about to let the man who'd abandoned his daughter on countless occasions, not to mention the whole of the last year, tell her that *she* was the bad parent.

'I went to the gym, Matt, not on a worldwide excursion to find myself. I thought that Lily was with Grace, as per the plan, otherwise of course I would have been there to pick her up. It's a misunderstanding, not a habit.'

'This won't look good for you.'

Certainly, on paper, this wouldn't look good for her. What if he managed to convince a judge that she was neglecting their child? Even the school would give evidence that they'd tried to call her and she hadn't picked up. Who would believe that a professional woman like her would let her phone battery die? No, no, this was ridiculous. *She* was the good parent. Nonetheless, she'd be packing two fully charged power banks in her bag from now on.

'Abandoning your daughter for a whole year won't look good for you either.'

'Lily should come and stay with me.'

'I don't want to,' Lily shouted from the door, a moment before she sprinted out to hug Ingrid.

'It's okay, baby. You won't have to. I'm so sorry I didn't realise that Grace couldn't fetch you. My phone died.'

Lily shook her head. 'It's fine, Mum. I knew you would've been there if you'd known. You've never not picked me up. I was more worried that something had happened to you . . .'

Ingrid hadn't considered this possibility and from the expression on Matt's face, neither had he. She hugged Lily tightly.

'Thank you, baby. I'm so sorry to make you worry about me. I forgot to take my charger today.'

Matt stood with his hands on his hips and watched them. 'Lily, darling, are you sure you wouldn't prefer to live with me? *I'll* never forget about you.'

Despite the seriousness of the situation, Ingrid let out a tiny derisive snort at Matt's utter cluelessness.

Lily shook her head.

Matt pointed at Ingrid. 'This isn't the last you'll hear of this.'

How had she let this happen? She didn't need any uncertainty in this divorce and now she'd given Matt ammunition. And he was certainly planning to use it.

19

Weekend

Ingrid sighed and leaned back in her chair to stretch as the figures on the page swam before her. This was a nightmare. It was taking much longer to decipher than she'd anticipated. They'd been at it since 9 a.m. and it was already 2 p.m. This was the time of day when she'd usually take a break to watch what Lily called an old movie, which was anything that predated her birth. Ingrid would've preferred to watch Marty McFly leap out of his time-travelling DeLorean for the hundredth time instead of looking at these figures again.

Was Matt right? Maybe she couldn't cope with all the competing responsibilities in her life. She'd triple-checked Grace's schedule to ensure that she could look after Lily while Ingrid was at the office today, but what if another misunderstanding occurred and Matt swooped in to take advantage of the situation?

She shook the thoughts out of her head and shifted in her seat as the waistband of the skinniest pair of jeans that she owned dug into her flesh. She'd told herself that she was being casual, pairing them with a figure-hugging short-sleeved cotton jumper, her hair arranged in a messy bun, but she'd spent longer picking out both pieces of clothing than she did her work outfits. Her messy bun had taken several attempts and enough hairspray to damage the ozone layer as she tried to make it look 'effortless'. And in Ingrid's opinion, the natural look took much longer to perfect than her usual full face of makeup.

Audrey might be right that a romantic relationship with Jacob was a bad idea, but Ingrid couldn't deny that she liked the way he looked at her. And if he was going to look at her, why shouldn't she make an effort? She'd take the boost to her self-confidence any day.

She looked over at Jacob, whose head was bent low over an open book with minuscule print. At least she wasn't the only one who'd made an effort. His slim, dark jeans and white linen shirt with the sleeves rolled up to expose his forearms were quite different from the casual wear he'd worn when in the Lake District.

The sound of Ingrid's ringtone pierced their studious silence, Grace's face flashing up on the screen.

'Hey, everything okay?' said Ingrid as she answered the call.

Jacob looked up. She mouthed 'my sister' at him and he nodded, returning to his book.

'Sis, I know I said I'd look after Lils, but I've got a chance at an audition for a show and I have to get there by five. Can you come home?'

'I haven't finished,' said Ingrid. 'And who holds auditions at five on a Saturday afternoon?'

'Someone's ill so they need a replacement for tonight's show and my mate Cassie recommended me.'

'Aren't there understudies, or you know . . . reserves for that? Why do they need someone new?'

'There are, but Cassie vouched for me and you know how much I've missed playing. It's a West End musical and decent money. Come on, Akki, you know I want a job.'

Ingrid tamped down her annoyance. She wouldn't have coped with the last year if Grace hadn't been there to help her with Lily. The weekend was usually the only truly free time that her sister enjoyed, and now Ingrid had encroached on that too.

'Yeah, sorry, Grace. I'm just snowed under. That's fine, of course you must go. It'll take me about an hour and a bit to get home, but I'll leave now.'

'You need to go?' Jacob asked as she ended the call.

'Yeah, I can't leave Lily alone. Listen, maybe we could do this online after all?'

Jacob shut his book and began to pack his rucksack. 'Why don't I come with you? It's definitely easier if we're in the same room.'

No way. She wasn't sure she wanted him to meet Lily, and she couldn't risk Grace making some smart remark.

'Hey, I don't want to impose. It's just that you're on a deadline here and it will take an unnecessarily long time to get through all this if we don't do it in person. But if it can wait, that's fine,' he said.

Ingrid didn't miss deadlines. Even the thought of it made her feel physically sick. And it would only take a couple more hours to get it done if he was there too. Would it really be that bad if he came with her?

Grace barrelled towards her as soon as Ingrid stepped inside the house, her coat on, bag in one hand, violin case in the other.

'Lily's upstairs. Says she's doing her homework, but she's probably playing Minecraft. She's had lunch and I just gave her a snack. Hopefully, I won't be back until late tonight. Sorry . . .'

Grace stopped and stared at Jacob standing behind Ingrid, at first curious, before recognition spread over her face like a sunrise. She gave Ingrid a 'you brought home the potential hot sex younger guy' look, and Ingrid was glad that she couldn't see Jacob's face.

'Hi,' said Grace, beaming at Jacob. 'I'm Grace, Ingrid's younger, more talented sister.'

'I see that,' said Jacob pointing to the violin case. 'I'm Jacob. Ingrid's . . . colleague.'

Grace raised her eyebrows exaggeratedly to her sister, the pause not lost on her.

'I'm sorry I had to drag you back here, but I have to seize every opportunity.' She waved the violin case at him.

'It's fine, Sis. Go. I really appreciate you watching Lily for me today. And break a leg. I know you'll get it.'

Grace kissed Ingrid on the cheek and whispered in her ear. 'Good luck to you too.' She headed out of the door. 'Love you!'

'Your sister's a musician?' Jacob asked as he removed his coat and added it to Ingrid's on the banister.

'Yeah. She used to play first violin in an orchestra in New York, but then the pandemic happened and she lost her job.'

'She lives with you?'

Ingrid nodded as she led him into the kitchen. 'I thought it would be a pain at first, but then Matt left and I don't know how I would have coped without her around. Although . . .' She groaned as she surveyed the kitchen, which looked as though it had been hit with a flour bomb. Muffin tins were stacked up in the sink, the mixing bowl had been left on the floury worktop, remnants of raisins were dotted everywhere, and the oven door was still wide open.

'This happens,' Ingrid continued. 'I'm sorry. I usually work at the kitchen table but it's a mess. Are you alright with sitting on the floor? We can use the coffee table in the living room.'

'Sure, anywhere's fine. Can I help you clear up?'

'No, it's okay. I'll do it later. But I'll see if I can find some of whatever they baked. My sister might be an indoor tornado, but her baking is amazing.'

She led him into the living room where Grace had lit three scented candles. Although there was plenty of light outside, the space looked altogether too intimate for business purposes so Ingrid reached for the light switch. Jacob stopped her hand with his own.

'No, please, this is nice. Really homely. I'm living in a soulless serviced apartment at the moment, so I'll take any home comfort I can get.'

'Um, okay then, but we should turn on the lamps at least. Your eyes may still be young, but I need a little extra light.'

Jacob sat on the floor next to the coffee table and took his laptop and the book he'd been reading in the office out of his bag while Ingrid switched on the lamps dotted around the room.

'I should go and check on Lily and then we can get started.'

'Mum?' Lily stood in the doorway, staring at Jacob. 'Who's that?'

Ingrid's maternal instincts kicked in. She didn't want Lily to feel threatened, or to think that Ingrid was trying to replace Matt, not that she was sure Lily would mind that. She rushed forward, putting her arm around her daughter's shoulders and moving her further into the room.

'This is Jacob. He's working with me at the moment.'

Jacob scrambled to his feet and extended his hand to Lily. 'Nice to meet you, Lily. I'm sorry to interrupt your weekend.'

Lily nodded, considering something. 'Can we have pizza?'

Ingrid laughed. Trust her daughter to use this situation to her advantage. 'Sure. But a bit later, okay?'

'Mum, Aunty Grace said she'd play Mario Kart with me.'

'Well, she's out now, so maybe another time. Besides, *she* told *me* that you were doing your homework.'

Lily rolled her eyes. 'It was easy. Finished in twenty minutes.'

'You're sure?'

'How about I play with you? Your mum was checking through something when we left the office and I can't help any more until she finishes that.'

'You look pretty old. Do you know how to play?' Lily asked as Ingrid laughed.

'Hey, I'm pretty good for an old guy. How about we see if I can beat you?'

'What do I get if I beat you?' Lily asked.

Jacob looked at Ingrid with a smile. 'Definitely your daughter. She knows how to make a deal.'

'How about you get dessert with the pizza if you beat Jacob? And if he beats you, you finish that homework you said you'd done?'

'How did you know?' Lily asked.

'Because I have mum superpowers. Deal?'

Lily nodded.

'Lead the way,' said Jacob.

'You don't need to do this,' said Ingrid in a low voice as he passed by her at the door. 'You're here to work. I don't expect you to entertain my kid.'

He put his hand on her shoulder. 'It's fine, Ingrid. You get on with checking those figures and don't worry about us.'

She watched them as they went to what had once been a dining room, but now served as a TV room complete with games console. Jacob laughed and joked with Lily, clearly at ease with kids, something Ingrid had never been unless she was related to them.

She instantly dismissed the picture-perfect fantasies that began to unspool in her head of Jacob, Lily and herself in the future. Honestly.

She had work to do.

20

Fun and Games

Ingrid finally finished checking the figures on her spreadsheet. She pulled off her glasses and rubbed her eyes, slowly adjusting to her surroundings, much like when she opened her eyes at the end of a yoga session. She'd tuned out everything else as she'd concentrated on her work, but now she heard Lily and Jacob shouting with glee as they continued to play games together. It was already 7 p.m. and she hadn't even fed her daughter. She should probably check if Jacob wanted to stay for dinner and then order the pizza that she'd promised Lily.

Jacob and Lily were sat on the floor, controllers in hand, both fixated on the screen as they drove their characters along an icy racetrack. He looked so much younger as he played the game, like a warning to Ingrid.

'So, who's winning?' Ingrid asked.

Jacob turned to look at her.

'Mum! You're ruining it,' shouted Lily.

'Story of my life as a mum, Lils.'

'She's crushing me,' said Jacob. 'Should be a professional.'

'Don't give her any ideas! Pizza and dessert it is then. I'll order and then you promised to teach me how to play this, Lily.' She couldn't forget why Jacob was there in the first place. It certainly wasn't to entertain her daughter. 'Jacob,

I've finished checking the numbers but I'm not sure if we've properly understood the structure of the fund and when payouts happen. Would you mind taking another look?'

'Sure,' said Jacob standing. 'Let's say you won that one too, Lily. I've got to work.'

'Can you stay for pizza?' Lily asked Jacob.

'Er, is that alright?' he asked Ingrid.

She shrugged. 'I wasn't the one who invited you.'

'Okay then, Lily. I'd love that,' he said.

'And when you finish work, maybe you can teach Mum how to play better.'

'Alright, alright. Enough of that, young lady. Come and choose your pizza. Are you allergic to anything, Jacob? Any preferences? And I'm warning you that if there's a hint of pineapple anywhere near the pizza, we'll no longer be friends.'

'I wouldn't dare,' said Jacob with a laugh. 'No allergies, no preferences.' He headed off to the living room.

'Mum, here, you can use this controller. Let me show you how to choose a character.'

'What about this little dinosaur chap?'

'That's Yoshi. Let's choose his car. What about this one?'

Ingrid watched her daughter's delighted face as Lily helped her set up to play the game she'd been desperate for Ingrid to learn. Why hadn't she done this sooner?

Once they started the race, it was patently clear that Lily had not inherited her gaming abilities from Ingrid.

'What's going on?' Ingrid shouted. 'Where is everyone? Am I really in front? And why do I keep being turned around by this giant hand?'

Lily began to giggle. 'Mum! It's doing that because you're going the wrong way.'

'No, I can't be! Really?'

'Press this button,' said Lily, leaning over to show her. 'Mum, it's not a real car, you don't have to move it like a real steering wheel.'

Ingrid laughed. 'Oh my God, I'm so bad at this.'

'We're all bad at this on our first time. Don't worry, Mum, I'll help you.'

Lily took the controller from her hand.

'Here, watch me, I've got this.'

Ingrid laughed and ruffled Lily's hair. 'Thank you, darling. I'll have to practise.'

'Promise?'

She kissed her daughter's cheek. 'Promise.'

Ingrid watched her daughter as she laughed and joked with Jacob and realised that she hadn't seen Lily like this in over a year. She was carefree and radiating a happiness Ingrid had thought that she and Matt might have destroyed. Jacob had such an easy-going manner that it was impossible for anyone to resist him. Maybe she'd been foolish to imagine that it was something more, when perhaps all he'd been doing was turning his general charisma onto her.

They'd devoured the delicious sourdough pizzas and Ingrid had begun to clear the pizza boxes away when the doorbell rang. She wiped her hands on her jeans.

'It's probably Grace forgetting her keys,' she said, heading for the door and praying that it wasn't her mother. Nothing could have prepared her for the face that met hers as she flung the door open.

'Matt?'

He was wearing another version of the stupid scarf and grey jeans. Didn't he realise it was the middle of July? 'Can I come in?'

Ingrid tried to close the door a little. 'Now's not a good time. Look, I know we haven't discussed this, but you should give me some notice before you come over. You can't just drop in.'

'I wanted to see Lily for a bit. She said she needed a new memory stick for school, so I brought one over,' he said, brandishing the small piece of blue plastic.

'Hey, Mum said I could have two scoops,' Lily yelled from the kitchen.

'You're eating? It's late,' said Matt.

'I'm pretty sure that she said *one* earlier,' said Jacob, his low tones echoing down the hallway to Matt's ears.

'What's going on?' Matt asked, his expression hardening, his body tensed for a confrontation.

Shit. She could definitely do without this, especially as everything was perfectly innocent.

'Just a work colleague helping me out with some stuff for a deadline.'

'By serving ice cream?'

He pushed her aside and stormed down the hallway into the kitchen while Ingrid shut the front door and paced after him.

'Who the hell are you?' Matt almost shouted at Jacob.

Ingrid saw the joy slip from Lily's face.

Jacob stood and extended his hand, keeping his voice characteristically calm and friendly.

'Hi, I'm Jacob Ellis. I work with Ingrid.'

'And what are you doing in my house?' Matt asked.

'Matt, you're being rude. Jacob is here to work and we stopped to have dinner with Lily. Not that I owe you an explanation.'

'I need to know when you introduce new men to my daughter.'

'*Our* daughter. And I'm not introducing "new men" to her. Jacob is a colleague. We were working in the office, but Grace had to go to an audition so we came home.'

Some of the steam seemed to evaporate from Matt. Ingrid expected Jacob to bolt at any moment. No one wanted to be in the middle of a domestic argument like this. But he stayed put, the ice cream scoop still in his left hand.

'Matt, can we speak in the hallway please? Jacob's right, Lily. One scoop before bedtime.'

Lily nodded and Jacob looked down to smile at her. In that moment, Ingrid was incredibly grateful for his presence in her home.

She shut the kitchen door and moved Matt towards the front of the house.

'Listen, Matt. Lily is your daughter and you absolutely should see her, but it's not helpful for her if you turn up unannounced on a Saturday night and act like this. In the future, we can work out a schedule, or you can give me at least twenty-four hours' notice so I can make sure that she's here. She has other things to do too.'

Matt's eyes were a little glassy as he stared at Ingrid. 'You just don't want me to catch you with your toy boy there. I mean, how old is he? Thirty? Does he know how old you are? Come on, Ingrid. I expected more of you. I never thought you of all people would end up a cougar. Wait, is he the reason why you weren't there to pick her up yesterday?'

She counted to ten very slowly in her head, ignoring the sharp stab of guilt at his words. No, she would not give him any ammunition for his nastiness. There was no way she could lose her cool with him, but really, he was beginning to make her blood boil.

'As I've already said, he's a work colleague. There's no reason for you to be so hurtful.'

Matt put his hands on his hips and regarded her. 'I saw the way you looked at each other. You know men like that will be expecting a lot more than someone like you can give.'

Tears pricked her eyes.

'He probably thinks you'll be experienced and teach him a thing or two. Little does he know that—'

She wasn't going to listen to any more of this poison. 'Stop it. You don't get to come in here and talk to me like that.'

'Unless you've already done it and he prefers the frigid type.'

She wanted to slap him so badly, but she wouldn't sink to his level. He'd never said anything so despicable to her before, but clearly this was what he'd really thought of her. Try as she might, she couldn't stop the stray tear that escaped down her cheek.

She wouldn't allow Lily to be in the middle of such hatred. She would swallow her angry words for the sake of her child. Pushing him away, she dug deep in her reserves to be civil to this man who'd once shared her bed.

'Please leave, Matt. Let's talk when you're ready to be more reasonable.' She opened the front door and gestured that he should exit through it.

'I'll be telling my lawyer about this. Another failure for you as a mother.'

'You do that. But please go now. We'll set up a time for you to see Lily.'

'This isn't over,' he said as he slammed the door behind him.

Ingrid wiped down the kitchen countertop as she tried to calm the anger that was threatening to engulf her right now. Who the hell did he think he was, barging in here and telling her that she was a bad mother? *She* wasn't the one who'd gone off around the world for a year. Who had banged the interior decorator – *in their bed* – and forgotten Lily's birthday. She hadn't even been able to look at Jacob when she'd re-entered the kitchen. Thankfully, Lily had tugged at his arm, asking if he'd play one more game with her.

Ingrid had taken the opportunity to engage in some household chore therapy, cleaning up Grace's baking mess while she processed it all. She had to try and make Matt see the effect that his antagonism towards her was having on their daughter.

Meanwhile, how mortifying to have Jacob witness her domestic upheavals. He'd even been caught in the crossfire. She had no idea what she could say to him other than to apologise.

'Are you alright?' Jacob asked.

She turned to see him at the door and nodded.

'I'm sorry if my presence here made things awkward.' He leaned on the door frame and crossed his arms.

'No, you're not to blame for Matt's imagination. *I'm* so sorry that you got caught up in it all.'

'I tried to keep Lily occupied, so I'm pretty sure that she didn't hear anything.'

Ingrid sat on one of the hard oak chairs. 'God, why is he being like this?'

Jacob came to sit next to her. 'He's angry.'

'But he's the one who left. Why is he angry with *me*?'

'Because you weren't supposed to move on. He was the one forging a new path while you were left behind. He thought leaving you was all about him, but instead of crying in your pyjamas, you're thriving.'

'That's very insightful for someone so young.'

'Or someone who's had a lot of therapy.' He smiled.

They sat in silence for a while as Ingrid softly rubbed at the table with her microfibre cleaning cloth.

'I'm thirty-two, by the way.'

'Sorry?' said Ingrid, thinking that that was very young.

'The only bit I heard was him shouting about how old I was.'

'He's such an idiot,' she exclaimed throwing the cloth onto the table.

'I'm sorry you're going through all this,' he continued. 'But it will get better. In the meantime, I think you need a friend to help take your mind off things.'

'I swear to God, if you suggest another retreat, I may have to kill you.'

He laughed. 'No, nothing that drastic. But you need to have a little fun.'

'You mean you didn't find tonight's entertainment fun? I thought it was a hoot.'

He put his hand on her arm. 'Come out with me tomorrow.'

He'd said 'friend' earlier, right? He wasn't asking her out on a date. Not that she'd have said yes in light of this debacle.

'Now that we've finished the work, I was hoping to spend the day with Lily.'

'Look, I don't want to encroach on your mother–daughter time, but I was thinking we could do something together.'

'What do you have in mind?'

'Why don't I pick you up at 9 a.m. tomorrow and you'll see. I promise, you'll both love it.'

It was crazy to do this when Matt was threatening lawyers over finding Jacob in their house, wasn't it? But she wasn't going to let him walk all over her anymore. Jacob was offering friendship and God knows she could do with a little of that.

She smiled, warmth rushing through her at the prospect of a surprise day for her and Lily with this lovely man. 'Okay.'

21

Sunday at the Climbing Wall with Jacob

Ingrid took a nervous sip of water from her bottle and peered out of the window as the Uber that Jacob had hired pulled up outside the Westway Sports and Fitness Centre. Clearly Jacob's idea of fun and relaxation involved rigorous physical exercise while Ingrid's was more along the lines of lying on sofas and streaming romcoms. She tried not to let the disappointment show on her face as she read the board boasting the myriad of activities available. What torture did he have in store for them? On the plus side, trying to get through whatever activity he had planned was bound to be better than thinking about the humiliation of last night.

'Are you coming out?' Jacob asked, holding the door open, his hand extended while Lily bounced next to him.

'I'm thinking about it,' said Ingrid, aware of the antsy driver in the front who wanted to leave to pick up his next fare.

Jacob crouched to speak to her. 'I promise, you don't have to do anything you're uncomfortable with, and I'll be with you the whole time.'

'We'd better not be playing five-a-side football,' she said, reading the board again.

'There's three of us, so no.' He tugged her hand. 'Come on, it'll be fine. And look at your daughter.'

Lily was busy taking photos of herself with the fitness centre in the background. Ingrid had banned her from social media so she briefly wondered where those photos might be going. It was highly possible that her tech-savvy daughter had found a way around her parental controls and had her own Instagram account. She made a mental note to do a little snooping later. Ingrid's life had been so much simpler without the intrusion and pressure of social media and the constant need to be photographed. She'd been allowed to live in comfortable ignorance of beauty trends and the need to look good every time she'd stepped out of the house. She didn't want Lily exposed to it all before she was mature enough to handle it, although Ingrid wasn't quite sure if there was a specific age when that happened.

Ingrid stepped out of the car, which sped off almost as soon as Jacob shut the door.

'I'm guessing your rating's gone down. Sorry,' said Ingrid as they watched the red lights disappear.

'I'll live with it. Now, are you coming?'

'Are you going to tell me what we're doing?'

'Have you ever been climbing before?'

'Like rock climbing?'

He nodded.

'From the little you've known me, do you think that's likely?'

'No, that's why I thought you might try it. It's a great way to get out of your head, not to mention a brilliant total body workout.'

'I'm still aching from the boxing. Are you trying to send me a message?'

He looked her up and down so slowly that she thought she might melt right there and then on the pavement. 'Maybe not the one you're thinking of. I just thought you might want to try something new. To forget.'

She remembered Matt's face last night, the nasty words still ringing in her ears. Perhaps Jacob had a point. Exercise as therapy seemed to be his thing.

'But don't you need to know how to climb to go to a place like this?'

'Not at all. You can book classes and stuff. But you guys don't need a class because you have me. I've done my rope competency check here so I can guide both of you today.'

Was there anything that he didn't do?

'Mum, come on! I want to have a go,' Lily called as she bounded towards the centre.

'Will she be safe?'

'Absolutely. I'm a trained instructor and I wouldn't let anything happen to either of you.'

Ingrid wasn't so sure. She was fit, but she wasn't too sure about heights.

'You don't look like you believe me,' said Jacob.

She turned to face him. 'I'm an accountant, Jacob. I assess and manage risk on a daily basis and I'm not sure a climbing wall cuts the mustard.'

He smiled at her. 'Is that one of your old people's sayings?'

She gave him a playful shove. 'Hey, watch it, or I'll smack you with my walking stick. Anyway, aren't you afraid that with my rapidly advancing age, I might break a hip or something?'

He pushed her forward. 'I've seen you boxing, remember? You're fit and healthy and you can absolutely do this. No broken bones or hip replacements for you yet, although I could arrange for some slippers and a newspaper to be ready by the time you come back down.'

'And tea, don't forget that,' she said with a smile.

'And tea.'

A noisy group of teenagers barged past them, yelling at each other despite only being a foot away from each other, phones waving.

Ingrid curled into herself a little, groaning. 'Oh God, I don't think I can take all those children in there laughing at me trying to get up a wall.'

He bumped his shoulder with hers. 'I happen to like children.'

'*I* don't.'

'But you have a child.'

'I like *her*, of course. And my niece and nephews, but that's where I draw the line. And anyway, you probably like children because you're closer to them in age.'

'Who knew you'd be such a curmudgeon?'

'You mean my sunny disposition when cold, wet and muddy in the Lake District didn't tip you off?'

Jacob laughed, dragging her to the entrance. 'Those children always tend to get a lot less mouthy when they get to the top and have to abseil down.'

'But won't they . . .'

'If you're about to run down a list of risk factors, don't. It'll be fine. I'll make sure it's fine. And you're with me, so of course you'll have fun.'

'What makes you so sure of that?'

'Gotta back myself. And honestly, Ingrid, I know what I'm doing here and I promise you and Lily will love it.'

'Full disclosure,' she said, drawing to a halt just inside. 'I'm not so good with heights.'

'Not so good as in vertigo, crippling fear, or just don't really like them?'

'Um, the last one.'

'We can work with that. I'll get Lily started and come back for you.'

There really was no getting out of this. Ingrid sighed in resignation and let Jacob lead them to the equipment hire desk.

Ninety minutes later, Ingrid had her head between her knees, thankful for only having had a coffee this morning or her breakfast would have revisited her. Jacob knelt in front of her and handed her a bottle of water that he'd already opened for her. She shook her head, feeling that she was likely to throw up if she drank it. He took her hand and pressed the bottle into it.

'Sip it. You'll feel better.' And as she continued to ignore him, he took the bottle and put it to her lips, forcing her to take a sip.

The cool liquid slipped down her oesophagus, annoyingly making her feel a little less nauseous and proving Jacob right.

'Thanks.'

'I'm so sorry,' he said, his face a picture of abject contrition. 'I should've taken your fear of heights more seriously.'

She shook her head. 'Honestly, I didn't know quite how bad it was until now.' Jacob fed her another sip of water. 'At least Lily is having a ball.'

They both glanced at the children's climbing area where Lily was scooting up and down the wall like a spider monkey.

'She's definitely not a coward like her mother,' said Ingrid.

Jacob stroked Ingrid's head, lifting it so she could see his eyes. 'You're not a coward. You knew you were scared and you still gave it a go. That's the definition of brave.'

She remembered the time when she'd felt dizzy and nauseous at the top of the Eiffel Tower with Matt and the way that he'd mocked her for the rest of their short so-called romantic break. Jacob's warmth and sincerity were an entirely new experience for her.

'I think I'll take those slippers and a cup of tea now,' she said with a weak smile.

'Sure.' Jacob gestured to his friend, Rob, who was belaying Lily as she scrambled up the wall, then led Ingrid to the cafe.

'You've had a terrible time. I'm so sorry,' said Jacob as he watched Ingrid take a sip of sweet hot tea.

'No, no. Even if I couldn't quite do it, it's wonderful seeing Lily away from that computer and doing something active. She's been so ecstatic all day that even if you made me climb a hundred of those bloody walls, the smile on her face would make it all worth it.'

'I'm not so sure it was worth terrifying you. But Lily's a great kid, Ingrid. You've done such an amazing job with her.'

Ingrid stared at him for a moment. He'd said something similar to her when he'd first appeared in the office.

'Thank you for saying that, Jacob. It really means a lot.' No, she wouldn't cry. 'Holding down a full-time job while trying to be the best mother I can be has left me with a permanent sense of guilt that I've been a bit shit at both.'

He leaned forward in his seat. 'You don't become a partner at a firm like yours by being rubbish and your kid wouldn't have turned out as well as she has if you weren't a wonderful mother. It's a tough gig. And you've been doing it on your own for the past year. You should give yourself more credit.'

Ingrid felt as though she had been parenting alone for all eleven years of Lily's life.

Jacob moved his seat next to Ingrid and leaned closer to her.

'I get the impression that you're the one supporting everyone in your family, so I think you deserve a little yourself,' said Jacob, placing an arm around her shoulder. At first, she sat stiffly, feeling a little silly in the sport centre's cafe, but he gently pressed her arm, the warmth of his palm calming her. And it was so tempting to relax and completely surrender to this unfamiliar feeling of being held, but she shouldn't become accustomed to this. Whatever Jacob was offering, whether it was friendship or something more, it came with an expiration date. And while that was fine for her, it wouldn't be good for Lily, whose soaring expectations needed to be managed.

'Stop that,' said Jacob in her ear.

'What?'

'I can feel you thinking.' He pushed down her shoulders, which had crept up to her ears.

'Lily likes you,' said Ingrid.

'Is that a problem?'

'Definitely. You're a colleague and you're leaving the country in less than six months.'

'I thought I was a *friend* who *might* leave the country in less than six months.'

'Didn't you say you had accepted the offer?'

He shrugged. 'Nothing is ever set in stone.' He pulled her closer to him, bent to speak into her ear. 'Is it?'

She pulled away to look at him. 'What does that mean?'

'It means that when I first received the offer, I didn't have much to keep me here.' He looked at her steadily. 'But that's changed now and things aren't so clear cut.'

Feeling a burst of something like adrenaline, Ingrid considered and discarded all the questions that rushed into her head. Maybe he had decided to stay for his mother's sake. Ingrid certainly shouldn't expect anything from him. Besides, she was carrying enough baggage to fill the hold of a transcontinental airline. There weren't many men, let alone ones as young as Jacob, who would be willing to take on that.

And yet, here he was at the weekend, with her and Lily. Yes, they were doing something he loved, but he had also brought them here to take their minds off the drama of yesterday. And he was no fool – he must have known what Lily might assume from it all. After his own experience, she didn't think he was the type to toy with a child's emotions. And she couldn't ignore the way he looked at her. Those eyes that never veered away from hers, as if he could see the real Ingrid. Eyes that promised her the type of life that she longed for, with laughter, fun, adventure and freedom, but preferably without heights.

Would it really be so foolish to hope that this might be something?

22

Friday is the New Thursday

Almost a week later, Ingrid massaged her temples and checked her watch. How was it only 8 p.m.? The last hour had passed at a snail's pace, the minute hand inching forward as though she'd lost herself in some time loop. She usually rushed home to Lily after work each day, but tonight it was her turn to be the boring old partner with the credit card for this team dinner. Her job was to show her face, pick up the tab and go home before the fun really started after 9 p.m. Would it get back to Chris that she'd ducked out early if she left now?

She was too tired to be sociable. Her brain ached from thinking about Jacob. The way he'd lingered on her doorstep with her last Sunday after Lily had skipped back into the house. His lean into her as they talked in her office. She couldn't help but read hidden messages into every word and gesture, as if she were a fourteen-year-old girl. She had to stop.

It was definitely time for her to leave, so Ingrid grabbed her bag, ready to escape, just as Trent wearily skipped down the stairs into the dark, cavernous restaurant and made a beeline for the empty seat next to hers.

'Hey,' he said, reaching for the bottle of wine in the middle of the table. 'I thought you might need a little backup, so I hurried over as soon as I sent that contract to my client.

157

Would you believe he's had us redraft it eighteen times? *Eighteen*. I need this drink.'

He took a long gulp of wine and leaned closer to her, a conspiratorial look on his face. 'So, what have I missed?'

Ingrid dropped her bag. She had barely paid attention, trotting out the same script to two or three juniors who'd ventured a career-enhancing conversation with the partner.

'The usual. Why haven't you gone home to a warm shower and much nicer wine than that?'

He shrugged. 'I prefer spending some quality time with you.'

She laughed. 'I can think of better places.'

'So name one. We'll go,' he said, smiling broadly.

'Sure. We haven't been to lunch in a while, have we? Let me know when you're free and I'll get Kerry to book something.'

Trent looked at her for a moment and then nodded.

She felt a warmth next to her in the other vacant seat and turned to see Jacob, his hair still a little wet from the shower she assumed he'd had after heading straight to the gym after work. Then she imagined him in the shower. Ingrid grabbed her glass for a deep sip of the Japanese whisky she'd nursed for the past hour, hoping her thoughts weren't written all over her face.

When she placed the glass back on the table, his shoulder bumped hers as he stowed his black gym bag under his chair. He reached over and picked up her glass, bringing it to his lips, a quick nod of acknowledgement in Trent's direction.

'How's this?' he asked, his eyes on hers as he took a sip.

She raised her eyebrows at him. A smile flirted at the edges of his mouth, and as she looked up into his eyes, she knew he'd caught her staring. Something intangible passed between them. 'You tell me.'

'I wouldn't have expected whisky to be your drink of choice.'

'What did you expect me to drink?'

He put the glass down and placed his elbows on the table. 'Hmm, maybe something more practical, like a gin and tonic.'

She smiled. 'Do you mean old? I like to surprise.' Which wasn't true at all. Gin and tonic was absolutely her middle-aged drink of choice, but in her spirit of trying new things, she'd decided to sample one of the many bottles of Japanese whisky and sake displayed on the shelves behind the bar. She retrieved her glass.

'Hey, man, how's it going?' said Trent, smiling at Jacob as though sharing some inside joke.

'Good thanks, Trent. Did you get that contract out?'

Trent nodded. 'Finally, thank God. I thought I'd pop in for a quick drink with Ingrid,' he said before draining his glass. He looked at first at Ingrid, then Jacob. 'And now I'd better go home, have a shower and a much nicer glass of wine,' he continued with a wink at Ingrid, who smiled. 'Bye, guys. Be good.'

They both waved him off and Ingrid felt the heat of Jacob's thigh against hers under the table as he moved closer, his hand wrapping around her glass again. Ingrid turned her face to his.

'Jacob!' said Erin, one of the junior members of staff who was at least twenty years younger than Ingrid. Erin had launched herself into the empty seat and draped herself over Jacob's left shoulder.

Ingrid didn't have anything against Erin, but the sight of her all over Jacob suddenly had her fighting a strong urge to shove Erin off him.

Jacob removed Erin from his shoulder with as much tact as possible. 'How are you, Erin? Need some water?'

'I'd rather have some of your drink,' she said, licking her lips.

Ingrid had to admire a girl who knew what she wanted and went for it. Honestly, who had Ingrid been kidding? Whether or not they'd just shared a moment, Erin was much more suitable for Jacob than her. She needed to act her age and duck out of this gracefully.

'Actually, this is Ingrid's drink. She let me have a taste,' said Jacob, looking at Ingrid and grinning.

Erin's eyes ping-ponged between them both, assessing the situation and quickly concluding that nothing romantic could be going on between two people with such a big age gap. She laughed.

'Yeah, my dad drinks whisky too and tries to get me to taste it. But it's an old person's drink, isn't it? Like gin.'

Ingrid raised her eyebrows at Jacob. 'Well, this old person should go,' said Ingrid, before she was tempted to pour her geriatric drink over the young woman.

Jacob put his hand on her arm, anchoring her to the table. 'I've only just arrived. Don't leave.'

Erin watched them again, searching for an explanation for their familiarity. 'Oh, you knew each other, didn't you?'

Ingrid was so embarrassed that she had to look away, but then she remembered that everyone thought that she and Jacob had met at a conference, rather than on a hill in the Lake District.

Jacob looked at Ingrid and winked. 'We go way back,' he said.

'Something like that,' she said. He was young, so a couple of months might seem like 'way back' to him.

Jacob flagged down a waiter. 'Please may we have two more of these, lots of ice on the side.'

'I'm not sure I'd like whisky,' said Erin.

'It's for Ingrid, er, so sorry, I can't remember your name,' said Jacob, knowing full well that he'd just addressed her by it a minute ago.

Ingrid swallowed the wry smile threatening to appear on her face. But Erin was undeterred. She grabbed Jacob's arm again, pulling her chair closer to him as she did so.

'It's Erin.'

'Right,' he said, plucking her hand off his arm once again. 'Erin, I have to talk to Ingrid about something, would you excuse us?'

Erin's face fell. 'Can't you talk about it in the office?'

Ingrid couldn't stop her snort of derision and coughed dramatically as she tried to cover it, while Jacob turned his face away from Erin and winked at her. There was no way that Ingrid would have made a comment like that when she was a junior, and certainly not in front of a partner who was paying for the entire evening out. But then young people didn't look for the same longevity in their careers, so even unfiltered, ill-judged comments weren't so career limiting.

'We could, but we're flying out to New York for the pitch on Sunday, and time is of the essence,' said Jacob, still looking at Ingrid.

'Yeah, course. I'll see you in a bit,' said Erin, looking downcast for a moment before sloping off and leaving them to talk.

A waitress placed the two glasses of whisky in front of them and Ingrid raised her glass in a toast.

'Nicely played, Mr Ellis,' she said.

He clinked his glass with hers, moving his chair even closer. 'You know, I did actually want to talk to you about something work related.'

Ingrid felt the flush creep up over her breastbone, over her neck. 'Oh.'

'Just kidding,' he said.

She elbowed him playfully. 'You seem very practised at letting women down easily.'

'Do I?'

'Oh come on, you must know that you're handsome and that attracts people.'

He leaned closer. 'So you think I'm handsome?'

She took a large gulp of whisky. 'I think we can safely say that this is a fact. And Erin is part of the data,' she said, pointing her glass in Erin's direction.

'Do *you* think I'm handsome?' he asked.

There was no way in hell that she was going to give him a straight answer on that one.

'Have you seen *When Harry Met Sally* . . . where he tells her that she is empirically attractive?'

He shook his head. 'I'm assuming that's some black and white movie.'

Ingrid rolled her eyes. 'Seriously, are you so young that you don't know that movie?'

He laughed and bumped her shoulder. 'Who hasn't seen the famous orgasm scene?'

She felt herself blush at the mere mention of an orgasm in Jacob's presence. And then she blushed again as she imagined a scenario in which she had one with him.

He smiled as though he knew exactly where her brain had just gone. 'So you were saying that you find me handsome.'

'*Empirically* handsome.'

He laughed. 'Okay then. As are you.'

She shook her head. 'Sadly, I'm a middle-aged woman, Jacob. This is the phase of my life where I don the cloak of invisibility.'

'Nonsense.'

'Yep. Even my husband didn't want me and *he* was contractually obliged to.'

'We've established many times that he's an idiot.'

Ingrid was suddenly aware that Jacob was very close and people were beginning to notice. No doubt Erin would reappear any moment now.

'Actually, I should get going. I don't like to stay at these things for too long.' Avoidance had always worked for her in the past. Why change now?

'Stay, please.' There was something in his expression that made her wonder if he thought that she was going after Trent. Would it hurt if he did? Oh my word, she really was fourteen again. Was that the last time she'd felt like this? Butterflies in her stomach, something buzzing in her veins . . . Perhaps it was the whisky.

Ingrid realised she'd been gazing at him again and quickly snapped back to herself. 'I've been here for quite a while now and I think I've overstayed my welcome.' Even she knew she sounded old, but then she was. Wasn't she?

'Rubbish. They're planning to do karaoke in a bit.'

'No, nope, absolutely not.'

'That was pretty definitive.' He grinned.

'I don't sing. Do you have any idea of the damage my singing could do to my professional reputation?'

Jacob laughed. 'I bet it isn't that bad.'

'Oh it's bad. You'd never think of me the same way again.'

'I don't think a bad song could change what I think of you,' he said, looking into her eyes again.

She took another deep sip of whisky to steady her breathing. If she didn't leave now, she would be in trouble.

He put his hand on hers briefly. 'Stay.'

Ingrid simmered in the corner of the karaoke room that she'd commandeered as soon as they'd arrived. What on earth had she been thinking when she'd agreed to come to this neon-infested hellhole? Of course she was here for Jacob. She hadn't been able to resist his voice asking her to come with them, the touch of his hand, his smile, the way he looked at her as though she were the only person in the room.

But Erin, fuelled by several pornstar martinis, had assumed limpet levels of attachment that even Jacob was having trouble shaking off. He stood awkwardly in the middle of the room as Erin tried to drape herself over him.

'Would you like sex on the beach?' Erin shrieked at him over a rendition of 'We Are the Champions', shoving the drink in his face before immediately dissolving into a fit of giggles that seemed to require clutching Jacob's upper arm as she pressed herself up against him, a little of the sticky concoction spilling over them both.

Jacob glanced over at Ingrid who instantly looked down at her phone screen as though preoccupied with something important. She wasn't jealous, she insisted to herself. No, she was just annoyed that she'd swapped a quiet night in bed with her book for this fiasco.

She began a determined doom scroll of Instagram, swiping between reels, trying not to look as though she was ready to escape at any moment.

'I'm sorry,' said Jacob, breathing into her ear and causing Ingrid to almost have a heart attack.

'Bloody hell! Where did you come from? Last I saw, you were pretty intimate with Erin over there.'

Ugh – sometimes she wished that her mouth came with a rewind button. Why had she said that?

He grinned at her, highly amused by her words. What did he think was so damned funny?

'What?' she asked, unable to keep the annoyance from her voice. He grinned even more.

'I really am sorry for dragging you here. You clearly hate it, and I honestly wasn't expecting Erin to be so . . . persistent,' he shouted over the racket.

'Why did you ask me to come here, Jacob?'

He moved so close that Ingrid felt the heat of his body. She tried not to shift away, or worse, move closer, staying as still as possible as his hand pushed a small section of her hair behind her ear so he could speak into it again.

But he was suddenly yanked off the seat by Erin. Jacob tried to extract his hand from her iron grip, but he was slightly off balance, so she was able to drag him away before he could dig in his heels.

After all her years in business, Ingrid knew when it was best to walk away. She wasted no time in grabbing her tote bag from the seat and left the room, cheeks flushed with indignation, and yes, unmistakable jealousy.

She ducked into the bathroom and braced herself against the cool porcelain of the basin as she looked at herself in the mirror. What had he been about to say? Did she really want to know?

She wiped an end-of-day smudge of mascara from under

her eye and swiped lip balm over the remnants of her lipstick. She had to stop this fantasy. She would pay the bill and head home. Jacob could take care of himself. And Erin.

Ingrid finally emerged into the hot and sticky London night, her retinas still imprinted with the garish neon signs from inside. She checked her phone to see that her Uber was approximately one minute away.

She felt a pang of regret for having left Jacob with Erin, but she told herself that he deserved it, particularly as he hadn't come to find her. And that was a good thing, wasn't it? All this evening had done was prove to Ingrid that she was definitely too old for him.

She heard the scuffle of shoes on the pavement next to her and looked up to see a couple locked in an uneasy embrace, as though trying to get their bearings on a boat. This wasn't an uncommon sight outside a bar in London on a Friday night.

Wait. The broad back in that white shirt, that dark hair, those trousers, and shoes. And now a very familiar giggle from the woman who clutched him tightly. Ingrid couldn't see her too clearly, but she seemed to have her head tilted back.

Her stomach roiled as the car pulled up by the kerb. She yanked open the door and jumped in as Jacob turned and saw her, his face stricken as he registered her expression.

She was a fool. A middle-aged, fantasising fool.

23

Orange Wall and Red Faces

Ingrid stared at the bright orange wall in Audrey's living room, speechless.

'It's fabulous, isn't it?' said Audrey, clearly delighted with her wall that looked as if it had been Tangoed.

'Um,' said Ingrid, searching for a response that wouldn't trigger her sister's temper. 'What does Nathan think?'

She felt a little guilty for shifting the onus of commenting on this monstrosity onto her brother-in-law, but she figured that Nathan could take it. He was used to Audrey constantly coming up with new projects and organising everyone else's lives. Although even he might not be up to handling a redecoration based on the Stabilo highlighter colour scheme.

Audrey scowled. 'We all know that he has no taste, and besides, he's always at the hospital, so his opinion doesn't count. But Millie loves it, don't you, darling?'

She held up her phone where Millie, her middle child, filled the screen. Millie's backdrop was a gate at Ibiza airport. Her eyes were tired behind the black-framed glasses that topped off her now signature look of scraped back hair and no makeup, which she'd adopted for life among the Imperial College science bros.

'Er, I didn't say that, Mum. But you do you,' said Millie, clearly horrified.

Lily ran into the room.

'Hey, Lily!' Millie said from the screen, while Lily rushed forward to take the phone from Audrey.

'Are you really coming home now?' Lily asked excitedly.

'Of course. I wouldn't miss it for the world. We can play Fortnite together.'

'Yay!' Lily squealed.

Her happiness made Ingrid feel a little better about leaving her daughter to go to this pitch.

'Mum, I'll see you later. Love you,' said Millie.

'Love you,' called Audrey, while Lily ended the call and returned the phone to her.

Ingrid embraced her daughter. 'Are you all set, got everything you need?'

Lily nodded.

Grace entered the room, looking chic in a Breton-style T-shirt and white linen trousers, ready for her week in Paris.

'Bloody hell!' she said, her eyes wide in disbelief. 'Have you developed colour blindness or something? Seriously, Sis, that wall is giving me a headache.'

'Ingrid likes it,' said Audrey, pointing at her.

'Did I say that?' said Ingrid.

'Aunty Audrey?' said Lily.

'Yes, darling?'

'*I* like your wall.'

'See? Ingrid, your child has great taste.'

'She's eleven, so she still goes out in neon tutus and leggings, Akki,' said Grace, who'd now donned her sunglasses for emphasis.

Audrey crossed her arms and peered at her psychedelic wall. 'Oh God, it's hideous, isn't it?'

Grace and Ingrid exchanged an eye roll. It was best for Audrey to slowly reach her own conclusions.

'What's going on?' Grace asked.

Audrey sighed. 'I need to do something. Now the kids are

gone for most of the time, I haven't got a clue. I'm not cut out for this ladies-who-lunch lifestyle.'

'I see that,' said Grace.

'Could you go back to medicine?' Ingrid asked.

Audrey shook her head. 'God, no, I don't want to go from too much time on my hands to questioning my existence on minimal sleep.'

'Why don't you paint the wall cream again and then sign up for a creative writing course or something?' Grace said.

Audrey began to glare at Grace, but adjusted her expression as she visibly warmed to the idea.

'I hate to admit this, Gracie, but you might be onto something,' said Audrey.

'And you're less likely to damage the house,' said Ingrid.

'I'm hungry,' said Lily.

'There's a plate of flapjacks on the kitchen table, darling. Let me show you,' said Audrey, standing and leading Lily into the kitchen.

Ingrid stared at Grace.

'What?'

'Sometimes, just sometimes, you're a genius.'

Grace laughed. 'I'll take sometimes. Do you remember how she used to write all those stories on Mum's old typewriter? All that annoying tap-tap-tapping while we were trying to sleep? Maybe she should've been writing all this time.'

'Yeah, but did you ever read any of it? Was it any good?'

'Don't you remember? She used to get better marks for English than the sciences, but Ammi went nuts when the teacher suggested she studied English Lit and forced her into medicine. And Audrey's so bloody good at everything that she didn't find the switch too hard.'

'I dread to think what she'll write about. What if it's about us?'

'Shit, I didn't think about that. Sorry. Not like she'll take my advice anyway. So, are you ready for your trip?' Grace asked.

What on earth was she going to say to Jacob when she saw

him? She had no claim over him, and he certainly didn't owe her an explanation. It annoyed her how much she bristled every time she remembered Erin all over him.

'Are you ready for yours?' Ingrid asked, deflecting.

'I'm sorry I couldn't get out of it.'

'You should go and enjoy yourself in Paris, Gracie. You've done more than enough for me.'

'I assume you didn't tell Matt you were off to New York for your pitch?'

'I thought about it, but he's been acting so irrationally, I couldn't guarantee that he wouldn't abscond with Lily. I can't imagine he'd try and pull any shit with Audrey. Can you?'

Grace nodded. 'Yeah, she'd paint him orange or something. But you seem pretty nervous. Haven't you done loads of these pitches before?'

She weighed her options. If she mentioned something to Grace, her easy-going approach could help her to make sense of what she'd seen. But she couldn't risk Grace letting something slip to Audrey, or worse, to Mum, and Ingrid could happily skip the resulting lectures on not being a silly, middle-aged woman with an overactive libido. Both Mum and Audrey were convinced that women should 'age gracefully', which in their book meant cover up, put up and shut up. Although ironically neither of them managed the last two.

'I'm just worried about leaving Lily at the moment.' Which was the truth.

'You can't avoid work. And you'll need the money once you split, won't you? Don't worry, Sis, Audrey and I will pick up the slack for you. It will all work out.'

The front door slammed shut and Mum's far from dulcet tones rang out in the hallway. 'Putha, I'm here. I've made some roti.'

Ingrid and Grace froze. Neither of them understood why Audrey had given their mother a key to come and go as she pleased. Even when Ingrid had been desperate for help with

Lily over the past year, there was no way she would ever have granted Mum unfettered access to her space with a licence to lecture at will.

Mum rounded the corner and entered the living room. 'Ah, good, you're still here,' she said to Ingrid, before almost dropping the foil-covered plate as she spied the orange wall.

'I'm just off now,' said Ingrid, who really did have to run to be able to check in on time.

'What on earth has she done?' said Mum, pointing at the wall.

'You'll have to ask Audrey,' said Ingrid, speed-walking to the hallway, Grace close on her heels.

'Why is she here so early?' Grace hissed in Ingrid's ear.

'No clue, but let's get out while she's distracted by the wall. Lily, I've got to go now.'

Lily barrelled out of the kitchen, flapjack in one hand, spraying crumbs down the corridor like Gretel. She flew into Ingrid's arms.

'I'll miss you so much.'

Ingrid's heart broke a little more with every separation; the guilt of maintaining a career while being a mother, a perpetual weight on her shoulders.

'I know, baby, I'll miss you too, my Lilypad. But it's only three nights. Be a good girl for Aunty Audrey and no gaming after nine p.m., okay?'

Lily nodded. 'Don't forget to go to the Nintendo store.'

Ingrid nodded and ruffled Lily's hair. 'I won't forget. I have all the photos of what you want on my phone.' The least she could do was buy Lily's favourite Pokémon to lessen the blow of their separation.

'And, Aunty Grace, don't forget to bring me macarons from Ladurée,' said Lily, grinning at Grace, who stuck out her tongue at her niece.

'How is it that your child is as bougie as you? Ever since you brought home that client gift, she's been bugging me for them.'

'That's my girl,' said Ingrid, kissing Lily on the cheek.

Mum stood in the living room doorway shaking her head. Ingrid and Grace had seconds to escape. They began a hopeful sprint to the front door.

'You shouldn't be going anywhere now,' called Mum.

Ingrid turned back reluctantly. 'I have to. It's a pitch and it's very important to my career and the amount of money I make.'

'If you'd stayed at home more, maybe your husband wouldn't be leaving you.'

Ingrid pointedly looked at Lily as if such subtlety was likely to shut up her mother.

'I should go, or I'll miss my flight.'

Mum glared at her. 'You know this job was half of the problem.'

Ingrid wondered what the other half was – her probably. But she wasn't going to engage.

She grabbed Grace's elbow. 'We should go, the car must be here. I'll drop you off at the Tube on the way.'

Audrey emerged from the kitchen, her face falling as she spotted Mum in the hallway. She was probably trying to work out how to get that key back. Grace slunk through the door, trying to avoid Mum's radar.

Ingrid gave Lily one last kiss and hug and followed her sister out of the front door.

As she checked her watch for the hundredth time, huffing with frustration, Ingrid wished she'd taken the much more reliable Tube with Grace instead of tackling the perpetual car park that was the M25 in her executive Uber. She tried to calculate the time she had to check in, get through security and make it to the gate. She really should have asked Grace to drop Lily off at Audrey's and got to the airport in good time for her flight, but her guilt over all the heartache her daughter had been going through had compelled her to stay with her until the last possible moment. And now she was in serious danger of missing her flight.

Finally, the taxi inched its way to the M4 exit where the traffic flowed better and within twenty minutes, they pulled up by the passenger drop-off zone of Terminal Five. Ingrid hopped out of the car, thanked the driver as he extracted her bag from the boot and placed it on the pavement, and hurried into the vast terminal building.

She was still annoyed with herself for staying up most of Friday night, replaying that little scene between Jacob and Erin outside the karaoke bar. Was she so out of the loop with these things that she'd completely misread the situation, reading more into every look and gesture between herself and Jacob that night?

Then she'd spent Saturday night telling herself that she had no business dwelling on Jacob's kiss with Erin. He was too young for her. For God's sake, he'd been *three* when she'd taken her GCSEs, in primary school when she'd taken her A levels and gone to university . . .

She needed to show him that she was unaffected by what she'd seen. She'd banked on meeting him in the lounge where a conversation to break the ice might have been possible, but now it was likely that nothing would be said until they reached New York.

She handed over her passport to the woman at the check-in desk and bent to pick up her battered Rimowa suitcase to place it on the luggage belt, but another hand grasped the handle and lifted it.

'You're cutting it a bit fine too?' Jacob asked with a tentative smile as he handed over his passport.

Ingrid stared at him, cursing the flush travelling up her chest, which she hoped he'd think was due to her brisk walk through the terminal. He kept casting glances at her. The first time she'd seen him look less than confident.

'I'll be as quick as I can, Mr Ellis,' said the woman at the desk whose name, according to the tag on her uniform, was Marian. Marian's smile to Jacob was infinitely warmer than the welcome she'd given Ingrid moments earlier.

'The traffic was awful,' said Ingrid, keen to keep the conversation as banal as possible in front of Marian.

'Yeah, I should've got the Tube, but a mate gave me a lift.'

Ingrid nodded, careful not to look at his face.

Marian went through the usual security questions and handed them their boarding passes.

'You'll have to hurry. They're about to board,' she said, pressing Jacob's passport into his hand.

'Thanks, Marian,' said Jacob, eliciting a brilliant smile from her.

Then he placed his hand on Ingrid's elbow and steered her towards security.

'Excuse me, mate, we're about to miss our flight, could you let us through?' Jacob asked the bored Heathrow worker perched on a stool by the entrance to security.

'Sure.'

Clearly Jacob's charm extended to all airport personnel because Ingrid was spared her usual additional random security check.

They said nothing further to each other as they both removed shoes and watches, unpacked laptops and so on, then ran to the shuttle that would take them to their gate.

'How was your day with Lily yesterday?' Jacob asked as they gripped the yellow handrail in the shuttle.

'Wonderful, thanks,' said Ingrid, wishing they didn't have to talk right then.

'That's great,' he said, smiling tentatively at her as they swayed with the motion.

Should she say something to dispel the awkwardness? She looked up at him and was about to open her mouth when the shuttle came to an abrupt halt, nearly throwing her into his arms instead. Mercifully, she managed to avoid contact and they disembarked and sprinted to the empty gate where the attendants gave them reproving looks before ushering them quickly through.

As they shuffled onboard, Ingrid was guided to the opposite side of the plane to Jacob, who waved before taking his seat. She should have felt relief at being spared the conversation, but not having said anything left her feeling awkward and apprehensive. And now she'd be feeling like this for the next seven hours.

Great. Ingrid took out her business-class eye mask and hit the recline button.

24

Getting Acquainted

Ingrid smoothed down the skirt of her white cotton sundress and slipped her feet into the sky-high white Louboutin heels that she'd treated herself to after winning the last pitch. She checked her bright-red lipstick in the mirror, flicked her hair back over her shoulder and tried to muster as much courage as possible before she headed out to dinner with Jacob.

She absolutely wasn't dressing for a date, especially after what she'd seen on Friday night. She looked at herself in the full-length mirror. Should she swap her shoes for the flats? Should she wipe off the lipstick? Maybe some nice, sensible trousers would look better. But no, let him see her for who she was. *What he's missing*, said the voice in her head.

Her phone vibrated.

I'm in the lobby. See you soon?

Be right down.

As she stepped into the elevator, her heart was beating so loudly that she was sure that the elegantly dressed lady who'd come from a higher floor could hear it. She had to say something to Jacob to defuse the tension between them so that it wouldn't affect the pitch tomorrow.

She exited the lift and turned left into the lobby with its giant white wire sculpture of a head by the door and saw Jacob chatting amiably with the doorman. He turned as she approached, his eyes widening a little as he saw her.

What was that micro-expression? Did she look like mutton dressed as lamb? Was he comparing her to Erin? She pushed back her shoulders and walked towards him with as much confidence as she could muster.

Ingrid looked around the tiny, dimly lit restaurant, which was decorated in an interesting mix of subway tiles and ornate chandeliers. Jacob had picked it and unlike the brightly lit steak places that she usually frequented for her New York business dinners, there was an intimacy to the space. Just like the day when he'd visited her home, she wasn't the only person who'd dressed up. Jacob wore dark jeans, loafers and a tailored blue linen shirt.

'Is this place alright?' he asked, noticing her looking around the restaurant.

'Oh, yes, yes, it's great,' she replied, crossing her legs under the table and brushing her ankle against his leg as she did so.

Instead of moving his legs out of the way, he extended them out, maintaining contact.

'It looked good online and wasn't far from the hotel so I thought you'd be able to get here in heels if you wore them.'

Had he been helping Erin as she stumbled on her heels? Is that why he'd fallen on her lips? *Stop it, Ingrid.* She pushed her hair back behind her ear and took a deep gulp of the cold water that had been placed in front of her.

She should have had a plan for this meal. What she would say, how she would be. Ingrid wasn't good without a plan, which was probably why the last couple of months had been such a mess. And yet, she'd felt more alive than she had in years. Plans took the spontaneity out of life and she was beginning to see that life could be a lot more thrilling if she let it happen rather than trying to control and tame it. But she wasn't sure if she wanted to deal with the consequences of spontaneity, like awkwardly sitting here with this man right now.

Jacob looked up from the menu and took a deep breath. 'I need to talk to you about Friday night,' he said.

'Jacob, it's okay. You don't owe me an explanation.' *Explain. Please.*

'I do. *I* was the one who made you go there and then I couldn't shake that girl off and then you saw us outside, and—'

She held up a hand, assuming her best nonchalant consenting adult expression. 'We've all had a little fumble outside bars on a Friday night. You don't need to explain yourself to me, Jacob. I was just a little surprised because I thought you weren't really into Erin.'

'What?'

She met his eyes, which were puzzled.

'You were kissing Erin.'

He laughed. He actually laughed and Ingrid fought the instinct to stand and stalk out of the restaurant there and then.

'The only person I wanted to kiss on Friday night, on any night since we met on that hill in the Lakes, is you, Ingrid.'

They stared at each other for a few moments as his words hung in the air between them. Had he just said that he wanted to kiss her? That he hadn't kissed Erin? She took a deep breath. She hadn't been wrong all those times she'd wondered if he was feeling the same attraction?

'But Erin . . .' was all she could manage to say.

He rubbed his face, then set his elbows on the table as he leaned forward.

'I came out looking for you. Erin must've followed, and she launched herself at me. I was just trying to get her upright when I saw you leaving in that cab and, God, Ingrid, I can't tell you how many times I wanted to come over to your house this weekend and tell you, or call you, but I didn't want to interrupt your precious time with your daughter over something like this. Not when I knew you'd understand as soon as I explained.'

'Well,' she said, trying to appear calm and sophisticated while her heart and mind raced. It hadn't been what she'd thought. Would she be a fool to trust him? Her brain sifted through memories from the past week, and she knew that she should.

'I mean, I thought I was making it so clear. How much I'm attracted to you. Ever since we met, I've been thinking how lucky I was that I stumbled upon such a beautiful, kind, driven, strong, independent, funny and incredibly sexy woman that day.'

Ingrid was suddenly very aware of her jaw, which seemed to have frozen wide open like a boa constrictor. She snapped it shut and shifted in her seat. Did people really make confessions like this in real life? She had to say something, but what? Where were all her words?

'Um . . . it's just that you're kind of like that with most women, so it was a bit difficult to tell. And if I'm honest, I'm shocked that someone like you would be interested in me.'

'Someone like me?' He gave her a mischievous smile. 'Ah, yes. You said I was handsome the other night.'

She gave him a playful shove, knocking one of his elbows off the table. He straightened with a laugh.

'*Empirically* handsome.'

'Hmm,' he said with another smile, which made her look at that perfect mouth. He noticed and his smile was even broader. 'You must know that *you're* so beautiful. Every man in that lobby was looking at you when you emerged from the lift in that dress.' His eyes ranged over her. 'I'm fairly sure that Trent is into you.'

She was worried that she might spontaneously combust from his words alone. She fanned her face with her hand. What was that he'd just said about Trent? 'Trent is a friend.

Like Erin is to you.' She couldn't help herself. Forty-five and still petty.

'You know she's not even that to me.'

Ingrid took a deep breath as she processed all this information. And the risk assessor in her couldn't help herself.

'You know, this isn't so easy for me to jump right into. I have to think of Lily. And I'm worried that maybe I'm too old for you and I have too much baggage for whatever this is between us to be a thing.'

'Personally, I think the age thing is irrelevant. And everyone has baggage.'

'Some of us have older baggage.'

'But age doesn't mean anything when it comes to baggage. Some young people have experienced more pain than many much older than them.'

He traced the condensation down the side of his glass of water.

'I like you, Ingrid. A lot. And I think we could have something good together. Don't you?'

It was almost a superhuman effort to stop herself from nodding.

'Jacob, I have to consider Lily. She's had such a rough time of it with Matt being a crap father, always absent and now this crazy behaviour of his. She likes you, and it worries me. I don't know how she'd cope if we broke up or if you went off to the US. It wouldn't be fair to her.'

Jacob nodded. 'I understand. I know that we don't know where this could go yet, so how about we keep it low-key in front of Lily until you're sure? But I'm not saying that because I'm looking for a fling. I want to be in a relationship with you, Ingrid, and I know that means Lily is a major part of that.'

Was that relief? Assurances were worthless in relationships. After all, Matt had promised to love and be faithful to her until they died. Nonetheless, Jacob's words had made her feel more at ease.

He caressed her forearm as he read the menu and Ingrid fought to ignore the electric current that zipped across her skin. How was it possible for his touch to have that effect on her? She cleared her throat.

He looked up and smiled, his gaze dropping to her lips.

She touched his leg with her own and looked into his eyes again.

'Are you ready to order?' said the young waitress who'd appeared by their table while they'd been in some kind of highly sexy staring contest. She ignored Ingrid, addressing Jacob with a smile.

Ingrid wondered if he noticed all this special attention.

'Have you decided?' Jacob asked Ingrid. 'I've been too distracted to actually take in the menu.' His hand touched her leg under the table.

Her stomach growled. Ingrid never ate on planes and it had been a while since she'd had her coffee this morning. She took a quick look at the menu.

'I'll have a steak, medium rare, a mac 'n' cheese side and a green salad. And . . .' She thumbed through the book that contained the wine list. 'A bottle of the Margaux.'

'What about you?' asked the waitress, turning to Jacob with a coquettish smile, which was entirely lost on him because he was grinning at Ingrid.

'I'll have what she's having.' He winked. 'See, I told you I'd seen that old movie.'

Ingrid laughed. 'And a large sparkling water please.' She couldn't afford a hangover with the pitch the next day.

The waitress bit her lip, considering. 'Can I add you on Insta?'

'Oh, I don't use social media,' lied Jacob.

'Your number?'

Ingrid didn't even attempt to hide her amusement at this girl's persistence.

Jacob grabbed Ingrid's hand. 'I'm not sure my girlfriend would like that.'

The waitress's face turned strawberry red as she looked at Ingrid, who read judgement in her eyes. If she let this thing, whatever it was, happen with Jacob, she would have to get used to that expression.

'Sorry. I didn't realise.'

'No problem,' said Jacob.

'I'll bring your drinks right out.'

'Does that happen to you a lot?' Ingrid asked.

'Not really.'

'Liar. And what was that about a girlfriend?'

He laughed. 'Let a man have some hope!'

As they walked back to the hotel, the air between them was thick with more than the humid August heat. Once they'd both confessed their feelings, the rest of their meal had been peppered with searing touches, as hands grazed knees, or fingers caressed arms, each one increasing the temperature between them. Now, as they tried to maintain a conversation about the next day's pitch, eyes straying to each other's lips, they both knew that they no longer wanted to talk. Their fingers were intertwined, shoulders bumping periodically. Ingrid felt as though she was in a pressure cooker.

As they waited for the elevator to arrive, Ingrid's brain raced through possible scenarios of what lay ahead, each one a little terrifying for someone who had been out of the romance game for as long as she had.

The elevator was empty when it arrived, Jacob gesturing to Ingrid that she should board first, and they each pressed the button for their respective floors with Ingrid on the floor below.

As soon as the doors closed, Jacob turned to her, his eyes on her lips once again. Before she could take a breath, he pulled her close, cradling her cheek with his hand as his lips met hers, the force of his kiss propelling them against the wall.

Ingrid hadn't been kissed for almost two years, and it had never felt like this when she'd kissed Matt. Or anyone.

Jacob's lips were firm and insistent as they fitted on hers, pulling her bottom lip between his teeth, coaxing her mouth open. Ingrid's entire body was instantly on fire as she dropped her bag to the floor and her hands linked behind his neck, pulling him closer. Her chest pressed against his, their hips fused together. She couldn't get close enough.

The lift doors opened at her floor and they jumped apart. She pointed at the open doorway.

'I should go.'

He nodded, then picked up her bag and handed it to her, his fingers lingering on hers.

'You have my lipstick . . .' She made a circular movement around her mouth.

'At least this way I'll know that I didn't just dream that,' he said with a smile. 'Sleep well, Ingrid. See you tomorrow morning.'

The lift doors closed.

Sleep? She wondered how long the fire in her body would take to burn out before that happened.

25

Pitch Perfect

Thank God for jet lag. Despite the almost heart-stopping kiss with Jacob, exhaustion claimed Ingrid as soon as her head hit the plush hotel pillow and she sank into the crisp white sheets. She awoke with a clear head, and battle-ready. In the bright New York sunshine, the previous night seemed like a fever dream, all hazy heat and potentially bad decisions.

Would they be able to interact on a professional basis for the duration of the pitch, even though she had never been kissed like that in her life? Did young people really do things so differently? He'd set her whole body aflame. Even a cold shower hadn't quite dissipated the effect. And she wanted more.

But she needed to focus.

Her makeup was light, with a neutral lipstick. Her dress a dark green shift with a matching jacket that cinched in at the waist and tan suede shoes that were effectively nude against Ingrid's brown skin. She checked that her laptop was fully charged before packing it into her tote bag. Then headed downstairs, checking her reflection for remnants of lipstick on her teeth.

Jacob sat on one of the chairs in the lobby, dressed in a dark blue suit with a white shirt and burgundy polka-dotted tie, pushing his glasses up his nose as he read the newspaper. Ingrid stopped and caught her breath, her eyes dropping to those lips that she'd felt on hers. No, she must not think of the kiss. She had to win this work. After finally making a fuss in the office, she couldn't fall at this hurdle and undermine her position.

She steeled herself and walked towards him. Jacob looked up and smiled, folding up his newspaper.

'Sleep well?' he asked.

'Like a log. You?'

He stood. 'Not really,' he said with a heart-stopping smile, enough for her to know exactly why. 'But I'm ready for this. Don't worry, I won't let you down in there.'

'Okay then. Let's do this.'

Ingrid returned to her hotel room and took off her jacket with a sigh. Despite the arctic air conditioning in the conference room, she'd felt the sweat trickling down her back as she'd presented their pitch to a roomful of dark-suited men. She was no stranger to being the only woman in the room, but she hadn't cared as much as she did this time. Her professional reputation was on the line and she couldn't afford a failure.

Apart from one hair-raising minute where her laptop had spontaneously shut down in the middle of her slide show, she thought that the whole thing had gone well. She'd answered their questions with detail and plenty of evidence. Everything now depended on how the other three firms performed before things were narrowed down to the final two. All they could do was wait for the call. Ingrid kicked off her shoes and went to shower.

Jacob had gone straight to a meeting with the bank that had offered him a job, and the thought that he might not be in London for much longer made her feel vulnerable. How was it possible to feel so connected to someone in such a short time? It wasn't just their physical attraction to each other. When she was with him, her worries receded and her burdens lightened. But she couldn't ask him to stay for her. They had only just met. Had she made a mistake last night?

The cool shower was a huge relief. New York City in August was like walking around in a cauldron. It was no wonder the wealthier inhabitants of the city decamped to the cooler beach climes of the Hamptons every weekend.

She wrapped herself in a plush white robe and stretched out on the bed, grabbing the new Nintendo Switch she'd bought for Lily on the way back from the pitch. Thankfully, it came partially charged. She loaded up Mario Kart, determined to be better at this before she went home. At least this time she seemed to be going in the same direction as everyone else. But, as she played the game, the dull ache of missing Lily sharpened, and she stopped to check the time to see if she could call her. She dialled Audrey's number, but it was Lily who answered, no doubt handed the phone by her aunt.

'Mum! I miss you. What's that you're hiding behind you?' asked her hawk-eyed daughter as soon as she saw her.

Ingrid moved to hide the Switch better. 'I miss you too, Lilypad. It's just the pillow.'

Lily was about to ask another question when Audrey appeared on camera behind her. 'How was it?' she asked.

'Good, I think. I mean, it couldn't have gone any better. And Jacob was great with the numbers.' She bit her lip.

'Has he been to the Nintendo store yet?' Lily asked.

'Why does *he* need to go there? Didn't you send me a list?' Ingrid asked.

'Er . . .'

'Lily, have you asked *Jacob* to buy you things? You can't do that. I work with him.'

'But, Mum, he promised me.'

'Who's Jacob?' Audrey asked.

'Someone Mum works with,' said Lily. 'He came to our

house to work and Dad went mental, but then he took Mum and me climbing and he was really nice.'

'Climbing? Aren't you terrified of heights? Why haven't I heard about this?' Audrey asked, face close to the camera.

'Relax, Audrey. I work with him, that's all,' said Ingrid, hoping that the blush on her cheeks as she remembered their elevator kiss would be masked by the bad lighting on her end. 'What did you do today, Lils?'

Lily bounced excitedly on her seat. 'Harry and Millie took me to Comic Con.'

Ingrid groaned. Lily had been pestering her to take her for ages, but she'd never relented, not least because the ExCel centre was the other side of London and was a nightmare to get to. But mostly because she knew that Lily would bankrupt her as she tried to get her hands on every Pokémon plushie she could find.

'And how was it?'

'Oh my God, it was brilliant! I used my birthday money to buy loads of stuff. And don't worry, they're all different to the ones I asked you to get.'

If she had to be away from her daughter, there was at least some solace to be had in seeing her joy.

'Here, darling, have some cake,' said Audrey, sliding a large slice of chocolate cake towards Lily.

'Not too much sugar, Audrey,' said Ingrid.

'You can do whatever you like at home, but when my lovely niece is with me, I have the right to spoil her as much as possible.'

Ingrid smiled. It was the line she'd used on Audrey when taking care of her children and filling them up with sugar before sending them home feral.

'Well, I'll be home the day after tomorrow so normal service will resume.'

Lily's gaze became distracted, no doubt reading a message that had cropped up on the screen of her mobile phone. Ingrid had resisted Lily's pleas for one for as long as possible, finally relenting as her daughter started secondary school. Now she regretted not buying a sturdy Nokia brick with no internet capability instead of being persuaded by Grace that her daughter might attract ridicule and bullies if she was seen with something so ancient.

'Mum, Harvey's asking if I can play Minecraft with him. Can I go now?'

'Remind me who Harvey is again?'

Lily rolled her eyes impatiently. 'He's a boy in my class, Mum. I told you before. Can I go?'

'Alright, darling. See you in a couple of days. Love you.'

'Love you, Mum,' said Lily, before racing out of the room.

'I figured you wouldn't mind about the comic thing since you're not here,' said Audrey, who was no stranger to Mum Guilt.

Ingrid couldn't disagree. 'How much tat was purchased?'

'Um, whatever you think is a lot times about two. It took all three of them to carry stuff home. But they loved it. Hey, you okay?' Audrey peered into her phone camera.

'Yeah, just tired and apprehensive.'

Audrey peered at her, and Ingrid tried not to look evasive. 'Hmm. Fine, I'll take your word for it.' Ingrid was sure that her sister had clocked that she was in a hotel bathrobe in the middle of the day, and was probably checking the background for signs of a man. Right on cue, the doorbell rang on her hotel door.

'Listen, I have to go, but I'll see you soon. Give Lils lots of kisses from me.'

'Will do. Safe journey, Sis.'

Ingrid peered through the peephole. Jacob.

As she opened the door, Jacob smiled, eyes raking over her robe. 'May I come in?'

She wasn't sure of the etiquette when greeting someone you'd kissed passionately and then gone to an important meeting with as a professional the next day, especially

187

when wearing only a plush hotel robe. She pulled the belt tighter.

'Ingrid? You okay?'

'Hmm? Oh, yes,' she said, stepping aside to allow him inside the room. 'How was your meeting?'

He nodded slowly, taking off his jacket and tie and draping them over the arm of the sofa at the foot of the bed.

'Good. I think. They seem like really great people I could work with.' He undid the top two buttons of his shirt and breathed deeply as she watched, mesmerised.

'So you've made a decision.'

'I'm not sure it's just my decision to make anymore.'

'Right, your mum.'

'It's not just my mum,' said Jacob, taking a step towards her.

'Jacob, you really shouldn't be making any decisions based on a single kiss.'

'Oh but it was a spectacular kiss.'

God, it really was.

'And I'm hoping it wasn't a *single* kiss,' he said, eyes on her lips.

He was so close to her that she instinctively took a step back.

'I know that you have a lot going on in your life. So do I. But this type of attraction, this feeling, doesn't happen that often. I don't know. I can't explain it properly, but I feel like I would be making a big mistake if I walked away right now,' he said, stepping closer.

Ingrid's phone rang and she leaped to answer it. 'Hi, Will, have you heard anything from the guys in New York?'

'Yeah, actually, they wanted to call you, but I asked if I could let you know.'

'Yes . . .'

'They were really impressed with your pitch. In fact, they said you were the top choice and they could see why I backed you. Anyway, long story short, they're inviting you to the second round. Most likely in London and they'll want to see the rest of your team.'

'Will you be there too?'

'Probably not. I don't want the decision to include me. I think it's best you win this on your own. And they really liked that guy you brought with you. Any chance he'd be working with the client?'

She glanced at Jacob who was following the conversation closely.

'He's a consultant, so no, he won't be.'

'Shame.'

'He's one of your lot, actually. A banker.'

'Interesting. I'll mention that to the others. Anyway, must go and well done. I knew you'd nail it.'

'Thanks for giving me the heads-up, Will.'

He hung up and Ingrid turned to look at Jacob, unable to contain her elation and relief.

'We did it?' Jacob asked.

She nodded and then she was in his arms as he twirled her around.

Even though the air conditioning was at full blast, the moment he touched her, the temperature in the room was scorching. He looked down into her eyes, a silent request for permission. The moment she smiled, his lips were on hers. His hands threaded through her hair to clasp the back of her head, holding it in place as he kissed her. Her arms grabbed his shoulders, her brain shutting off as she leaned into the intoxicating sensation of the kiss. He backed her towards the bed and they both fell onto the mattress, lips fused. Then he kissed her neck, her collarbone, and Ingrid leaned her head back as she craved more contact.

It was as if someone had lit a match to her dormant libido, waking it with a force that almost scared her. She hadn't been touched like this in over two years, maybe never, and the overload of sensation made her head spin. Jacob's teeth grazed the tender skin between her neck and shoulder as his hand crept inside her robe, seeking her breast, the weight of him on top of her bringing her back to reality.

She pushed at his shoulders. 'Jacob, please, stop.'

He pulled back instantly and stood, running his hand through his now dishevelled hair. 'I'm sorry.'

'No, *I'm* sorry. It's too soon.'

He sat on the edge of the bed as she pulled her robe tighter. 'I shouldn't have moved so fast. I'm sorry, Ingrid.'

'I'm not sure any of this is a good idea.'

'I want to be with you.'

'I have a daughter.' As much as she wanted this, Lily's needs came first.

'I understand. Honestly, I do. I would never want her to be hurt or confused because of me either. But can't we see how it goes before we shut it down? One thing I'm absolutely certain of is that I like you, Ingrid. A lot. And I think that if those kisses are anything to go by, we'd be amazing together, but how will we ever know if we don't try?'

She watched him, so earnest as he sat patiently at the end of the bed. She thought about how she'd felt moments ago in his arms until her brain pulled her back yet again. All this checking and restraining hadn't brought her joy as she'd lived a measured and uneventful life. When Jacob had kissed her, every molecule in her body wanted him and she felt a surge of excitement and anticipation within her at the thought of what life could be like with him. Why was she denying herself? They were literally a continent away from Lily, and she'd already decided it was time to leave her self-sacrificing ways behind her.

'Okay,' she said. 'Let's try. Let's see where this goes.'

They were such alien words for Ingrid that she felt as if she were shedding a previous version of herself, and walking into a new phase of her life. It felt dangerous, but so good.

Jacob moved closer to her, pulling her into a hug. Then his lips sought hers again for a soft kiss.

'Jacob,' said Ingrid, 'can we take it slow? I . . . God, this is so embarrassing. Look it's been a long time since I last had sex, so I want to take this slowly.'

He pulled back, his eyes roving over her face. 'You never have to be embarrassed with me, Ingrid. And thank you for trusting me. We'll go as slow as you need.'

'Can I ask you something?'

He caressed her cheek. 'Anything.'

'Last night, at dinner, it was as though you wanted to say something, but you changed your mind.'

He shifted so that her head rested on his shoulder and twined his fingers with hers and sighed.

'I came back from Singapore because my younger brother, Marcus, died.'

Ingrid gasped, moving to look into his eyes. 'I don't know what to say. Sorry doesn't feel like enough for a loss like that.'

Jacob moved her head back to his shoulder and took a deep breath. 'He was a mountain guide in the Alps, you know for skiing, climbing, winter sports, and he did mountain rescue. It was April and he was trying to rescue some people who'd gone skiing despite an avalanche warning, and he got caught up in one himself.'

So that's why he hated casual walkers on hills without the correct gear.

She wiped away a tear from his face with her thumb. 'What was Marcus like?'

The edges of Jacob's lips turned up in a half-smile. 'He was five years younger than me, and you know, a typical younger brother, more adventurous, carefree. Didn't think much about financial security, whereas watching Mum counting the pennies each week after Dad left made me hell-bent on earning well so I could take all that worry away.'

'And were you close with him?'

'Very. As close as you can be when separated by thousands of miles. We went climbing and stuff, you know? I was helping him set up his guide business, was even thinking of spending a bit of the season with him next year.'

'Oh, Jacob, I'm so sorry.'

'I wish I'd been there to help him, to even look for him. I should've done a better job of trying to protect him.'

She pulled away and knelt on the bed, facing him. 'But you know that it's not your fault, don't you? You couldn't have known that something like that would happen. You couldn't have changed things.'

He shrugged. 'I know it isn't rational, but it's how I feel.'

'And are you wavering about the job here in New York because you think you should stay with your mum?' she asked.

'Mmm. At least I was . . . I've tried to spend as much time as possible with her since I've been back, but she's not happy about this job offer and wants me to settle down up there. But I can't do my job in the Lake District and even though the guilt of leaving my mum alone is sometimes overwhelming, I keep reminding myself that what happened to Marcus is proof that life is so short and can disappear in the blink of an eye. I can't live so carefully that I miss out on other wonderful things. It's so tough seeing Mum heartbroken. We were her life.'

'I think that a large part of motherhood is preparing your children to live without you. As much as we want to claim our children as part of us, they're individuals with their own hopes and lives, and we have to let them live. Your mum is grieving now, but with a little time, she'll take the pressure off you. She's scared of losing you too, I suppose.'

He took her hands in his once again and stared at them. 'Yeah. I know, but I wonder if I haven't been a good enough son. She went through so much for us, maybe it's time for me to do something for her.'

'Mothers don't have an emotional ledger of debits and credits between them and their children. At least, most of us don't. The things we do for our children are a privilege, never a sacrifice, and never something that requires repayment in kind or otherwise.'

He looked at her, holding her gaze for a moment. 'I'm really glad I met you, Ingrid.'

'I'm really glad I met you, Jacob.'

26

Hide and Seek

By the time Ingrid finally entered the Everyman cinema at Baker Street, she'd already walked past it twice. Okay, so the entrance was much smaller than most of the shopfronts on the busy road and easy to miss, but honestly, she couldn't make out much from behind the oversized sunglasses she'd chosen to obscure almost her whole face for fear of being spotted by someone from the office. Now she was hot and a little sweaty, and feeling decidedly unsexy for her date with Jacob, who stood in the air-conditioned lobby waiting for her as though he were posing for some designer lookbook. He peered at her for a moment before laughing, and Ingrid began to turn away towards the exit. Jacob sprinted towards her and grabbed her hand.

'Don't leave, Ingrid.'

She tried to pull her hand out of his grip but he held firm. 'This is ridiculous.'

'I agree. No one is going to recognise us here, so you can ditch the sunglasses.'

'I meant all the cloak and dagger stuff.'

'*I* wasn't the one who insisted on it.'

He was right. She was the one making this so complicated by not allowing anyone to know about them. But there could be difficulties both at work and at home if it came out.

'I'm sorry. I have my reasons.'

'All of which make complete sense to me, otherwise I wouldn't be participating in this secret squirrel stuff.'

He pulled her into a hug.

'I've missed you,' he said. He'd moved into his own office when they'd returned from New York two weeks ago, so their moments together had been limited.

'I'm all sweaty,' said Ingrid, trying to angle her body away from him.

'I don't mind. I'd even go so far as to say that I'm really looking forward to the time when I'm the one who makes you all hot and sweaty.'

She looked up at him, feeling the strength in his arms as he held her. She very much wanted him to make her hot and sweaty, so why on earth was she holding back? Fear. Saying she was making changes in her life was a different thing from doing it.

'Strictly speaking, you've already made me all hot and sweaty by picking the most inconspicuous cinema in London. I walked past it twice.'

'You know what I mean. But I'm not pushing. I'm happy to wait.'

'Happy might be overstating it. But I appreciate the patience.'

'Although, I really need to kiss you.'

'Does that mean you've booked us into the back row?'

'What do you take me for? An amateur?'

She laughed and pulled away. 'Definitely not. That's why you booked the cinema with the sofas, right?'

'Damn straight.' He took her hand. 'Let's go.'

The cinema was a series of plush two-seater sofas interspersed with the odd single armchair. Jacob hadn't been joking about booking the back row. They nestled into their sofa as a member of staff placed their wine on a small wooden table next to Jacob.

Jacob stretched out his arm across the back of the sofa until his hand landed on Ingrid's shoulder.

'I see that your generation still likes to use all the oldies' tricks,' said Ingrid with a laugh.

'We don't like to throw out the stuff that works.' Jacob squeezed her shoulder and brought his face close to hers. 'It works, doesn't it?'

'It works,' she said, looking at his lips.

Jacob closed the small distance between them and kissed her, a soft press of his lips against hers, and because of their recent lack of contact, it quickly turned into something more incendiary.

'Ingrid?'

Ingrid paused for a moment. She could have sworn she'd heard Audrey's voice. Obviously her Catholic guilt over this relationship was now manifesting in illusions of disapproving family members. Jacob's lips became more insistent as he continued to kiss her and Ingrid's hands found their way into his hair as she pulled him closer.

'Ingrid?'

Ingrid opened her eyes. Audrey and Nathan stood in the row in front looking down at them. If Audrey had been one of those Marvel characters, Ingrid was fairly certain that the stare she was giving her would have turned Ingrid into a pile of ash. She pushed Jacob away from her.

Jacob used his thumb to wipe Ingrid's lipstick from his mouth and Nathan handed him one of the napkins that was absorbing the condensation from his cold beer with an apologetic look.

'Audrey!' Ingrid exclaimed, before jumping out of her seat, which was no mean feat when it was a slouchy sofa close to the ground.

'And who's this?' Audrey asked. She gave Jacob a tight smile, like she might have given the troublesome relative of a patient when she worked in A & E.

'Um, this is Jacob.' In an instant, she'd regressed to being a child, as though she'd been caught doing something naughty by one of her parents.

Audrey stared so hard at Jacob that Ingrid was inclined to step in front of him in case he turned to stone.

'Hi, I'm Jacob Ellis. You must be Ingrid's other sister, Audrey.' He smiled and Ingrid swore she saw a small crack in Audrey's armour.

'Have we met before?' she asked, still staring, her internal facial recognition software determined to place him.

'Jacob is currently working in my office on a short contract,' said Ingrid.

Audrey's eyes widened in recognition. 'Oh, I see!' She crossed her arms. 'So, how long has this been going on for?'

'Not long,' said Ingrid.

To Ingrid and Nathan's surprise, Audrey nodded, standing down from DEFCON 1 in seconds. But then she didn't know Jacob, and even Audrey had enough of a filter to not lose it in front of an outsider, not to mention in a public place.

'It's nice to meet you, Jacob.' She leaned over to grab Ingrid's wrist. 'Would you excuse us for a moment? I just need to have a quick word with my sister. Nathan, you can keep him company for a bit, can't you?'

Nathan nodded dutifully and shook Jacob's hand.

Ingrid let herself be dragged to the side.

'Why am I only hearing – no, correction – seeing this now? Don't you trust me?' Audrey asked, looking so hurt that Ingrid felt a pang of guilt.

'Sis, it's not on purpose. It's so new. Just a couple of weeks and even *I* don't know what this is. It's strictly low-key until we work it out because I have to think of Lily.'

Audrey chewed her lip for a moment, then nodded. 'Okay.'

Ingrid was confused. 'Aren't you pissed off?'

'I am, but not because you're seeing him, because you didn't tell me. I bet Grace knows.' She huffed petulantly, aware that Ingrid and Grace shared a lot more between them since they'd begun living together.

'You know that if I had to pick one of you to keep a secret from Mum, it wouldn't be Grace.'

'Oh shit. Mum! She'll lose it if she finds out about this.'

'Another reason why we're here, trying not to run into people. And what the hell are you two doing here? Isn't this off your beaten track? How come Nathan even has the time?'

Audrey instantly looked very pleased with herself. 'I got accepted onto a Masters for creative writing and Nate wanted to take me somewhere different to celebrate. Someone is covering his shift.'

'Seriously? That's amazing, Akki! I had no idea that you'd taken Gracie's suggestion to heart.'

'Yeah, well, the more I thought about it I realised she was right. I'm so excited, and Nate's been super supportive, although part of me thinks that he just doesn't want me to redecorate any more rooms in the house . . .'

'He's a good egg.'

Audrey looked over at her husband with affection. 'He is.' She put her hand on Ingrid's arm. 'Hey, I know you've had a rough time of it and you absolutely deserve some happiness, but I have to ask. How old is he? He seems so young. And what about the divorce?'

Ingrid sighed. 'He's thirty-two. And I'm still getting divorced. I don't see how this changes things.'

Audrey nodded slowly. 'I suppose not. Did this happen when you were in New York a couple of weeks ago? I knew something was going on when we spoke that time. You were in a bathrobe.'

'Believe it or not, nothing like that has happened between us yet.'

Audrey's mouth fell open. 'What? You mean you haven't . . . ?'

'Shhh, they might hear you. No, nothing like that.'

'Wait, isn't that the point of finding a younger guy? For all the hot sex? Are you not sure about him?'

Ingrid rolled her eyes. 'It's more than a sex thing,' she

hissed. 'I really like him, Aude, but I have to be careful, for Lily's sake.'

In truth, Ingrid knew she couldn't continue like this for much longer. Lying to her daughter about her whereabouts wasn't a good feeling.

'I get it. I'm not telling you what to do here but, take it from me, Sis, kids know a lot more than we give them credit for.'

'The thing is that she really likes Jacob. And she's had enough men disappearing on her.'

'Just one man. Are you saying this one is likely to disappear?'

Ingrid didn't want to tell Audrey about Jacob's possible plans to leave the country.

'You never know, right?'

'I suppose.' She looked over at Nathan and Jacob who were chatting amiably. 'On a lighter note,' she said, conspiratorially, 'that man is seriously hot!'

Ingrid grinned. 'Maybe too hot for me.'

'Stop that!' Audrey said, smacking her arm. 'My sister is utterly gorgeous and he's bloody lucky to be anywhere near you.'

Nathan caught Audrey's eye and came to join them. Jacob's arm snaked around Ingrid's waist, pulling her close, while Audrey and Nathan exchanged a smile. Ingrid had expected fireworks and disapproval, not this.

As people began to jostle around them with boxes of popcorn and drinks, each couple headed to their seats.

'All good?' Jacob whispered.

'Yeah, but I think we might have to keep the kissing to a minimum.'

'Damn, remind me to get a refund.'

Ingrid and Jacob strolled up Pinner High Street towards the parish church, now beautifully illuminated for the evening. The air was humid, the trees in full leaf, the heat shimmering above the pavement.

Jacob hadn't said much on the Tube ride home, not that conversation was ever easy on the Underground. Even now, he was lost in thought.

'My family can be a bit much, I wouldn't blame you if you wanted out,' said Ingrid. Her tone was light but she'd been through enough break-ups in her life to know that this kind of silence was usually a prequel to a dumping.

Jacob stopped and turned to look at her. 'Sorry?'

Ingrid bit her lip and looked down. 'My family are a lot.'

He raised their clasped hands to his mouth and kissed the back of hers. 'No, actually. I was just thinking how nice it would be to talk like that with my brother.'

She pulled him into a hug. 'I can't believe how insensitive I am.'

'You aren't.' He pulled away and took her hand again. 'Was she fine with us?'

Ingrid nodded. 'Believe me, you'd have known if she wasn't! But she's a bit worried about our age difference.'

'And you're not?'

'I'd be lying if I said it didn't matter. I worry you'd miss out on a lot of things with me.'

'Or I could miss out on a whole lot of other things not being with you.'

'And I'm worried that this is temporary. That you'll be gone soon.'

He pulled her close. 'It isn't temporary. I know you don't believe me. You probably think that I can't wait to skip off to New York and leave you and Lily behind, but I won't. I've never met anyone like you, Ingrid. I know it won't happen again, and I know it's early and I probably wouldn't say this at this stage if that job offer wasn't hanging in the air, but I have no intention of walking away.'

She might not have believed him if he hadn't included Lily in his speech.

'Have I convinced you?' he asked.

She shrugged. 'Maybe. But you told me yourself that you like to live your life for yourself.'

'Being with you would fall into that category.'

'And my daughter?'

'*And* Lily.'

What more could she expect at this stage? A written contract signed in his blood? At some point she had to accept his word.

They continued to walk down the street, hand in hand.

'So tell me about Audrey,' he said.

'She's a lot more like our mother than she'd ever admit. Strong, opinionated, organised, bossy – but she loves with a ferocity that's almost scary. She used to be a doctor working in a hospital until she and Nathan had three kids in quick succession. But now that they're older, she's just decided to do a creative writing Masters. She was a brilliant doctor, but seeing her face earlier when she told me she'd been accepted onto the course made me realise how much happier she'll be doing this.'

'So the three of you are pretty different.'

'I suppose so. Not sure how that happened, but maybe we're all a total stereotype. You know, the eldest responsible one, the middle appeaser and the carefree baby.'

'And what's your dad like?'

'Mum is larger than life, so he supports her really. He's quieter and kind, and the only person she listens to. Actually, it's their fifty-fifth wedding anniversary in a couple of weeks. I don't know how they've done it.'

'From what I can see, marriage is a lot of work. I guess that every day you keep making the choice to be together.'

'And how would you know, youngster?'

He touched the tip of her nose with his finger. 'I'm incredibly perceptive. And not *that* young.'

'Yeah, maybe you're right about that.'

'I'm right about a lot of things.'

They'd reached Ingrid's house. The solo violin from one of Bach's violin concertos filtered out through an open window and, as beautiful as her sister's playing was, Ingrid hoped that it wouldn't wake up Lily.

Jacob tugged her behind the hedge that bordered the front of her house.

'We were interrupted earlier,' he said, drawing her close.

'What if someone sees?'

'Let them look.'

His lips found hers. Her brain was vaguely aware of the music stopping, but their kiss deepened, and everything else receded as she lost herself in him.

'Welcome home,' said Grace.

They both jumped.

'I promise I'm not a perv or anything. The Ring camera notifications kept buzzing, so I came out to investigate. The Neighbourhood Watch has been banging on about car thefts and stuff. Nice to see you again, Jacob.'

'Hi,' he said, a little embarrassed this time. 'But don't you think that might have been a bit dangerous?'

Grace shrugged. 'I could've taken 'em,' she said, brandishing her bow.

Jacob laughed. 'I should go.'

'You should come in,' said Grace. 'You're always welcome and you don't have to play hide and seek with me. I totally know that you two are dating.'

'No shit, Sherlock,' said Ingrid, wiping her lipstick off Jacob's face with her thumb, thinking it must be incredibly bad luck to have not one, but two sisters interrupt her kisses in the same night.

'I don't want to confuse Lily,' said Jacob.

Ingrid touched his hand. 'I'll see you tomorrow.'

He nodded. 'Sleep well. Bye, Grace.'

'Bye,' said Grace with an exaggerated wave.

Ingrid took a step forward but Grace held out her bow to stop her.

'I should let you know, Lily's still up.'

'Shit,' said Ingrid, 'why isn't she in bed?'

'She wanted to see you.'

'Has Matt been round?'

'Not that I know of, but Mum was round here earlier, remember? When I had that audition for *Hamilton*.'

Ingrid groaned. This was not good.

27

Permission

As soon as they entered the house, Grace dragged Ingrid into the utility room. Ingrid looked around for more accidentally tie-dyed clothes, or a leak, but nothing seemed out of place. The sound of the dryer masked any conversation from Lily's curious ears.

'Something happened. Tell me,' said Grace, placing her hands on Ingrid's shoulders.

Was she so readable? 'Audrey and Nathan were at the same cinema. By the way, did she tell you about the creative writing course she was accepted onto?'

Grace nodded distractedly. 'I spoke to her on the phone earlier. It's great, but stop trying to divert attention away from you. What happened?'

'Jacob and I were kissing.'

Grace crossed her arms and nodded, grinning. 'You two are really into the PDA, huh?'

'Argh, enough,' said Ingrid, embarrassed.

'All I can say is that I really like this guy if he's loosening you up. So was Akki upset about the kissing or *who* you were kissing?'

'She was more upset that I hadn't told her about him.'

'Ditto! Just because I have Miss Marple skills and know all the signs of someone sneaking off to see their boyfriend, doesn't mean that you shouldn't have told me. We live together. Did you really think I wouldn't have noticed?'

'We're still trying to work out what this is. It didn't feel like it was time. But I guess you know now.'

She hadn't said anything to her sisters because until he made a decision about it, the job in New York hung over their heads like an hourglass, the sand slowly slipping down as their time ran out. Her risk-averse brain kept telling her that she and Lily were in for heartache if Jacob left, but her heart was telling her to believe him when he said that she and Lily were part of his decision.

'To be honest, it's getting pretty exhausting trying to hide it from everyone. And it isn't as though we've done anything more than kiss.'

'*What*?'

'Some of us don't move that fast.'

'Some of us don't move that slow.'

'Shut up.'

'Mature. So, what are you going to do?'

'First, I need to talk to Lily. And then I need to tell Matt.'

Grace grimaced. 'Rather you than me. Do you think he'll go nuts?'

'Probably. But it's the decent thing. I wouldn't be happy if the shoe were on the other foot.'

'And then Ammi and Thatha?' Grace asked, shrinking into herself a little at the mere thought of enlightening them on Ingrid's love life.

An idea popped into Ingrid's head. No, it was mad. She couldn't do something like that. Audrey was the creative writing student with a flair for the dramatic. Ingrid was the boring accountant. Except . . .

'So, I've just had this idea. But it's mad.'

'Go on,' said Grace, intrigued.

'Depending on how well it goes with Lily, and after I tell Matt, why don't I bring Jacob to Ammi and Thatha's anniversary party in a fortnight's time?'

Grace placed the back of her hand on Ingrid's forehead. 'Are you sick?'

Ingrid batted her away. 'I'm serious. Ammi is less likely to kick off in front of all those people and it's a good way to show everyone that this isn't just a fling but a relationship.'

'So it's a relationship?'

Jacob had brushed off her allusions to this being temporary and it was time to believe him. This hare-brained plan was a statement of intent.

'Yes. He's my boyfriend.'

Ingrid fished the Nintendo Switch out of her bag and headed up to Lily's room where her daughter lay on her stomach watching anime on her laptop in bed.

'Mum, you're home,' said Lily sitting up. 'Is that a Nintendo Switch?' Her eyes glittered with anticipation.

'Yep. I actually bought it when I was in New York, but I wanted to practise a bit before I gave it to you.'

'You've been practising Mario Kart?'

Ingrid nodded.

'So you can play with me?'

Ingrid smiled, and Lily launched herself into her arms.

'You're the best.'

Ingrid kissed the top of Lily's head and stroked her hair. 'I know how much you love it and I wanted to be a bit less rubbish at it.'

'It doesn't matter if you are. We can play on the same team.'

'I'd love that, baby. Listen, I really need to talk about something with you.'

'Is Jacob your new boyfriend?' Lily asked.

Once again, Audrey was right. Kids really did pick up on more than you expected.

'Why would you ask that?' Ingrid asked.

'Alicia said that if Jacob took us climbing and brought me Pokémon from America, then he must want to date my mum.'

Alicia was far too precocious for Ingrid's liking, but somewhat helpful in this instance.

'Would you be upset if we dated?' she asked Lily.

Ingrid watched her daughter carefully for a micro-expression that might tell her what she was really thinking. Lily ran her fingers through the end of her long ponytail, her forehead fixed in a frown, lips pursed as she considered. When had she grown up so much? For Ingrid the last few years had passed in a haze of laundry, signing permission slips and mad dashes to school, against a constant backdrop of never feeling able to give her daughter quite enough time and attention.

'I don't think so. He's nice.'

She hugged Lily. 'Jacob and I would like to be together, but if you feel uncomfortable about it, then we'll stop seeing each other.'

'As long as you and Dad don't get back together.'

'Why do you say that?'

'We were a lot happier when he wasn't here.'

'Lily, darling, I know he's hurt you by being away, but he's still your dad and he loves you. But no, Dad and I won't be getting back together.'

'He doesn't really love me. If he did, he would've been here more.'

This was a tricky one. She'd often wondered the same thing. 'You know, Lily, grown-ups make mistakes sometimes. We don't always know the best way to be parents. And I think Dad regrets his mistakes and wants to know you. But it's your choice. No one will force you into anything.'

'It's so boring when I'm with him.'

'I think he just doesn't know enough about your life, darling. It will get better.'

'Jacob's nice, Mum. If you want to date him, you should.'

'I'd like to.' The latent worry that he might leave remained, but again, she told herself to trust him.

'Can we play a game now?' Lily asked, taking the Switch.

'Just one, then bed.'

* * *

Ingrid sat in the bay window of her bedroom while she dialled Matt's number. The call was cut almost immediately, which meant that he'd probably seen it was her and rejected it. She tried again but got the same.

For God's sake, the man was making it impossible to communicate. Should she send him a text or an email? But what on earth would it say? No, she had to speak to him.

She would try again.

But for now, she called Jacob, who picked up on the first ring.

'Hey,' he said, his voice sleepy.

'Did I wake you?'

'No, but I was just about to go to sleep.'

'So I spoke to Lily about us.'

She heard the rustle of cotton. 'You did?' His voice was instantly alert.

'You told me that this wasn't temporary, and my sisters know now. It's a matter of time before other people know and I wanted her to hear it from me. I tried to call Matt too, but the bastard isn't taking my calls.'

'That's a big step.'

Her heart thundered in her chest. Did that mean she shouldn't have done it?

'I'm happy you finally trust what I've been telling you, Ingrid.'

She did, didn't she? Otherwise she would have sworn her sisters to secrecy and carried on. It was time to take this type of risk in her life.

'Um, there's something else I want to float past you.'

Ingrid had warmed to her somewhat insane idea. She would be killing several birds with one stone, but it was also possible that she could kill this relationship before it even had a chance to get started. Could Jacob handle the full force of the Pereras?

'Okay.'

'My parents are having a fifty-fifth wedding anniversary party in a couple of weeks and I was wondering if you wanted to come with us. Obviously, you can say no. I mean, Audrey is a pussycat compared to Mum. I just thought that telling my parents about you with loads of people around might mean Mum couldn't freak out,' said Ingrid, a little embarrassed.

'I'll be there,' said Jacob without hesitation.

Ingrid was in shock. She'd braced herself to do a little persuading and then drop the whole thing. 'Did you just say yes?'

'I told you many times that this isn't temporary. I can't wait to meet your parents.'

Ingrid couldn't help snorting. 'You might change your mind about that. I warn you, it won't be easy. And you'll meet all the nosy aunties and uncles desperate to know who my boyfriend is.'

'So I'm your boyfriend now?'

Ingrid recoiled at the word. 'I know, it sounds ridiculous at my age, doesn't it?'

'I like it.'

'Yeah?'

'Yeah. And don't worry about the party. I've got your back.'

So much confidence. The poor lamb had no idea about Florence Perera.

28

You Get Less Time for Murder

Ingrid stared wistfully at the car as the valet climbed in and drove off to park it. Grace, looking elegant in a wine-coloured satin dress, glanced at her, checking once again whether Ingrid wanted to go through with this madcap idea. The truth was that ever since she'd made the decision, she'd thought of countless ways to backtrack, not least because Matt hadn't been taking her calls, so she hadn't even told him. But with both her sisters questioning her sanity, she couldn't back out now.

Jacob stood next to her, looking sleek in a tuxedo, and Lily was decked out in a deep red sequinned dress accessorised with what she called her Dorothy ruby-red glitter shoes. After agonising over an outfit, Ingrid had settled on a deep pink off-the-shoulder mermaid dress that hugged her curves and flared out at the hem, and she knew that she'd picked the right thing when she saw Jacob's appreciative gaze as she opened the door to him. They couldn't waste all this effort by listening to her instincts, which were screaming at her to head to the nearest McDonald's drive-thru instead of staying for the hotel's rubber chicken at seventy pounds per head.

Despite the slightly cooler September air, Ingrid's palms were clammy. All the changes she was bringing into her life seemed so straightforward in theory, but were accompanied by heart-pounding fear. She turned away as if looking for the way to the party and took the opportunity to breathe deeply, trying to calm her anxious heart.

Jacob's arm snaked around her waist and pulled her back against him as he lowered his mouth to her right ear.

'We're in this together,' he said.

She covered his hand with her own and nodded.

'I mean it. I've got you.'

He'd said this before and she knew from experience that he meant it, but there was little he would be able to do to protect her from everyone's judgement. Probably sensing her discomfort, Grace sidled up to them.

'Last chance to cut and run, Sis. Are you sure about this?'

Ingrid stepped out of Jacob's embrace and shook herself. She couldn't be worried about the opinions of others, even her own family. They weren't the ones living her one and only life. She had to dig deep for her stores of courage. She would face this. Ignoring the significant part of her that was saying 'absolutely not', she rolled back her shoulders.

'Go big or go home,' she replied, with what she hoped would pass for a smile.

'What about you, Jacob?' Grace asked in one last effort to avoid Armageddon.

'If Ingrid's up for it, then so am I.'

'I knew I should've invested in a flak jacket,' said Grace as she followed them into the hotel lobby.

Florence Perera had been in sole charge of all the arrangements for tonight and it looked like Thatha had relinquished any hope of maintaining a budget. Things had probably begun to spiral out of control when Mum had booked The Grove, a luxury hotel just outside of Watford with a sweeping driveway, lush championship golf course and upscale entertainment spaces. The florist's bill alone was probably higher than Ingrid's monthly mortgage. Tropical flower displays had been placed in the centre of each table and strings of deep pink orchids fell from the ceiling. Mum clearly thought it was her wedding.

Florence stood in the centre of the dance floor wearing an oyster satin floor-length dress, every inch the bride. Audrey's son, Freddy, was in tow, looking handsome in his tuxedo and no doubt being introduced as the Cambridge graduate who'd overcome the uselessness of his English literature degree to study law. Freddy had adopted the usual frozen smile required for all of Florence's meet-and-greets at these things, his eyes occasionally wandering wistfully towards the bar. They were surrounded by a variety of fawning aunties in a selection of jewel-toned saris and dresses.

Florence's eyes rested on Ingrid a matter of seconds after they'd entered the room, darting immediately to her and Jacob's clasped hands, then to the proximity of Lily and Grace, both clearly at ease with him. Florence's eyes narrowed and she nodded absently to the person speaking to her, her entire body tensing as Lily held Jacob's free hand.

Ingrid tracked her mother's gaze, which quickly moved across the room as if she was looking for someone. Aunty Colleen no doubt, who could be relied upon to be the most vocal in her outrage. She watched her mum's eyes dart to and fro until they found their target. Ingrid glanced across to see who Florence Perera was most concerned about.

Oh my God. What the hell was Matt doing here? Ingrid felt rooted to the spot as he pinned her with a stare that took in both her and Jacob, his face incandescent with rage. *Shit.* Without looking away, Ingrid extracted her phone from her clutch bag and gestured to it, as if to explain, but Matt wasn't looking receptive.

What on earth had her mother been thinking to have invited him there when she knew that they were divorcing? This should not be happening. She tried to take a deep breath, but her heart was racing.

'My girls!' said Thatha, breaking the unbearable tension as he approached them from behind. He pulled at his collar, clearly uncomfortable in black tie. His jacket was a little too big for him, the trousers a little baggy, but Ingrid could see the shadow of the handsome young man he'd once been. It was hard to believe that he was the same person that featured in Mum's stories about how he would come to visit her at university, always accompanied by a gaggle of admirers.

Grace gave him a warm hug while Ingrid waited her turn, taking furtive glances at Matt, trying to prepare for his advance. Thatha's eyes widened as he saw Jacob next to Lily.

Ingrid embraced her father, feeling the curiosity burning in him. 'This is Jacob, Thatha. He's my . . . boyfriend.'

'It's good to meet you, Mr Perera. Thanks for inviting me,' said Jacob, shaking Thatha's hand, knowing full well that it was Ingrid who'd extended the invitation.

Thatha looked around for his wife, clearly checking to see if he'd been spotted exchanging pleasantries with someone whom she'd consider the enemy.

'Um . . . yes, of course, you're very welcome,' he said, eyes still searching the room before settling on Ingrid. 'She knows?'

This had been a terrible idea, but it had been hers and now she had to see it through. 'Let's just say that she's finding out around the same time as you.'

'You thought that was a good idea?'

'I know, I know. Believe me,' she replied, instinctively scoping out the exits.

'Seeiya!' Lily exclaimed, hugging her grandfather. 'Can I take Jacob to meet Millie and Harry at the chocolate fountain? Mum says I have to wait until dinner's over, but it's a party and that's boring.'

'Of course, putha,' said Thatha. 'Do you mind?' he asked Jacob.

Jacob checked with Ingrid who nodded. 'Not at all. It was nice meeting you. And happy anniversary.'

Dad smiled warmly as they skipped away.

'Is that man Ingrid's toy boy?' shouted someone at a nearby

table. Her attempt to speak above the volume of the music meant her comments were broadcast to everyone in the vicinity. 'I heard she's getting a divorce from that other one, shame on her. Look at Florrie, acting like the queen over there, dragging that poor boy around. What does she have to boast about? A failed doctor, a failed musician . . .' she was counting these points on her fingers, her head shaking from side to side '. . . and now a failed marriage. I could never hold a big shindig like this considering all that . . . It's embarrassing. Here, pass me some of those vol-au-vents.'

Thatha pulled them away from the table. 'You'll always get people like that.'

Ingrid could never understand why her parents kept people like that in their circle of friends. Always sour-faced and ready to drip condescension and criticism in equal measure, their opinions were the reason why her mother went over the top with her celebrations, as if something swanky enough would prevent the negative comments.

Despite knowing all this, their words stung.

'You shouldn't let them bother you. Know that I'm proud of all three of you. So is your mother, it just comes out a little differently with her. Why don't you both go over there and get a drink. You'll need one,' Thatha said, pointing to the bar.

'Love you, Thatha,' said Grace kissing him on the cheek.

He grinned, thrilled. 'Love you both too. Where's your sister?'

Audrey was never on time to these things, as though she wanted to get it all over and done with as quickly as possible by staying for the least amount of time. And who could blame her? In her parents' friends' eyes, she was the doctor who couldn't hack the cut and thrust of the medical world. The comment that they'd just heard was the tip of the iceberg compared to some of the things people had said to her face.

'Not here yet,' said Ingrid. 'Happy anniversary. Fifty-five years is quite an achievement, isn't it?'

'You know you get less time for murder,' he said with a

wink. It was a well-worn joke in their family but sometimes Mum was so much that it was a little too on the nose. 'So, he seems . . .'

'Nice?' Ingrid supplied a possible adjective.

'Young.'

'He's younger. But not immature.'

'And Lily likes him.'

'And he likes her.'

'And you're sure?'

'I am.'

'Okay then, see you later.' He sauntered off, shaking hands with random uncles as he passed, looking back occasionally.

Ingrid tugged on Grace's arm. 'How long do you reckon until Armageddon?' Ingrid asked.

'As long as it takes her to get away from that lot.'

Ingrid held onto her sister. 'You promised you'd have my back.'

Grace's eyes shifted from left to right, planning her escape. 'Did I?'

'Grace!'

'Fine, fine, I'll try.'

Ingrid spotted Matt again and cringed. 'I really wasn't expecting him to be here.'

Grace almost choked on the strawberry macaron she'd just stuffed into her mouth as she finally noticed Matt. 'Why is *he* here? Did you invite him? Oh wait, it's Mum, right? I might have to rethink that backup promise, Sis. I hadn't factored Matt into the equation. He looks so pissed off.'

'He's been avoiding and ignoring me for the past two weeks. I've been trying to tell him about Jacob, just so he knew – not because of today. It never occurred to me that Mum would invite him *here*.'

'What is he playing at?' Grace looked over Ingrid's shoulder. 'Oh . . . incoming in about five, four, three, two . . .'

'What on earth do you think you're doing?' Florence hissed from behind Ingrid, who whirled around to find her mother scowling at her. Her hands were so tightly balled into fists that Ingrid was sure the diamond ring on her finger was cutting off her circulation.

'Happy anniversary, Ammi,' said Ingrid, trying to muster up a smile.

Grace stepped a little behind her as Jacob returned at that moment with Lily, who was armed with a bowl of marshmallows and strawberries that he'd helped her dip into chocolate.

'This is Jacob.' She took a deep breath. She'd come this far, she might as well say it. 'My boyfriend. He's an investment banker.' She really hoped that Jacob would understand the introduction by profession as a requirement for most South Asian parents.

Jacob extended his hand to Florence and flashed one of his megawatt smiles. 'Thank you so much for inviting me, Mrs Perera. It's lovely to meet you. I can see where your daughters get their beauty from.'

Jacob, of course, knew that he hadn't been invited by her mother, but clearly he'd picked up on Ingrid's cue re the best way to defuse her.

Florence hesitated, not completely immune to Jacob's charm. 'It's nice to meet you too and I'm glad you could come. Did Ingrid say you're an investment banker?'

Ingrid exchanged a smile with Grace.

'Yes, that's right.'

'Which bank?'

Jacob was a professional at this because he didn't even stop to look at Ingrid. 'I was at Morgan Stanley in Singapore for a while and I've recently moved here.'

Ingrid released the breath she'd been holding. Her mother didn't need to know about Jacob's plans, whatever they might be.

Florence looked suitably impressed and she visibly softened towards him. 'It must be a bit of a culture shock coming back.'

Jacob put his arm around Ingrid's waist, Florence's sharp

eyes noticing. 'A little, but Ingrid, Lily and Grace have really helped with that.'

'They have?' As her gaze alighted on Ingrid and Grace in turn, the all too familiar annoyance was clearly displayed in her features.

'Aachi, you look so beautiful!' Lily exclaimed, trying to balance both her chocolate bowl and a large glass of the cola that Ingrid usually banned in their home. Florence kept a close eye on both in case they ended up covering her dress. 'Jacob's great, isn't he? Although he still can't beat me at Mario Kart even though he claims he's been playing it for years.'

'Really?' Florence responded, her smile tight. 'Lily, Jacob, would you mind if I had a word with my daughters alone? I just want to ask them their advice on something.'

Jacob squeezed her waist and she watched them go.

Florence's gaze followed them as they chatted like old friends, and then turned to her daughters, aware of several sets of eyes on her.

'You two certainly have been busy, haven't you? You aren't even divorced yet and here you are flaunting another man in front of everyone,' said Mum with a tight smile.

'I'm not flaunting anything.' She sort of was. 'I just wanted the person I'm seeing to meet you all.'

Florence rolled her eyes. 'And you thought that this was the most appropriate place for that? What has got into you, putha? You've been acting unhinged lately.'

Ingrid glanced at Grace who shrugged. She was sure that she was not the only one who had been acting unhinged lately. Still.

'Do you think I'm unhinged because I'm living my life without worrying about what you or anyone else has to say?' Wasn't Ingrid the one who'd been doing just that moments ago?

A few people nearby had begun to pay attention to their conversation – something that wasn't lost on her mother who smiled and laughed falsely as though she were in an amateur dramatic performance rather than talking to her children. Ingrid wasn't in the mood to play along. She crossed her arms.

'Why is Matt here?'

'He's your husband.'

'Not for much longer. You know we're divorcing.'

'People don't need to know that.'

'Why did you invite him here?'

'You should be trying to get him back, not cavorting with some child.'

'Ammi, stop. People can hear you,' said Grace glancing around to confirm that many people were indeed listening to them.

Ingrid's mind worried at her mother's last comment. 'Ammi, I know we're here to celebrate your long marriage with Thatha, but not everyone gets there. Some relationships come to a natural end and that's where Matt and I are now. And please don't insult Jacob. He's a grown man with a steady job. And yes, he's younger than me, but that's our business, not yours.'

'He's lovely, Ammi. You should be happy that she's found someone who appreciates her and Lily. And haven't you noticed all the aunties fawning over him? He's pretty handsome,' said Grace.

Ingrid squeezed her sister's hand in gratitude.

'And you . . .' Florence began.

'Ammi, leave her alone. It's me that you're annoyed with, not Grace. Jacob is a good, kind man and he likes Lily.'

'You're still married.'

'In name only.'

Florence huffed, but was unable to say anything due to Matt's arrival.

'You should talk to your *husband*,' said Florence, grabbing Grace's arm. Grace tried to squirm out of her grasp, but Mum held firm and tugged her. 'Don't make a scene,' she hissed as she pulled Grace away.

Grace shot Ingrid an apologetic look. Ingrid nodded

in understanding – it was impossible to withstand the gravitational pull of a mother in high dudgeon.

Since when had Matt owned a tuxedo? He'd gone to every other function that had required black tie in a lounge suit while railing about the excesses of the bourgeoisie before returning to their bougie house in Pinner. She had to admit that he looked good in it. But he'd also developed a real love of scarves because, once again, he'd accessorised with a dark burgundy silk one.

'We need to talk . . . *darling*,' he said, casting a glance at their audience of aunties and uncles who smelled the chum in the water as they gathered around them.

His hand clamped hard around her forearm, his eyes flashing with anger, his smile menacing. He tugged, but she stood her ground and shrugged his hand off her.

'Funnily enough that's why I've been calling you for the past two weeks. Follow me.'

She didn't look back to see his no doubt shocked face and stalked out of the room.

29

Face Off

Taylor Swift's 'Karma' played in the background as Ingrid stared at Matt. How dare he grab her like that?

'What the hell is he doing here?' Matt practically spat the words in her face.

Ingrid extracted her phone and showed him the fifty-seven rejected calls she'd made to him over the past two weeks.

'If you'd bothered to answer any one of my calls, then we wouldn't be having this conversation here, would we? Why did you reject them all?'

'Because I didn't want to speak to you.'

'What if something had happened to Lily? You need to pick up, Matt. I don't care if you hate me, but you're still her father.'

'And as her father, didn't I have the right to know about this man before you brought him here?'

'Why do you think I've been calling you? And why are you here?'

The door behind them opened and Jacob appeared.

'Everything alright?' he asked.

'It's fine,' said Ingrid.

'I knew you weren't just a *work colleague*,' Matt shouted, jabbing his finger at Jacob.

'He's my boyfriend, Jacob,' said Ingrid, keen to keep this between herself and Matt.

'Yeah, *boy* is about right. How old are you? You're such a fucking cliché, Ingrid. Trying to regain your lost youth, are you?'

Jacob was about to speak but Ingrid pushed herself forward into Matt's line of sight. Maybe it was the shock of having Matt manhandle her in that way, maybe it was the anger over him thinking that behaviour was acceptable, maybe she'd had enough of people in her life thinking that she could be pushed around to do their bidding and think what they wanted her to, but she wasn't standing for it any longer.

She didn't need anyone to protect her or speak for her. She saw Jacob take a step back, his eyes on her as if to say that he was there if she needed him.

'Don't speak to me like that, Matt. Whatever you might think of me, I'm the mother of our child and we spent fifteen years together. I don't deserve it. And I can promise you that if you ever touch me like that again, I'll call the police and have you arrested for assault.'

She moved forward into his personal space and the look on her face must have been so unfamiliar, so fierce, that he took a step back.

'Yes, Jacob is my boyfriend and if that makes me a cliché, so be it. But that's my business.'

'You look very pleased with yourself for an adulterer,' said Matt.

Ingrid laughed. 'Are you joking?'

'We're still married.'

'It's interesting that you didn't feel that way when you were enjoying sex so much with other women over the past year – not to mention in all the years before.'

She saw Jacob tense in her peripheral vision.

'We were on a break last year and there was no one before.'

'Who's the cliché now, Ross Geller? *You* were on a

break, Matt. I was still living my life here, with Lily. And seriously, don't insult my intelligence. I know what you were up to.'

'You lied to me when I came to the house that time,' he growled, clearly trying to reclaim the upper hand. 'You said you weren't seeing each other.'

'I didn't lie, Matt. We weren't together then.'

'Why did you bring him here?' he yelled. 'And how come he's so comfortable with Lily? You should be checking if that's alright with me first!'

'I tried!'

Ingrid knew she'd be annoyed if Matt introduced a new woman into Lily's life without telling her. He had a point, but he needed to pick up the damned phone.

'Jacob is here because he's a significant person in my life and this is a family event.' Although even she was currently questioning her judgement on that one. 'I tried to tell you about our relationship when it developed. But he met Lily before we became anything, actually on the same day you met him.'

'You know that he's too young for you,' Matt hissed, leaning into her.

This again. She did know. She worried about it every day, and there was a never-ending procession of people waiting to tell her the same thing. But she wasn't going to let Matt of all people tell her what was right for her. He'd left her alone for a year and been emotionally absent for years before that. He'd never been satisfied with the life that they'd built together, never asked her what she wanted out of her life, constantly pushing her to work harder while complaining about the time she spent doing it. Had he ever loved her? She wasn't sure that he had. She'd been the next stop on his life journey until he found something better.

The now familiar anger began to burn through her and instead of pushing it down and out of the way, minimising her emotions, she let it rise.

'What exactly is your agenda here, Matt? You're the one who moved on more than a year ago. You're the one who wanted a divorce. What is it to you if I've found someone else? Why does his age matter?'

'Because you're making a fool of yourself,' he said, his lip curled. 'And I don't like him around my daughter.'

'Jacob is kind, intelligent, funny and wonderful with Lily. You're telling me that being with someone who is consistently there for me and my daughter makes me a fool? Where the hell were you for the past year, Matt? You abandoned us. *You're* the one who made a fool of me, but you'll be pleased to know I won't be letting that happen again. Ever. So don't stand there with a holier-than-thou attitude now.'

Matt sneered at her. 'It was your fault that I left in the first place. Haven't you considered that you were the one who was absent, Ingrid? You were always working or with Lily. There wasn't any room for me. Too tired for sex and when we did it, you were barely present. How was I supposed to live with that?'

She rolled her eyes. The reality was, he would never take any responsibility. He was such a child himself. Thirteen years younger, Jacob had already proved himself to be twice as mature.

'I'm not taking the blame for your bad behaviour, Matt,' she said, staring him down. 'I might've turned a blind eye over and over again, but don't mistake that for weakness. I just wanted to get on with my life. Not once was it my fault that you disappeared. So shut up.'

'Hear, hear,' boomed Audrey's voice from behind her as she clapped.

They whirled around to see Audrey and Nathan arriving late.

'I'm curious, Matt, why are you even here? Bored? Nothing to do? You know this is a family event, and now that you're divorcing my sister, you're not welcome,' said Audrey.

'Always interfering, aren't you?' Matt barked at Audrey.

'Always being an arsehole, aren't you?' Audrey snapped back. 'You should leave.'

Matt stared at her and sneered again. 'Your mother invited me. Apparently to her we'll always be family.'

'Well, she's wrong. You'll always be Lily's father, but you're not family anymore,' said Ingrid.

'I'm more family than he is,' said Matt, pointing to Jacob.

Nathan came over to shake Jacob's hand.

'Good to see you, Jacob,' said Nathan, using his other hand to clap him on the shoulder.

'You too, Nathan,' Jacob replied.

Matt's head ping-ponged between the two men. 'You know each other?'

'Of course they do,' said Audrey with a snort, as if it was obvious. 'He's my sister's boyfriend.'

Ingrid gave her sister a slight nod of thanks, grateful that she knew how to read the room.

'How come everyone else knew before I did?'

'They're my family. No one else knew.'

'Until you paraded him here.'

'How many times do I have to say it? Fifty-seven calls, Matt! Regardless, you should leave,' said Ingrid.

It was like watching the steam release from a pressure cooker as Matt fought with his feelings, choosing his next move. 'Fine, I'll go. But I'll be telling my lawyer all about this.'

'As will I,' said Ingrid.

Matt shot her a vicious look, then stalked off, knocking Nathan off balance as he did.

Grace emerged from the banqueting room in time to see Matt's retreating back. 'What's going on?'

'You okay?' Jacob asked Ingrid, pulling her close. 'That was a lot.'

She shivered a little as the shock set in.

'I've never seen you like that with him,' said Audrey with admiration. 'My little sister has grown up.'

'I've been grown up for some time. You just haven't noticed.'

The weight of Jacob's palm was calm and reassuring and she leaned into him. A small worry hovered at the edge of her consciousness. Was this all too much too soon for him? Did she simply have too much baggage for someone so young? But none of this was reflected in his expression. For someone who'd only been in her life for a few months, he seemed very much at ease with the situation.

'What did he say?' Grace asked.

'What was I doing here with Jacob? The usual obsession with his age.'

'If he'd answered any of your calls, he might have saved himself all that anguish,' said Audrey. 'It was fun to see him squirm a bit though. He's taken the piss with you for such a long time, he had it coming. Well done, Sis! I'm proud of you.'

Ingrid didn't feel too great. Yes, it felt good not to cave into Matt, but she'd wished things hadn't unfolded in this way.

'How's Mum? She must be fuming in there. I mean, everyone must've had a field day when you walked in together,' said Audrey.

'Yeah, something like that,' said Ingrid, now weary before the party had even started.

'Right then. United front it is,' said Audrey.

'Er, not sure if this is a good time to bring this up, but my friend Cassie just messaged me with this.' Grace held her phone up to Ingrid and they all crowded around her to see.

There was a photo of a shirtless Matt on the dating app Bumble. He'd been matched with Grace's friend Cassie, whom Ingrid knew to be in her late twenties. According to the few words on his profile, he was looking for fun. And his age preference ranged from twenty to thirty-five.

Ingrid laughed at the hypocrisy.

'Bastard!' said Audrey.

'Send me a screenshot for Cheska, will you?' Ingrid said. 'At least it will totally shut down any rabbit holes about relationships.'

'Done,' said Grace. She stared at Ingrid. 'Now I think we should go back in there before Mum comes out here.'

'We'll go first,' said Nathan, ushering Audrey and Grace into the hall as Jacob and Ingrid collected themselves. More guests straggled in past them, most of whom recognised Ingrid, giving her a wave and staring at the handsome man with his arms around her. The raised eyebrows assured her that she'd be the hot topic of conversation tonight.

The staff discreetly shuffled around them, carrying in trays of canapés and bottles of champagne, pretending not to have witnessed the argument that had just taken place.

Jacob had respected her space and her right to deal with her own problems, and now he reassured her with his embrace.

He kissed the side of her head. 'I can hear you thinking that this is all too much for me.'

She pulled back to look at his face. 'How do you do that?'

'Because I'm beginning to know you a little, Ingrid, and you're always more concerned about other people than yourself.'

'Maybe . . .'

'It's not all too much, you know. I knew what your situation was from the start. And I'm here.'

She nestled back into his chest. 'Thank you, Jacob. Really.'

Ingrid hugged him tighter for a moment, then put her hand in his and strolled back into the banqueting hall, which had filled up in her absence. They made their way to their designated table, where Mum sat with Lily, their backs to Ingrid, heads leaning together like two birds, engrossed in conversation. No one would win any prizes for guessing the topic.

'So you like this Jacob then?' Florence asked her granddaughter.

'Yep. He's really nice, Aachi. He takes us to cool places and plays games with me. And he makes Mum smile. She's been so sad for so long, I'd forgotten her real smile. You know, the one where her whole face lights up. She does that when he's around.'

Florence sat back in her seat, clearly nonplussed by Lily's unexpected insight and maturity.

'And you don't mind him being with Mum?'

Lily shrugged. 'Not really. He's nice.'

'And what about your dad?'

'Mum says that he'll always be my dad. But he's been gone for so long and he didn't even remember my birthday or me going to Year Seven and he's really hurt Mum. So . . .'

Florence stroked her granddaughter's hair. 'And what about your friends? Don't they say things about your parents getting divorced?'

Ingrid couldn't see Lily's face from where she was standing, but she could swear she could hear her daughter rolling her eyes.

'Aachi, *loads* of my friends' parents are divorced. It's not a big deal. Alicia says that I'll get two birthdays and Christmases and that both her parents try a lot harder to spend time with her now that they're divorced.'

Florence clasped Lily's hand in both of hers. 'Sweet girl. But don't you think that Jacob is so *young*?'

'But he's a boomer like you, Aachi.'

'He most certainly isn't.'

'Everyone older than me is a boomer, Aachi. Including Jacob.' Lily turned her head and spied Ingrid and Jacob behind them. 'Mum! What happened with Dad?'

'He had to leave, Lilypad. He's sorry about that.'

Lily nodded and Ingrid searched her daughter's

expression for sadness, but there was none. It wasn't her responsibility to mend Matt's relationship with Lily. All Ingrid could do was provide love, support and stability. A nagging doubt about Jacob worried at the edge of her consciousness, but now wasn't the time to entertain it. She pushed it away.

'Hey, Lils,' said Freddy, Millie and Harry in unison, clearly dispatched by their mother Audrey to keep their cousin company. 'Let's go and check out the magician.'

Was her mother hosting an anniversary or children's birthday party?

'Mum, can I?'

'Of course, darling. Enjoy.'

Lily rushed off with her cousins.

Florence examined Ingrid's expression, her visceral maternal instinct telling her that something was awry. 'What happened?'

Ingrid glanced at Lily and shook her head. 'You should go and be with your friends, Ammi.'

Florence approached her and cupped Ingrid's face with her palm. 'Are you alright?'

It was at moments like these, which were few and far between, when Ingrid felt the force of her mother's love. Too often, it was smothered under layers of concern about the opinions of others or her own expectations, but Ingrid had always known that this was Florence Perera's way of loving her daughters, of wanting their experiences in life to be better than hers, of trying to shield them from the pain of insecurity because of a lack of money, or exclusion because of the colour of their skin.

Ingrid nodded slowly, her eyes meeting her mother's. 'And Jacob was there to help me.' It wasn't strictly true, but it would help her old-fashioned mother appreciate him a little more.

Florence glanced at him. 'That's good,' she said. As she left them, she put her hand on Jacob's arm. 'Make sure you eat well, Jacob. And also, try and keep Lily from falling into that chocolate fountain.'

There was a beat before a surprised Jacob responded. 'Yes, Mrs Perera.'

30

Truths

Ingrid looked around the home that she'd shared with Matt. Unlike other couples, she couldn't say that they had built it together. They'd never gone to test out the comfort of sofas or tried out mattresses. Matt had decreed that Ikea was off-limits, so they hadn't crawled through the labyrinth becoming distracted by gadgets that seemed perfect in the moment but would remain in a drawer or cupboard once they made it home. They hadn't chosen the huge Venetian mirror that hung in the hallway, or the mirrored console table that rested beneath it. The only expression of their intertwined lives lay in the photographs dusted around the house in discoloured silver-plated frames. Or the detritus of their daily lives: the unopened envelopes by the front door, Lily's trip-hazard trainers lying abandoned at the foot of the stairs, a forgotten jumper draped over the back of a kitchen chair, a collection of clothes on the bedroom floor.

Unlike previous homes, she didn't see the spot where her waters had broken, or where she and Matt had curled up on the sofa to watch the latest television series, or the corner of the living room where he'd dropped to one knee and asked her to marry him. All those memories had been left in those places as they'd moved on. As though every new home papered over the images, obscuring them, making them both forget what they'd once shared. In the year that he'd been gone, his presence had also faded into the background as his things were tidied away in boxes so that Ingrid couldn't see and smell them, couldn't remember that he'd abandoned her. And Grace had replaced him. It was strange that in that short time, she'd left more of an indelible stamp of herself on this house than Matt ever had.

Ingrid switched on the kitchen digital radio, letting the sounds of jazz fill the room. She rubbed her wrist where Matt had grabbed her, a bruise beginning to form. With his actions, his words, and the dating profile that Grace had shown her, it was becoming easier to take Michelle Obama's high road. Matt was becoming pitiful in her mind.

Jacob padded around the kitchen, clearing up the empty cups from the hot chocolate that Lily had insisted they all drank as soon as they'd got home. He had an easy, calming presence, the polar opposite of Matt. He didn't hover, waiting for her reaction or to provoke one. He let her be alone in her thoughts, staying in the background, wordlessly telling her that he was there for her. She couldn't understand how they were at this stage so soon. It had only been a month since they'd agreed to take this relationship further and now he'd been introduced to her entire family, he was involved in all their drama and still wasn't showing the slightest sign of bolting. Was it all too good to be true? Ingrid was old enough to know that there was always a tipping point in relationships. That moment from which there was no return. Would it be soon for them?

'I think that Lils might be in a chocolate-fountain-induced coma,' said Grace, popping her head into the kitchen. 'I'm heading off to bed too. See you both in the morning.' They heard her trudge up the stairs to her room.

Jacob raised an eyebrow at Ingrid. 'I'm staying over?'

Grace's casual comment was an indicator of how quickly family opinion seemed to have turned for them, but it also released something from within Ingrid. A heaviness lifted from her chest. However much she might tell herself that she needed to free herself from the weight of other people's opinions, she still cared. With Grace's words in her ears, she could take another step closer to him with a lighter heart.

'Aren't you?' Ingrid asked.

Jacob watched her for a moment, then came up behind her and hugged her, his hands clasping around her stomach, his chin resting on her shoulder. 'If it's alright with you. We'll go at your pace.'

She turned to face him, resting her hands on his shoulders. 'I'd like us to sleep together. But I mean actually sleep, not a euphemism for sex.'

He chuckled. 'I'd like that too. You went through a lot this evening.' He smoothed a loose strand of hair back against her head. 'You must be exhausted. Do you want to go straight to bed?'

She nodded. 'I really need to get this dress off,' she said, clutching at the sides of it. 'I could barely breathe in it before I left and now after all the food and champagne, I feel like a zeppelin.'

Jacob took an exaggerated breath. 'You look amazing in that dress, but I'd prefer you breathing, so I'd be more than happy to help you out of it, even though I know that it's going to test me.'

'Thank you for saying that,' said Ingrid. As a middle-aged woman, she spent a lot of her time beating herself up about her changing body, but Jacob didn't judge her in the same way at all. His compliments lit up parts of her that had remained dormant for so long.

'Let's go.' She took his hand and led him out of the kitchen, into the hallway and up the stairs to her room, stopping before they entered. Although they'd spent time together in a bed in New York, this was something quite different. It was a step into her space, another move further into her life. She wasn't sure that it was as momentous for him, but she collected herself before pushing the door open and walking in.

Jacob looked around, no doubt taking in the decorator's

choice of dark blue walls, crystal chandelier over the bed and super-king-sized bed facing the window that looked out over the back garden. The door to the en suite was ajar, revealing the tale of Ingrid's frenzied preparation for the party, with towels strewn on the floor, makeup scattered around the edge of the basin, and lip-imprinted tissues that had missed the bin.

He approached her back and wordlessly began to unzip her dress, pressing a soft kiss to her shoulder as he did so.

'Wow,' he said as the zip reached its limit and he had a full view of the pale pink bustier and matching underwear that Ingrid had squeezed herself into with Grace's help. 'You should've warned me what was under there.'

All Ingrid had been able to think about was the relief she would feel when she was released from the dress's confines. She hadn't given a thought to Jacob's reaction. She blushed, placing her cool hand against her hot cheek.

'I promise, no mixed signals. I didn't think.' She bit her lip. 'I'm so sorry about this, but I'm going to need some help getting out of this too. There are so many hooks and eyes I can't do it on my own.'

Jacob gulped as his fingers brushed her skin and he began to detach each mooring. Every touch melted another part of her resolve, but this wasn't the right time to take the next step with him. Not with her daughter and sister sleeping down the hallway. She clutched the front of her dress to her and headed to the safety of the bathroom, grabbing her pyjamas on the way.

'Feel free to change and get into bed,' she said, instantly aware that Jacob had nothing to change into other than the sweatshirt and pants that he'd lent her when they'd first met.

He smiled and pulled off his tie, beginning to unbutton his shirt. She swiftly turned and ducked into the en suite.

When Ingrid emerged from the bathroom half an hour later, feeling more like herself after scrubbing off her makeup and showering, she fully expected Jacob to have dozed off while waiting for her, but he was sitting up, propped on pillows, reading the book that she'd left beside her bed. She blushed for two reasons. The first was that her reading material over the past year had been heavily *Bridgerton* influenced. She liked the steamy historical romances, which were so far removed from her everyday existence. And if she couldn't experience heart-pounding passion in the flesh, she could at least partially satisfy its absence by reading about it. The second reason for her blush was that it was the first time that she'd seen Jacob without a shirt. He was lean, with defined abs and pectoral muscles. Was she gaping?

He shut the book with a thud as she climbed into bed next to him. 'So that hasn't helped to calm me down. I'm seeing a whole new side to you, Ingrid Perera.'

She plucked the book from his fingers and replaced it on her bedside table. 'Are you judging my reading material?'

'Appreciating, not judging.' He pulled her to rest her head on his chest. 'How are you feeling after tonight?'

Ingrid sighed. 'My family's a lot, huh?'

'Aren't all families?'

'I suppose so.'

Jacob rubbed her shoulder. 'Has Matt always been like that?'

Ingrid looked up into his eyes. 'I tried to ignore it for so many years, but yes, I guess he has. I just didn't want to see it.'

Jacob stroked her hair. 'He says some nasty stuff to you.'

'I can handle it,' she said, feeling the liberating truth of her statement. 'But I have to admit that some of his comments hit home. I mean, I love being with you, but why are you with *me*, Jacob? There must be so many younger, more suitable women out there for you.'

He placed his hands gently on both sides of her face. 'Physically, I'd find you attractive at any age, but I also like that you know who you are and you're straightforward. There's no guessing games or wordplay and you're funny, intelligent and compassionate. And when I kiss you, it's like the rest of the world fades away and it's just the two of us. And I've never felt anything like that before in my life.'

Could words melt you? Her face flushed.

'I mean it,' he said, bending to kiss her.

He was right. Their kisses were unlike anything else that Ingrid had experienced. He lowered her flat onto the bed, their legs tangled together. She'd been explicit about not wanting sex tonight and she knew that he'd heard her and would soon stop, but she didn't want to get carried away herself and have their first night together be tainted by their interaction with Matt. She pulled away.

'So, about the sex thing,' said Ingrid, sitting up to look at him. 'It's not that I don't enjoy it, like Matt said. It's just been so long since it happened. And I really want to. But after tonight . . .'

'I understand. It'll happen at the right time. And I know you haven't been sure about jumping into a relationship so soon after deciding to divorce. I won't push you.'

'Why exactly are you waiting like this? Most men would run.'

He clasped her hand. 'Because I know that what we have is pretty rare and if I didn't, I'd regret it for the rest of my life. People always talk about bad timing, but I think that's just a form of giving up. If something is worth it, you owe it to yourself to give it a shot and to work out all the logistics between you.'

'And by logistics, you mean imminent jobs in New York?'

'We'll work it out, Ingrid.'

He leaned over to kiss her. Soft and reassuring.

'I need to go up to the Lakes next Friday to see a lawyer about my brother's estate. Would you come with me? I thought we could stay at the cottage and maybe visit my mum.'

Was this how Jacob had felt when she'd invited him to their major family party? She was a grown woman. Why was she so nervous? Perhaps because she might be closer in age to Jacob's mother than she was to him . . .

'Would your mum be up to meeting a new girlfriend? Especially one my age?'

'Of course she will. And if she thinks that you're likely to keep me here, she'll welcome you with open arms.'

She wasn't sure if she should be spending the time away from Lily. But Jacob couldn't be the only person making all the effort in this new relationship of theirs.

'Okay.'

31

Snake in the Grass

It was a truth universally acknowledged that a woman who needed to leave work on time for a weekend away with her boyfriend, would be delayed at every turn by annoying tasks, major disasters and supercilious posh wankers. Ingrid walked back to her office after fighting the most recent fire with a junior who had sent confidential information to the wrong client, to find Tim Woodstock inside. Unlike a normal person who might have left upon finding the office empty, he was hovering around her desk, peering into her moleskin notebook, before leaning over and clearly trying to guess the password on her computer. She bit back the curse on her tongue and watched him for a moment more.

He extracted his phone from the inside pocket of his jacket and began to take photographs, his signet ring glinting in the desk light. Ingrid was a big fan of the clear desk policy as a rule, locking her computer even when she stepped away to get a coffee, always in anticipation of a moment like this. He was probably looking for the materials for the pitch in New York, which were stored away on a memory stick that she carried with her on a keychain. Tim was currently photographing her calculations of how she would be able to manage financially after her divorce. Ingrid decided to get some evidence of her own and took some photos of his snooping in case she might need them in the future.

'Can I help you?' she said from the doorway.

Tim jumped and dropped his phone. 'Ah, you're here. Chris asked me to check up on how the proposal was going.'

Ingrid leaned on the doorjamb, adopting as nonchalant a posture as possible. 'That's odd. I filled him in on it this morning.'

Tim sneered at her. 'Maybe he wanted me to verify. After all, it's a key proposal and he probably wants to make sure that you're not going to mess things up.'

Ingrid reminded herself that she didn't have to spend her entire time as a partner in this firm being grateful for the privilege of occupying the position. She'd earned her place and she was no longer going to let the likes of Tim Woodstock make her feel like she owed them.

Ingrid entered the room and picked up his phone from the floor, holding it to his face to unlock it. She glanced at the photo and then showed it to Tim. 'Then perhaps he should have sent someone a little more competent. This is my personal financial budgeting sheet.'

Tim grabbed the phone from her to see the photo for himself and was unable to hide his wince as he realised his mistake.

'I don't need to update you on anything, Tim. You're not involved in this proposal.'

'You know that you're only doing it because your boyfriend persuaded Chris to let you do it.'

Ingrid stared at him. Did he know about Jacob? But how would he be relevant? Jacob didn't persuade Chris to give her the chance for the pitch. Realisation smacked her in the face and she laughed.

'You mean Trent?'

'Of course. Why else would he be sniffing around you? It's obvious that you're sleeping with him. Frankly, it's despicable how some of you women think that's the only way to get ahead at work.'

The old Ingrid would have walked away from this misogynist idiot, not wanting to create waves. But that was not who she was anymore.

'It must be so hard for someone like you to adapt to a changing world, Tim. It'll come as a bit of a surprise for you but, women can be good at their jobs too, and in my case, I'm much better than you are.'

'You haven't denied sleeping with him.'

'I don't need to dignify your wild accusations with an answer, but even if I were, it would be none of your business.'

Tim stepped closer to Ingrid. 'You know, Ingrid, if you were looking for a little extracurricular, you could've come to me. I imagine someone as uptight as you are in the office would be wild between the sheets.' To her absolute disgust, he stroked her cheek.

Ingrid smacked his hand away. It wasn't the first time that someone had touched her inappropriately in the office. When she'd started work in the late nineties, there'd been comments about the length of her skirts, the opacity of her blouses, stray hands on her legs and her breasts, and many attempted kisses after a few too many in the pub on a Friday night after work. And she'd always been on the wrong end of the power dynamic, always unable to make a fuss. Things were different now.

'I'll give you a pass this time, Tim, because clearly you're stupid. But I'm warning you that if you *ever* touch me or say something like that to me again, *or* photograph my private documents, I'll report you. And honestly, the thought of being intimate with you makes me feel physically sick. Leave my office now.'

There was a knock at the door and Trent's head appeared round the frame. 'Hey!'

She rolled her eyes. He was the last person who she needed to be here right now.

'I see your . . . protector has arrived,' said Tim, giving her what he probably thought was a significant look.

'Come in, Trent. Tim was just leaving.'

'Yep. Leaving,' said Tim, sneering at them both and leaving the room. 'Remember what I said, Ingrid. The offer's there if you want it.'

She barked out a laugh. 'It'll be a cold day in hell, Timothy.'

'What was that about?' Trent asked, as soon as Tim was a safe distance down the corridor.

'That loathsome cretin was snooping around for details on the proposal while I was away from my desk. And after I caught him, he accused me of sleeping with you to help my career, after which he offered himself as tribute.'

'He what?'

'It's fine. I can handle the Tim Woodstocks of this world. Here I was thinking he was some evil mastermind when actually he's just a lecherous twat.'

'Shouldn't you report him?' Trent settled himself on the edge of Ingrid's desk.

'I'd rather beat him the old-fashioned way, by winning that pitch.'

'But what if he's doing it to other people? Who aren't as badass as you.'

She hadn't considered that. 'How about I document it and you do the same and if it happens again, I'll report him. I don't want anything to detract from my work right now.'

'Alright. I have to admit I'm a bit flattered that he thinks you might be interested in me.'

Ingrid raised her eyebrows at him in surprise, reminded of the Wendy Cope poem. Her life had been devoid of any interest from men for so long and now all of a sudden they were arriving like overdue buses.

'You know I see you as a trusted colleague, right?' Would she have seen him as more if Jacob hadn't arrived? Perhaps . . . But she'd waited so long for an ally in all of this that she wasn't keen to give it up.

'It's mutual,' he said, nonchalantly.

Jacob appeared at the doorway. 'Hey, are you nearly done? Oh, Trent, hi.'

'Hey, Jacob. You good?' Trent asked, standing and walking to the door.

'Great, thanks,' said Jacob, assessing the situation he'd walked into.

Trent looked between them. 'Ah, I see,' he said with a smile. 'Hope you both enjoy your weekend. See you next week.'

'Did I interrupt something?' asked Jacob as he watched Trent leave.

'I'll fill you in on the way. I've just got to put all my stuff away and I'll be good to go.'

Jacob watched Ingrid for a moment and, looking up from her desk, she was surprised that for the first time in their relationship he was the one who looked insecure. She pulled him to her and kissed him on the cheek, leaving an imprint of both her lipstick and her intent.

32

The Next Step

Ingrid stepped into the hallway of the cottage that she'd visited three months ago and watched Jacob as he switched on lights, opened windows and took both of their bags into the master bedroom. He was so self-assured, exuding a calm goodness to which Ingrid was fast becoming addicted. Apart from the times when he made her heart race, he was so easy to be with, his quiet presence supportive and kind. She could really get used to this feeling of having someone to lean on. But what would she do if his mother didn't approve? Could she walk away?

She was more than a little nervous about meeting Jacob's mother, knowing that if she were in her position, she would struggle with this relationship. Ingrid knew that as a mother she often had to shield her daughter from her true thoughts, choosing her words carefully. And she was sure that Jacob's mother would be polite to Ingrid without showing Jacob her true feelings, keen not to alienate her only remaining son. Would it bother Jacob if his mother didn't approve? Would he even notice?

Jacob emerged from the bedroom with a key, which he used to unlock a cupboard in the hallway full of bottles of hand soap, shower gel, toothpaste, towels and even bedlinen.

'Wait, is this *your* cottage? You weren't renting it?' Ingrid asked with sudden realisation.

He extracted a large box from the base of the cupboard, which no doubt held all his favourite products, and carried it into the kitchen, setting it on the table, which was painted in white, of course.

'I bought it a couple of years ago when I came home for a visit. I rent it out, hence the cupboard. Why did you think it wasn't mine?'

Ingrid looked around at the space, which was totally devoid of any personality, let alone Jacob's. It all made sense now she knew that it was his rental property.

'There's hardly anything personal in here, you know? Like art or photographs.'

'Hmm. On purpose though. It's a bit weird to have personal stuff up in a rental.'

'Not even art?'

Jacob sat on the edge of the kitchen table and crossed his arms. 'Do you think it needs some?'

'Maybe some photos of the Lakes or the hills?'

Jacob pulled her to stand between his legs. 'I like that. How about we pop into Keswick tomorrow and see if we can find some?'

She put her arms around his neck. 'Sounds good. But what if we have really different taste?'

'I'm pretty indifferent to art, so you can pick whatever you think is best.'

'You trust my judgement?'

'Implicitly. Besides, I assessed the data, which tells me that you're a smart woman with good taste and I wouldn't go wrong leaving decisions like that to you.'

'Hey, don't judge me by *my* house. I didn't choose anything there. In fact, I'm sure that Matt slept with our interior designer in the bed that she sourced for us.'

'You're joking, right?'

She shook her head.

He caressed her face. 'You know I thought he was an idiot before I met him, but now that I have *and* I hear

243

stuff like this, I may have to downgrade his status to total arsehole.'

She pressed her forehead to his. 'Mr Jacob Ellis, to date, I've never heard you use language like that.'

'I save it for people who deserve it. And he really does. But I have to admit that I'm grateful he's too stupid to realise what a good person he had, because you're here with me now.' He slowly swiped across her bottom lip with his thumb. 'And you're easily the sexiest woman I've ever met.'

He pulled her into a hug. He was warm and solid against her, and she felt her shoulders relax as she told herself to be in the moment and stop thinking about all the things that could go wrong. Here, in the present, she could enjoy the simplest yet most glorious parts of life, like a rain shower, or the smell of freshly brewed coffee, or Jacob's warmth seeping into her skin.

He extracted his phone from the back pocket of his jeans. 'Selfie?'

Ingrid inclined her head towards Jacob, who kissed her on the cheek as he took the photo. As with all millennials, he took several shots, which was infinitely more sensible than Ingrid's usual one-and-done that invariably pictured her with her eyes shut or out of focus.

'Can you send that to me?' Ingrid asked, thinking that a photo of them together would be something she could pull out whenever the doubts struck.

'Done,' said Jacob. 'I'm going to print that out and frame it.'

'Ditto.'

'We're official now,' he teased. 'You're stuck with me.'

She laughed. 'You're crazy, sticking with *me* even though my family's nuts.'

'I like them,' he said, pulling her close.

She rolled her eyes in disbelief. Sometimes even she wasn't sure *she* could put up with her family.

'No, seriously. You all love each other so fiercely. Maybe

sometimes that comes out in a negative way, but the intention is good.' He looked away, perhaps thinking of his own family, and started unloading from the box. 'Hey, why don't you call Lily while I unpack all of this. I'll get some dinner started, then maybe we can just chill?'

How did she deserve this man? Perhaps she took her family for granted. Her parents' long, stable marriage, her sisters with their strength and insight, even their interference. It was all love.

Jacob extracted toiletries and thick fluffy towels and went about the cottage putting everything in its designated spot. Time and again he'd shown her that he was serious about them, from taking care of her and her daughter to interacting with her family, and still she'd doubted their relationship. Because of what? Her insecurities about her age, her imminent divorce?

The most important things were good between them. As she watched him pack away groceries, reaching for a high shelf, the muscles in his back evident through the thin fabric of his T-shirt, she knew that she was ready to take the next step.

Ingrid thought about the black lace lingerie that Grace had packed in her bag. Perhaps her sister knew her better than she knew herself. But she was so out of practice that she had no idea how to initiate things. All she could do right now was hope that the temperature between them would be anything but chilled.

As Ingrid watched Jacob's hips sway to the music playing in the kitchen while he cooked, her skin heated. She was so nervous that her palms were a little clammy and she reached for a tea towel to wipe them. What if young people had sex differently? After all, Matt had enjoyed it so much more with other younger women than with vanilla Ingrid. Should she have paid more attention to those sex position games they played on *Love Island*?

No, it wasn't that difficult. She'd had plenty of sex in her life, even if the past two years had been entirely solo and battery-powered.

She looked at the piles of chopped herbs and vegetables in tiny bowls, the chicken that had been diced into precise cubes and tossed in a sauce that Jacob had probably made himself, and she knew that she had to wait a little longer. She grabbed the glass of water on the counter and gulped it down, while Jacob stirred something on the stove.

She approached him and put her arms around his waist, resting the side of her face against his back.

Jacob turned down the heat on the stove and faced her, placing his hands on her hips. He looked her up and down.

'This outfit . . .' he said, adding a low whistle.

'What about it?' she asked, glad that the navy dress with its tight skirt with a thigh-high split and very deep V-neck was having the desired effect.

'How am I supposed to concentrate on cooking dinner when you're wearing that?'

'This old thing?' It was brand new, of course. An item like that wouldn't have had a place in her wardrobe prior to Jacob.

He bent to kiss her neck, inhaling her scent. Then he moved her to one of the stools and perched her onto it, retreating to the other side of the kitchen where an open bottle of red breathed.

'Wine?' he asked.

'Please.'

She looked out of the kitchen window at the lush rolling hills as she heard the glug of wine into a glass. 'How did you leave here? Living in a place like this is good for the soul.'

'It loses some of its charm when you don't have money. And in some ways it's no different to London with the reams of tourists.' He stirred the sauce and looked out of the window. 'Marcus loved it here, and the mountains generally. I suppose you could say he thought it was good for the soul too.'

'But not you?'

'As far back as I can remember, all I did was plan how I was going to leave. I wanted to see the world, to prove that I was more than some country boy.'

'And did you?'

He laughed softly. 'The distance made me realise how lucky I'd been to grow up somewhere like here with Marcus and Mum. I guess it's why I bought this cottage. A sort of anchor, you know?'

Ingrid would give anything to not be so anchored to the things in her life. It was as if she were a hot air balloon, held down by ballast for decades and, one by one, she was cutting the ropes. Maybe she and Jacob could meet somewhere in the middle?

'I get why you might need to feel connected to home, having been away for so long. I think I'm the opposite. Most of my life is about home.'

'Am I your escape?' His brow furrowed.

'Not an escape.' She considered for a moment. 'More that I'm allowing myself to do the things that I want without the worries and responsibilities of home preventing me from doing so. And I want to be with you.'

He put down his wine glass and approached her, then tilted her chin up and kissed her. He pulled back to see her face clearly. 'Dance with me?'

She looked around the kitchen as if expecting a glitter ball to descend from the ceiling. 'Here?'

'Here.'

Billy Paul's 'Me and Mrs Jones' played on the Bluetooth speaker as she slipped off the stool and settled into his arms.

'Appropriate,' she said with a wry smile.

'I didn't plan it, I swear,' he said, pulling her close.

'What about the food?'

'It's fine for the moment.' He began to sway.

She looked up into his eyes and they both remained like that for at least a minute. She'd never looked into someone's eyes for so long before Jacob had come along, and this time, the intimacy of it knocked her off balance. How had these intense feelings developed for him so fast? Were they lust, or something deeper like love? She suspected a little of both. And then she told herself to stop overthinking and sank into the kiss he planted on her lips. A kiss that deepened as his tongue explored her mouth, as his hands swept up to her waist and lower to cup her bottom, bringing her even closer to him. Her hands were in his hair, holding his head close to hers as their kiss intensified. Soon she was pressed up against the breakfast bar and grabbing at the hem of his T-shirt, pulling it up to feel his skin beneath it, the hard line of his muscles.

He pulled back to look at her.

'Am I misreading the signals here?'

'No.'

Jacob reached behind him to turn off the stove, then lifted her into his arms and carried her to the bedroom.

33

Call It Love

Jacob looked at her.

'Just to be clear, you want to have sex with me, right?'

In all her life, no one had ever asked her for permission and the fact that he had made him infinitely more attractive.

'Yes.'

She tugged his T-shirt up over his head, then traced her finger down the lines of his muscles to his belly, stopping at his waistband. She looked up at him. His eyes brimmed with tenderness as his hand cupped her face and he bent to kiss her softly.

'You're so beautiful,' he whispered in her ear, kissing along her jawline, down her neck. 'I thought so from the moment I met you.'

She pulled back to look at him. 'Really?' Now wasn't the time to mention that she'd been covered in mud.

He nodded, his eyes more heated as he tugged her closer, kissing her.

She leaned away. 'I'm worried I won't be enough for you. That I won't be good enough at this.'

'We can take it as slow as you like, Ingrid, but know this, you are more than enough for me. More than I could ever have imagined. And we'll be amazing together.'

She pulled him to her and kissed him, infusing every

press of her lips with her desire for him.

His hand slipped through the split in her skirt and as he touched her bare skin, all thoughts flew out of her head as she gave in to the sensation.

'I told you so,' he whispered with a smile, as Ingrid's breath quickened. 'And you're safe with me. Always.'

Those words were all she needed to finally let go of the doubt and fear.

Her fingers found the buttons on his jeans, pulling them free and pushing the denim down past his hips, her hands on his skin. It had been so long since she'd touched anyone like this, but instead of it being an alien sensation, every caress felt as though she was coming home. She was where she was supposed to be, with this man, in this place.

Jacob unzipped her dress, pulling it down and baring the black lace strap of her bra, which he took between his teeth and nudged off her shoulder. His hands roved over the fabric of her bra, his lips following as he pulled down the dress and discarded it entirely.

He stood for a moment as she lay on the bed, taking in the black lace balcony bra and matching pants that Grace had had the foresight to pack for her, his gaze heavy with desire.

'Is something wrong?'

He shook his head. 'I'm just thinking how incredibly lucky I am that you came into my life. I never thought I would feel this way about someone.'

Her heart leaped as he climbed back on top of her, pushing her hair back off her face and kissing her passionately. Her hands were in his hair as his mouth found its way to her breasts and before long, her bra was discarded.

It was as though no one had ever touched her before, the intensity of the feeling making Ingrid grip his shoulders, melting into his arms like ice in water. Time slowed. He was in no hurry to move ahead, savouring her, whispering to her how beautiful she was, making her feel cherished, valued, loved.

And then he was on his knees pulling her underwear down, his eyes burning into hers. She couldn't look away in embarrassment or even shame, as so often had been the case in the past. Before, she'd felt as though she were selfish to seek any kind of pleasure for herself, that she didn't deserve it. But his words and the way that he looked at her, touched her, gave her the confidence to accept him, to give herself permission to be vulnerable with him.

This was more than a physical act for them both, as though in doing this, they were baring their true selves to each other.

And Jacob needed no instruction, his mouth and hands bringing her to the edge of a precipice that she'd never experienced with another person before.

'How did you know what I like?' she asked, struggling for breath.

'Because I know *you*. I know the sounds you make when you're happy. Especially that tiny little sigh just before I kiss you, and that catch of your breath when my fingers brush your skin.'

Words were definitely her love language. In moments, she was over the precipice, her body trembling with the force of the explosion.

Jacob kissed her belly, tracing his way back up to her lips, then reached over to extract a condom from the bedside table drawer before settling his weight on top of her.

'Is this still okay?' he asked, propping himself above her, his face hopeful.

'Do you usually leave condoms for the people who rent this house?'

He smiled, then used his teeth to rip open the wrapping. 'I put it in there earlier just in case.'

'You're pretty sure of yourself.'

'I'm sure of how I feel about you.'

She pulled his hips closer to her. 'So am I.'

She sighed as he pushed inside her, her legs clasping around his waist, his mouth on her neck. Even in this, they were in synch as their bodies moved, each wanting to be as close to the other as possible. She felt the heat of his breath at her ear, heard his soft, punctuated moans, and then his words in her ear. 'I love you.'

She pulled his head to face her, looked into his eyes as he continued to move inside her. 'I love you too.'

34

Family Ties

Jacob parked the car in front of a modest bungalow with shades-of-brown exposed brickwork and a grass-green front door that blended with the surrounding scenery. The air was filled with the squeals of joyful children playing in the sunshine and the distant, muted bark of neighbourhood dogs. Ingrid stared at the house, unable to get out of the car just yet. Was that the twitch of a net curtain at the latticed window in the front? Ingrid couldn't blame Jacob's mother for taking a peek at her before they met officially. In fact, she was relieved. She doubted that Jacob had prepared his mother for how old and brown she was, and she preferred it if any surprise was kept under wraps and away from her.

Jacob knocked on the passenger window, jerking her out of her thoughts. She scrambled in the seat well for her bag, pulled the visor down to check her face in the tiny, slightly distorted mirror, and reluctantly stepped out of the car.

'This is very interesting,' said Jacob, moving closer to look into her eyes.

Ingrid straightened her bag strap. 'What?'

His hands rested on her hips, pulling her closer. Her skin heated in the cool September breeze as she recalled his hands on her last night.

'You're nervous. Quite the opposite to that cool calm woman in the multimillion-dollar pitch.'

'I'm not nervous.'

They both knew she was lying, but Jacob leaned forward and kissed her.

'Alright, let's say that you're not. But just in case you are, don't be. My mum is a sweetheart and she'll love you.'

'She'll think I'm too old for you.'

'She might at first, but as soon as she gets to know you and sees how great we are together, she'll see past that.'

Ingrid had subconsciously reached back to grab onto the car door handle, only noticing how hard she had gripped it when Jacob's hands covered her own and tried to prise them away.

'Ingrid, it'll be fine. I promise. If you're uncomfortable, we'll make some excuse and leave.'

For a moment, she was tempted to agree to this modified plan because it appealed to her fight or flight instinct, but she wasn't a quitter. She'd stuck at a job that was determined not to love her, likewise her husband, and the last thing she could be accused of was running away when the going got tough. What happened to living in the moment and being happy? She let go of the door handle and stood up straight.

'No, I'll be fine. Sorry. Just a wobble. I want her to like me.'

'And she will.'

She admired his optimism.

As much as Ingrid tried not to obsess over the age gap between herself and Jacob, it was hard when confronted with her boyfriend's mother who was indeed closer to her age than to her own mother's. Ingrid saw Jacob's features in Lorraine's face. They had the same deep brown eyes, the same elegant nose. Her hair was thick, dark and wavy, and she had the athletic physique and slightly weathered skin of someone who spent a lot of time outdoors. Dressed in a deep blue shirt and light denim jeans that accentuated her thin legs, she didn't look old enough to have a child Jacob's age.

She beamed as her eyes alighted on her son, hugging him tightly. Once she released him, she turned her curious, cautious eyes to Ingrid and extended her hand in greeting.

'I'm Lorraine, Jacob's mum.'

'I'm Ingrid.'

'My girlfriend,' Jacob added.

Lorraine's eyes widened a fraction, but she rallied quickly. 'You didn't tell me that you were dating, Son.'

Ingrid flashed a surprised look at Jacob. At least she'd told him in advance that her parents had no clue about his existence. Would she have agreed to come here if she'd known? Perhaps he already knew her better than she thought.

Jacob avoided Ingrid's eyes and kissed Lorraine's cheek. 'I'm telling you now, Mum.'

'I'm sorry, it must be a bit of a shock. I'm sure I'm not what you would have been expecting,' said Ingrid. In a situation like this, she found directness preferable to avoid the awkwardness that comes from half-spoken truths.

Lorraine was surprised. 'To be honest with you, Ingrid, you're right. But it doesn't mean that you're not welcome. Come in, love. It's almost time for lunch.'

A woman's voice called out from an adjacent room, presumably the kitchen, moments before she appeared. 'Lorraine, where do you want me to put the roasties?'

'Chlo?' said Jacob, his tone flecked with surprise. He glanced at Lorraine who smiled and looked away.

'On the table next to the gravy, lovely,' said Lorraine, grabbing Ingrid's arm and propelling her towards the dining room.

'Jacob!' Chloe exclaimed, putting down the dish and launching herself at him.

Ingrid stood behind one of the dining room chairs and watched. Chloe was about Jacob's age, lithe with long straight dark brown hair falling down her tanned back in a shimmer. Her dress was minuscule, the type of thing that Ingrid with her curves and age could never wear.

Who was this girl? Friend or ex-girlfriend? From the sheepish look on Lorraine's face, Ingrid assumed the latter.

'Hope you don't mind me being here, but Lorraine said you were coming home for the weekend and that I should join you.'

Jacob extricated himself from the hug and went to put his arm around Ingrid's waist, pulling her close.

'It's good to see you, Chloe. This is my girlfriend, Ingrid,' he said, confirming Ingrid's suspicions.

'Oh, right,' said Chloe, who wasn't as adept as Lorraine at hiding her shock. 'But you're . . . er, sorry, but you seem a bit older than us.'

Rude, thought Ingrid. If this girl didn't have a filter, this meal was going to be excruciating.

'Let's sit, shall we?' Lorraine said, before Jacob could respond.

The dining room was compact, the table just big enough for the four of them. The furniture was all country oak and there was even a dresser up against one wall. The window was huge, with a panoramic view of the hills behind the house, but it was only Ingrid who stared at them. Her London existence was a palette of greys with the occasional splash of green accompanied by the rainbow of cars with their white and red lights, and the bright yellow of streetlights. The landscape of the Lakes was spring green and azure blue with dashes of espresso earth and the vibrant colours of nature. She could look at it forever. And to be honest, she would've preferred to do so now rather than face this meal with these people.

'So, Ingrid, where are you from?' Lorraine asked.

Here we go again, thought Ingrid.

'London?' Lorraine continued.

Ingrid was momentarily lost for words as Lorraine supplied Ingrid's standard response rather than them disappearing down the no-where-are-you-really-from rabbit hole.

'Um, yes. That's right.'

'And how long have you two been seeing each other?'

Jacob grasped Ingrid's hand. 'It's still quite new, Mum.'

'Right,' said Lorraine, spooning peas onto everyone's plate, her lips pursed together in consideration. Ingrid guessed that she'd be revealing her true thoughts to Jacob later.

Chloe's eyes were on their clasped hands. 'You've certainly changed since *we* went out, Jacob.'

Ingrid tried not to smile at such an obvious ploy. She might have been nervous about Lorraine's opinion, but an ex-girlfriend's wasn't going to sway her either way. The advantage of being older was that she didn't have time for these games. Besides, dealing with Chloe wasn't nearly as bad as Jacob having to deal with Matt.

'I'm sure we both have, Chloe.'

'You definitely didn't like PDA back then.'

Jacob lifted their clasped hands to his lips and kissed the back of Ingrid's hand. 'I do now.'

Chloe's eyes were still on their hands. 'Where did you meet?' she asked Ingrid.

'Here actually,' said Ingrid. 'I was injured on a hillside and he helped me out. Then we met again for work in London.'

'Yeah, I was kicking myself after we first met that I hadn't asked for her number. Then a few weeks later, I walked into a boardroom in London and there she was. It was like fate.'

Lorraine snorted and carved into her roast lamb. 'I don't believe in fate. I just lost my son. I won't believe that was fate.'

'Of course not,' said Ingrid. 'I'm so sorry, Lorraine. I can't imagine how you must feel. Losing a child must be the greatest kind of sorrow.' She tried to convey all the emotion she felt into her words, but she still worried that they sounded flat. What could one say in these circumstances? 'Jacob told me about Marcus. You must be so proud of your two boys.'

Lorraine looked at Ingrid. 'Thank you for saying that. So many people don't want to talk about it, or they avoid the subject altogether. You speak like a mother. Do you have a child?'

'I do. She's almost twelve.'

'Ah. And where's her dad?'

'We're getting divorced. It's not easy.'

'Oh I know, I've been there, love. Are you saying you aren't divorced yet?'

'Isn't it too soon for a new relationship then?' Chloe said, unfolding her napkin and placing it across her lap.

Ingrid tried to hide her irritation at this young woman questioning her life choices. She had enough of that within her own family.

'No, I'm not divorced yet,' said Ingrid, choosing to ignore Chloe.

Lorraine shot Jacob a look.

'It's fine, Mum. They were separated for a year before they decided to divorce.'

Lorraine nodded, but her expression belied her scepticism. 'Let's eat, shall we?'

Ingrid shifted in her seat, ready to put one of the many exit strategies she'd planned in her head during this incredibly awkward meal into action at any moment. She'd tried her best not to be bothered by Chloe's incessant chatter as the archetypal stereotype of the ex-girlfriend determined to one-up the new woman with her in-depth, out-of-date knowledge of Jacob. And Ingrid had reached her limit of the number of times this child would find some way to reference her age, as if she needed reminding.

She felt the disapproval rolling off Lorraine in waves, even if she was too polite to vocalise it. On the surface, Lorraine was welcoming and cordial, asking if Ingrid wanted any more potatoes and making sure that her wine glass was topped up. She listened to whatever Ingrid said with apparent interest, but it was those stolen glances at her, eyes unsure as she assessed her son's lover, that made Ingrid want to be anywhere else.

Clearly Jacob was also uneasy, checking on her, making

sure to touch her regularly. His eyes told her that he couldn't run away from his mother so quickly. Maybe he had a type of survivor's guilt when it came to their relationship. But she didn't blame Lorraine for wanting to keep Jacob close. The grief that she must feel as she opened her eyes each morning and had to make it through another day without her son was unfathomable to Ingrid and she decided that she could put up with a little awkwardness to give Lorraine time to process this relationship.

Lorraine excused herself and left for the kitchen.

Ingrid squeezed Jacob's hand. 'I'll go and help your mum.'

'Sure?' he asked, glancing towards the open dining room door.

She nodded. 'You guys should continue catching up.'

'Oh my God, do you remember Shaz? You'll never guess what she's up to now,' said Chloe.

From the look on his face, Jacob had no interest in guessing Shaz's life choices. Ingrid smiled and went to find Lorraine in the kitchen.

Baking trays soaked in the sink, but other than that, the kitchen was spotless. Jacob's mother was clearly the type of cook who cleared up as she went along. Lorraine stood by the window next to the kettle, her thoughts far away as she waited for it to boil. Should she leave? She didn't want to intrude, but she thought that perhaps it was best if Lorraine was able to say what was on her mind.

A floorboard creaked as Ingrid stepped forward and Lorraine turned around.

'Oh, it's you, love. Would you like some tea? We only have the builders' kind, I'm afraid.'

Perhaps she thought that Ingrid drank the elegant, yet slightly dishwatery Earl Grey or some other pretentious tea blend.

'Builders' is perfect, thank you. Let me help you. Where are the cups?'

Lorraine pointed to a cupboard above the toaster and

Ingrid extracted four mugs, thinking that things between her and Jacob were so new that she had no idea how he took his tea.

'I'm sorry if I've been a bit weird,' said Lorraine. 'Jake didn't tell me that you were coming.'

Ingrid nodded.

'I wouldn't have invited Chloe if I'd known. She's always carried a torch for him and they were so good together, even though it's been years now. But it must be very uncomfortable for you, and I'm sorry about that. I shouldn't be interfering in his life, but . . .'

'But now that Marcus has passed, you'd like your son to be in the same country as you at least?'

Lorraine faced her with watery eyes and nodded slowly. Ingrid stepped forward and pulled her into a hug. At first Lorraine remained stiff-backed, but in a minute, relaxed a little.

'And I must have been a bit of a shock,' Ingrid said as she stepped back.

'A little.' Her face said that it was a lot. 'He's always been older than his years, you know. I think it's because his dad left when he was so young and he felt like he needed to be the man of the house.'

'He *is* very mature and responsible. You did a great job, Lorraine.'

Lorraine looked as though she were warring with herself internally, weighing her words.

'So I suppose it isn't a surprise that he picked someone like you. But . . .'

Jacob appeared in the doorway. 'Mum, we're meeting Colin and his wife a bit later, so we should get going if that's okay. I'll be back soon, promise,' he said.

He glanced at Ingrid, willing her to go along with his story. She hadn't been the only one dreaming up exit strategies. She nodded at Lorraine to confirm the appointment, relieved that she wouldn't have to hear what came after that 'but' right now.

'Of course, Son. Remember to call me, will you?'

Jacob hugged her tight. 'Definitely, Mum. You know I love you, right?'

Ingrid couldn't help the tear that snaked its way down her face as she watched them.

35

For Old Times' Sake

There was nothing like the comfort of her own bed, thought Ingrid as she snuggled into the pillows that dipped in just the right spot and pulled the sheet over herself. She listened to the cascade of water from the en suite as Jacob showered, stretching her aching limbs and thinking about the past forty-eight hours. The visit to Lorraine's had been a lot to process, and she and Jacob had studiously avoided the topic for the whole of Sunday and during the long drive home. He'd kissed her as soon as they'd returned to her empty house, backing her up the stairs and into the bedroom, not giving her time to think, to speak, as if he were trying to erase any doubts that might have arisen during the trip.

If she was honest, she'd been grateful for the distraction because it had saved her from agonising over Lorraine's words and gestures. She wasn't sure how Jacob would continue with this relationship if he knew how disappointed his mother seemed by the fact that Ingrid was thirteen years older than him and unlikely to have another child. Yes, he was much more used to following his dreams without letting family tie him down to a location, but that didn't mean that he wouldn't want to make Lorraine happy.

All this thinking made her temples throb. Even if Jacob could live without his mother's blessing, could Ingrid?

Putting herself in Lorraine's shoes, she knew that she'd have a problem with this situation. Could she deprive another mother of her son and future grandchildren? And if she ignored all these things, would the karma fairy visit her in the future when Lily brought home a much older man.

Jacob emerged from the bathroom with droplets of water falling from strands of wet hair onto his skin, a towel around his waist. Ingrid couldn't help but stare. Speaking of karma, she must have done something really good in a previous life.

He grinned at her. 'Can't get enough?'

'If I said no, would you come back to bed?'

'What time is Lily back from Matt's, and Grace from wherever?'

Ingrid glanced at the clock. Matt would be back there for seven. 'We have about an hour.'

Jacob tossed his towel aside. 'Well, that's just about enough time.'

Ingrid laced her hands around Jacob's neck as she stood on tiptoe to kiss him goodbye for the fifth time in the hallway. Her lips had barely touched his when they were both startled by a fist thumping on the front door. From the shape of the silhouettes visible through the frosted glass panes, it looked like Matt and Lily.

'He seems angry. Want me to stay until he's gone?' Jacob asked.

Ingrid touched her forehead to Jacob's and sighed. There was a time when she'd have welcomed a Matt who was desperate to see her, but that had long passed. Now, she simply didn't want to deal with him.

She pulled away and shook her head. 'No, it's fine. He'll probably behave with Lily here. I'll call if I need you.'

He released her reluctantly as Matt continued his assault on the front door.

'I don't like this,' he said, picking up his backpack from the floor.

'I know. But honestly, it'll be fine. You'll be late for your meeting.'

Jacob's forehead furrowed for a moment, then he nodded and opened the door. Matt, who had been about to pound on it once more, was propelled forward into the hallway and fought to find his feet underneath him.

He straightened, pushing back the hair that had fallen into his face as he fell and shrugging his shoulders as he tried to relocate his dignity.

'What are you doing here at this time of the morning?' Matt spat the words at him, but Jacob remained calm, turning to Ingrid and kissing her temple before stepping through the doorway to leave.

'Good to see you, Matt. I'm just leaving.' He turned to Ingrid. 'I'll call you later.'

Ingrid nodded, her eyes on Matt.

'Hey, Lily. Did you have a good time with your dad?' Jacob addressed a sulky Lily.

'It was okay,' said Lily, slouching into the house. Clearly the relationship between father and daughter hadn't improved much.

'Don't forget to pack your PE kit,' said Ingrid as she watched Lily stomp up the stairs.

'Right then. I'll be off.' Jacob nodded at Ingrid, then called after a retreating Lily, 'See ya, squirt.'

The door closed behind him, leaving Ingrid alone with Matt in the hallway.

'He stayed the night?' Matt asked.

'He's my boyfriend, so yes he did.'

Matt scowled and Ingrid scoffed.

'What?' he asked.

'It's not like you were even interested in me when we were together.'

'I was interested. It was *you* who never had time for me between your precious job and Lily.'

Not this again. She wouldn't assume the blame for the

demise of their marriage. That was on him. *She'd* tried. But there was nothing to be gained from another argument.

'Let's agree to disagree on that one. Did you want something else?' She didn't want to deal with Matt's feelings at this time of the morning. She had to drop Lily at school and get to work.

'Actually, yes.'

Ingrid crossed her arms and waited for the next bomb to drop.

'It's just that you're so different these days.'

She nodded. As annoying as the selfish bastard was, he'd been the catalyst for Ingrid to take a good hard look at her life and the supporting role she'd been playing in it.

'And I was thinking that this divorce is going to be hard on all of us, not to mention the financial nightmare of selling the house and splitting everything. Then there's Lily.'

Ice crept through Ingrid's veins. Was he actually going to say that they should call off the divorce and he should move back in? Did he have such a low opinion of her that he thought she would accept that after all he'd said and done? Maybe he just couldn't bear to see her thrive alone.

'You're not seriously suggesting what I think you're suggesting, are you?' Ingrid asked, trying to keep her voice as steady as possible.

'Why not? Don't we owe it to ourselves and to Lily?'

'That's a question you should've asked before taking yourself off for your gap year.'

'I'm asking it now. We could be good together, babe. Like the old days.'

'We've *been* together, Matt, and the old days were shit. Look, you were right to call it quits when you did. I'm happier than I've been in a long time.' She was finally finding the real Ingrid who'd lived quietly inside her all this time, waiting for her moment to shine. She was making decisions that benefited herself and she was finally taking ownership of her life.

Matt took a step towards her, and she backed away, her palms up.

'No. You no longer have the right to touch me,' she said, and he reared back as though she'd slapped him.

Ingrid gave herself a little mental high-five.

'Think about it, Ingrid. You know that guy's too young for you. He's just playing with your emotions.'

Ingrid laughed. 'Oh, the irony. You've played with my emotions for years, Matt. But Jacob isn't the point. Whether I'm with him or not, I know that I don't want *you* anymore. Just like you worked out the same about me.'

'Don't throw away all those years without thinking about it, Ingrid.'

Matt was the epitome of a person who wanted the new shiny toy that everyone was talking about. He hadn't been interested in her when she was his wife, but as soon as Jacob had shown an interest, he suddenly wanted her back.

'Look, Matt, we can't go from you calling me names, telling me you want a divorce and that you want custody of our child, to expecting me to want to be with you. I'm not a masochist, although I understand that our fifteen years together might indicate otherwise. I've moved on. Let's just draw a line under all of this now.'

She gestured towards the door and he began to move towards it.

'I won't give up,' he said, opening the door.

'You should,' said Ingrid.

36

Offers and Acceptances

'Congratulations, we've decided to award your firm the work,' said the finance director of Blue Mark over the phone.

Ingrid turned to Jacob and mimed clapping her hands as he beamed back at her.

'And we've accepted the fee arrangement.'

Ingrid allowed herself a moment to stand and punch the air, and then said, 'I'm delighted to hear that. And we're honoured and excited to be working with you. I'll send you over an engagement letter in the next few days. Thank you so much for choosing us.'

'We'll speak again soon, Ms Perera.'

Yes. She had really needed this win. She was taking back control of her career and her work and there was no way that Tim could insert himself into this project and claim any of the credit for winning the client. Things were finally beginning to look up and she was beside herself with joy.

Jacob pulled her into a tight hug.

'You were amazing, Ingrid! They'd have been idiots not to say yes to that proposal.'

'I couldn't have done it without your help.'

'Nonsense. It might have taken a little longer, but you really didn't need me.'

He looked into her eyes and held her gaze. She didn't

need him. But she *wanted* him. And that was so much better than the dependent relationships she'd had in her life to date. With Jacob she could be herself. Unapologetically and confidently. He wasn't emasculated by her career success because he had his own and he actively encouraged her to make her own decisions.

'I really want to kiss you right now, but there are about a hundred curious eyes out there and they've seen enough,' she said, pulling herself out of his embrace.

Jacob grabbed his jacket and bag and pushed her towards her own things. 'Then let's go back to my place and celebrate.'

'Or you could come to mine.'

He shook his head. 'Too far. I can't wait that long.'

Ingrid had no idea how long the taxi journey to Jacob's place had taken. Nor was she aware of how they got from the lobby to the door of his flat, against which she was now pressed as they continued to kiss, their lips seemingly fused together since they'd left the office.

Jacob used a free hand to unlock the door and they stumbled into the hallway, bags falling on the floor, hands fumbling on buttons and zippers. Jacob kicked the door shut, peeled off his shirt and lifted Ingrid into his arms, curling her legs around his torso and carrying her to a room at the end of the short corridor.

'Wait, I want to see your flat,' said Ingrid, trying to look around.

But Jacob shook his head. 'Later.'

They looked into each other's eyes, their passion for each other burning clear and strong as he carried her to the bed.

Ingrid padded out of the bedroom towards the smell of cooking emanating from the kitchen. She was a little self-conscious dressed solely in Jacob's shirt, but she hadn't felt like the tight dress that she'd been wearing that day. And although she felt like a walking cliché, she was joyous.

A few months ago, her life had been a disaster, her career going nowhere, her husband rejecting her, her family's moods and expectations dictating all her life choices, and now she was genuinely happy and empowered. And she had a hot, younger boyfriend who was cooking for her after making love to her.

She smiled as she watched him shake the pan, glossy slices of ginger, garlic and red onion leaping into the air before landing back in the fragrant oil. He turned as he heard her footsteps.

'Well, I won't be washing that shirt any time soon,' he said, his gaze raking over her.

She laughed. 'Do you mind?'

'I love that you feel comfortable enough to borrow my clothes.' He turned back to the pan. 'Is frittata good for you?'

'Perfect, thank you.'

She approached the breakfast bar, which was the only dining space in the tiny flat, and her fingers brushed the stack of correspondence that Jacob had opened and left in a neat pile.

'So I suppose that winning the pitch means that your job with us is over,' she said, trying to cover the hesitation in her voice. She wasn't going to be the needy girlfriend asking her boyfriend to stay with her.

Jacob poured the egg mixture into the pan, swirled it, turned down the heat and leaned over the breakfast bar so his face was inches from Ingrid's. He gently poked the middle of her brow with his index finger.

'What's going on in there? You don't want to say something, but you can tell me anything. I'm not going anywhere.'

She looked up into his eyes, which gazed steadily at her. 'But that's just it, isn't it? You *are* going somewhere. To New York.' She shook her head. 'I'm a realistic person. I knew this might happen, I just didn't expect . . .'

'To have fallen head over heels for me, right?'

She shoved his arm and scoffed. 'Always so sure of yourself.'

The pan sputtered behind them and Jacob turned to check on the frittata. 'I've told you before that I'm sure of you. And even if you haven't fallen head over heels, I have,' he said as he gently prised the posh omelette away from the sides of the pan with a spatula.

Ingrid could tell from the way that Jacob's shoulders tensed and his grip on the pan tightened, that he was waiting for her response. She could tell how he felt, with every touch, every kiss that they shared. And she knew that despite her rational brain telling her to take things slowly as he might have to leave, her feelings had run free, falling as deeply in love as he had. A part of her had accepted that the experience of loving him was worth the inevitable heartbreak if he left, while also hoping he'd stay, not least because of the effect that his departure could also have on her daughter.

She looked down, her eyes focusing on the pile of correspondence, snagging on the words *'we're delighted to offer you the position of MD in our London office'*. She grabbed the letter to take a second look and then slammed it down on the counter as she realised it was incredibly rude to read his letter without his permission. Their eyes met as she looked up.

'I'm so sorry. I had no right to read that.'

'I was going to tell you, but if you remember, we were a little preoccupied when we arrived earlier.'

'You're staying?' This time she lost the battle to keep the hope from her voice.

He switched off the heat and came around the breakfast bar to hold both of her hands in his.

'This just gives us options.'

Us? 'Jacob, this is *your* life, and I can't be the person holding you back from a glittering career in New York.'

'But you could be the person giving me a glittering life in New York *or* London. I know you might not be able to go with me, with the divorce and everything, so I thought it was sensible to explore alternatives. It's only the middle of September, we have time, and I want to be with you and Lily.'

Ingrid closed her eyes, trying to process the emotions threatening to overwhelm her. She had never expected to fall in love at this stage of her life. She certainly hadn't dared to hope that Jacob would consider altering his plans for her.

Jacob pulled her against his chest and looked down into her eyes.

'That's if you'll have me,' he said. Although his expression was soft, there was tension at the edges of his eyes.

She didn't need to think about it at all. 'I will.'

37

Can't Sleep, Won't Sleep

So this was what people meant when they talked about walking on air, thought Ingrid. She turned up the sound on her digital radio, singing along with Sharleen Spiteri about her 'Inner Smile'.

'Mum?' Lily's head popped around the door frame.

Ingrid continued to sing, although that was definitely a loose term for the sound she was making, and pulled Lily into the room, beginning to dance with her.

Lily giggled, no doubt because Ingrid was tone deaf. And she joined in, hopping and skipping to the music, Ingrid's joy clearly infectious.

'Someone's happy,' said Grace from the doorway, sleepy but without a trace of annoyance at having been woken up so early. Since she'd secured a job playing in an orchestra for a West End show, her nights were longer.

Ingrid sang the lyrics at her sister while Lily laughed.

'I love it when you're happy, Mum,' she said.

Ingrid floated down the street towards the office, coffee in hand, still relaxed from a weekend that had given her an irresistible glimpse of what it would be like to be in a long-term relationship with Jacob. They'd done a grocery shop together, taken an initially reluctant Lily to the cinema, then played board games like a real family, arguing and bargaining in order to win. Then Ingrid and Jacob had snuggled in front of the television together with a large bowl of popcorn and a bottle of wine. Her nights had been filled with a new type of passion. No longer as frenzied in the knowledge that they had to take what they could get, but slower and more tender, knowing that this was just the beginning of their journey together.

Ingrid smiled to herself as she stepped into the elevator and took a sip of her coffee.

'You're looking particularly smug this morning.' Tim's irritating drawl assaulted her ears, curtailing her daydreams.

Ingrid's skin itched at having to share such a confined space with the odious man, but nothing was going to dim her mood. She flashed him a broad grin. 'Absolutely.'

'We'll see how long you manage to keep them as a client, shall we?'

Was this the best that he could do? She was simply too full of the joys of her life to engage.

'We shall,' she said, taking another sip of coffee and clearly not giving Tim any more oxygen for the fire of his envy as he struggled to find a comeback for such a response.

Thankfully, the doors opened at their floor, sparing her from another display of misplaced testosterone and she skipped lightly out of the elevator towards her office.

Kerry gesticulated wildly at her before she could open the door.

'Did you have a good weekend, Kerry?'

'Oh, you know, had the out-laws round so it was a little fraught, to be honest. That woman had me running around from morning till night and nothing is good enough for her. I'm glad to come to work for a rest.'

Ingrid patted her on the shoulder in empathy. She definitely knew that feeling, but it was usually her own family giving her grief and making her run around like a dervish.

'I'm so sorry, Kerry. That sounds tough.'

'Unlike you, missy. You look like the cat that got the cream.'

Ingrid felt herself blush. 'My weekend was great.'

She was finally wholeheartedly, blissfully happy without waiting for the other shoe to drop. Even her body had relaxed as the tension of the past few years ebbed out of her, her shoulders no longer slumped, her teeth no longer grinding.

'Well, that's just wonderful, Ingrid. I'm so happy for you. And I suspect that that gorgeous man you were sharing your office with is partly responsible for that smile on your face.'

Ingrid laughed. Nothing got past Kerry. Of course she'd have noticed how close they'd become. 'Maybe a little.'

She turned to carry on into her office.

'Wait, Ingrid. I wanted to tell you that there's someone to see you in your office. A Ms . . .' she looked down at her notepad to refresh her memory, 'Lorraine Ellis.'

Ingrid was sure that she actually heard the other shoe drop.

Ingrid opened the door and stepped into her office, telling herself that Lorraine could be here for any number of reasons. Maybe she wanted to get to know her better, to apologise for how she'd made her feel in the Lakes, or maybe even to plan a birthday surprise for Jacob. But as she saw the grim, pinched expression on Lorraine's face, all of those reasons faded into the background.

'Ingrid. I'm sorry for intruding like this, but I didn't know where else to find you and we need to talk.'

Ingrid nodded, indicating for her to sit down. 'I see Kerry's got you something to drink already. What can I do for you?'

'Break up with Jacob.'

Ingrid stared at her, surprised at the blunt statement, but equally admiring of Lorraine's no bullshit approach to matters.

'Shouldn't you be talking with him?'

Lorraine shook her head, clasping the strap of her handbag tighter in her lap. 'I know what that boy is like. If he's in love with you, which I suspect he is from the way he looked at you, then nothing short of an act of God would stop him. No, *you* need to be the one to end it.'

Ingrid felt as if she were in a Christopher Nolan movie and time had come to a halt, droplets of water suspended in the air as her brain tried to process Lorraine's words. But then, hadn't this been inevitable? Why had she thought she could be happy without considering the effect it would have on the people around her?

'You know that I lost my other son, Marcus.'

'Yes, I can't imagine the pain you must be going through every day.'

Lorraine nodded. 'I know that you understand, as a mother.'

Ingrid mirrored Lorraine, nodding as the weight of their conversation sank in. Jacob looked so like her, but instead of the tension that was as much a part of Lorraine's physique as the shape of her nose, Jacob was relaxed and easy in his body.

'And because now I only have Jake, I have to think of what's best for him, even if he can't.'

Ingrid felt tears prick her eyes. She let Lorraine continue, because honestly, there was nothing she could say right now.

'He says that he doesn't want children, but that boy doesn't know himself. You should see him with them, he lights up.'

Ingrid knew how he was with Lily. It was one of the many reasons why she'd wanted to be with him.

'And he should be a father, but you know, with you, that's . . . unlikely.'

Ingrid sat as still as possible. She was forty-five. Although the newspapers were full of women her age giving birth, she knew that this was an unlikely scenario for herself and Jacob.

'If you carry on with this relationship, then you'll be stopping him from living the life that he could have. I know you'll hate me for this. But I'm his mother, and if I don't act in his best interests, then who will?'

Me, thought Ingrid. *I will act in his best interests.*

And as Lorraine spoke, Ingrid knew that it was precisely because she had fallen so deeply in love with Jacob, that she had to break up with him. Lorraine had confirmed every deep-rooted thought and doubt that she'd had about their relationship. She wanted Jacob to have all the wonderful things in life that were possible with a woman closer to his age. She was being selfish expecting him to alter his plans so he could be with her. She'd been living a fantasy.

'I know you understand where I'm coming from, Ingrid. It's honestly nothing against you as a person. You seem lovely. But you must know that this relationship isn't good for him in the long term.'

Ingrid sat poker still, the words resonating as Lorraine fished for something in her capacious handbag. The pain etched on her face was hard to see.

'Strawberry jam. I make it myself. I thought you might like a jar.'

Lorraine nodded, not waiting for a response, and swiftly left Ingrid's office. Ingrid stared at the jar that had been placed on her desk.

As if the sweetness of the condiment could eliminate the sharp tang of regret.

3 a.m. Ingrid blinked at the time on her phone and turned over in bed again. Lorraine's speech replayed itself over and over in her head, but with different scenarios. What if Ingrid had argued with her? Or tried to persuade her? Why had she sat there and taken it? One moment, she'd been congratulating herself on taking control of her life and the next, she'd completely given in to Lorraine.

Ingrid was sure of Jacob. She knew that they were in love, but because of this, she also wanted the best for him. And Lorraine had touched the growing doubt in her that perhaps Ingrid wasn't what was best for him. At least not for future Jacob who might change his mind about children and the life he thought he wanted.

Ingrid knew from bitter experience that the life she'd envisioned at thirty-two hadn't turned out that way, and that even at her age, people didn't always make the best decisions for themselves. She was being selfish wanting this man for herself. Particularly as she was in the midst of a divorce with a different man who'd now decided that it would be much easier all around if they called the whole thing off. She hadn't even had the chance to tell Jacob about that piece of Matt's delusion.

Was she taking the easy way out?

No, this was the hardest possible way. She and Jacob had had one weekend of being sure of each other. One delicious, addictive glimpse into the future that they might have had and that made it all the harder to walk away. But rationally, she knew that it made sense. And she knew that he wouldn't be the one to do it.

She got out of bed and went downstairs to make herself a coffee. She wouldn't be sleeping tonight anyway.

38

Swings, Roundabouts and Dead Ends

'You look terrible,' said Matt as she opened the door to him on Saturday, unable to hide his delight.

'Just what every woman wants to hear first thing in the morning,' she said, wishing that their loose custody arrangement that saw him spending time with Lily on alternate weekends involved a more neutral drop-off point that didn't require her to interact with him. He watched her as she moved around the hallway picking up Lily's things.

Ingrid pretended not to see him, her hackles rising despite her sleepless night. The man had a nerve to suggest that they get back together, and then find joy in seeing her miserable. The contrast with Jacob's kindness was stark, and her heart hurt to think about what she was about to give up. She'd spent every night that week replaying her conversation with Lorraine, that expression on her face. Ingrid couldn't be responsible for causing her any more pain. This was the right thing to do, and although it would be excruciating, she'd survive it. She had to. Matt's presence reminded her that she was able to get through any emotional upheaval.

'He dumped you, didn't he? I knew it.' *Was he bouncing with glee?* She looked away. 'He was too young for you. And dare I say it, far too handsome for someone like you.'

278

Matt was an utter bastard, but his words could no longer hurt her.

'No, he hasn't,' she said. Technically the truth. She'd rather cut off her arm than tell Matt that *she* was about to break up with Jacob.

'But you know it's only a matter of time, don't you? You really should stop making a fool of yourself and get back with me. Come on, Ingrid, we're good together. You know it.'

He was such an idiot that his narcissistic brain really expected her to welcome him back with open arms. She'd had enough.

'Listen, Matt. I've said this before but it didn't seem to take with you, did it? In the words of Taylor Swift, we are *never, ever* getting back together. I've realised far too late in the game that you're a wanker and I should never have married you in the first place. Lily is the only good thing that's come out of this sham of a marriage. There will be no reconciliation. And my relationship with Jacob is absolutely none of your business.'

He straightened and walked towards her. Ingrid pushed back her shoulders, lifted her head high and stood her ground as he stopped in front of her, searching her eyes for weakness. She stared back defiantly until he finally registered that he couldn't intimidate her. Then she turned and called up the stairs.

'Lily, Dad's here for you.'

'I'll be there in a minute,' Lily shouted back.

Ingrid shoved the rucksack into Matt's hands and pushed him towards the front door.

'You should wait outside.'

'One day, you'll be begging me to take you back and I'll have moved on.'

'One day, it will register in that head of your s that *I've* moved on. Now go. And make sure that Lily's back by five today. She has a piano lesson.'

'Bitch.'

She wouldn't rise to it. She shut the door behind him, rubbed her face with her hands and sighed. That had been the easy part of today.

'You don't like the food?' Jacob asked, his eyes following her hand as she relocated her now limp and soggy salad to another quadrant of her plate.

She shook her head and bit her lip for the four-hundredth time. Should she wait until the meal was over? Should she even say anything in this busy restaurant? Should she wait until they got home? All options were awful. There was no easy way to do this. She'd avoided him for most of the week, finally accepting his invitation to dinner on Saturday.

Jacob hadn't said anything about her straggly hair with its light greasy sheen, or her un-ironed blouse. He'd merely been gentler and kinder than usual, pulling out her chair, checking that she wasn't too cold under the air-conditioning vent, that her herbal tea was warm enough, and with every gesture, another small crack appeared in her resolve. How could she move on from him? Was that even possible? She was destined to become a pitiful old woman from a Victorian novel, clutching her bottle of gin and wandering through memories of when she once had something, but sacrificed it for the greater good.

She shook herself out of her reverie, her fork clattering onto the plate. Jacob looked up at her, his expression expectant.

'I need to say something,' said Ingrid.

Jacob's hand shot out to cover hers, which had begun tapping on the tabletop as if she had no control over it. She pulled away and straightened herself in her chair.

'So say it,' said Jacob, gently, looking at his empty hand.

'We should break up.' She couldn't look at him, because if she did, she'd probably take it all back.

Jacob leaned back in his seat with a sigh. 'I knew

something was up, but I couldn't put my finger on it. We've been so great together, I never thought it would be this. What happened, Ingrid?'

Your mother happened, she thought. But she wouldn't throw Lorraine under the bus like that.

'So many reasons,' she said as every single one of them flew out of her brain.

He folded his arms and stared at her as she continued to avoid his gaze. 'Okay. Tell me.'

Ingrid fixed her eyes on the next table where a family sat, the parents sharing a bottle of wine while their children scrolled through iPads encased in huge rubber cases that would probably survive a drop from the top of a building. This was what Jacob would be giving up if they continued this relationship. Granted, it didn't look all that appealing to Ingrid, but she knew the joy of having Lily in her life and she simply couldn't deprive him of the possibility.

'I'm too old for you, Jacob. I have so much baggage that I'm holding you back from this amazing job in New York. I'm dragging you into this divorce with Matt and I'm landing you with a child who isn't yours. You should be living your life so differently. Not with someone like me.'

'Isn't it up to me how I live my life?'

She nodded. 'But you're young and maybe you don't quite know what you want at the moment, but in the future, you'll probably change your mind and it will be too late.'

He ran his fingers through his hair and rubbed his scalp as he considered her words. This was one of the things she loved about him. The way he thought through his responses instead of lashing out at her.

'Wait, have you been talking to my mum?'

Ingrid's fight or flight instinct kicked in. She had to get out of here before she caved and revealed everything.

'It's not that. Let's just call it a day, Jacob. This was all a mistake.' She looked at him as she grabbed her bag from the floor and stood. Her heart broke at his expression, and she wanted to hug him and tell him that she didn't mean it. But you couldn't take back words like that. Could you?

'Ingrid,' he called after her.

She couldn't look back. If she did, she'd have thrown herself into his arms and begged his forgiveness for her foolishness. She had to remember Lorraine. The mother and son relationship was far stronger and more important than the one she had with Jacob. She pushed past chairs and tables in haste, almost knocking over a lady by the entrance as she fled the restaurant. She almost cried in relief as a black cab with its light on came into view. As she climbed into the taxi, she resisted the almost unbearable urge to turn back.

Ingrid kicked off her shoes by the front door and padded towards the kitchen in order to splash some water on her face and find a couple of ice cubes for her puffy eyes. She'd cried the whole way home, in the kind of way she couldn't remember doing since she'd been a child. Her chest had heaved with the strength of her sobs, her already wrinkled blouse now stained with the tears she hadn't been able to stem with her tissues. She'd ignored the glances from the taxi driver in his rear-view mirror as she gave in to the grief, and she couldn't help but notice that she hadn't felt even an iota of the same emotion when Matt had ended their marriage. Of course, that only made the tears worse.

'Jesus, you look like shit,' said Grace, who stopped flicking through the *BBC Music Magazine* as she looked up at her from her seat at the kitchen table.

'Thanks,' said Ingrid.

'What happened?' Grace asked. She pushed back her chair and stood, walking towards Ingrid. She stopped right in front of her and Ingrid resisted the urge to step back. Then she reached out and wiped a stray tear from Ingrid's face, and waited.

'I broke up with Jacob,' said Ingrid after a moment or two.

Grace crossed her arms and nodded, not in the least bit

surprised. 'I suppose it was only a matter of time before you pressed your self-destruct button.'

'What's that supposed to mean?'

'There's more Catholic in you than you'll admit, Akki. You know, all that delayed gratification and your reward will be waiting for you in the afterlife. So, at any hint of pleasure or happiness, you self-destruct.'

'That's a load of rubbish. Name one time when I've done this,' Ingrid challenged, instantly thinking of the time when Rob Harding, the crush she'd had through the whole of university, finally asked her out and after a blissful month together, she decided that she had to break up with him instead of always waiting for the inevitable break-up that would follow.

'That's not the important thing right now, and I can see from your face that you know of at least one occasion. So, why did you break up with him?'

Ingrid groaned and ran her fingers through her already straggly hair. 'His mum asked me to.'

'Are you joking?' Grace laughed, then fixed her gaze on Ingrid, her smile slowly wiping itself off her face. 'You're joking, right?'

Ingrid shook her head. 'She wants her son to have a life that might include his own children one day. And Jacob's brother died recently, so he's her only hope. And in case you haven't noticed, I'm too old for all of that. My eggs are literally in their death throes as we speak.'

'He can't have been too happy to hear about his mum interfering like that.'

'I didn't tell him. There was no point in hurting their relationship.'

Grace raised her eyes to the ceiling and sighed again. 'You're too nice for your own good, Sis. But, really, doesn't Jacob have a say in this?'

Ingrid had considered it for a moment, but Lorraine had triggered every doubt and insecurity within her, and Ingrid had decided that it would be better if she ended it all before things became more complicated. 'She thinks that he doesn't know any better and he'll change his mind in the future.'

'So what if he does? Isn't it his choice?'

'Grace, it's done. There's no going back.'

Ingrid pulled out a chair and plonked herself onto it. She had no energy left to even think about it anymore.

Grace knelt by her side. 'I'm so sorry, Sis. He's great and I just loved seeing you so happy. But there's always a way back.'

Ingrid was about to wave her away when her phone rang. Audrey. She couldn't deal with telling her right now. She muted her phone, but a moment later, Audrey called again. They both stared at the screen as the call went to voicemail.

Then Grace's phone rang.

They looked at each other. Audrey was a persistent person when she had a bee in her bonnet about something and neither of them was keen on being stung by her.

Pick up. Please. Code Red.

The texts pinged on both of their phones simultaneously. Grace answered her phone on the next ring and put it on speaker.

'Akki, what's going on? Where are you?'

They heard a sob and then Audrey cleared her throat. 'Northwick Park Hospital. It's Nathan. He's had a heart attack. Can you come?'

'Jesus,' Grace said. 'He's . . . er . . . is he alive?'

There was another sob, such a strange sound to come from their usually indestructible sister. 'Yes.'

They both heaved a sigh of relief. 'Akki, we'll be there as soon as possible. I just need to get someone to take care of Lily,' said Ingrid.

'Okay, but not Ammi. I don't want her to know and then appear here with all her weeping and wailing and rosaries and stuff.'

Ingrid looked at Grace. 'Understood. See you soon.'

'I'm coming with you so don't even think of asking me to stay here,' said Grace. 'Can't we bring Lils with us?'

'No, I don't want to freak her out. Hospitals are awful places.'

'Matt's out, I suppose. What about Jacob?'

'Are you high?'

'It's an emergency.'

'I just dumped him, Grace.'

'I know, but desperate times and all that. Or I could call Matt.'

After their altercation yesterday morning, she didn't want Matt there. She could just ignore Audrey and call Mum, but she knew that Florence was the last person they needed when things were so uncertain.

'Let me call some of Lily's friends' parents and see if they can help out.'

'There's a big swimming competition today. They're all at that.'

'Shit, shit, shit.'

'Shall *I* call him?' Grace asked.

'No!' Ingrid looked at the phone. They had to get to the hospital and they were losing precious time. 'Okay.'

It had definitely crossed her mind to shoot out to the car and wait for Grace there, but she couldn't tell Jacob that he was too young for her and then act like an adolescent herself. She had to put on her big girl pants and face this incredibly awkward situation.

Besides, here he was, looking impossibly handsome again in low-slung joggers and a white T-shirt. Other men would have laughed and told her to get lost, but not him. And she was the idiot who'd let him go.

'How's Nathan?' he asked as he kicked off his shoes in the hallway.

No preamble. Good. It was easier this way. Or was it? The

sight of him alone made her heart ache, her hands tingling with a longing to pull him close, feel the skin of his neck against her face, the scent of his woody cologne.

'We don't really know. But I'll keep you posted from the hospital. Thank you so much for doing this. Especially in the circumstances.' She bit her lip and looked down, then felt his fingers on her chin, tipping her face back up to look into his eyes, which were tinged in red around the edges, the skin underneath a little puffy. Had he been crying?

'I'll always be here for you, Ingrid. And we'll talk about the other stuff another time. But you can't make a unilateral decision that concerns both of us like that and expect me to accept it.'

Her heart thudded in her chest. Was it hope, or fear? 'But . . .' She thought of all it had taken her to get those words out of her mouth.

Grace appeared with a bag that she'd packed with toiletries, underwear and clothes in case Audrey had to stay in the hospital overnight and beyond.

'Good thinking,' said Ingrid.

'She'll never believe that I haven't used these pants before, but I literally took them out of the packet yesterday.'

Ingrid smiled. Grace had a knack for defusing taut atmospheres.

'We should go,' said Ingrid. 'Lily's in her room.'

'Any rules I need to be aware of?' Jacob asked.

'Just love her,' said Grace, before Ingrid had a chance to respond.

Jacob looked at Ingrid. 'That's an easy one.'

39

Life and Death

Accident and Emergency at Northwick Park Hospital buzzed with activity on a Saturday evening with injured drunks, mothers with babes-in-arms who had no open doctors' surgery to go to when their children inevitably developed fevers over the weekend, and the usual aches, pains and breakages.

Audrey was waiting for them in the space that separated the waiting area from the treatment bays. She looked drained, her hair hastily pulled back, loose strands around her face and neck. The usual Audrey, in control, calm, impeccable, had disappeared. Here was a woman who was untethered from the steady rock in her life, Nathan.

Ingrid and Grace hugged their sister, the three of them locked together, as doctors and nurses scurried around them, sharing their strength to get through whatever this was.

'They've moved him to a ward and then tomorrow he's going to Harefield,' said Audrey.

'Can we see him?' Grace asked.

Audrey nodded. 'Yeah, I just need a minute.'

Ingrid looked around the chaos of A & E. 'Let's find somewhere to sit and talk. You look like you could do with something to eat and drink. You're going to need your strength if you have to sit around here. Is there a cafe or something?'

'There's a Costa,' said Audrey.

* * *

Twenty minutes later, the three of them were huddled around a tiny table with the coffee and cake that Grace had insisted was vital at times like this. Ingrid and Grace waited while Audrey sipped her drink and picked at the dry carrot cake, both hesitant to ask this unfamiliar version of their sister questions about Nathan's condition.

After ten minutes, Audrey set down the fork and looked up at both of them, her eyes glistening. 'I just can't get the image of him out of my head. One minute we were talking about going to Barcelona for a weekend and the next, he started sweating, looked grey and then clutched his chest. I swear, I thought he was going to die right there in the kitchen.'

Ingrid placed her hand on top of Audrey's which had begun to tap the tabletop. 'It was a good thing that you were there, Akki. And you're a doctor. I bet you didn't panic and did all the right things.'

Audrey nodded. 'I was on autopilot. But all I could think about was what if this was it? What if I'm about to be on my own, without him? Does it even matter that he's never home to take out the rubbish, or that he never shuts a cupboard properly so it looks like we have a poltergeist in our house, or that he keeps the same sodding teaspoon out to stir his coffee for over a week like there aren't loads more in the drawer? I'm petty and annoying and keep forgetting how amazing it is that I found him in this world.' Tears pooled in her eyes.

Ingrid and Grace looked at each other, both clueless about how to manage the situation.

'What's the prognosis?' Grace asked carefully.

'He needs surgery. That's why they're moving him to Harefield. I suppose there's an advantage to being a cardiologist needing heart surgery.'

'I brought you some things,' said Grace. 'I figured you wouldn't be leaving.'

'Do you want me to call the kids for you?' Ingrid asked.

Audrey shook her head. 'Already called them. They're on their way.' She clasped their hands briefly. 'Thank you for being here.'

'We're always here for you,' said Ingrid.

Audrey nodded and sighed. 'I'm exhausted. Can we not talk for a bit? Just sit here?'

'Sure,' said Grace, rubbing Audrey's arm.

They watched the ebb and flow of clientele, while listening to the coffee shop jazz in the background. A strange little oasis in the middle of the hospital.

'Something like this makes me realise that I've been worrying about all the wrong things, you know?' Audrey grabbed Ingrid's hand. 'You're happy. And I see that you haven't been until now. And it shouldn't have taken my husband almost dying for me to really understand what people mean when they say that we don't find that kind of happiness often in this life, Nangi.' She looked into Ingrid's eyes with her own teary ones. 'You have to seize it while you can.'

Grace looked at Ingrid with an almost imperceptible shake of her head.

'I will, Akki,' said Ingrid, her stomach churning.

Audrey stood. 'Right, that's enough time away. Let's go.'

At 3 a.m. Ingrid parked the car and sat in the dark for a moment, trying to collect herself. Emotions swirled in a huge, tangled mess within her and just like the annual untangling of the Christmas lights, she had no idea where to start with it all.

Freddy, Millie and Harry had arrived together, all shell-shocked to see their father in such a different state. Audrey had hurried them home, telling them that it was more important for them to be at Harefield during the operation the next day, but they knew that she was trying to spare them the stress of listening to the constant blip of the heart monitor and his laboured breathing. They'd sloped away reluctantly, but only when Ingrid and Grace had assured them that they wouldn't leave Audrey alone.

Then Audrey had obtained special permission for herself, Grace and Ingrid to stay with Nathan in the private room she'd arranged when he was admitted. Nathan was as much a part of their family as they were, and no one wanted to leave him. Even though Ingrid picked up and put down her religion like a handbag, she couldn't help suggesting a quick prayer. She'd expected the usual disdain for her Catholic superstition, but both of her sisters had joined in with the Our Father, the words burned deep into their hippocampus from countless childhood chants.

In the quiet moments, Ingrid's thoughts had wandered to Jacob. What if it was him lying on that bed, with tubes attached to him and monitors beeping? So pale, and vulnerable. Could she bear it?

As she thought about her possible loss, she thought of Lorraine. What would Ingrid's loss be compared to his mother's? Surely that trumped anything that she might feel. Yes, it was the right thing to do. Lorraine was already experiencing the unfathomable loss of one child, and Ingrid couldn't rob her of all her hopes and dreams for the remaining one.

At 2 a.m., Grace had sent her home, pushing her out of the door, whispering to her to talk to Jacob about their issues. But there was no use in talking. What was done had to stay done. She looked at the flickering lights coming through the slats in the blinds and steeled herself. She couldn't relent, even if every part of her wanted to sink into his embrace.

But as she padded softly into the living room, she could not have been prepared for the sight before her. Lily was curled up on the sofa, her head in Jacob's lap, clutching a hot water bottle to her stomach. She was fast asleep while Jacob sat still and a little slouched so as not to disturb her, one arm slung over the back of the sofa. The tableau gave a swift punch of oxytocin to her brain. Even though she'd cruelly and abruptly ended things with him, here he was comforting her daughter, showing up for both of them again.

Jacob looked up at her and gently moved Lily's head onto a cushion, creeping off the sofa and tiptoeing towards her.

'Thank you for this,' she said, trying not to look into his eyes.

'No problem,' he whispered. 'How's Nathan?' Jacob ran his fingers through his hair and Ingrid swayed towards him slightly as her hand wanted to follow his.

'Still touch and go. He needs surgery later this morning. Audrey's found one of his consultant friends to perform it at Harefield, so they're moving him. We just have to believe that he'll be alright.'

Jacob rubbed her arm. 'Of course. Nathan's strong and resilient. I'm sure he'll be in excellent hands.'

'Audrey did say his friend is one of the best.' She smiled weakly, then pointed at Lily. 'Why is she out of bed? And what's the hot water bottle for?'

'Ah, well, she started her period earlier,' he whispered.

Lily had only just started menstruating so things weren't at all regular. 'Oh God. I should've been here. It's still so new to her.'

'Don't worry, she's okay. She was a bit embarrassed because you were out of pads, so I popped to the late-night chemist and picked some up with some painkillers and a hot water bottle. She couldn't remember where you kept yours. We watched some TV and then she didn't want to be alone, so I kept her down here with me. Hope that's alright?'

The universe was sending her all sorts of signals about this man. He'd treated her daughter with kindness and empathy even though her mother had just rejected him. Was she doing the wrong thing? It was only hours ago, but felt like years since she'd left him in the restaurant. From that moment she'd been unsteady, a little nauseous. Was walking away from him as crazy as it felt?

As she looked at her sleeping daughter, Ingrid couldn't help herself and threw her arms around Jacob, pressing the length of her body against him and transferring all her gratitude, love and yearning to him. His arms wrapped around her, pulling her closer, rubbing her back, and she began to sob – for Nathan, for Audrey, for Jacob, for Lily. For herself.

They stepped away after a while and looked into each other's eyes. Ingrid wondered if hers reflected the same hurt, fear and love as Jacob's.

Jacob pulled out his phone to open the Uber app. 'I should go.' He flicked her a look, and quickly looked back at the screen.

Ingrid put her hand on his arm. 'You'll never get a car at this time. You should stay.'

40

Clarity

Ingrid rolled over into the warm hollow next to her. As her brain began to wake from her all too few hours of sleep, the reality of yesterday's events crashed down on her. Nathan. She prayed that he would survive the operation today and leaped out of bed to check her phone. A text from Kerry to say all her meetings that day had been cancelled and one from Grace confirming that the operation was already under way. Ingrid decided to forgo a shower, rushing around her room, jumping into the jeans that she'd discarded on the bedroom floor earlier, grabbing a fresh T-shirt from a drawer, slipping a sweatshirt over her head and realising that it was one Jacob had left behind from another overnight visit. She inhaled his scent, keen to keep it with her throughout what she knew would be a difficult day of waiting.

She probably shouldn't have spent the night with him, but she couldn't have sent him away after all that he'd done for her, for Lily. And if she were honest with herself, she'd needed his comfort, the safety of his arms, the surety of his kiss, even if it would kill her to let it all go again.

She trotted downstairs, following the aroma of coffee like a bloodhound. It was emanating from the kitchen, where Jacob was pouring a strong-looking espresso into a tiny cup from the Moka coffee pot that he'd insisted was a necessity.

He looked up as she entered the room and passed her the cup. 'You off to the hospital? I can take care of Lily again if you like.'

'I can't ask you to do that. I should call Matt.'

'No, it's cool. I'm not working today and I'm guessing you don't want Matt here.'

Matt's aversion to all sanitary products would make him virtually useless to Lily.

'Maybe I should stay. Grace is with Audrey. I should probably be here with Lily.'

Jacob put his hands on her shoulders. 'She'll be fine with me. You be there for your sister. And let me be here for you.'

'But we broke up. It isn't fair for me to rely on you like this.'

'*You* broke up. *I* didn't. You didn't even give me a chance to say anything. And I'm telling you and showing you here and now that I'm not giving up on us, Ingrid.'

Apart from Lily, this man was easily the best thing that had ever happened to her.

'But I can't do this to . . .' She stopped herself just in time.

Jacob rubbed his face and exhaled loudly. 'Mum.'

Ingrid couldn't look him in the eye so he placed a finger under her chin and tipped her face up.

'What did she say?'

'I can't, Jacob. I promised her. And I don't want to be the reason that you and your mum fall out.'

'Okay, but if we fall out, it will be *her* fault because she really should mind her own business and also . . . we won't fall out because she's just scared.'

'But she made a good point. I mean, I'm old. I can't give you children.'

He sighed. 'You're older, not old. And who said you needed to give me children? What kind of an old-fashioned notion is that? You have Lily and she's wonderful. And look, if we have another kid that's awesome, and if we don't that's also awesome because I want to be with you and not your uterus.'

She tried to ignore the hope surging within her. 'But after Marcus died, you're her only hope.'

'For what? Breeding? That's ridiculous. You know better than me that a parent's job is to equip their kids to live in the world without them, not *for* them. Mum may hope for stuff, but it's my life, isn't it?'

'And what about New York? Are you really going to give up such an amazing opportunity for me?'

Jacob picked up his rucksack from where he'd left it resting against the table leg the night before and extracted three glossy brochures with photos of uniformed schoolchildren.

'Actually, I was looking into schools for Lily. I told them that I had a daughter and the company sent me some details of schools and they'll help with admissions. Of course, you don't have to say yes, but I thought it could be an option. And all the accommodation would include both of you. But if you want to stay here, then there's the London job. I just want to be with you, Ingrid.'

She was floored. She was always the one who explored options, the one who was willing to compromise, to put her dreams aside. She had never been the person who was thought about, considered. Her husband had disappeared on his own without a thought for their daughter or for Ingrid. And even as he wanted to reconcile, it had nothing to do with either of them – merely a convenient financial solution for a man who blamed all his shortcomings on everyone else.

'Look, I know that you have empathy for my mum. It's one of the things I love about you. But nothing is going to erase her grief, and I can't live my brother's life to make her happy. I'll talk to her and make her understand.' He stopped and heaved a deep sigh.

'I should've talked to her before you met. I know that lunch was awful for you, and that's on me. I guess I didn't want the third degree from her, so I dodged the conversation and then it was awkward and she invited Chloe, and now this. I shouldn't have ignored it. We might've avoided all this. Look, Mum's not usually like this, but losing Marcus has changed both of us.'

Jacob and Matt were in different universes when it came to considering the feelings of others in their lives.

'It felt as though I was taking you away from her.'

Jacob stepped closer and took her hands in his. 'I'm not a parcel, Ingrid. I can't be taken from anyone to anywhere. I make my own decisions and sometimes, those aren't going to align with what my mother thinks is good for me. But I'll always discuss them with my partner because *you're* the person I'm sharing my life with.'

He caressed her cheek with his palm. 'I know you were trying to do what you thought was the right thing, but you really hurt me. Not just from the break-up, but because you didn't think that I was worth having a discussion with before you made your decision.'

She looked down as his words pierced her heart. It was true – she'd been high-handed, even patronising, as she'd decided that Jacob was too young to know any better and that she should make the decision as the older person in their relationship. Perhaps she was more like her own mother than she thought. But she would change.

'I'm sorry. I was wrong.' A tear snaked down her cheek. 'I thought that I loved you too much to let you waste your life on me.'

He pulled her into a hug. 'Waste? A life with you would be a privilege.'

'I'm sorry,' she said, her voice a little muffled by his jumper.

'So, we're still together right? I didn't misread last night? Now?'

She looked up at him and nodded. 'But I need to speak to Lily. And I need to think about New York. Matt will have a cow at the thought of it.'

'How about I throw in a regular plane ticket for him to come and visit us?'

'You'd do that?'

'If it makes your life easier and we get to have an amazing adventure together, then I'll do whatever I can.'

'And what about my job?'

'You have an office in New York, don't you?'

'Partner transfers are pretty rare.'

Jacob's expression fell for a moment before he quickly recovered. 'Then I'll take the London job. I just want us to be together.'

'But then we just won that pitch,' she continued, the possibilities now racing around her head, 'so I might have a reason to be in New York for a while. But gosh, what about my family? Grace? My parents? And then there's Audrey and Nathan.'

Jacob pulled her close again and stroked her hair. 'Let's deal with one thing at a time. You get to the hospital and I'll take care of Lily. We can deal with the rest later. But the important thing is the "we" part, yes?'

41

Mother Love

Nathan looked disgruntled as Audrey fussed around the bed, checking medication, plumping pillows that didn't need plumping and snatching his mobile phone out of his hands if he dared to pick it up from the bedside table. Grace and Ingrid smirked at each other, enjoying the little tableau as well as being relieved to be able to witness it. Nathan's operation three weeks ago had been a huge success, but the lengthy recuperation time, first in ICU and then on the ward, was testing his patience.

And yet, they were perfect for each other. He knew that she'd been scared witless by this crisis and that her fussing was a coping mechanism. And she knew that he secretly loved the attention, catching the small smile at the edge of his lips or the way he looked at her as she tucked in the corner of a sheet.

'So, what did you decide?' Grace asked Ingrid, patting her on the leg to bring her attention back from the lovebirds.

'I haven't decided one hundred per cent.'

'What's stopping you?' Audrey asked, pausing as she popped a couple of pills from the blister pack by the bed.

'Well . . .' said Ingrid, knowing full well that it was fear of the unknown.

She'd never considered living in a different country from

the one in which she'd been born and bred because it seemed too risky. And yet, she wanted it badly. She'd spent hours imagining them living family life there, dropping Lily off to school, heading to the office hand in hand, spending weekends having picnics in Central Park, or whatever it was that Manhattanites did when the sun shone. But she was scared of making the leap.

'If there's one thing I know after what I've just been through,' said Nathan, 'it's that you have to grab the life you have with both hands and live it. You and your daughter have the opportunity for the most wonderful experience and you're stopping to think about everyone else. Do something for yourself, Ingrid. London will still be here.'

Audrey looked at her husband, her eyes soft with love for him. 'As usual, my husband is absolutely right.'

'I thought you'd be against it,' said Ingrid.

'I was never against it, just worried. Live *your* life, Ingrid, not Mum's, not Jacob's mum's. You only get one, so don't waste it.'

Grace nodded. 'Ditto. It might be difficult to sort out, but it'll be worth it.'

There was a commotion outside the room and they heard Mum's voice in the corridor pestering an already harried nurse to find a vase for some flowers. They exchanged glances, bracing themselves for her arrival.

'Nathan, how are you?' Florence squealed as soon as she entered the room, a burdened Thatha behind her carrying two Tesco Bags for Life full of Tupperware.

'I'll get there, thanks, Ammi.'

Mum began to pat down the sheets. 'Are they making you comfortable? I hope this one isn't making things worse for you.' She pointed at Audrey, who opened her mouth to retort but thought better of it and closed it again.

'I've brought some food because you know this hospital food is disgusting. And you've had a heart attack, so I've used only a tiny bit of salt and cut off all the fat.'

Thatha turned to leave with the bags. 'I'll see if I can get someone to put these in the fridge.'

'Let me help you,' said Ingrid.

'Oh, you're here,' said Mum, blocking her path. 'Where's Lily?'

'With Jacob.'

Ingrid waited for the usual scowl, but it didn't come. She looked at Grace and Audrey, who both shrugged.

'He's a good person, isn't he?'

'Um . . . yes,' said Ingrid, unsure of what was coming next.

'He came to see me.'

Ingrid couldn't hide her shock.

'He told me that he wants to take you and Lily to New York for a few years, showed me the brochure for that excellent private school and photos of the apartment. He's a lot more grown up than he looks, isn't he?'

Ingrid could only nod. Jacob didn't know her mother. All that information would be used as ammunition against him. But it didn't matter now what crafty scheme Florence Perera had up her sleeve, Ingrid's decision would be her own.

'You should go.'

Ingrid briefly wondered if she would be the one requiring cardiac surgery next. She was sure that her heart had stopped for a moment.

'What?'

'Yeah, Ammi, Nathan's just recovering from a heart attack, you shouldn't be inducing another,' said Audrey.

Mum shot her a hard stare, which had the desired effect of Audrey shrinking back into the plastic seat next to Nathan's bedside.

'I met up with Sarasa last week and she told me that she saw you and Matthew at our anniversary party. That he looked like he was about to hit you. She was going to come and help but then Jacob was there, and the rest of you, so she didn't. She thought I knew all about it but not one of you said a word to me. How could I have known what Matthew was like if you don't tell me?'

'It was your special night. I handled it and there was no point in spoiling it. Besides, would you have listened?' Ingrid asked.

Mum shrugged. 'Anyway, Sarasa saw it. And I don't like it.'

Ingrid sneaked a glance at her sisters and Nathan, who looked equally puzzled. In a way, it was a relief that there was some sort of line in the sand for her mother when it came to Matt.

'And this Jacob seems very different. I still think he's too young for you. But he seems mature for his age, and he's very good with Lily. And . . .' She shook her head. 'I don't know, you're *different* with him. More like the girl we used to know when you were young. You were so carefree and full of life. Some of that seems to be back since this man has been around. It's all I ever wanted for all of you.'

The sisters looked at each other again, incredulous. Their mother would never admit that her parenting style left a lot to be desired, but in her way, this was as close to an apology as any of them would get from her.

'And if you need to go to America with him, you should.'

Ingrid stared at her mother, open-mouthed. 'Why?'

Mum turned to face her properly. 'Because I thought that I was protecting you all this time. That you'd be happy with this life that you built, but do you think it gives me pleasure to see you so down all the time? These two give me no end of headaches, but look at them, so happy in their lives. You should go and do this, if Matthew agrees. I can talk to him if he gives you trouble.'

Ingrid smiled, and pinched herself just to make sure that she hadn't accidentally stepped into *The Matrix*.

'Okay, Ammi.'

'How did it go?' Ingrid asked Jacob two weeks later as she met him at Euston station.

He kissed her cheek and grabbed her hand, and they began to make their way down towards the Tube.

'She asked if you liked the jam.'

Ingrid winced at the reminder of her breach of contract. 'Seriously, Jacob, was she alright? Does she really hate me?'

'She definitely doesn't hate you. She's just trying to hold on as best she can at the moment. And I made her see how wonderful it will be having you and Lily in her life. How we're no longer alone. She's really sorry for doing that to you, you know.'

Ingrid stroked his arm as they walked. 'I know. What about kids?'

'Look, obviously, she wants me to have my own kids, you know? Little Jacobs running around, but that's never a guarantee with anyone and she understands that this is *my* choice to make, not hers.'

Ingrid guessed that this wasn't an easily overcome hurdle for Lorraine. But they had time. Things would work themselves out.

'I'm glad you talked with her. And by the way, when were you going to tell me that you'd spoken to my mum?'

Jacob looked a little sheepish. 'Ah. She told you. I'm sorry, I know I should've said something, but I wasn't sure it had gone well, so I kept putting off telling you.'

Ingrid nodded. 'Well, that charm of yours should be bottled and sold because you managed to win over Florence Perera.'

Jacob smiled in surprise. 'I did?'

Ingrid beamed back at him. 'You did. But, honestly, in future please tell me before you go and do something like that again. She's not easy to handle without backup from Dad. But I hear my hypocrisy. I should've told you about your mum's visit.'

'Noted. But I think we could also look at it this way. We really love each other, and that's what I believe your lot call a blessing.'

'Ahh, I see. A Catholic gibe. You really are becoming one of the Pereras.'

42

Don't Look Back in Anger

Matt's face was almost beetroot red as he processed her words, and Ingrid waited for the inevitable combustion. She glanced at Cheska beside her, who had on her best, slightly bored poker face. Matt's lawyer looked as though he couldn't wait to be done with this case, adopting a disinterested, distant air, going through the motions for an unreasonable client whom he couldn't wait to get rid of.

As before, Ingrid had tried to contact him in advance of this meeting, hoping to tell him about her plans over a coffee or maybe even a glass of wine, but she imagined that he was still smarting over her most recent rejection and as a result, had declined every call. She'd even texted him, but all her messages remained unread. If Matt was going to be petulant, then she couldn't avoid blindsiding him in front of these lawyers.

'Matt, I know that this is a bit of a shock and I'm sorry about that. But I'm asking you to do this for our daughter. It will be such an enriching experience for her and I'm happy to pay for you to come out and spend time with her. I don't want to run away from you or prevent you from seeing her. And I know that however angry you might be with *me*, you're a great dad.' Okay, she was lying now, but needs must. 'And you want the best for Lily. We'll be back before you know it.'

The colour slowly began to drain out of his face, his chest that had initially puffed out in indignation, deflating. He turned to his lawyer. 'Can you leave the room, please? I'd like to speak with my wife in private.'

His lawyer looked over at Cheska who checked with Ingrid before they both left the room, hovering on the other side of the frosted, opaque glass wall.

Ingrid waited as Matt took a few deep breaths. Perhaps he'd been to anger management classes or something.

'You're serious about this guy?'

She nodded.

'And he doesn't mind that you have a kid?'

'I wouldn't be with him if he did.'

Matt rubbed his face with his hands. 'Shit, how did this happen to us? Weren't we happy once?'

Were they? She wasn't sure. Maybe he'd been the happy one because he'd never had to compromise on anything. She wasn't going to remind him again that he was the one who'd walked away over and over. He was the one who had put all of this in motion and now he needed to accept that this was finally the end of their marriage. She stayed silent.

'I'm sorry,' he said, knotting his hands in his lap and not looking at her.

She was confused. Was he saying no? Or was he genuinely apologising for something?

He looked up at her and heaved another deep breath, before standing and walking to the other end of the room. 'I felt as though with every trip away I was having all these experiences, and you . . . weren't. They changed me in small but significant ways, but here you were, always unchanged. And we didn't fit together anymore. So while I was away this last time, I decided it was time to call it a day. But then once I asked for a divorce, you were suddenly different. I didn't expect that. At all. And I suppose I didn't react well.'

Ingrid took a sip of her water, processing his words.

'Ingrid,' he said turning to face her. 'I'm sorry for

everything. For treating you badly, for running away, for the things I said. Everything. Life when I came back didn't turn out the way I'd expected and I know now that I've directed some of that frustration at you.'

Ingrid resisted the urge to cross her arms while listening to his confession. It was all too little too late. But she had to remember that she was working towards her future here, and she couldn't afford antagonistic body language.

'Thank you.'

'And I have to accept that our marriage is over. I suppose I knew when I left, but I wasn't honest with you. I let all my resentment build up over the years until there was really no salvaging us. And then not only did you move on, but it was with that young guy. You're different with him, you know? Relaxed and free. I realise that I've never seen you that way. You were always so guarded. I guess I was never the right person for you.'

Since when had Matt been so introspective? She wasn't going to knock it. It was definitely a huge relief that she didn't have to explain any of this to him herself.

'Look, I'm not over the moon about you all going to the US, but the truth is, I'm struggling to get work and I don't want Lily to have to be in the middle of that, so I'll accept your offer.'

'I appreciate the apology, Matt. And thank you for agreeing to New York.'

Matt nodded. 'I'll let James know that I agree to your terms. I wish you all the best.'

She stood and nodded at him, astonished at the tears that pricked her eyes. 'All the best to you too, Matt.'

Lily turned another glossy page on one of the school brochures, bending to peer more closely at the photographs of smiling students playing violins, or dressed in lab coats and holding test tubes to Bunsen burners, or wielding hockey sticks. She'd been preternaturally quiet as Ingrid had presented New York as a possibility to her.

'What about my friends?' Lily asked.

'You'll make new ones, darling, but I suppose, some of your good friends could come and visit. And we'll be back sometimes too to see your grandparents and Aunty Grace and Aunty Audrey. We don't have to go at all if you hate the idea.'

'When would we go?'

'Possibly spring or summer. You and I can decide on the best time between my work and your school. I know it won't be easy, but a couple of Jacob's new colleagues have kids the same age in that school, and they said they would help you to settle in.'

Lily nodded. 'This looks like the school in *Gossip Girl*.'

'When have you watched that?' Ingrid asked, horrified.

'Alicia's house. Her mum lets her watch it. She says it's educational.'

Ingrid raised her eyebrows. At least she wouldn't have to worry about Alicia's influence for a while. Or perhaps if this really was like the *Gossip Girl* school, she'd have a whole host of other problems.

'So, what do you say, Lilypad?' Ingrid asked.

'Let's do it.'

Ingrid snuggled into Jacob's shoulder as he smoothed her hair back, the only light in the bedroom a slice of white through the gap in the curtains from the streetlight outside her house. Things were moving fast, but she didn't feel disoriented or apprehensive. She couldn't remember the last time that she had anticipated life with such excitement, and without a careful risk assessment. And she was finally free. She sighed.

Jacob soothed her brow with his thumb. 'Why the big sigh?'

'I'm happy. And it feels wonderful.'

'I'm glad. Things seem to be slotting into place.'

She adjusted her head to look up at him. She traced the bridge of his nose with her index finger, running it down to his lips, and his tongue darted out to lick her finger.

'I'm just sorry I can't give you a child of your own.'

'It's not like you're ancient.'

'But it's unlikely.'

'So if it happens it's great and if it doesn't, it's also great.'

'You want a baby?'

'Want is a strong word. I think maybe never say never is more like it. *And* I think that maybe we need to keep practising.'

He rolled her onto her back and looked down at her.

'God, that's such a cheesy line.'

'Did it work?'

She laced her hands around his neck, pulling him closer. 'Absolutely.'

Acknowledgements

A lot of life happened to me in between the publication of my first novel and this one. My father died, my kids left for university one after the other, middle-age and all its ailments (some more serious than others) sucker-punched me, and a whole other novel was written and put away. There was a moment there when I thought that I couldn't write another word. Gratitude has been a huge part of my healing journey so it's only right that I take this opportunity to thank the small village who supported me and encouraged me to get back on my literary feet.

The greatest thanks, as always, goes to my wonderful agent, Hayley Steed at Janklow & Nesbit UK. From the moment we began our relationship as mentor and mentee to now, I have felt supported, encouraged and challenged in the best way. Thank you for your patience, kindness and honesty. I'm so fortunate to have you by my side in this journey. Thank you also to Mina Yakinya for reading my manuscript and giving me feedback.

Of course, I wouldn't have been able to get to the stage of publishing this book without my wonderful editors Jane Snelgrove and Melanie Hayes at Embla Books. I truly appreciate your understanding and patience, your willingness to brainstorm to help kickstart my creativity again and your kindness and good humour. Jane, it has been an absolute honour to work on this book with you.

Thank you to everyone at Embla Books including Emma Wilson, Emma Kiesling and the audiobook team, Vishani Perera and Katie Williams for publicity. To Sandra Ferguson for your copy edit, and to Kay Coleman and Rachel Eley for your proofreads.

Nigar Alam, Sophia Spiers, Sophie Jo, Francesca Robbins and Avione Lee, my fellow Madeleine Milburn Mentees – I couldn't have made it through all of this without our daily texts and our all too rare meetups. Thank you so much for telling me off when the negative thoughts overwhelmed me, for cheering me on as I picked myself up again, for supporting and listening throughout. Much love to you all.

Thank you to Faith Eckersall for your constant friendship and support and your tireless efforts to publicise my work. I continually thank whatever higher power made me overcome my usual introversion and compelled me to introduce myself to you on that first day of our MA at Brunel.

Thank you to my mum for her constant love and support. And to Jude and Noah – I'm forever grateful that even as young adults you still want to talk to your old mum and that I don't have to ask you for proof of life! Thank you for your love and support through a difficult couple of years. I'm so proud of the people you've become.

Thank you to Malcolm. As ever, I couldn't have made it through without you. And even though I'm a bit annoyed that you wouldn't let me properly research this book (😂), I'm so grateful to have spent so many wonderful years with you as my best friend and the love of my life.

And to all my readers – thank you so much for reading my books, even more for leaving reviews and for recommending it to others. It still feels surreal that my work is out there in the world, and the thought that you enjoy reading it makes the journey worthwhile.

About the Author

Ronali Collings was born and bred in West London, has a degree in English Literature from King's College London, studied law and then worked in finance for many years before becoming a stay-at-home mother. As her brain began to atrophy from her main company being two small children, she rediscovered her passion for writing and graduated with a MA in Creative Writing from Brunel University under the supervision of Bernardine Evaristo.

You can follow Ronali on Instagram @ronalicollings

About Embla Books

Embla Books is a digital-first publisher of standout commercial adult fiction. Passionate about storytelling, the team at Embla publish books that will make you 'laugh, love, look over your shoulder and lose sleep'. Launched by Bonnier Books UK in 2021, the imprint is named after the first woman from the creation myth in Norse mythology, who was carved by the gods from a tree trunk found on the seashore – an image of the kind of creative work and crafting that writers do, and a symbol of how stories shape our lives.

Find out about some of our other books and stay in touch:

X, Facebook, Instagram: @emblabooks
Newsletter: https://bit.ly/emblanewsletter